Adam flashed her a stunning grin.

A minute later he was sliding his long legs into his car, and then he had purred out of the semicircular driveway. Louise was left standing there, wondering why her heart was beating harder, wishing it weren't. There was a saying, wasn't there, about even the longest journey having to start with a single step?

One day, I want love. I want it all, she knew. But I'm still so scared of going down the wrong path. The first step terrifies me. . . which is a good reason to make myself take it, I suppose.

Take it with Adam Van Curen? If he was offering. . .

Lilian Darcy is Australian, but on her marriage made her home in America. She writes for theatre, film and television, as well as romantic fiction, and she likes winter sports, music, travel and the study of languages. Hospital volunteer work and friends in the medical profession provide the research background for her novels; she enjoys being able to create realistic modern stories, believable characters, and a romance that will stand the test of time.

MIDWIFE'S DILEMMA

BY

LILIAN DARCY

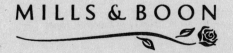

MILLS & BOON

*MILLS & BOON, the Rose Device and LOVE ON CALL
are trademarks of the publisher.
Harlequin Mills & Boon Limited,
Eton House, 18–24 Paradise Road, Richmond, Surrey TW9 1SR
This edition published by arrangement with
Harlequin Enterprises B.V.*

© Lilian Darcy 1995

ISBN 0 263 79258 7

*Set in 10 on 11 pt Linotron Times
03-9508-58569*

*Typeset in Great Britain by CentraCet, Cambridge
Made and printed in Great Britain*

CHAPTER ONE

HOSPITALS didn't sleep. . .and some cynics might have said that the patients in them didn't either. There was a time of quiet, though, that came late night. Most wards were darkened, and night-lights glowed at the nurses' stations. Patients in pain had been given the sweet relief that followed the late evening drug round. Casualty was still busy, and somewhere, often, there was an operating theatre with a surgical team intently at work on life-saving emergency surgery. There was one more department that was routinely busy at this hour as well: Maternity.

'It'd be nice if babies kept nine-to-five hours, wouldn't it?' drawled Mary Rigmore, the midwifery sister in charge of this shift in the new maternity unit at Morleyvale Hospital in West London.

'Quite a few do, these days,' answered Louise Redding on a chuckle.

She twisted a thick knot of soft dark hair back up on to her head as she spoke and wound a black elastic band around it, stuck in some pins and added a tortoiseshell comb or two for good measure, still not confident that it would do as it was told. New to her job, after several years away from nursing then a short refresher course, she had got out of the habit of putting it up.

'At least we'd probably get more understanding from the powers-that-be when it came to staff allocations,' Mary was saying, following her own train of thought. 'They never seem to realise that a night can begin quietly, so it looks as if we're doing nothing, and three hours later we've got twelve mums in active labour and

5

half the midwives we need. Now, if all deliveries were
scheduled Caesareans——'

'Then we'd all be out of a job,' Louise teased, raising
neatly arched eyebrows above dark brown eyes.

'That, or mere handmaids to the consultant obstetricians, which wouldn't suit most of us.'

'And anyway, there's something about nights. I like
them.'

'The drama, or something?'

'Yes, and the. . .holiness?' she hazarded. 'But that
sounds silly.'

'No, I know what you mean.'

'Mm.' Louise threaded in a final comb and looked
out of the window for a moment. She could see a car
park, fluorescent-lit and almost deserted, and beyond
it the hospital's casualty department and main
entrance. One o'clock in the morning. The rest of the
world slept, it seemed, but here in the hospital's state-
of-the-art maternity unit, opened only six months ago,
human drama unfolded almost hourly.

Even as she watched she saw a car come screeching
into the ambulance bay in front of Casualty. A frantic
man leaped from the driver's seat and hurried to open
the passenger door, helping out a woman who looked
so pregnant it was a wonder she had managed to fit
into the small Ford at all.

'This must be our latest arrival,' Louise commented.
'And it looks as if the husband's afraid they might have
left it too late!'

'That'll be Mr and Mrs Stelton. Good. Third child,
so it's likely she *will* go fast. Lynette can take her,
because she's only got Mrs Lewis, who's hours away
yet, and Mrs Petrie, who's even further and we probably should have sent her home.'

'Why didn't you?'

'She was so nervous, poor thing, and I think her
mother-in-law was there fretting and refusing to go to

bed. I don't know why there's all this talk about home birth these days. That's the last place I'd wanted to be. By my second I'd cottoned on to the fact that hospital was the only place I'd get a break for the next twenty years!'

'Speaking of breaks, mine's over, so I'd better get back,' Louise said, summoning her energy again.

'Off you go, then.' Mary stifled a yawn. 'Goodness, I wish I could go to a hotel for my sleep after nights. The children never leave me alone. . .'

'Right, time for me to check you again, Mrs Hilliard,' Louise told her patient, back in Room Three. 'Let's see if you've made some good progress, shall we?'

Inherited from Maria Thomas on the afternoon shift, Mrs Hilliard was having her first child, and had already been in labour for some hours.

'It must be getting close, surely?' her husband said. 'She's getting pretty tired.'

They seemed like a very nice couple, professional people in their early thirties, who had tackled the pregnancy and their coming parenthood with great enthusiasm.

'Let's have a look and a listen,' Louise said. It didn't take long. The baby's heart-rate was hovering around a hundred and thirty beats per minute, healthy and strong. Now for the internal examination. She draped a sheet carefully over Mrs Hilliard's lower limbs and the huge mound of her pregnancy as she performed the pelvic exam.

'You're almost there,' she said after a minute. 'Nine centimetres' dilation, and head nicely descended.'

A contraction came almost at once and Mrs Hilliard could not answer as she panted raggedly, unable to keep to the rhythm she had been practising over the past weeks. Her husband had given a muttered, 'Thank God!' at Louise's report, and was now pressing his hands into her back to counter the pressure of the baby.

'If she needs to push, do call me straight away,' Louise told him. 'It really won't be long now.' She squeezed the labouring woman's hot hand.

'Two more admissions,' Mary Rigmore said as Louise left the couple alone once again.

'Don't give them to me,' Louise answered. 'She's almost fully dilated and the baby's coming down nicely. She won't be long at all.'

'I'll take one, then. She's a couple of weeks early, and contractions every three minutes. Gaby can have the other.'

And so, against the deceptive backdrop of darkness and quiet outside, their unit was suddenly in full swing. Louise was barely aware of it over the next hour, though. Mrs Hilliard was ready to deliver at last, and pushed with such determination that little Brian Michael was out after only fifteen minutes of work, and cord and placenta were delivered uneventfully a few minutes later.

What a wonderful time it was! The little red creature was so well-equipped for life that it rooted for the breast as if it had been doing so for weeks, and then sucked lustily as if drinking in life itself with the greatest possible relish.

There was something about nights. Nothing to disturb this magic moment. No visitors. No ward rounds. The couple were bathed in a glowing mixture of exhaustion and exhilaration which rendered them almost oblivious to Louise's quiet, matter-of-fact presence as she checked the baby for any signs of weakness or ill-health. This was just as she liked it. She had no desire to intrude, and the safe delivery was the best kind of thanks.

Here in the new unit, too, where the mothers were able to labour, deliver and spend their post-partum recovery time all in the same room, staff intrusion could be kept to a minimum.

She was just finishing when Mary Rigmore appeared again. 'We've got another admission,' she said, sounding a little worried this time. 'Can I give her to you?'

'Of course. No problem here at all.'

'It's twins. And early, too, by four weeks. No problems as yet, but she looks huge and she's been a bit slack about clinic appointments. Hasn't been seen for four weeks—goes to her GP—and hasn't had a scan since week thirteen. . . Look, the more I talk about it. . . Would you like to take over my girl in Room Fifteen and I'll do this one? If it's tricky——'

'If it's tricky, I'll call in the registrar, of course. And if it's *very* tricky the consultant. . .'

'Adam Van Curen's on tonight. He's *very* good.'

'Yes, so I've heard, and I've seen him on rounds. Look, I know you and Barbara and Judy have been giving me the easy ones because I'm new,' Louise said firmly, 'but that can't last forever. I've delivered twins before, and I've assisted in Theatre with a Caesarean of triplets. It was all several years ago, but——'

'All right,' Mary came in. 'Go ahead. We *have* been giving you a light load, you're right, but if you feel ready——'

'I do.'

'Good luck, then!'

Louise spent a last few minutes with the Hilliards, and would return at intervals to check that mother and baby were doing well and that the uterus was contracting as it should. Then she washed thoroughly once more and went to her new patient, who was already settled in Room Ten. Settled, but not particularly relaxed or comfortable. 'Better to walk around?' Louise asked.

'So far.' The husband, a tall, gangling man, stood beside the bed, green-gilled and saying nothing.

'You're not having a contraction now?'

'No. Just restless. I'm going to hate this. I hate hospitals.'

'She does. She always has,' Mr Peterson intoned.

'Well, let's get you on the bed and see how you're coming along, shall we?'

'I didn't want to come in yet, but my GP said when the contractions were five minutes apart. . .'

'Who is your GP?'

'Dr Gordon.'

'Right. I don't know him, but——'

'Well, he doesn't do many pregnant ladies. He stopped about ten years ago, really, but he's so nice. I persuaded him. I've had him for years.' A strong contraction gripped her and she stopped speaking until it was over, then went on, 'He's the only doctor I've ever been able to stand.'

'He is.' Mr Peterson again, in a monotone. 'She hates doctors. Dr Gordon told us there's far too much fuss about giving birth these days anyway.'

'Look,' Mrs Peterson said, 'do you mind if I chatter on while you're doing that? Keeps my mind off it—— Ouch!' Louise's hand had approached the new patient's thigh but had gone no further.

'Another contraction?' she asked quickly.

'No. Your hand's cold. Gosh! Is that my legs shaking? Isn't that silly?'

'Not silly at all. Very normal,' Louise soothed. 'Sorry about my hand.'

Although she knew it wasn't particularly cold, she rubbed her gloved palms quickly together, knowing that labouring women often had a heightened sensitivity to such details.

'Oh, no, it's just me,' Mrs Peterson was saying. 'This sort of thing always happens to me.' She kept talking in a nervous, high-pitched voice until another contraction, perceptibly longer and stronger, took her concentration. They were coming really thick and fast now. When it was safely over, Louise put one hand on the huge abdomen to try and relax her patient a little, and managed to feel the cervix. 'Seven centimetres.'

'Is that good? That's good, isn't it?'

'Pretty good. Might be a bit of a way to go yet. Now let's just feel. . .'

Yes, there was one head nicely descended into the lower pelvis, and here, sticking out frontways, was its little bottom, a good classic vertex position, head down with the baby facing the mother's spine. Now, the other baby. A good firm palpation indicated the other head in not such a good position, over towards the left side with its bottom way up under Mrs Peterson's distended breasts. Odd that it should be so much over to this side. Louise had another firm feel. Had she made a mistake about that first one? No, she could definitely feel it. . . Another contraction. . . But what was this over on the right side? It felt like. . .

'Another head,' she muttered aloud. 'It can't be.'

'What? What was that?'

'Who told you this was twins?'

'She had the scan at thirteen weeks. We saw the two babies. They looked like little jelly beans with legs and arms. We saw them!' Mr Peterson was indignant. 'You mean it's not twins?'

'We've bought two bassinets.'

'Oh, it's definitely twins.'

'Then what do you mean by——' He stopped as his wife clutched at him, moaning through a fiercely painful contraction.

She took the opportunity to duck quickly out of the room. She met Mary outside, and the latter said, 'Everything fine?'

'I'm calling in the consultant.'

'Already? Louise. . .!'

'Unless she ate a whole cantaloupe for dinner, I think it's triplets.'

Adam Van Curen was groggy on the phone for about fourteen seconds, then he clicked into gear and told her in a cool drawl, 'I'll be there in five minutes.'

Giving him the benefit of the doubt, Louise mentally tripled that. A flustered SHO had also been summoned, and the ob-gynae theatre put on stand-by just down the corridor. Vaginal delivery of triplets? It could be done. It wasn't, often, these days, although the incidence of triplets was on the increase, due to the effect of some fertility drugs.

'And I could be wrong,' Louise realised. 'That'd be a nice embarrassment, wouldn't it—getting the consultant out of bed at three in the morning for nothing?'

When she got back to the Petersons, another contraction was in progress and the pregnant woman was weeping openly. 'They're not stopping. There's no rest in between. Can I have something?'

'Yes, of course you can. . .' She began to put up a drip, talking as she worked, and hooked up an external monitor. 'Listen. . . That scan you had at thirteen weeks might have missed something.' The monitor gave forth a cacophony of heartbeats, including the mother's, and was of little use. 'I'm pretty sure I can feel a third head in there——' She tried a listen with the foetal stethoscope, but again it was impossible to distinguish three separate foetal hearts. Scary. If one of the babies was in distress. . .

'Oh, my God!' the gangling father-to-be groaned.

Another contraction, and, in the brief interval between it and the next one, time for another exam. Almost fully dilated now. With the uterus filled to capacity, the first baby's head was pressing down strongly with each contraction, maximising their effect. Any minute now. . .

'I need to—I can feel a bowel movement coming. No! I need to push!'

And the consultant wasn't here yet.

'OK, breathe through this one, Mrs Peterson,' Louise said urgently. 'Pant. That's right. Let's get you into position first.'

'Is there a birthing stool? I feel I might like to squat.'

'I don't think Mr Van Curen is going to want you squatting,' Louise told her gently. 'Not for this delivery.'

'Van Curen?' Mr Peterson said.

'The consultant. He's——'

'Here,' came a voice from the doorway.

Louise didn't have time to turn round. She flung a brief explanation over her shoulder. 'She's fully dilated. Ready to push. The external monitor was useless.' Then, 'Here, Mrs Peterson, now try to rest your legs on these stirrups. They look a bit ghastly, but they're padded at the thigh and they're actually quite comfortable. Now take a deep breath. Yes. Now push. Down through your bottom, love. *Down*. . .'

Behind her came the snap of gloves. 'The head's crowning already.' A voice gravelly with fatigue, wasting no words. A faintly familiar voice, as she'd heard it echoing in the corridor, or on the phone in the office, although chance was such that she hadn't yet officially met the man in her two and a half weeks on the job.

'Yes, you're doing really well, Mrs Peterson,' she told the patient, and then, as the contraction subsided, 'Just rest now, breathe.'

'I saw its hair. It's got hair, Janey. . . Or *this* one has,' Mr Peterson added gloomily, clearly daunted by the fact that there were two more to come.

'We'll forget the monitors for now.' The low voice again, even huskier this time, and closer too. 'I'll try a listen with the foetal stethoscope.'

'I just got a mess of sounds there, too.' She still hadn't actually looked at the man.

'This one's not far off, then it'll be easier to check on the state of the other two. Paediatrician been called?'

'Registrar's on his way.' This was Mary Rigmore, reporting from the doorway. She disappeared again.

'Do make sure there *are* two more,' Louise murmured.

'*What*?'

'Previously undiagnosed. I didn't explain on the phone. . . Yes, that's right, Mrs Peterson; here it comes again. Breathe now, and push. Keep it up right through the contraction. I know you're tired. Hold your legs. . .'

'Then——?'

'I felt a third head.'

She got a chance to look up at him at last and got the same fleeting impression she'd got in the corridor a couple of times of dark, unruly hair untainted by grey, dark eyes, straight brows, strong shoulders. . . It didn't really sink in. They were both too busy.

Turning from her, Adam Van Curen palpated the abdomen as she had done—classic presentation, little bottom lower now, and an odd hollow beginning to form in that round white stomach as the first baby moved through the birth canal. If there were two more in there, they'd move a bit now to fill the space again.

Another contraction came, and the head was crowning dramatically now, no longer sliding back when Mrs Peterson stopped pushing, as it had done before.

'Yes, you were right,' Adam Van Curen murmured. 'Why wasn't it diagnosed?'

'She's been missing her clinic appointments. Ducked a scheduled scan. Gather the GP's a bit rusty, too.'

'OK, well, here goes the first. . .' The head was half out now, small enough that the stretched perineum was in no danger of tearing. The respite between contractions was only seconds long. 'Pant through this one, Mrs Peterson,' he said. 'Keep that head from going back. Can you feel it?'

'Can I *feel* it? You have to be joking! It's like a——Ah!'

'Deep breath, and. . .'

The head was out. A baby. That blessed miracle again. Its eyes were tightly closed and its face purplish and wet and waxy. In sleep, yet it wasn't like sleep but like a brief suspended trance. First shoulder rotated and slipped out. Second shoulder. Then Mr Van Curen guided out the torso and spindly legs. Smaller than the head, they came much more quickly.

'Ah. . .!' came again from Mrs Peterson.

Now. . .a boy, mouth open, eyes screwed up, bawling in protest, as healthy pink gradually reached his extremities. The slippery blue-white cord, still pulsating. . .

'You have a beautiful boy, Mrs Peterson,' Adam Van Curen said. 'Now. . .'

Louise took the little thing into her hands, having suctioned out nose and throat while the consultant held him. He looked good, red and frog-like, still crying lustily. The pain medication Mrs Peterson had taken had barely had time to cross the placenta. She added up his Agpar score—two for heart-rate, two for respiratory effort. . . His cries subsided as he was laid on his mother's still huge stomach for a brief, wonderful moment. Then she weighed, wiped and warmed him. Five pounds, two ounces.

Adam Van Curen was busy with monitors. He had managed to clip one on to the second baby's head and attached it to the screen. 'OK. . .' Two careful, controlled syllables. He was trying to get as close as possible to the second baby's heart with an external monitor, but kept getting interference from the mother's heartbeat, much slower. 'Hang on. . .'

He had it now and Louise could hear that it was far too slow, and it dipped still further as the relentless uterine contractions began again. 'Let's get her to Theatre.' This time Adam Van Curen's voice had the sharp report of a gunshot and the lusty and timeless miracle of birth became the very different modern miracle of technology triumphing over dark fate.

Mrs Peterson's contractions were fiercer than ever, but this time there was no head being pushed down against the cervix. 'This one's in a transverse lie.' The consultant pointed at the internal monitor. 'And the third. . .feels like the smallest. . .is being squeezed way up on the left side.'

'Here comes the placenta from the first. . .'

It was safely delivered and Louise examined it carefully. It had come away complete. Add a tick for that to the tick for one healthy baby. Still some nagging question marks. . .

The anaesthetist had arrived in Theatre. The paediatrician was on stand-by. Gaby Driver was scrubbing up, and so was the SHO.

'Can I. . .? What should I. . .?' Poor Mr Peterson had been swept aside like a leaf in a current.

'You won't be able to come in, I'm afraid.' Adam Van Curen's voice was low and serious. 'There just isn't time. We'll be putting her under general anaesthesia. . .'

Louise was already giving a catechism for the anaesthetist's benefit. Had Mrs Peterson ever had surgery? Was she allergic to any medicines? When had she eaten her last meal? Drunk her last fluids?

Moved to a wheeled stretcher, Mrs Peterson had another contraction which tightened her abdomen and showed up on the monitor. That second heartbeat had dipped alarmingly again. She was raced down the corridor. Louise put a drip into her hand and attached a bag of fluid high on a stand. The anaesthetist calculated his dose and added it through a tap-like opening to the clear tube that was taped to Mrs Peterson's hands.

A sterile field. Bright lights. Theatre greens. Far too many people. The SHO frowning and exhausted-looking. . .

The first baby, Neil Patrick, was already in Neonatal Intensive Care, although the parents had been assured that this was only routine. He seemed extremely healthy, but he was four weeks early, and with those other occupants fighting for space and nutrients in the womb. . .

'Heart-rate on number two is forty-eight now,' Louise pointed out quietly.

'We're nearly there.'

Then suddenly there was the dark green-black of meconium in the fluid that leaked on to the draped table and the urgency increased still more. There was something about nights. Perhaps it was the sudden wash of adrenalin into tired bodies. The faces around the operating table looked stark, with tightly pulled lines. Louise's heart was beating faster now, and she felt a determination that was almost, but not quite, exhilaration.

Mrs Peterson was out now, blessedly, fully draped. The consultant palpated the first baby with his gloved hand. 'Still that transverse lie. Seems pretty tight. I could turn it, maybe, if there were more time, but there isn't. That rules out a low transverse incision.'

Instead, the far more dramatic classic vertical incision. Retractors held back the skin and with a fine balance of speed and control Adam Van Curen cut through the layers of muscle and moved the bladder out of the way, then gradually deepened the incision through the uterus until the foetal sac of the larger baby showed through. Lying sideways, its position was extremely tricky, and Louise had a moment to be thankful that Alan Peterson could hear nothing through the sound-proofed glass window that gave him a view of his inert wife. The SHO swore then began to whistle thinly under his breath. Gaby Driver gave a tense cough into her mask.

'I don't want that incision any bigger,' Adam Van Curen muttered, 'and yet. . .'

The head was pulled free after what seemed like much more than the few seconds it really was, and then the shoulders. Louise was ready to suction out the mouth and nose, and did so as soon as she could get a hand in. With the meconium staining in the amniotic fluid, the danger of the baby breathing it into his tiny, tender lungs and developing a serious lung infection was very real.

'Good,' came the consultant's voice when she had finished.

The baby breathed, cried, writhed, but less lustily than her brother. This was a girl, and at least a pound smaller. The paediatrician stepped in and took the child, and within a few minutes she was in a humidicrib, with a respirator and heart monitor in place. Meanwhile, Adam Van Curen had already pulled the third child from the open incision, and they could all see at a glance that this was the smallest and most endangered of the three. Another boy. Only about three pounds, and with limp muscle tone and irregular breathing.

A nurse from Neonatal Intensive Care suctioned out this one's nose and throat and it was immediately whisked away.

'Touch-and-go,' Dr Slattery, the paediatrician, said very quietly.

'We've done a good job,' Adam Van Curen murmured on a growl. 'It's. . .unfortunate that she missed her appointments.'

'She doesn't like hospitals, apparently,' Louise put in.

The consultant gave a wry shrug, then addressed the inert patient with surprising gentleness as he began to stitch the delicate yet resilient uterine membrane closed. 'My love, haven't you heard the saying a stitch in time saves nine? Please, please remember it next time.'

'Tell her that when she's awake.'

'I will. . . Or her husband.'

'He certainly seemed to be supporting her attitude,' Louise said.

Closing the wound took far longer than actually getting the babies out. Adam Van Curen worked neatly and carefully, aware of the prominent line that would be left arrowing down Mrs Peterson's lower abdomen. Louise assisted him, tired now. It was hard when a delivery ended like this, a question mark hanging over the health of the babies, a helpless father staring miserably through the glass at them, and the new mother unable to enjoy her well-earned sense of satisfaction.

Twenty minutes later, it was all over.

'Thanks, everyone.' Mr Van Curen was brisk now as he tossed his gloves in the bin. 'Three babies and a recovering mum. Staff Nurse. . .' He looked around, found Louise's name-badge and finished, 'Redding.'

'Yes, Mr Van Curen.'

'I'll talk to the dad for a minute than you can take him across to NICU.'

So they left the theatre together, pulling their masks off at the same time, and Mr Peterson came towards them, looking rather grey around the lips. 'Is. . . Are. . .?'

'It went well, Mr Peterson. The babies have been taken to Neonatal Intensive Care. The third one, the other little boy, is small and had rather a hard time.

He'll need some special care. The first one is a splendid chap and will be able to go home with your wife in about five days or so. The little girl needs to do some growing before she's safe to leave. That's going to be hard on you and Mrs Peterson. I gather. . .'

'She hates these places.'

'Yes, and can you see now why that's all the more reason for her to keep her clinic appointments? If we'd known in advance that there were three of them——'

'She just wanted it all to go smoothly. She just couldn't face coming in until she had to.' The point didn't seem to be sinking in. The consultant's gaze, dark-eyed with a flash of fire, met Louise's very briefly, acknowledging a defeat that, she felt sure, was only temporary.

She came in, 'If you have any questions, Mr Peterson, I'll try to answer them for you. Let's go over and see the babies now. . .'

They did so, and Mr Peterson stared at them mournfully with nothing to say until Louise felt she had to jump in with explanations about respiration and posture, reflexes and tone, just to fill the space.

'Peter's half the size of Neil,' he said at last. 'He's got some catching up to do.'

'He may always be a little smaller. Is your wife planning to breast-feed?'

'She wants to.'

'That's good.'

'She knows it's better. . .but she thinks she'll hate it.'

When pressed, he said he wanted to stay for a while so she left him and returned to her own wing, only to be greeted by Mary Rigmore once again. 'I'm sending you in with Adam again.'

'Another admission?'

'There's a full moon.'

'Another one of those myths that you'd swear was

true, wouldn't you?' Louise laughed. 'On full-moon nights——'

'I'd certainly swear it! This one's a patient he's been seeing all along—second pregnancy after a six-year gap, needed surgery for endometriosis and fibroids before she could conceive. Now it's breech and a bit early.'

'Another Caesarean, then?'

'No, he doesn't believe in routine Caesareans for breech deliveries.' She spread her hands. 'His Caesarean rate is extremely low, and he's proud of it, and I must say he's never made a mistake. If you'd rather Gaby. . .'

'No,' said Louise firmly, determined to get rid of this 'new girl' image. She didn't like special treatment. 'But I'll check Mrs Hilliard first. . .'

Five minutes later, she was washing thoroughly, ready for the new patient. To be honest, she wasn't thinking a lot about the impending delivery, nor about Adam Van Curen. To be *more* honest, she was mainly thinking about her own bed, and how it was only a few hours now until she would be in it. There was something about nights. . .but at this pre-dawn hour she had trouble remembering what it was.

She thrust open the door of Room Six and suddenly her low ebb was over. A woman sat on the bed, twisted forward with her face buried in a dark man's shoulder. Her pretty pile of auburn hair was tumbled all over the place, and the man. . .presumably her husband. . .was getting the shoulder of his shirt all wet as he made soothing noises from deep in his throat.

'Having a hard time, are you, my love?' Louise began as she moved briskly forward to get the patient settled. She wasn't yet gowned, there was no equipment in the room. . . Lots to do.

Then she stopped abruptly as the man lifted his head and looked around.

Not the husband at all. Adam Van Curen. He was no longer in theatre greens, and hadn't yet donned the sterile gown that would cover his clothing later on during the delivery. His unruly dark hair curled freely against the collar of a dark red shirt worn above black twill-weave trousers that were slung closely over his hard hips and muscled waist. He must have been somewhere in his middle thirties, and he had such very dark eyes, pooled with concern for his patient, and very white teeth in a generous, firm-lipped mouth. . .

I didn't look at him before, Louise realised. I didn't *see* him at all until just now, when I thought he was a husband.

And. . .there was definitely something about nights. . .she wished quite strongly that she weren't seeing him so clearly now.

Because he was far too good-looking, and prickles of wariness travelled up her spine. Was it stupid that she still distrusted herself whenever she felt the faintest physical response to a man? Probably. Possibly. The reason for this reaction stood out glaringly in her past and ambushed her once again, more freshly and vividly than it had done for a long time. Seven years ago, at twenty-one, she had mistaken physical infatuation for love. . .

'I'm sorry,' she said quickly now. Not the time to be distracted by self-doubt. She added, 'Should I wait a while, Mr Van Curen?'

But it was the patient, Mrs Dace, who answered, 'No, Nurse, I'm fine now. I'm sorry. It's just that this is two weeks early and my husband's away in Stockholm on business.'

'He's probably already at the airport, madly trying to charter a flight home,' the consultant said, and a smile like thin sunshine after rain came to his patient's face.

'He didn't want to go, but I made him.' Her voice

wavered again. 'And now I wish I never had. I'd counted on him so much. . .'

'Don't you feel you can count on us, Mrs Dace?' Louise asked gently. 'You can, you know.'

'Oh, I know, but it's not the same.'

'We talked at your last two appointments about trying for a normal delivery even though we knew the baby wasn't going to turn,' the consultant said to his patient. 'But that's not set in stone. Without your husband's support, if you feel you'd like to go in for a Caesarean. . . Many obstetricians these days would take that route automatically.'

Mrs Dace didn't answer, as a strong contraction built in her body and she sat rigid on the edge of the bed, trying to breathe through it but not succeeding very well. When it had passed, she said, 'No, I don't want the Caesarean. When I had Gwen six years ago it was so. . .magnificent, really. I'd like to do it that way again. But I do think I want the epidural.'

'Yes, we talked about that. I want to put it in anyway in case we do have to rush you off to Theatre, and if you'd like it in straight away let's do it. Staff Nurse Redding. . .' he had had to look at her name again. '. . .will get you settled, while I go and tell Peter Craven—he's our anaesthetist tonight—what's going on.'

He left and Mrs Dace sighed. 'He's not James. . .my husband. . .but he's good. Isn't he?'

She turned to Louise, who answered steadily, 'Oh, yes. He's the best.' And she found that she believed it as she said it, although she couldn't really know about him yet. He had seemed focused and caring during Mrs Peterson's long delivery. That was about all she knew.

Another contraction came, and it was time to get to work. This new maternity unit was marvellous, a far cry from the hundred-year-old Nightingale wards that labouring mums had used up until just a few months ago. Mrs Dace was able to use a small but private bathroom that opened straight from this room, and by bringing equipment in on wheeled trolleys when it was needed they could ensure that her delivery took place here, even when epidural anaesthesia was used. After the birth, the equipment would be wheeled away again, the curtains opened in daylight, and the room would be hers until she was discharged, with the new baby in the room with her for as much of the time as Mrs Dace wished, but able to return to the nursery if she needed extra rest.

Now Louise opened the bathroom door. 'There's even a shower if you'd like one.'

'Um. . . I don't think so. Just the toilet. It's getting. . .'

She stopped and began to pant, too tightly gripped by pain to keep on walking. Another contraction took hold on her way back from the bathroom to the bed and Louise thought, Second child, contractions every two minutes. I hope we have time to get that epidural in.

Mrs Dace's blood-pressure, temperature and pulse were all as they should be, her cervix was paper-thin and seven centimetres dilated. Leaving the patient alone, reluctantly, Louise went to get monitoring equipment and the trolley and warming bed that would be needed for the baby later on. She met Adam Van Curen in the corridor. 'Craven's finishing another Caesar, so there'll be a bit of a delay. How is she?'

'Progressing. Comfortably settled. Doesn't want to be alone.'

'I'll go in again and put up a drip. She may have a long second stage with the presentation she's got. Membrane ruptured yet?'

'Not yet.'

'I'll wait a bit before doing that if it doesn't go on its own, or it will speed things up and Craven will get here too late.'

The drip was in by the time Louise got back and she attached the two belts of the external monitor around Mrs Dace's abdomen—one for foetal heart-rate, the other to measure the contractions—then moved the first belt around until she found the rhythmic pulse she was listening for. It was in the right range, hovering around a hundred and thirty a minute, good and strong.

The consultant had remained with Mrs Dace until all this was done, but left again now. Louise didn't know why. Perhaps for coffee. Perhaps paperwork. He didn't explain. Consultants often didn't. They were lordly creatures, which was fine. They'd worked hard to get where they were. She was wary of this one, and wanted her unexpected and too sudden awareness of him to please, very nicely, just go away. . .

Things were really hotting up now. Mrs Dace couldn't rest or gain any comfort between contractions, and since there was no husband there for support Louise didn't want to leave her alone again. The membrane ruptured suddenly, releasing a flood of warm water. No meconium staining, which was good. No sign of cord prolapse, which could be a danger in breech presentations. The labouring woman gripped Louise's hand and moaned through each tightening rack of pain, asking as each one ebbed, 'Is the anaesthetist nearly ready? Won't he be here soon?'

At last he was, with Adam Van Curen hard on his heels, and Mrs Dace pulled herself together a bit now that she could see the end of the pain approaching. It took some time to get the cannula into her back. She had to slump forward to open up the space between the vertebrae, and once the spinal catheter had been inserted the thing had to be taped up her back and out of the way before the drug could be put in.

Sweat darkened the auburn hair now, and her gown was open and falling off one shoulder. Like most women at this stage, she couldn't care less. At last

Peter Craven looked at Mrs Dace from beneath his bushy, sand-coloured brows and said, 'This next contraction should feel less intense.' It did and Mrs Dace relaxed back against the bed and watched her pain on a monitor.

'Marvellous!' she said. 'I really don't know what this natural childbirth is all about. I did it with Gwen, but never again. The actual birth was wonderful, but the lead-up? Yuck!'

The consultant gave her a quick internal examination. 'Almost there,' he said. 'And if Peter's done his job properly you should still feel enough lower down to tell you when to push.'

The anaesthetist glowered at the suggestion that he might *not* have done his job properly, then left.

'Don't expect this to go fast,' Mr Van Curen warned.

It didn't. With the baby's healthy-sized little bottom wedged tightly down in the pelvis for some weeks now, there had been no chance that it would turn on its own, and Mrs Dace had to work hard to push it through the birth canal. A glimpse of the little purple cheeks came at last, then they slipped back, appeared again.

'Her pushing's still not efficient enough,' Adam Van Curen said in an aside to Louise, his dark eyes fixed on her beneath a frown that rippled his high brow. Mrs Dace had been at it for over an hour already, and was tiring and getting discouraged despite the relief given by the epidural. 'Can you coach her harder? I don't want to bully, but——'

'She's trying.'

'She's not trying enough. At this rate. . . Look, the heart-rate is dropping during each contraction now. Not dangerously, but measurably. She can do this. I don't want to stop now and head off to Theatre, but. . . Don't you have any coaching tricks up your sleeve?'

'I'll try.' She turned to the patient. 'Can you do something for me, Mrs Dace?'

'No. . .'

'Yes. Listen. I want you to think of a car's accelerator. When you push on that, you don't stick it flat to the floor in the first second or two and just leave it there, do you?'

'No. . .'

'Instead you keep pressing steadily, pushing it further and further down. Can you try that for me now? Don't even think about getting a baby out. Just push steadily harder and harder as the contraction builds.'

'Yes. . . OK. . . Like an accelerator pedal.'

Adam Van Curen was frowning still, his mouth tucked in at one corner, clearly sceptical of the analogy. Louise spread her hands and gave a rueful, upside-down smile. How did you explain these things? She'd remembered another labouring mum who had said this worked for her, imagining a car's accelerator. Some women described it in cruder terms. Others had an instinct for it and couldn't describe what they were doing at all. Louise had never done it herself. . .

'Here goes,' said Mrs Dace, and she began to strain, and this time the baby didn't slip back but kept on coming. And with the next push it came further. And again.

'Don't push through this one, Mrs Dace,' the consultant said. 'I don't want you to tear deeply so I'm going to put in a bit of local anaesthetic and cut you neatly in the spot where it will heal best. . .'

Louise prepped the dose of anaesthetic, then coached Mrs Dace to pant through the next contraction as it was administered. Next, she was ready with the instruments that Adam Van Curen needed, and soon a neat slit had widened the perineum enough to get that bottom through.

'If only James were here. . .'

'OK, here we go.'

It was awkward, and lasted through three contractions. First came the little bottom, skilfully helped on its way by Adam Van Curen's gloved hands, then the legs, stiffly held from their weeks of being squeezed against the baby's chest in the frank breech position. Finally—and in a breech presentation this was the trickiest part—the head appeared. 'It's coming. Keep pushing, Mrs Dace. You're doing it. It's coming. It's here. . .'

'You have a beautiful boy,' Louise whispered, and Mrs Dace began to cry.

So did the child. He was wet and slippery and completely perfect, and when he was placed on his mother's abdomen her tears became coos and sighs and she held him and caressed the darkly wet hair that covered his little head. She looked damp and exhausted, yet the picture she and her baby made together was so beautiful that Louise thought, not for the first time, I want that to be me one day. I do!

It wasn't a new realisation, but something she had always known. She held it within her like a guiding star, ignoring the pain that the knowledge sometimes brought her, and she could only try to forget the past, when she had thought, for a while, that it was going to happen.

How do I get there from here? she wondered now. At the moment, it still seems like such a long way. . . But oh, it's beautiful!

She smiled and yawned and caught the consultant's eye. He was smiling too, and when he saw her hand covering her open mouth it was contagious and he did the same. Mrs Dace didn't notice. She was saying her baby's name. 'Little William. William James. . .'

Louise and the consultant both had work to do, but for another minute they didn't do it, just watched.

'There's something about birth, when it happens like this, no complications when there easily might have

been, and when it's wanted and healthy and loved,'
Adam Van Curen said softly, watching her.

'Mm,' Louise agreed, suddenly near to tears.

'Something about the stillness. . .' he went on.
'Something about it when it happens at night. . .'

CHAPTER TWO

IT WASN'T night-time any more. The September sun was up and Louise had given her report, put on her light coat and gone down in the lift to leave. It was a glorious morning, actually, and there was something about mornings, too, after that long night shift from nine-ten till seven-thirty.

She stopped outside the main door when she felt the first rush of fresh air in her face and stretched her tired shoulders, closed her eyes and smiled up into the sun that warmed her face. The bed that had seemed so desperately, wonderfully comfortable and important a few hours ago didn't beckon nearly so strongly now. She started to walk, out of the car park and down the hill, past the bus-stop where she had alighted last night. Sensible to take the bus up at night, but now it would be so much nicer to walk the short distance. . .

Except that a car had purred up beside her and someone was offering her a ride. Adam Van Curen.

'Oh. . .' She was so surprised that she stopped dead on the pavement and didn't say yes or no.

He laughed, recognising her astonishment for what it was. 'Um. . .normally I'd have driven straight past, yes.'

'Yes, or you'd be a chauffeur service,' she laughed. 'There's usually quite a cluster at the bus-stop and a good straggle of us going down the hill to the Broadway.'

'I know. You must have been a bit late off. You had such a jaunty walk at this hour——'

'The fresh air revived me.'

'And it caught my eye, the way your hair bounced

30

and rippled round your shoulders now that you've loosened it.'

'Oh, it always falls down when I walk. . .' She was catching at hairpins even as she spoke.

'Then I recognised you and well, it was an impulse.'

'Impulses can be good.'

'Then you accept? Or shall I putter away home and hide my spurned transport in the garage?'

'Putter? This car couldn't putter!' It was a vintage Italian sports car, lovingly maintained in forest-green and polished chrome.

'Nice comfortable leather seat, too.' He patted it invitingly. 'Come on.'

'OK. . .'

He leaned across to open the door for her and she slid in beside him, smelling the leather and polish now, mingled with the crisp, slightly smoky autumn air. For some reason it suddenly made her hungry. Mm. . . She sat back and closed her eyes for a second. Several seconds. The car had started so smoothly that she was scarcely aware of it, although it was quite loud here inside, and they were round the corner of Holmhill Street and halfway down Mountjoy Road before she knew it.

And there was her house, flashing past on the right as he took the bends in the street with creamy-smooth control.

'Um. . .' she began ineffectually. The bus took five minutes to get from the hospital to her stop, and this car had done it in about thirty-five seconds. She felt silly, and almost laughed aloud. To have let him go past her own house!

'Now, where can I drop you?'

'Oh, on the Broadway, just where the shops start,' she improvised quickly. Easy enough to slink back up the hill after he had gone.

'By the Four Seasons Café?'

'Yes, fine.'

'Ah, so you're not going home at all,' he teased. 'You're going to duck in for a cream bun or two?'

'I — Yes, actually.' Why not?

'Want some company?'

What could she say? 'That would be nice, yes. . .'

He had to wait a moment for the traffic to clear, then made the left turn, and found a parking place that was about six inches too small, getting into it with a combination of will-power and manoeuvring that must have left his shoulders sore and taken several months off the wear of his tyres. Louise got out, her coat falling open across her knees.

This is silly! she was thinking. Why did he ask? I hardly know the man. Why did I accept? *Why* did I let him drive past my house? Still, there's no sense in being stiff now. I'll put on my best manner. . .

She liked the Four Seasons, and headed automatically for her usual table by the window, then hoped, as she sat down with her back to the light, that he hadn't had another spot in mind. He looked worried somehow.

The waitress came. 'Hello, Louise.'

'Hello, Trudy.'

Across the table, Adam Van Curen was suddenly and visibly relieved, and Louise hid a smile. So he hadn't noticed her first name, and now he knew!

'Your usual, love?' Trudy was saying.

'Yes, thanks.' She shrugged out of her coat. There! He had her whole name-badge in view now, to prompt him, as she hadn't changed out of her uniform to go home.

'I'll need the menu,' the consultant growled, but he only flicked a quick glance at it before asking for coffee and an apricot Danish pastry. 'You've established your status as a regular pretty quickly,' he teased mildly when the waitress had left. 'How long have you been in the job? A couple of weeks?'

'Actually, I've been coming here for years.'

'Really? I thought——'

'I've lived in the area. . .well, all my life, apart from a break or two.' A break of two and a half years, in fact, when she had lived in Australia. But that wasn't an interlude she cared to discuss just now, although it was very much in her mind.

'Where do you live, then? I'd assumed some nurses' digs round the corner next to the laundrette or something, but——'

'I'm embarrassed, Mr Van Curen,' she said with a reluctant smile.

'Why?'

'We drove right past my place, halfway up Mountjoy Road, but your car was so much faster and smoother than the bus, I didn't manage to tell you to stop in time, so I pretended——' She broke off and spread her hands. 'What a confession! Can I blame it on being tired after the night?'

'I prefer to take it as a compliment to my driving and my car.'

'Please do, then! Your car is marvellous.'

'Ah, a woman who knows when to be impressed!'

'I was impressed because it's better polished than my furniture. . .'

And so she slowly relaxed so much so that she followed his lead after about half an hour and ordered a second cup of coffee and another scone. Somehow they were talking about farming now. 'I grew up on a sheep farm further north,' he told her.

'And you didn't become a vet?'

'I thought about it. My younger sister's one. But, while I don't mind getting up in the night to come to a nice warm civilised hospital to bring babies into the world, the thought of getting up to go out to some draughty barn or boggy field for the sake of lambs and calves. . . For all their faults—and for all the helpless, adorable *wooliness* of lambs—I like humans best.'

'So do I,' she agreed, then thought of a similar discussion she had had one night with her father, one of their many satisfying wrangles in those years before his second stroke, when his verbal skills had still been unimpaired. 'Humans often sin and fail in such interesting ways, don't they? Animals don't.'

'Their owners do,' he pointed out, leaning forward so that a lock of dark hair fell across his high forehead. 'But I know what you mean. Those little ships I help to launch into the current of life—silly metaphor!—I'm fascinated by the thought of where they'll all end up.'

'Washed on to terrible shoals, some of them,' she put in soberly. 'That saddens me.'

'On the other hand. . .' His lean fingers curled around the handle of his cup for the last time as he finished his coffee. 'I keep a set of albums with all their pictures and names, and the names of their parents. It's too early yet, but in my dotage I expect to be able to boast that I delivered a Nobel prize winner, or the singing sensation of the year 2019.'

'So you must be grateful to the parents who call their babies things like Sutcliffe or Dawn Angel,' she suggested. 'You'll never remember that you delivered Jane Brown if she hits the front pages.'

'But will Dawn Angel Brown ever make a mark in life?' he countered quickly, with one brow raised just a little. 'Surely she'll be so embarrassed about her name that she'll slink into the profoundest obscurity she can manage?'

What happened to farming? They never got back to it. She hadn't remotely expected to enjoy herself this much, and guessed—as he looked at his watch in astonishment and horror—that he hadn't either. His firm lips were very expressive. 'My God, I have a clinic at half-past nine. But you live in Mountjoy Road. Good. I can drop you home and still make it. Nice for you to be so close to the hospital.'

'It is, yes. I did my general training here at Morleyvale, too.'

'Let's go.'

This time he roared up the hill and into the driveway that she just had time to point out to him. The morning sun was hitting the mellow pinky-orange brick of the wide front, and the brick-paved front yard was darkened by moss and gently undulating underfoot as she climbed out. He climbed out too, after glancing at his watch and finding that he had time to be polite. 'Great place,' he commented, then amended as he peered through the bay windows, 'If a bit of a mausoleum inside. What? You have a little flat, subdivided off the top floor?'

'No,' she answered simply. 'It's mine.'

'Hell, and I said it was a mausoleum. Sorry.' He tensed his strong shoulders in discomfort.

'That's OK. You were right. It is.'

'You must have inherited it.'

'Yes. From my father. Six months ago.'

'I really am sorry.'

'It's *all right*,' she stressed. 'It needs a lot of work, inside and out. He was too ill. We both wanted to wait. Then after he died I had to get back into the workforce, all the legal stuff, too. It's only just got done. Now I'll do just as you suggested and divide the top two floors into flats. The ground floor is going to be professional rooms, if I can get a tenant. Dad got council approval and plans drawn up for it all several years ago, before he had his stroke. Most of the houses in this street are going that way. Like me, most people can't afford to keep them as single-family dwellings.'

'And you'll live in one of the flats?'

'Yes. The sunny one at the front on the first floor.'

She kept waiting for him to get back in the car and drive off, but he didn't, and was wandering closer and closer to the house as they talked.

'So these stairs at the front here open off their own entrance?'

'Yes.'

'And this front yard is all paved apart from those three lovely rose-beds and the holly trees. Room for — what? — four cars?'

'Five, I'd say, if you count the space in front of the garage down the side there.'

'When do you think the conversion will be done? Have you any possible tenants lined up for the professional rooms?'

'Not yet, no,' she answered. 'I've had other things on my plate.'

'Of course.' His sympathy was matter-of-fact, but very genuine.

'Do you think it'll work?' Suddenly, she was interested in his opinion.

'Yes, it's ideal. People don't always want to go to the middle of a busy shopping street, where there's no parking, and since the bus comes past here too. . .'

He was still looking thoughtfully at the house. His eyes were narrowed, his strong chin jutting forward a little, and his mouth, which was mobile in conversation, was very serious now.

'Thank you for breakfast,' she said, not sure if he was waiting for his cue. 'It was nice.'

'Yes. Thank *you*!' He collected his thoughts and flashed her a stunning grin. 'Bye. . .'

A minute later he was sliding his long legs into his car, and then he had purred out of the semicircular driveway. Louise was left standing there, wondering why her heart was beating harder, wishing it weren't. There was a saying, wasn't there, about even the longest journey having to start with a single step?

One day, I want love. I want it all, she knew. But I'm still so scared of going down the wrong path. The first step terrifies me which is a good reason to make myself take it, I suppose.

Take it with Adam Van Curen? If he was offering. . . Somehow, her emotional antennae must have been pretty sharp this morning, because she had sensed his interest which of course might be very fleeting. . .

It's just the first step. There doesn't necessarily have to be a second one. I will, if he asks. I *need* to! she told herself.

'You haven't met Mr Henslow yet, have you, Louise?'

'No.' Although the name had been ringing bells whenever her busy mind had alighted on it in passing as she caught up on paperwork. 'He's been away since I started.'

'Well, he's back, and with a vengeance,' Judy Smith said. An experienced midwifery sister of thirty-five, she had swapped rosters with Mary Rigmore this shift.

'My goodness,' Louise responded to Judy's last phrase. 'With a vengeance! Why?'

'Oh. . .' The older nurse shrugged. 'I don't like him, that's all. He shouldn't be an obstetrician. He doesn't care enough. In my opinion.' Abruptly spoken. Sister Smith could be short-tempered and abrasive at times, Louise was beginning to discover.

Now she tried a gentle tease to restore the atmosphere. 'And all this is a preliminary to telling me he's waiting for my assistance in Theatre right now?'

'Exactly, and the man has the patience of a tired two-year-old, so get your skates on.'

It was night-time again. A quarter past two in the morning, to be precise, but somehow this was turning into one of those *other* kinds of nights. The kind when she had to fight hard just to stay awake and involved, fight to remember just why it was that she had decided that midwifery was the career for her, and the kind when everyone was in a bad mood—including the babies!

They had had two teenage mums already, both too young for parenthood and neither with any good economic or personal prospects. One of them had screamed through her entire labour and delivery—fortunately rather quick—and the other had scarcely looked at her baby.

Louise thought of Adam Van Curen's metaphor yesterday morning—little ships launched into the current of life. Well, two little ships had been launched tonight, but it made her angry and sad to think of the stormy passages ahead for them. Let his little spirit be resilient, she had almost prayed over the one she had delivered. Let it survive.

Judy had attended the other birth, the screamer, and had been tight-lipped and taciturn ever since, which didn't help to turn the night around. *And* it was raining, chilly, relentless buckets of the stuff. The wetness had plastered down the thinning hair of the man coming towards Louise now in the corridor outside the theatre suite. He looked impatient and irritable and he had to be Mr Henslow.

'Are you doing this with me?' he growled at Louise, but before she could reply his tone and his manner suddenly changed. 'My God, it's Louise Redding, isn't it?'

'Yes, it is, but. . .' She frowned and smiled politely at the same time. Had she ever met. . .? Then recognition dawned. 'John Henslow!' Gracious, she would never have known him in a crowd, and even the sound of his name on Judy's lips hadn't jogged her memory at first.

'John Henslow at your service.' He bowed with studied gallantry, and a slick of long wet hair flopped over to the wrong side of his parting, reaching almost to his shoulder, exposing the bald spot it was so carefully designed to hide. 'You didn't recognise me, did you?' he accused.

'It's been so long,' she responded feebly. Over seven years. 'And your hair was wet.' She went on quickly, 'To be honest, in the middle of the night, on my way to an emergency Caesarean, I wasn't thinking about faces from the past.'

It was here that they had met, during her training. He had been a student on rotation in the same department—Paediatrics—where she had been working then, and he must have liked the hospital, as she did, because now he was back here on staff as a senior registrar. Obstetrics. It *was* a choice that surprised her, and she remembered what Judy Smith had said. 'He shouldn't be an obstetrician. He doesn't care enough.' Seven years ago she had got the impression that he would go into something more convenient or more lucrative.

'No, well, neither was I,' he was saying. 'But you haven't changed much.' A flicker in his very attractive light blue eyes told her that he approved of her appearance.

They entered the theatre suite together and began to prepare, scrubbing up and putting on theatre greens. The patient was still on her way by ambulance, apparently.

'Bloody nuisance,' was John's comment. 'I had her scheduled for tomorrow anyway. She's breech. We tried to turn her from the outside at thirty-six weeks but it wouldn't budge. Now—typical!—she goes in the middle of the night, and the membrane's ruptured and the cord's prolapsing. . . But anyway, where have you been all my life? You disappeared on me!'

'I——' She stopped. Yes, she had disappeared. She had gone to Australia. But she didn't want to talk about it now! His casual dismissal of the imminent patient, in labour and with her cord prolapsing, had repelled her. Babies could and did die that way. 'Um, it's not really the time for catching up on the past, is it?' she told the senior registrar.

'No. You're right, of course,' he said, more soberly now. 'We should get together properly, shouldn't we? Do this serendipitous reunion justice. Are you on again tonight?'

'Yes, and for the rest of the week.' It was designed to put him off. She sensed a date in the wind—that 'first step' she had thought about the other day—and didn't really want to go out with him. She'd done so, seven years ago, and even back then she hadn't been bowled over, in spite of a blue-eyed senior medical student's cachet with some of her fellow nurses.

But John Henslow had taken her words the other way. 'On tonight,' he echoed. 'So how about dinner beforehand, then I'll drive you on up here?'

They were ready to go into Theatre now; the rest of the team was at work, and a commotion down the corridor told her that the ambulance and patient had arrived. 'Dinner would be nice,' she said, forcing herself, remembering her recent resolution to start that long journey.

'I'll pick you up at six forty-five, then. Now, I don't suppose you're at Mountjoy Street still?'

'Actually, I am.'

'Hmm! In that case, no need to tell me the address.' He said this last bit conspiratorially, nudging her shoulder with his, and then they were plunged into the emergency operation.

In surgery, John Henslow was very competent. The words of reassurance he flung to the mother were necessarily brief. She was put in a special position to keep the pressure off the cord, while being prepped as quickly as humanly possibly. Oxygen was given, and general anaesthesia, which was far quicker to administer than the epidural used in more relaxed circumstances.

Louise's job, once the patient was unconscious, was simple: continue to stop the baby's presenting part from putting pressure on the prolapsing cord. John moved fast to make his incision, and used an even knife-stroke to open the tissue beneath the skin. When the uterine incision was completed, in what seemed just like a few seconds, Louise moved quickly to apply external pressure as the senior registrar manipulated the presenting part through the incision.

'OK, I think we've got her in time,' he said, and out came a smallish girl. About six pounds, Louise estimated. 'Ugly, but healthy?' He held the baby up and flicked her heels, then passed her to the paediatrician as her cries started up. The assisting SHO administered a drug to assist the uterus in contracting while John manually delivered the placenta. 'Now,' he cracked, 'if only you could close 'em as quickly as you open 'em up!'

The circulating nurse, Naomi Johnson, snickered dutifully, but Louise couldn't manage to. He had always been intelligent and capable, she remembered grudgingly. He was at work now, closing the uterus with textbook suturing technique and careful attention to detail, and in the background the paediatrician was saying, 'She's in excellent condition. Good work, John, getting her out so quickly.' The man's social graces and sense of humour, on the other hand. . . And she was going out with him tonight! The very thought made her want to take to her bed, and she clamped her jaws around a gaping yawn.

'So, the sands of time and all that. . . What have *you* been doing?'

They'd both nearly finished the solid if uninspiring dinner at the local steakhouse, and Louise had managed to keep him busy for most of the time with questions about his life. She had found out why he went into Obstetrics.

'*Chercher la femme*,' he had said. 'I was after a certain woman at the time, and that was her field. Cold meat in the end, she turned out to be—and I'm glad, *now*. . .' His glance was meaningful. 'But by the time I found that out it was too late. I was a FRCOG and stuck with it. . . Well, I exaggerate, but you know what I mean. After putting in six months, it seemed a waste to switch to something else. Sometimes, like getting called out this morning for that cord prolapse, I *know* I made a bad decision!'

He'd gone on about this at some length and she'd almost thought she was going to get away with revealing little of her own life, but it was not to be. The sands of time. She had to tell him something. . . While she paused to sift through what she wanted to say and what she had to say, he helped her out.

'Nothing much, evidently, if you're still in the neighbourhood. Yet you haven't been at the hospital all this time, or I'd have seen you. I've been there over a year now.'

'No, I've only just started, as you say,' she answered him. 'I took—um—several years off to look after my father. He was elderly—he was nearly fifty when I was born—and he'd had a stroke.'

'To look after him?' John echoed, his blue eyes wide. He had been good-looking seven years ago, but that had been superficial, and very easily watered down with the years. His face looked weak and lacking in character, and only his eyes really retained their charm. He was exclaiming now, 'You mean you gave up work and stayed home with him, shut away in that house like some Victorian spinster with an invalid relative in a bath chair?'

'If that's how you want to put it, yes,' she said coolly.

He back-pedalled. 'Sorry, that sounded rude. I didn't mean. . .But you know what I meant, don't you?'

'Oh, yes—yes, of course.'

She let him off the hook, wondering inwardly if this was how other people saw her: a Victorian spinster with a father in a bath chair. It hadn't really occurred to her before, and it didn't coincide with her sense of self at all. She had loved her father, owed him an enormous amount, and he had needed her, that was all. And if she'd told John how good those years with him had been, especially after what had happened in Australia, she sensed that he wouldn't really believe her.

Since she didn't want to tell him about Australia anyway, she let it slide. If John Henslow thought her a social anachronism, so be it.

And clearly he did. He had stopped giving her those distinctly syrupy blue looks with his pale, handsome eyes. Knees which had been nudging hers under the table were suddenly coyly paired at the edge of his seat. 'I'd better get going,' he said. 'You don't mind if I drop you at the hospital a few minutes early, do you? I have to get off. . .papers to write up; I've got a conference in a couple of months. . .'

'No, that's fine.' A few minutes early? It was barely eight, and her shift didn't start till ten past nine.

'You can have coffee before you start,' he suggested helpfully.

'Yes, I will.' With the newspaper, in the little cafeteria tucked between the main building and the new maternity wing.

He commandeered the bill with an impatient gesture, then said with distant gallantry, 'I'll get it. Don't worry.'

And since his income was probably at least twice the size of hers, and this whole thing had been his idea anyway, she didn't worry in the slightest.

'Good to catch up with you,' was his final assessment

of the event as he pulled up outside the maternity wing. 'Nice to have a familiar face in the unit. We'll have to keep in touch.'

Some inner demon prompted her to say with a wickedly plaintive intonation. 'Aren't you going to kiss me? For old times' sake?'

'Oh—er—of course.' And he planted a peck on her closed lips with a reluctance that made her wonder if he thought her supposed 'spinsterhood'. . .for that read virginity. . .was catching.

The cafeteria was nice and quiet, and, as she had hoped, there were a few newspapers left, so she got her coffee and plunged at once, with relish, into the foreign news section.

As she read about the dramas of humanity and nature in far corners of the globe, painful emotion caught her unawares like an unexpected rain squall, and she had to swallow back tears for a time. I miss Dad and our talks, she thought. He knew so much. . .

She stopped reading for a minute, remembering. Her father had been a foreign correspondent for years, until his late marriage at the age of forty-eight, and right up until his last stroke, a few months before his death, he had retained a zestful interest in the world, at home and abroad. Not just war and politics, but art and popular culture as well. Physically, they had led such circumscribed lives together during those last four years of his life, but mentally they had voyaged to the stars. . .

He was gone now, and she missed it all, missed him, missed him.

Gulping some hot black coffee, she recovered, put her mourning aside until the next time, and went on reading, a fashion supplement now, concentrating fiercely now to keep sadness at bay. It worked, and soon she was laughing and shaking her head at some of the ludicrous creations that the featured designers were trying to foist upon the female population this year.

When she looked up at last, some minutes later, she saw that someone else had come in with a paper too, and was at the next table, sitting back and holding the rustling pages high, as she was doing, to discourage intrusion. At first, all she could see was a pair of long legs in dark trousers, some lean fingers curled at the edges of the pages, and the top of an unruly dark head, but then he lowered the paper a little and she saw that it was Adam Van Curen.

Quickly she lifted her own paper again. He obviously wanted to be alone, as she did. She didn't want him to feel that he had to talk, or even say hello. Her paper rustled as she found another article to read. His rustled too, and then five minutes later they lowered their pages at the same time, finding it impossible to ignore each other any longer.

Their eyes met cautiously over the top of each set of newsprint. The corners of his firm mouth rose in a polite smile. So did hers. She almost put the paper down, feeling she ought to speak. Her mouth opened. So did his. Then, in silent agreement made somehow through the subtlest of body language, they each took a mouthful of coffee, lifted their newspapers again, and returned to their reading.

A moment later, very quietly and drily from behind his paper, she heard the consultant say, 'Louise Redding, you're a woman I could deeply respect!'

CHAPTER THREE

'THESE plans look just right for the place,' the builder told Louise. 'Do you know who did them?'

'No, I don't, I'm afraid, but you do think you could work from them?'

'Oh, no problem at all, love.' He began to stride from room to room so fast that Louise could barely keep up. 'Front room for the main office, I see. Wall opened here to give access from here to the scullery, which becomes a wash-room. . . This back room here for storage of files. . . Kitchen's not well-used, I notice, in the plans. You could dismantle it and use it to furbish the new ones you'll be building on the top two floors for the second and third flats.'

'No, I'd rather not do that,' Louise said quickly. Probably foolish, but she didn't want to feel that the house could never become home to a family again in the future. She went on, 'Would the conversion take long?'

'Including the two new kitchens and the bathroom upstairs, a couple of months, but if you just wanted to start with the ground floor. . . You say you'll be using the first flat up the stairs?'

'Yes. It's fairly small, but that's all I need.'

'And it already has the kitchen and bathroom.'

'Yes. I'd like a shower put in there later—it's not on the plan—but that could wait too if necessary.'

'I've got a job got cancelled on me at the beginning of next month. I could do your flat and the professional rooms then.'

'It. . .it sounds wonderful. I'll have to think about it.' She hadn't expected things to move this fast. This builder had done the dentist's surgery up the road, and was licensed and highly recommended, so she certainly didn't want to put him off, but. . .

'Think about it, then,' he told her, 'and give me a ring. That slot might fill up fast, and after that I'm booked solid till——'

'I know. I'm sure you are. I'll ring you on Monday.'

It was Saturday morning, and her last night shift for this duty roster had finished just three hours ago. For the next few weeks she would be back on a shifting pattern of mornings, evenings and days off, and in spite of the special quality of nights she was looking forward to it. It was hard to get enough sleep when your clock was running opposite to the rest of the country, and there was a tendency to try and squeeze in too many errands.

On Thursday she had talked to her father's solicitor about the legal aspects of acquiring tenants, and yesterday, when the builder had returned her phone call with unexpected promptness, she had jumped at the first time he suggested for coming round.

Now, with all she had to think about and plan for and decide on, she just wanted to go to bed. The builder, Ted Shaw, departed and she did so, sleeping soundly until three. Restored by a shower, she then put on jeans and a baggy cerise-coloured T-shirt and sat in the little conservatory that opened off the kitchen, reading. Not current affairs today, but an extremely light novel that was deliciously funny in all the right places.

It was a wonderfully mellow early autumn day. The leaves had not yet begun to turn and the roses were still lavish. The birds knew to make the most of it, as well. They were singing their heads off in the old pear trees at the back of the garden. The garden needed attention, but she had tomorrow for that. Right now. . . The question of the house hovered in the back of her mind but it didn't seem pressing or worrying. She stretched her shoulders and her toes, contemplated a cup of tea. . .

And the phone rang. 'Darn! If it's someone trying to *sell* me something. . .!'

But it wasn't. It was Adam Van Curen. He didn't waste any time in polite conversation. 'I wondered if you'd got any further with finding a tenant for your ground floor, because—I thought I should let you know as soon as possible—it's a tranquil, attractive place and it's so close to the hospital. . . I'm definitely interested.'

Half an hour later, he was climbing out of his low-slung car into her now shaded front yard.

Louise was at the door before he rang the bell, having heard his car. Her heart was beating rather fast and that seemed silly, but on second thoughts perhaps it was understandable. This was a business visit, not a personal one, not that first step she was having such trouble with, but it was important. If he liked what he saw, then she'd definitely have to get back to Ted Shaw straight away.

'I hope he *does* like it,' she murmured as he approached, insisting to herself that this was why her fluttering heart was fluttering even more. It could have nothing to do with the silhouette of the man in those faded hip-hugging jeans, or his lazy, lion-like walk, let alone the smooth lines of his neck and jaw as he raised his head in greeting. She distrusted any physical response to a man so intensely now. . .

'Thanks for letting me come at such short notice,' he said. 'But with our schedules I didn't know how long it might be before we'd manage to coincide so nicely again, and I'm anxious to get it settled.'

'So am I.' She told him what Ted Shaw had said, and he nodded.

They were inside now, in the cool hall that ran

straight through the house. With the sun shining full into the back garden, the house was bright today, and she could see a small flat mole on his cheekbone, like a fleck of chocolate. Apart from that, his face was very smooth. . .

'It's like a tour, isn't it?' she said quickly, once again too aware of him, although the hall was quite wide. 'Let's start here, and I'll show you the plans as we go. You'd need to paint. I hate this green!'

'Yes, it's like the old Nightingale wards we used before the new maternity wing was finished. But you hadn't started then.'

'No, but I remember them from when I trained. I don't think they'd changed the colour since the fifties!'

'1850s would that be?'

She laughed. 'I don't know why that green is so horrible, actually. You'd think it would be nice, like a shady garden, or something, but it's not, is it?'

'No, it's sickly and sterile, like a bilious complexion. I will paint. It should be——' He stopped and looked. 'Heck, I don't know. Sort of whitish? Or a pinky-yellow? What do they call that?'

'Peach,' she supplied drily. 'You're not a decorator.'

'No. . . And yet I don't want to get someone in and have it turn out like a gracious living magazine. That sort of thing can date so fast, or look fussy and inappropriate. Do you think I should go to a hardware store and get a colour card or two and sort of grunt and point?'

She laughed again. 'Don't you have a girlfriend who can help?'

'Not at the moment.'

And their eyes met, and somehow it was awkward, and she was sorry she'd asked, hadn't really intended him to answer seriously. She knew now that she had been wondering—secretly, not admitting it even to herself—if he was attached or unencumbered. Well, now she knew, and much good it did her. His interest must be purely practical, she had decided. That first step. . . She'd have to find someone else to take it with.

She said quickly, opening the door to the room on the right where her father had slept in his last years, 'As you see from the plans, this will be a waiting-room. It's large enough for a desk and chairs and magazine table.'

'What about files?'

'The next room. Look. . . There's no connecting door. The receptionist would have to go out into the hall again. Maybe that should be changed.'

'Not really a problem. She'd gather all the files for a particular surgery session and have them ready on the desk.'

'Yes, that would work, wouldn't it?'

They were both sounding a little *too* practical now. 'I'm sorry it's all so cluttered,' she said, waving a hand at the large, well-crammed bookshelves and the too abundant furniture. 'My father loved books.'

'He has some good ones.'

'And the furniture had sentimental value to him. He'd spent so much of his life travelling—almost thirty years—that when he finally settled down he ended up with too much.'

'Travelled? For his work? What did he do?'

'He was a journalist, a foreign correspondent, until the mid-sixties, then he worked for a magazine here in London after he married and I came along.'

'He married late.'

'Yes.'

'He must have seen some interesting things.'

'Oh, yes!'

'Europe?'

'And Korea, North Africa, the Middle East.' And since he seemed interested she told him more, so that they ended up standing there for about fifteen minutes, maybe longer, talking and looking at some of the books and not thinking about medical waiting-rooms at all.

He had a wonderful way of listening, she decided. Very intent and animated, his dark eyes alive yet not so fixed on her that it was disconcerting. Not fixed on her face, anyway. He did seem to be looking at other parts of her. Her arms, for example, as she gestured to make a point, and her hair as it fell into her face and she flicked it away.

'It must have been hard for you when your father died,' he said finally, when she came to a halt, and she nodded.

'Yes. . .and yet he was ready. He was in his late seventies, and he'd been in a wheelchair for four years. He was looking forward to seeing my mother again, too.'

'He believed in that? An afterlife?'

'Yes. Very strongly. Even after all the war and strife he'd seen. I thought it was wonderful.'

'Your mother. . .?'

'She died when I was six, so Dad brought me up on his own. I have some lovely memories of her. She was an actress, very cutting and funny and sharp.'

'Really? So's mine. Cutting and funny and sharp, that is. I doubt she's ever set foot on a stage in her life!' There was a silence, then he took a deep breath. 'This looks fine,' he said, gazing around him and away from her. It seemed to be an effort and she realised that they were standing closer than they needed to. He was stretching his shoulders, making sinew and muscle tauten and ripple under his loosely casual black T-shirt. At the moment he didn't look like a consultant at all. He didn't even smell like one. She caught a waft of musk and almond and male saltiness that was entirely untainted by anti-bacterial soap, and thought, This is a man who knows how to get away when he's not working.

She remembered the farm upbringing, and wondered what his interests were. They must include sports or the outdoors in some way. He looked so fit, walking ahead of her across the hall now, the seat of his jeans tight across two rounded loaves of muscle.

'This would be your office,' she managed from behind him, wondering where the frog in her throat had come from.

'I like the bay window.'

'Again, though, the colour. . . It dates from my mother's time. My father said her colour schemes always sounded like classical poetry but looked like high-school chemistry.'

'Or in this case calamine lotion.'

'My goodness, it is, isn't it?' She laughed delightedly. 'Exactly that shade. I expect it looked quite pretty in a one-inch square on a paint-card.'

'I'll take that as a lesson in my own endeavours.'

So. . .relaxed and casual once again. Carefully so. Their tour took another three quarters of an hour, and by the end both of them could see it.

'Desk here. Plenty of room for bookshelves. I'd need storage for equipment and supplies, but that needn't mean steel cabinets.'

'We could add some build-ins.'

'Yes, sure, and if you were planning to sell some of that furniture. . .'

'No reason why you can't keep surgical gloves and packets of syringes in an antique wardrobe,' she agreed.

'Now, I want to get my own ultrasound scanner. . .'

They ended up in the kitchen, and it was a quarter to six. 'A microwave!' he said. 'I can have a hot lunch.'

'Sorry, that's going up into my flat,' she told him, then to soften the blow, although she didn't quite know if she should be saying it, she added, 'Would you—um—like a drink, since we're here?' Taking the first step herself. Maybe this was the way. . .

'I would, yes, that'd be nice,' he answered, leaning his forearms on the kitchen bench-top. Then he cocked his head to one side. 'Unless you'd like to go out instead. To celebrate.'

'Celebrate?'

'Yes.' He met her look at last, still leaning on the counter-top so that the hair that fell across his face shadowed his dark eyes. 'I'm going to take this place, if you'll have me.'

Their eyes locked and held, and she saw in his gaze a little more than the pleasure of a medical man who had settled on his future rooms.

He's taken my first step and made it bigger, she realised. Ignoring her panicking cacophony of alarm bells, she said, 'I'll have you. I've never been a landlady before. And. . .dinner would be very nice.'

'Hmm. Problem, though.'

'What?' He'd remembered another commitment for the evening. She was absurdly disappointed. . .and at the same time intensely relieved.

But what was he doing?

'Clothes.' He pulled at his black T-shirt, and it came adrift from his jeans just above his hip so that she could see a little triangle of smooth skin, still lightly tanned from summer swimming. 'I'm qualifed for a pub meal, but nothing better, and somehow that's not quite what I had in mind.'

'Me too.' They made a co-ordinated pair, both in jeans and T-shirts, his black and hers pink as if they'd consulted each other before they'd dressed.

'Change,' he suggested. 'I'll wait. Then we'll drop into my place on the way and I'll change too.'

'On the way to where?'

'Don't know. Hadn't thought. You choose. Up-market Indian? Provincial French? Hearty Italian?'

'Up-market Indian,' she said, thinking already of the fragrances. Cardamom and cumin and chilli and cloves. Her sense of smell seemed heightened tonight. She had caught the scent of him once again as he'd pulled at his T-shirt, and it had been as complex and satisfying as the curries she could already taste in her imagination.

'Can I think and wander a bit more while you're upstairs?' he asked. 'Just want to make sure we've thought of everything.'

'If you have any suggestions about power points or light fixtures or anything, do write them down.'

'Sure. . .' He took the rolled sheets of draughting in his hands, and their fingers touched for a moment. The contact seemed to create heat.

Upstairs in the bedroom that would eventually become the living-room of the second flat, Louise peformed the classic dance from wardrobe to mirror that went by the name of 'I haven't got a thing to wear', and for several minutes she really felt that she hadn't. She didn't go out much now, although at one time she had had a very active social life. If John Henslow thought she lived like a Victorian spinster, then in that respect he was right these days. . .

Hang on, though. She didn't go out, but when she stayed in. . . Her father had had a circle of fascinating friends from his journalism days, most of them living abroad, but when they'd come to London Louise would put on a dinner that was deliberately elegant. Those soirées had given her father so much pleasure, until the last months when he was too ill, and she had always dressed for them. Would a black cocktail dress be too much? Up-market Indian, they had decided. It seemed appropriate.

'Thank goodness!' she breathed, taking her favourite

of the two black dresses from the wardrobe and holding it against her body.

Simple, silky, wide across her shoulders, short against her thighs. She tucked her hair loosely back with combs, sketched on lipstick and eye make-up, added touches of silver jewellery and black shoes that were just high enough in the heel to tighten her calves into a fluid line.

He did a double take when she came down the stairs and she smiled, and was scared at the same time. Is this too much? Have I given him a signal I'm not prepared to follow through on? Am I plunging in headlong again? she wondered.

The atmosphere between them was almost frightening. He should have spoken, and he didn't, just nudged her ahead of him down the hall and out to his car, with one set of fingertips so light in the small of her back that for a moment she wasn't even sure if that was what she had felt.

Then, perversely, the imprint of those fingers seemed to remain and intensify and she felt little prickles leapfrog their way up her spine. The elegant little dress suddenly felt too tight.

His flat, in a rather attractive modern block with landscaped grounds, was about ten minutes away on the other side of the hospital, and she shook her head at his suggestion that she go up and wait inside while he changed. She needed some time to catch her breath, her palms unnecessarily damp as she pressed them to the polished leather of the car seat. Catch her breath, slow down her beating heart, get a grip on herself. Remind herself of the lessons she'd surely learned from her past mistake.

'I will *not* be tricked into another relationship that's based on sexual attraction alone!'

Looking up out of the car, she saw him coming towards her and it was so ironic, in view of the stern

statement she had just made aloud to the car dash-
board, that all she could see was a tall, fluidly masculine
body, dark hair rumpled by an evening breeze, lips and
eyes and hips and thighs that made her want to explore
him very thoroughly with her hands for a very long
time.

Could she shut off her body's response like turning
off a tap? She was certainly going to try. By the time
Adam reached the car, she was sitting stiffly, the skirt
of her dress pulled down as far as it would go, her
knees locked together and her shoulder pressed hard
against the car door, to put as much distance between
them as possible. He wore dark grey trousers and a
white linen shirt that was open at the neck, and he
carried a discreetly patterned tie, which he shoved into
his pocket as he slid in behind the wheel.

'Hate ties,' he grinned, seeing the direction of her
gaze. 'Thought I'd better bring it, though. I rang and
made a booking, but forgot to find out their dress
policy. If they'll let me get away with just the shirt. . .'

'They will if they've got any sense,' Louise said
before she could stop herself. The glimpse of smooth
throat and the hollow at the base of it was tantalising,
bracketed by the open wings of his white collar.

She closed her eyes. 'Are you OK?' came his concerned voice.

'I'm fine,' she said, opening them again reluctantly.

'You look great. I didn't say so before.'

'Thanks. So do you.'

'Well, it's a celebration, isn't it? Of our new
relationship.'

'Rel—relationship?'

'Tenant and landlady.'

'Oh, of course.'

'And may it be to the benefit of us both. . .'

CHAPTER FOUR

ADAM decided sometime during their first course that he was going to kiss her. Until then, he had put up a valiant fight. There was something about her at times that signalled to him very clearly to go slow in that department. Oddly, it wasn't that she seemed uncomfortable with her own sensuality. But the cards had been stacked against him from the moment she had appeared on the stairs in that black dress. It set off the pale grace of her arms and echoed the dark complexity of her hair and. . . Yes, he was definitely going to kiss her!

The restaurant was busy enough to stimulate the senses, the food was fragrant and fabulous, and she ate with a mixture of good manners and hungry pleasure that fed all of his appetites at once. This decision to kiss her was a tactical one, borrowed from the Eastern martial arts he practised when he could: Turn your weakness into your strength.

Since he *wanted* to kiss her so much, it was futile to pretend that he didn't, and he would only exhaust his reserves of will-power in the struggle. Better to admit now that he was going to capitulate. . .later on, at the right time. . .and concentrate his remaining strength on exploring the other, less physical possibilities of their fledgling relationship together.

It would be one kiss, he decided. One very nice, very long, very delicious kiss, one positively fabulous, overwhelming kiss, and that would have to do for going on with, until he'd explored the reasons behind that reserve of hers. She definitely didn't look like a naturally reserved person. With that fluid body and wild hair, her creamy skin and those dark, sparkling eyes, she looked far more the type to plunge into life with a glow of laughter in her face.

He felt quite joyous about the idea of getting involved with a woman again, a woman with the grace and depth of this rather intriguing Louise. It was seventeen months now since he and Sandra Tancred had split up, and he had needed some time before feeling ready to start dating again. The narrow, downward spiral of his five-year relationship with Sandra could still cast him into a fit of claustrophobic gloom.

She was married now—Michael Sims, like Sandra herself, was an obstetrician, to no one's surprise, and Adam could almost hear the dinnertime conversations the two of them must have, the same pointless, totally informed, technical and up-to-date discussion about obstetric issues that had grated on him so much by the end of his own relationship with the ambitious doctor.

He and Sandra had had no life apart from obstetrics, no talking points at all, and in the end it had been more than he could stand, far more than he wanted to stand for the rest of his life. He had hurt her badly when he'd broken off their loose three-year engagement—she had married almost *too* quickly, six months later—but, hell, there was a world out there! He wanted a woman who didn't even know what a low forceps delivery was!

Well, being a midwife, Louise Redding didn't quite fit that description, but so far their conversations had been blessedly free of shop-talk. Tonight, for example. . .

Ordering their meal had led to discovering some shared tastes in cuisine and on to some hairy anecdotes about past experiences in restaurants that were a little *too* exotic. Their plates of mixed appetisers had arrived and they ate in a very pleasant silence for a while. The wine was very good and quite heady, somehow, and she was mesmerising him with the sensuous way she ran her fingers up and down the stem of her wine glass.

She didn't have reservations about this after all, he decided. In fact, her eyes had grown very dark and deep, and her lips were parted in a way that had him thinking very steamily once again of the kiss he planned. . .

Quickly, he searched his mind for something to say, remembered her delightful absorption in the newspaper the other day and asked what it was that had so drawn her attention.

'Fashion, actually,' she answered with a laugh, and they were away.

Fashion. Adam agreed entirely with Louise that the *haute couture* end of the spectrum was quite ridiculous these days.

'They ought to be working harder on finding fabrics that are as comfortable as cotton and silk but never need ironing!' Louise said.

'You don't like ironing?'

'Does anyone?'

He laughed and admitted, 'I must say, sending my shirts out to the laundry was an important professional milestone for me, about on par with getting that funny handful of letters after my name!'

Louise was so delighted with this nonsense that she laughed aloud, then they strayed on to half a dozen other subjects, and she saw their empty coffee-cups taken away at the end of the meal with uncomplicated reluctance. They had no excuse to stay here any longer. Pity. . .

He drove her home, and came with her as far as the front hall to help her turn on some lights. At night, when she was alone, the house was intimidating in its size and she was grateful that he had thought of this. The considerate gesture had its hint of risk, though, too. She had taken a first step tonight. There were several more that she couldn't and wouldn't take too soon. . .

'I won't ask you in,' she said. He had brushed past her in the hall. She had felt his warmth, smelt the muskiness of him again, and now. . .

'No, I wasn't expecting it, Louise,' he answered. 'But——'

'Mm?'

'Can I. . .?' He finished the question with actions, not words, touching his hand to her shoulder as he pulled her towards him and found her mouth.

She closed her eyes and turned her face upwards, parting her lips willingly to drink in his kiss. Pulses were beating in her ears, and her chest felt tight at first. Should she resist—not just him, but her own untrustworthy desires? No. . . Her determination wasn't worth a gram of paper. His jaw was slightly rough now, just enough to be delicious against her softer cheek, and when she stroked the back of his neck and ran her hand up his hair it prickled and feathered against her fingers, and released more of his scent—almond shampoo and musky male skin—into her nostrils.

The tightness and the pulses were gone, and all that remained was the fluid darkness of his touch. At first their mouths met gently, questing softly for the taste of each other. Then she felt the tease of his tongue and responded until she could no longer tell which was his mouth and which was hers.

He started to pull away. She could feel it—a stiffening, a cool thread of air fitting between them where just a moment ago there had been no space. A little sound of protest and disappointment mewed in her throat quite without her volition, and then he muttered something under his breath and pulled her hard against him once more, his mouth trailing hungrily down to her throat. His hands moved upwards, pushing aside the open collar of her gabardine coat until it slid down to her upper arms, exposing the narrow sleeves of the black dress that just capped her outer shoulders.

He buried his face in the warm flesh he had just uncovered, making a hot trail with his lips against the neckline of her dress. She felt it stretch and slip a little, revealing the first hint of the slopes of her small, firm breasts, and she shuddered at an intimacy of touch that she had not known for over four years. It was wonderful. . .treacherous. How could she have forgotten how quickly something like this could dissolve her will? And surely. . . Had she ever been touched. . .stirred. . . quite like this in the past?

Adam's hands were searing down her back now, and the silky barrier of her dress translated his touch into something almost as sensuous as skin against naked skin. He cupped the tautly female curves of her buttocks, then slid his hands still lower to her thighs beneath the hem of her dress, slid up again to discover the sensuous secret of her stockings and the cream of bare skin above them. Earlier, she had rejected wearing the confining waistband of tights. Now she had to wonder, Did I know this was going to happen? Did I want to feel his hands on my thighs?

Heaven help her! She pushed at his chest ineffectually, but the gesture soon became one of exploration, not rejection. He was fit. There was not an ounce of fat overlying those sculpted muscles. His shoulders, too, and his waist, and that tight male behind against her palms. She felt him shudder, felt the hard ridge of his arousal brush against her hip and was suddenly alarmed. Behind her, the house was empty, and they were adults with no one to answer to if this thing continued to its ultimate conclusion.

No one to answer to but themselves, that was, and she knew that she had to take control because no one else was going to do it for her.

'Adam. . .' she whispered against his mouth. Delicious. She whispered it again. 'Adam. . .'

This was getting her nowhere. Summoning all her will, she made a supple cat-like gesture and twisted out of his arms, hugging the dark coat around her and giving him her shoulder as she struggled to bring her breathing under control. 'Adam.' At last it was firm and clear, no longer a throaty invitation. 'I——'

'It's OK,' he growled. 'Don't say anything.'

'But——'

'Don't.' Gently, he turned her to face him again, and traced her lips with the ball of his thumb, then cupped her jaw. 'That was. . .so nice. All of it. Thank you.' His voice was deep—gruff, yet with a burr of velvet at the same time. His eyes glittered darkly with the arousal that she knew he was still struggling to control. He added, even more huskily, 'I'm not expecting anything more.' His fingers stroked her neck then left her and she wondered if he knew that every inch he had touched was like a lacy weave of tingling sensation.

'OK,' she managed.

'We'll talk on Monday.' Very practical.

'Monday?'

'About the lease.' He sounded quite cheerful and relaxed, while her own heart was still pounding, and her feelings were a dangerous cocktail of confusion. 'And the timing of it all. If you've talked to the builder.'

'Right. Of course,' she managed, glad that they had this practical matter to seize on. 'I'm on days off so I should be able to get things moving.'

'Great.'

There was a pause, a silence, and she couldn't help watching his firm mouth, now closed below his strong, straight nose. If he kissed her one last time. . .

But he didn't. He had turned now, and was walking to his car, the herringbone brick gritty and percussive under his feet. A puff of wind ruffled his dark hair just as her fingers had done minutes ago, and then, as he opened the car door, he turned and waved. It was a casual salute, and she wished she could still see his eyes in the dark, but she couldn't.

She was already very much regretting that she had let herself go this far, this fast, this soon. Time. She had to give herself *time*! Abruptly, she went back into the house and closed the door.

It was a busy morning in Morleyvale Hospital's maternity unit. There had been a full complement of labouring mums the night before—Louise was rather thankful that she was on mornings and evenings this week—and now, with only two women still waiting to deliver, the heaviest work fell in the area of post-partum care.

'Do you want to take the bathing class this morning, Louise?' Judy Smith suggested. 'I'll send Gaby in to scrub up for the scheduled Caesareans.'

'How many of those?'

'Five. Two for Van Curen and three for Henslow. As usual, Adam's are clinically indicated a hundred per cent, and John's are distinctly iffy.' Judy snapped out the last line.

'Iffy?'

'If you ask me, he's getting known as a doctor who'll treat it almost as an elective procedure. Apparently a couple of women have been asking for him by name. They say they've heard he's good, then it turns out they want to be delivered at ten o'clock on a Thursday morning with no pain and a nice neat scar, thanks.'

'No pain?' Louise returned drily. 'Haven't they heard that a Caesarean is major abdominal surgery? Most women need fifteen minutes just to manoevre themselves out of bed for the first couple of days.'

Judy shrugged. 'Don't ask me,' she said shortly. 'I don't know why half these women want children at all.

They don't seem to have a clue what they're getting themselves into.'

'You've got some of your own, then?' Louise asked with a little chuckle. She knew Judy was married, and at thirty-five she was certainly old enough to have a brood of troublesome pre-teens at home. Perhaps this was the reason for her frequent short temper on the ward.

'Children? Me? No!' There was a hard laugh. 'Why on earth would I want to, seeing what goes on here? No, I've got no kids.'

There was an uncomfortable silence as Louise wondered, If she's that cynical, why is she a midwife? Then she gathered her manners and said carefully, 'Anyway, yes, I'll take the bathing class. Any idea if many mums'll turn up?'

'Should be a few. Mrs Cartwright seems keen and involved. Mrs Heller hasn't got a clue but at least she's trying. I told her she *should* go. Never changed a nappy before, is trying breast-feeding but says her own mother's milk was no good, and hers is bound to be the same. And of course the whole idea of bad milk is a complete old wives' tale. Why these women can't do a bit of elementary reading about the most important job they'll ever do——' Judy stopped and snapped her mouth shut again.

'I'll set up now, then, shall I?' Louise said gently. 'They've all finished breakfast. . .'

'Yes, do, because no one will turn up later on if their visitors have come. And I'd better check on that dreadful Lisa Macarthur again. It must makes me sick——' She broke off once more and left the nurses' station without finishing her cryptic, emotive statement.

Poor Judy. What was wrong? She was a pretty woman, or had been. Louise guessed that her plumpness was a recent thing. Her lacklustre hair, too. An attractive strawberry-blonde rinse was almost grown out to reveal hair prematurely greying in parts. She ought to touch it up, or at least style it nicely if she had decided to be frankly grey. What had happened to her self-esteem? Why had she stopped trying? Louise wondered about discreetly asking Gaby Driver, who had been here for several years and who was starting to be a friend. Perhaps there were problems at home, or subjects, here in the unit, that ought to be trodden around carefully.

Dismissing the issue for the moment, or trying to, Louise went to prepare for the little class in infant bathing that was conducted every couple of days for first-time or rusty mums. She wheeled an equipment trolley into the conference-room that was used for the class, found the portable blue plastic bath in a cupboard and checked the trolley. Towel, wet wipes, liquid baby soap, cotton buds, lotion, gauze swab and spirit alcohol for drying out the cord. More gauze and petroleum jelly in case today's demonstration baby was a newly circumcised boy.

Something was missing. She knew it was. Ah, yes, nappy. This trolley normally had a stack of them but they'd all been used, apparently, and not replaced. She went out into the corridor, then through the small ward sister's office to the room where supplies of this kind were kept, her mind still half caught by the issue of Judy Smith's short temper and evident grudge against her work and her world.

Even further back in her thoughts was the hovering image of Adam Van Curen, and she couldn't help the warmth that filled her when she conjured him into her mind, although she tried to school it away. Nearly five days since Saturday's kiss. They had talked by phone on Monday night about the conversion of her house. He definitely wanted the place, Ted Shaw was booked to start in ten days' time and the Redding family

solicitor was very enthusiastic. A nice conversation,
though strictly business. Since then she hadn't seen
much of him, but would see him tomorrow at the once-
weekly general round, and couldn't help looking forward to it. Couldn't help dreading it at the same
time. . . Which made a lot of sense, didn't it?

She grabbed a pack of disposable nappies, then saw
that they were the premmie size. If Mrs Heller brought
her baby boy, who was a hefty nine-pounder, they
would be too small. She looked on a different shelf and
found the right size. . .then stopped as she heard voices
in the office just outside, in the middle of a conversation that must have begun in the corridor beyond.

'. . .a Victorian spinster with her father in a bath
chair. Bizarre! Made me really uncomfortable.'

She recognised John Henslow's voice at once. Not
difficult, since he was using the same line he'd coined
to her the other day, only this time without any
pretence that it was lightly meant. 'So. . .
disappointing.'

'Er. . .yes.' Another voice that she recognised as
well.

'But, as I say, I'm not in the market for initiating
prim little virgins. They tend to be a bit too grateful
about it!' John finished, and she didn't wait. She wasn't
going to skulk in here until they'd gone as if *she* were
the one with something to be ashamed of!

Head held high, so that the flame in her cheeks was
blazoned for all to see, she clasped the plastic pack of
nappies like a shield and marched past them. John
Henslow had his back to her and she didn't favour him
with a glance at all, but she couldn't help meeting
Adam Van Curen's gaze full-on, and knew that her
brown eyes were narrowed and emitting electric sparks.
He was silent and steel-jawed, but she just had time to
hear John's awkward splutter before her sweeping
stride carried her out of earshot and along to the open

conference-room door. She slammed it quickly shut behind her. If either of them tried to come after her to apologise or explain. . . If Adam came——No! This just proved how right she had been to be afraid of plunging in too fast.

Back in the ward sister's office, Adam wasn't going anywhere. 'You bloody idiot!' he rasped to his junior colleague.

'I didn't. . . I had no idea she was there,' John spluttered.

'That's not the point.'

'I'll apologise.'

'Don't. Aren't you due in surgery?'

'Yes, but it'd only take a few minutes to——'

'*Don't* apologise to her! Can't you see that would make it worse? Get on with your list, because I don't want mine running late. I've only got a couple of things to do here, but after Theatre I've got day surgery over in the other building straight afterwards.'

'Sure. OK.' The man left at last, still red-faced, his pale blue eyes rather wild in his discomfort.

Adam was burning with anger and regret. Why hadn't he managed to cut John off? He should have said something as soon as the senior registrar had started on the subject of Louise out in the corridor, in that slick 'man's talk' voice. Why hadn't he?

Because he'd been too taken aback, too consumed with his own thoughts: This man's a colleague. . .and he's being boorish. . . Louise Redding is none of his business. . .and he's treading on my turf!

Then they had arrived in the ward sister's office and she had swept out of that storage-room before he had even begun to think of a way to deflect Henslow without betraying his own interest. As he might have expected, she had looked magnificent, the high colour on her cheeks emphasising the neat bone-structure of her face in contrast with the brown eyes and the dark hair rebelliously confined with pins and combs beneath her cap.

Now. . .would she be off crying in a cupboard somewhere? He didn't think so. She had looked too angry for tears, and in any case he somehow felt that easy tears were not her style. Should he go and find her, then? No. He knew immediately that that would be the worst thing he could do. There was no way he could convince her that he was innocent of John Henslow's prejudice other than by showing her, over time, in his behaviour towards her. She would never believe mere words. Words were too easy, and the fact that Henslow thought he could dampen her fire with a quick, slick apology only proved this.

John is an idiot! And if he's ruined things for good between Louise and me I'll——'

Adam stopped short. Oh, lord, maybe I should find her and say something? I can't have this spoilt! If I point out that many Victorian spinsters have been fascinating people. . . Emily Brontë sprang to mind. And that woman who had trekked around the world painting botanical specimens and left her whole collection to Kew Gardens. Not to mention Miss Nightingale herself. . .

No, it wouldn't ring true. John Henslow *was* a fool!

I'm going to have to ask her out again as soon as I can. . .he decided.

'And there she is, all clean and nappied and swaddled,' Louise finished, handing a tiny, rosy little girl back to her mother, Vicky Hwang, who cuddled her and nuzzled her tiny button of a nose. Baby Celia had been very co-operative in her role as demonstration baby, and the four new mothers all looked markedly less nervous and sceptical about the whole thing.

Mrs Heller was still the most ill-at-ease. Her baby had been fast asleep when the class was assembled, which was a pity, as it could help a nervous mother to see the bathing routine done on her own child. 'That cord stump. . .' she said now. 'I'm sure Andrew's isn't as neat as that. When will it drop off? Before we go home? What if it gets infected?'

'It might take as long as two weeks to drop off,' Louise explained. 'So don't worry about that, and don't try to pull it off. Gradually it will get drier and more shrivelled, helped by the spirit alcohol, touched on it with the gauze pad like I showed you. Do try not to let it get on to the unhealed part beneath the cord, though.'

'And his circumcision. . . I'm wondering now if we were right to have it done. I know a lot of people don't any more, but my husband wanted to, and——It looks so red and raw and swollen now.'

'You'll be surprised at how quickly it heals, Mrs Heller. As for the decision to have it done, that's a very personal one. Some doctors feel it does help to reduce the risk of infection and a certain kind of cancer later in life. Others say the evidence isn't yet conclusive. So your husband's wishes are as good a guide as anything.'

'Well, that's good to know. . . But won't it sting when he pees?'

'Let's look at it together, shall we? Call me as soon as he's awake and I'll show you just what to do to make it more comfortable for him.'

The new mother seemed satisfied with that, and the little group drifted away, pushing the wheeled cribs that held their babies. Mrs Matthews moved very slowly still, after a Caesarean three days ago, but after a minute or two Louise was left alone to clean up. She gave a sigh of relief. The women had gathered for the class when her face had still been burning from John Henslow's overheard words, and her presentation had been lacklustre at first.

John's opinion didn't matter to her at all, but Adam's. . .*hurt*! That he could make a shallow judgement like that, stereotyping her so narrowly! The fact that it was far from being true was quite irrelevant, and, worst of all, it was an insult to her father's memory.

It only goes to show that I was right to want to keep my distance, she thought. And then the familiar self-blame set in. I'm certainly a poor judge when it comes to men!

She looked up, tight-lipped, and he was there in the open doorway, entering the room and quietly closing the door behnd him before she could protest.

'Hi. . .'

'Hello. I'll be out in a minute if you need the room,' she said, wilfully misunderstanding the reason for his presence. 'I just have to empty the bath-water.' There was a sink and draining-board in the corner and she went to it.

'Louise. . .'

'Yes, Mr Van Curen?'

'Cut that out!'

She gave up the pretence, left the baby bath on the draining-board and came towards him, her body held tightly in a mixture of pride and defensiveness. 'Yes, Adam?'

'Look, I. . .just wondered if you were free tomorrow night, that's all. We could do a movie and a late supper.'

'I've got an evening. I don't get off until nine-thirty.'

'Saturday, then.'

'Same.'

'Well, why don't you pick a night?' She could see how hard he was trying to control the exasperation that she was deliberately provoking. He was trying to soften her, butter her up. At least he had the grace not to try some lavish apology, which would have had all the substance of whipped cream.

'I'd. . .rather not,' she told him. 'I'm pretty busy at the moment.'

There was a silence and she stared down, knowing he was watching her with those dark eyes, searching beneath dark brows. 'Look,' he said at last. 'I wasn't going to bring it up. Henslow wanted to——'

'If you're about to apologise,' she interruped, 'don't! I really couldn't bear it.'

'Louise——'

'And anyway, that's not the point. John's thrown that spinster and bath chair line at me before.'

'God, he's even more crass than I thought!'

She ignored this. 'The point is that if you're going to lease my ground floor, *and* we're going to go on meeting here in the unit, then perhaps it's. . .inappropriate for there to be anything more personal in our dealings with one another. I was planning to say this to you anyway. . .'

Not really true, but it made a convenient excuse, since she wasn't prepared to talk about her real reason—her deep-seated fear of repeating a very bad mistake. The fact that she was so hurt by his shallow assessment of her now told her how far she had already gone in her attraction, beneath all her sensible inner cautionings, and she felt dizzy with regret.

'Hey! Inappropriate? Why?' he demanded angrily. 'Sure, there are risks involved, the chance of hurt or embarrassment, but we're adults, aren't we? Hell, how are two people ever supposed to connect at all if we're all going to be put off by the fact that we work together, or share a building, or whatever? There are other things at stake in our lives, surely? The challenge of——'

'What?' she interrupted coldly, turning anger at herself into anger at him. 'The challenge—exciting to a select few—of breaching the defences of the modern virgin? She's an anachronism, she is, a dying breed. I'm surprised you don't share John Henslow's view that it's not worth all the bother, and that if you *do* do her the ultimate favour she's going to turn round and cling to you like a limpet for the rest of your days. That's the prevailing idea, isn't it?'

'If it is, it's Henslow's problem, not mine,' he growled. 'God, Louise, do you think I'm that shallow?'

'I don't know. Possibly not. I'm prepared to give you the benefit of the doubt, since I don't want to lease my ground floor to someone I detest.'

'Well, I hope you don't detest me,' he said, carefully controlled, and she was impotently disappointed that he hadn't kept the energy of their shared anger high. Somehow, it had been very satisfying to snap and rage at him, but she could see he wasn't going to let her have the pleasure any longer. 'Perhaps you're right,' he continued. 'My asking you out was. . .ill-timed. As for the other thing, I'm sorry that you overheard John's conversation with me. That's all I can say.'

'Oh. Good,' she floundered. The dignity and under-statement of his apology was cutting the ground from beneath her feet and she badly wanted to forgive him.

There was a knock at the door, and Mrs Heller appeared, hesitant and uncertain. 'Um. . .he's awake.'

'Who? Oh, baby Andrew's circumcision. I'll be right there.'

'Sorry. . .'

'No, Mr Van Curen had a problem, but we've solved it now.'

'Have we?' he murmured in a dangerous aside. 'That's good. . .'

'I'll ring you, Mr Van Curen,' she said firmly, 'as soon as Ted Shaw has the final plans drawn up.'

'Good.' He nodded briefly. 'Just in case there's anything I haven't thought of.'

'Now, if you'll excuse me. . . .'

Adam watched her go, loving her pride, angry with himself for having handled the scene so badly, wondering whether there was any truth in what she had said about modern virgins. Could the male population be divided neatly into two camps? Those who were itching to do a woman 'the ultimate favour', as she had caustically phrased it, and those, like John Henslow, who cringed at the likelihood of inhibitions in bed and emotional repercussions out of it?

Which category do I fall into? he wondered, then decided with a spurt of anger, Neither, damn it! She's bright and attractive and interesting. I know there's a spark there for her too, in spite of what she said, and I'm going to ask her out again!

CHAPTER FIVE

LOUISE blessed the unseasonable sunshine and warmth of the mid-October Saturday. She was opening every window in the house to get rid of the overpowering smell of new paint. The builders were officially finished with the ground floor, and with her own little first-floor flat, tucked at the top of the front stairs that opened to the right through their own separate entrance. But Ted Shaw had another job now, and wouldn't be back to complete the other two flats until December. . .possibly even January, he had said.

This was a bit of a nuisance, as the rent money would have been nice, but she would have enough to tide her over until next spring if necessary, and could probably increase the amount of the bank loan that had financed the recent work. . .

The worries of being a real-estate mogul!

In fact, she had discovered quite a zest for the whole business. Ted Shaw was entertaining, and so was his crew. And the ground floor looked wonderful. . .or it would do, when all the furniture and bookcases were removed. With the builder's 'now or never' threat hanging over her a few weeks ago, she hadn't had time to deal with everything, and his crew had spent the first few hours of their labour shifting everything out of the way.

Now, alone amid the smell of paint, wallpaper paste and freshly cut or sanded wood, Louise contemplated it all. A ton of work to do. . .and Adam Van Curen was coming as soon as he could to help.

Over the past few weeks, they had arrived at a truce that Louise didn't quite trust. She held him at bay, both in her thoughts and when they had to work together. When it came to this place, too, they both managed a courteous and careful relationship, but she couldn't help wondering. He had told her that he wasn't imbued with John Henslow's shallow opinion of 'Victorian spinsters', and she wanted to believe him, but her fears ran deep.

She knew she had been looking for trouble and expecting to find it ever since the initial awareness of him. But how did she go about overcoming an emotional block like that? She *wanted* to trust him. . . and instinctively she didn't. Was this his problem? Or hers?

Now she found herself thinking automatically of her options for escape. Her lease to him was renewable yearly, and able to be terminated by either party, with appropriate financial compensation.

If this doesn't work out, I won't hesitate to exercise my option, and he'd better do the same! she told herself fiercely now.

Shoving the subject aside firmly for now, she cut the plastic ties on the stack of flattened cartons she had bought and started making them up into shape, then began to pack away her father's books, ruthlessly banishing the sentiment that would have had her lingering far too long over many of them. Adam would see some progress when he arrived!

He did. She had fifteen boxes neatly packed and closed by the time he appeared. Like herself, he was dressed for hard work. He wore old jeans and a T-shirt, white and paint-stained, that was thin enough to reveal the pattern of dark hair on his chest. The carelessly masculine look suited him too well. . .

'Cup of tea first, and then work?' Louise asked quickly, as a distraction from the awareness she so distrusted in herself. 'Or work first and a cold beer to finish?'

'Cold beer?'

'Beer. . .cold. . .whatever. Wine or coffee if you'd rather. I happen to like it cold, myself.' He had flustered her a little by querying her suggestion. The liking for a cold can of beer every now and then was one of the few remaining legacies of her years in Australia, which she was quite determined were her own business alone, and she felt as if he'd caught her out.

But he was unsuspicious. 'Sure. It's warm today. We might work up a sweat. Let's get to it now and treat ourselves later.'

So they did. He was as energetic and strong and tireless as she had known he would be, and they soon dealt with the remaining books, and the other contents of drawers and cupboards. Louise had packed up her father's clothes months ago, as well as the rest of his more personal belongings, but there were all sorts of his mementoes and curiosities here and she knew that Adam was aware of her frequent struggles against emotion. She had to be grateful for the way he handled it. He seemed to sense when she wanted to stop for a minute and talk about something they'd come across, and when she just wanted to pack it away and move on.

'Where are you going to put all this stuff?' he asked her quietly after another dozen boxes had been filled.

'Up on the top floor. There's a storage-room where the roof slopes too much to be habitable. It has access from the front stairs, so it won't be affected by the top-floor flat, once that's done.'

'You'll have to deal with it eventually, though.'

'Oh. . . . I could leave it for someone to rediscover in two hundred years,' she suggested with a grin. 'Valuable antiques from the late twentieth century.'

'Such as this?' He held up a hand-knitted tea-cosy in hot pink and green, in the shape of a rather pregnant mouse, which her father must have bought out of kindess at a church bazaar.

Louise laughed, then said seriously, 'But you never know, do you? Aren't people paying enormous sums now for comic books and Beatle memorabilia?'

'Yes, when I think that I actually *threw away* my old collection of 45 r.p.m. singles!'

'And my Rolling Stones T-shirts.'

'You were a Stones fan?'

'Why the past tense?' she grinned.

'So, obviously we keep the tea-cosy, packed carefully away in blue tissue paper.'

'Blue?'

'*Always* blue, according to the home hints column in the newspaper.'

'You read the home hints?'

'Sometimes.'

'Goodness, I knew you had a broad-ranging interest in current affairs, but. . .'

'They're hilarious, those hints.' He was on the defensive, and she was still laughing. 'The uses people think of for old stockings and margarine containers. Either that or they really are damned useful. For instance, did you know that if you take an old shoulder pad from one of your blouses you can use it to——?' He was folding the tea-cosy lovingly as he spoke.

'Stop!' She grabbed it from him. 'I'm going to be ruthless. I'm going to throw it away.' She dropped it unceremoniously into the big rubbish bag in the corner of the kitchen.

He shivered in mock-horror. 'Auction that at Christie's in eighty years' time and you could pay for your great-granddaughter's wedding.' He moved towards the rubbish bag, thinking to unearth the thing again.

She fended him off. 'Sorry. She'll have to get married on the cheap.'

'But seriously. . .'

'Yes?' she challenged.

'You're right. You've got to be ruthless. I've got my eye on this desk for my office and it isn't nearly empty yet.'

It had been written into the lease that he was to have the use of any furniture that Louise hadn't already earmarked for her own use upstairs, and what wasn't wanted by either of them would then be sold. Still lots to do. They attacked the work with renewed vigour until he said, 'These two bookshelves. They're empty and I've cleaned them and they're getting in the way. I know where I want them. Could we move them now? Are you up to it? Sorry, I should have thought and brought a mate or two.'

'Of course I'm up to it!' She was indignant and flexed her arms in a body-builder's posing routine, complete with macho music, hummed quite out of tune.

He looked at her sceptically, one eyebrow raised. She took on some even more outrageous poses. 'Look! I could match Conan the Barbarian!'

He struggled, looked to have it beaten, then collapsed in laughter. 'Do not, *ever*, go in for women's body-building, Louise Redding!'

'No? Oh. . . They're actually pathetic, then, are they—my muscles?'

''Fraid so. And *please* don't think I'd have it any other way!'

'But honestly, I'm sure I'm not as feeble as I look,' she insisted very seriously. 'Dad carted me off to classical ballet lessons for ten years. . .'

'Ah, that accounts for it, then,' he murmured, looking at her slim arms.

'What?'

'Nothing. . .'

She did an arabesque instead, and then a leaping jeté, to fetch up several feet closer to him, braking hard and adding quickly, 'And ballet takes some muscle power, believe me.'

He kept looking for another long moment, then said a light, 'OK,' and she snorted.

'I should think so!'

But there had been a moment of awareness in him just then that disturbed her. . .angered her because she had felt it too and she was so determined not to. She stepped back.

They moved the heavy shelves and she could tell that he was impressed, as well as a little amused again, by her stubborn show of strength.

'Want a rest?' A question from him halfway down the hall.

'No. . .' she replied, trying not to grit her teeth. She could see the tightly balled muscles in his shoulders and arms, then lost her concentration and felt her aching fingers slip. 'Yes!'

They put the shelf down and both had to pant and stretch and flex their hands. He had stunningly nice hands, strong and well-muscled but as smooth as a surgeon's hands had to be. His shirt was streaked with the grey dust he had cleaned from the shelves and he had a mark of the stuff on his face, too. He must have felt it, or seen the direction of her gaze, because he scratched at it and threw her a questioning look. 'Is that dust?'

'Yes. But you're just smearing it now,' she told him, then watched as he casually lifted the clean strip of his T-shirt that had been tucked into the front of his jeans and wiped his face thoroughly with that.

What a stomach! Tight and tanned and etched with just the right amount of hair. She closed her eyes against her own foolishness, felt her reluctance, like vertigo, then heard him say, 'Sure you're OK?'

'I'm fine.' Opening her eyes, she found that the

T-shirt was tucked back into place again, and the mark on his face was gone.

They moved both bookshelves that were ready, then finished emptying and cleaning out the desk, and moved that.

'Getting there,' he commented, surveying the room, with its fresh creamy paint on the walls and freshly sanded and varnished hardwood floor. 'Long way to go. I've got some more furniture and medical equipment on order, including an ultrasound scanner.'

'They must be expensive.'

'I'm selling my car,' he grinned.

'Oh, that gorgeous thing?'

'Hey, I've just proved my masculinity with my prowess in furniture-moving. I don't need the macho car any more.'

She laughed, then added, 'But I wasn't querying your personal financial arrangements. I meant. . . security.'

'Hell, yes, that's something we *didn't* consider.'

'With valuable equipment and confidential medical files. . . I've got someone coming in next week to update the locks.'

'He should do the windows as well,' Adam agreed. 'And perhaps you can find out about alarming the ground floor.'

'I'll give you a set of keys as soon as the locks are done so you can come here whenever you need to. . .'

It got late and their work went on. The sun lost its warmth and both put on thick cotton sweatshirts, which soon became as grubby as the T-shirts beneath. It was nearly six by the time they had finished with the kitchen. The room was empty and open again now, with furniture either moved into Adam's rooms or tarpaulined on the back porch ready to be taken away. The boxes of books were piled up on the top-floor landing ready for Louise to store. The first floor still had to be tackled, but that wasn't Adam's problem as he didn't plan to use any of the furniture that had been moved up there.

'So that's about it for what we can do together,' he said now, surveying the scene.

Louise nodded. They were both tired and grubby, hadn't even stopped for tea or the promised beer. It beckoned invitingly now, signalling to Louise that her throat was parched. She went to the fridge and got out two cans. 'Want one?'

'Yes, please.'

She tossed it across and he caught it quickly and for some reason they both laughed. 'You reveal surprising new talents every time we meet, Staff Nurse Redding.'

'What, throwing a beer?'

'Drinking it.'

'That's a talent?'

He shrugged, looking a bit uncomfortable and she thought, No! Don't tell me. . . It's the spinster thing again, isn't it? I'm supposed to be a teetotaller. Damn him! And when I was just. . .forgetting all about that, starting to trust him and enjoy him. I could tell him, she realised. Tell him every ghastly and oh, so modern detail of those years in Australia, but I'm damned if I will! Let him think what he likes! I don't have to prove anything to him about myself at all!

And then he undermined her anger say saying lazily, 'Sorry, not a talent. Wrong word. A taste. And we share it. Like that, I do.'

'Do you?' she said still a little cool and wary.

'Yes, I do. And I wonder if there are any more. . . tastes we have in common. Fancy some dinner?' There was a slow sensuality to his voice which seemed to be suggesting the possibility of more than just a meal.

She said quickly, 'Well, I'm certainly hungry, but would dinner fancy us? I mean, like this, no restaurant

would let us through the front door.' She gestured at
their mutual grubbiness.

'I was thinking more of take-away.'

'Not very cosy here.'

'Your flat upstairs? You're all moved in, aren't you?'

'All but the beer.'

'That's easily fixed. If we phone for a pizza, it'll be
here by the time we've got ourselves cleaned up.'

The suggestion made so much sense that Louise's
instinct was to say no to it at once. So why was it that
when she spoke it was to say a careful, 'That sounds
nice. There's a pretty good place down on the
Broadway that delivers. What toppings do you like?'

The issue required some negotiation as *she* liked
green peppers and he didn't, and *he* liked anchovies
and she didn't, but in the end they settled on an extra-
large ham, tomato and green olives, and polished off
the lot in about ten minutes flat.

'And I hate to say this. . .' he had downed the last
drops of his second beer, as well '. . .but I'm still
hungry. I didn't really eat lunch.'

'Same here.'

'Shall I nip out and find us some dessert?'

'I bought an iced bun this morning, if that would do.'

'With tea? I'm thirsty. . .'

'Nice, yes.'

And this stretched out the meal not just to the point
where they were replete but in time as well, so that
they had plenty of opportunity to talk, and it was after
nine by the time the teapot was empty.

'You're not on call, obviously. . .' They were both
flung out in the twin armchairs that faced the electric
fire.

'No, next weekend,' he answered. 'Meanwhile, I'm
going to try to come here during the week. Would odd
hours bother you?'

'How odd?'

'As odd as you can get. Six at night? Four in the morning? If I'm between deliveries. . .'

'I doubt I'd even hear you up here.'

'Great! So as soon as you can get those new keys. . .'

'Until then, I can give you a set of the current ones.'

'Thanks. I hate to rush you but I'd like to get a move on with this.'

'When are you hoping to open for business?'

'Week after next, if I can.'

'That soon?'

'Got patients clamouring for my services, I have,' he grinned.

'Nice for you!' There was a little pause, then she asked, 'What made you decide to branch out into private practice? Can I ask?'

'Of course. It's still a bit of a controversial decision in some circles, isn't it?'

'Medicine's like that.'

He twisted in the deep armchair so that his legs were flung over the wide arm-rest and Louise found that she was relaxing more, too, leaning forward and pillowing her chin and elbow on a cushion.

'A kind of burn-out,' he said, clearly feeling his way through the thoughts as they came. She liked this about him—that he was a thinker. 'I don't really want to use the term because that inflates what I'm feeling too much. But there are days when all I'll see are teenage girls who think a baby is a new toy that will prove they're grown-up, or. . .because consultants get the problems, so often, not the normal deliveries. . .pregnancies or labours that are in trouble because the mother was too slack or too ignorant to get the proper pre-natal care, or maybe she drank or she smoked or she took drugs. You can get cynical, or you get depressed. You stop caring, and I don't want that. I'm not saying I want to stop delivering those problem babies, those unwanted babies, because those babies more than anything at least deserve the chance to get born right——Hey! Am I making any sense?'

'Think so. Keep going,' she told him, aware that she was extremely interested in what made him tick. And perhaps that was good. . .

'But I decided I wanted to do more for women who are really passionate about having a child. The Health Service really can't make infertility a top priority. And there are women with health problems such as diabetes who can get a bit lost in the system. I used to think that private practice was just for the rich and snobby, but I don't any more. I can think of two or three couples I know right now who are *not* rich, but who'll spend their last pound on infertility treatment if they have to, and I really want to help them so that, whether they succeed or fail, it's not a totally soul-destroying experience.'

'So you'll concentrate on infertility with your private patients?'

'Problems in getting pregnant, and problems in staying and being pregnant, yes. Some gynae work too. At first I'm certainly not going to be in a position to turn patients away because they don't fit my profile.'

'You'll go private full-time eventually if you get the patient load?'

'No,' he grinned. 'I'll just be busy.'

'Hmm.' She digested what he had said, and had to approve, then said thoughtfully, 'We see things from a different perspective, don't we? Midwives and obstetricians. We see all the normal deliveries, you see all the ones that go wrong.'

'Which makes us panic too easily?'

'Maybe. It's scary, though, how quickly a delivery can go from being happy and easy and routine to being a nightmare. I'm always glad you lot are in the background.'

'So you don't think you'll ever set up shop on your own, purely doing home deliveries?'

'No.' She shook her head. 'For all its faults, I'd have to say I believe in the system, and I think even home deliveries have to happen within it.'

'Not a radical. . .'

'No,' she answered decidedly. 'Even a nightmare labour and delivery only lasts a day or two, and recovery from a Caesarean lasts a couple of weeks. But if a baby's not given the right help at the right time during delivery, if it's deprived of oxygen at a critical time, the effects of that can last for life. Wouldn't any informed mother choose technological hell, and a medical team in a frenzy, and no time to consider her finer feelings, if that's what's necessary to get a baby out quickly and safely? When it comes down to it, I think the baby is more important than the birth experience.'

'So do I. And that's a good way of putting it,' he said. 'I'll have to remember it.'

There was a lazy silence and Adam knew he ought to make a move to go. He didn't want to. . .partly because he was just too damned tired to move! She was a hard worker and they had got a lot done. He had been amazed and impressed by the strength in those graceful dancer's arms.

They had talked shop tonight, coming to it naturally through the need to deal with the practicalities of his moving in here, and he contrasted the friendly, lazy and not very technical discussion with all the countless shop talks he'd had with Sandra. Very different! Much easier on the tongue and on the mind. No sense of competition between them, and only now did he see just how competitive his relationship with Sandra had been.

He was strongly attracted to Louise—and she to him, if he'd read her graceful body's signals right. And they got on well together—witness all that silly discussion over the mouse tea-cosy and her body-building routine. There was still a reserve in her, though. Perhaps it was her inexperience, he decided. Only one way to deal with that. . .

'I should go,' he said, not really as a precursor to leaving but as a way of getting both of them to their feet so that he could kiss her again, move things forward a little, signal to her that he had intentions. 'Can I help. . .?'

He gestured at the debris from their meal, but she shook her head. 'No, it'll take five minutes to tidy up, and don't tell the mice but I'll probably just pile the dishes in the sink and leave them till the morning anyway.'

'OK.' He stood up lazily, knowing she would follow to show him out, and they met up in the doorway to the odd little room that served partly as entrance hall, partly as dining-room.

He reached out and took her confidently into his arms, full of a relaxed pleasure and anticipation, and for a long time he wasn't disappointed. She responded willingly to his kiss, winding her arms around him with a fresh, whole-hearted sensuality that plunged him at once into a state of heated and hungry arousal. . .

Louise felt everything that was coming from Adam and knew that her own body was matching it, answering it. At first it was just too nice to question. The warmth of him, the living scent, the mixture of urgency and lazy exploration in the touch of his fingers and mouth. His hands, warm and smooth and dry, came up beneath her sweatshirt to slip against the sensitive skin at her waist and brush the undersides of her gently sloping breasts, a gesture of questing and discovery, not possession.

She felt his thighs against hers, and their hips bumped. His mouth travelled over her face and down, and then she heard him laugh at the plain modesty of how they were both dressed.

'Wish we still wore chitons and togas and bearskins,' he murmured against her lips. 'Don't you? I'm sure they just dropped off at a touch. . .'

He nuzzled her with his nose, which was a delicious one, slightly widened across the high bridge, as if it had once been broken.

'Should we? Couldn't we manage to?' he was saying now, swooping in to kiss her neck and then darting his tongue against her ear. 'Take some of it off, I mean. I'd love to see you, touch you. Cotton is nice, lace is nicer. . .' he had found the soft cups that held her breasts '. . .but skin is nicest of all and you're so silky, Louise. . .'

She came to her senses. 'Adam, I didn't intend——'

'Didn't you? I did!'

'No!' She pulled away, hugging her arms around her middle in a defensive gesture that did nothing to still the tingling in her body.

This was just what she *hadn't* wanted. Teasing and delicious and easy, as if the response of two people's bodies were all that counted. It wasn't. It could fade too fast, as she knew all too well. There had to be more. Two people had to be right together before sex could be right, otherwise, no matter how good it had once seemed, it went sour incredibly fast.

Adam was still standing close to her, his fingers reaching out to clasp her very lightly around the waist, a gesture she recognised as support, not demand.

'Listen, it doesn't have to be now,' he said. 'I'm just saying. . .this feels nice, doesn't it?'

'That's not the point.'

'Then what is, love?'

She tried. 'It's my own body,' she began tentatively, groping for words. Her body. Her responses. She didn't trust them.

Adam saw the difficulty she was having and tried to
help her out, suddenly deciding what it was that must
be troubling her—that issue of her virginity, so crassly
dealt with by John Henslow, but an issue, a reality
none the less.

'Louise, it doesn't matter,' he told her gently.

He and his first girlfriend, Anne, whom he still
remembered with fondness, had initiated each other
into the ultimate physical experience, and since they'd
both been young medical students at the time it had
happened without very much ego or agony on either
side. Lots of laughter, actually, and a surprising
amount of total ineptness in both of them at first.

But it would be hard for graceful, lovely Louise, who
was in her late twenties now. It had been postponed
too long. He was aching, really feeling for her, *determined* not to scare her more. 'I'm not going to let it
frighten you,' he said. 'It won't be tonight. Absolutely
not tonight. . . Although do let me kiss you again! But
when we do, honestly, we'll take it so slowly. . . I've
done this before, you see.' He was thinking again of
Anne. 'You'd be surprised what there is to do to lead
up to it. You'll see. Lovely things. . .'

Louise listened to the low, cajoling speech, distracted by the delicious throaty timbre of his voice,
until she suddenly realised what he was driving at. Her
much discussed spinsterhood! And he was being *kind*
about it, gently, sincerely, carefully *kind*!

I have to tell him, she realised. That's step four, I
suppose. Telling him. Have I got there already? It
seems that way. . .

'Adam, you've got it wrong,' she broke in desperately. 'John Henslow got it wrong. I let him, but I can't
go on letting you. I'm not a virgin, timid and nervous
about sex. That's not the problem. Far from it. I've
been married.' There! It was out. 'I've been married,
and that was how it all started. . .with great sex!'

'You've been *married*?'

'Yes. And now I'm divorced. Divorced! I hate it! I hate being twenty-eight years old and already divorced. That's why I never tell anyone about it if I can possibly avoid it.'

About her meeting with Australian physical education teacher Brett Walker on a youth-hostelling trip through Devon and Cornwall when she was twenty-one. Their heady and very physical courtship. Their hasty marriage after less than two months, and then the two-and-a-half-year playing out of their disastrous life together in Australia. The fights. The reconciliations. The growing emptiness of their lovemaking. His flagrant infidelity. Her naïve belief that perhaps a child could cement things for them. The final, painful proof that she was wrong on all counts. . .

Adam's hands had dropped from their light, reassuring clasp around her waist. He laughed tightly. 'Well, that puts a new complexion on things, doesn't it?'

'You agree, then, that it's a failure.' They were still standing very close. She could have touched him if she had wanted to. She didn't.

'A *failure*?' he said.

'Yes! An enormous one! I married, and I failed at it.' The fact hung like an albatross around her neck, because any fool should have seen that what drew her to Brett was purely physical, and yet she *hadn't* seen it at all. This meant that, no matter what blame there was in Brett's faithless and insensitive conduct, she had to accept that the thing was her fault as much as his. Probably more.

'I wasn't thinking in terms of failure,' Adam was saying. 'I just meant that it explains, perhaps, the. . . reserve? Reluctance?. . . I've seen in you.'

'Yes,' she acknowledged. 'That's there. I'm. . . trying. I want to get over it, I really do. It's taking a long time.'

'How can I help?' He was holding her again, and she knew that she must feel as stiff as a board in his arms. How could his touch be so intoxicating, and yet at the same time so claustrophobic?

'Help? You mean you want to?' she demanded, amazed.

'Yes. Is that arrogant?'

'No! It's generous!'

'It isn't, believe me! My interest is a very selfish one. . .'

'Time?' she suggested after a moment. 'Isn't time the only thing that really helps?'

'Not. . .this?' His mouth swooped in to find hers and she gave a tiny moan as their lips brushed hotly together, then pulled her face aside so that his kiss left a sizzling trail across her jaw to her tautly stretched neck.

'No, not that,' she told him hoarsely. 'It reminds me too much. It's the problem, not the solution.'

'You really do need time,' he whispered, searching her face, seeing the flush that she knew burned on her cheeks. 'How long ago was all this?'

'My marriage? Seven years ago. The divorce. . .four and a half, just before my father had his first stroke.'

She turned away, holding her arms around herself, seeing something clearly for the first time: her father's long illness. Until now, she had seen it as a time to recover and put the past behind her, but it had been too special and private a time for that. Now that it was over and her father was at rest, she knew that she *hadn't* spent those years getting over her marriage and divorce; she had simply shoved the issues to one side so that now they were far fresher, far less well resolved than they should have been.

Adam must think her degree of reserve odd, after so long, she knew. 'I'm sorry,' she said quickly. 'I've still got a lot of sorting through to do. I won't blame you if. . .what's started to happen between us. . .has lost all its appeal for you now.'

'Nonsense!' he exploded. 'Do you think I'm the kind of man that's put off by the trappings of a woman's past? Or by the fact that it's important to you? It just seems. . .wrong to me that you're taking so much of the blame on your own shoulders, even after four years. Do you want to tell me more about it?' he asked gently.

'No,' she answered, still not looking at him. She felt tension knotted in her neck and shoulders as she sensed his gaze locked upon her. 'Not tonight, if you can be content with the bald statement of facts I've already given you.'

'Then let's take this at your pace, OK?'

'My pace?' She laughed a little. 'Snail's pace. Friends, Adam?'

'Friends. . .'

'Such an insipid word in this context, isn't it?'

'But it's all you can offer. . .'

'At the moment.'

She was able to turn back to him at last, wondering what she would see. Many men would reject the tepid suggestion she had just made. Brett would have done. He would have laughed in her face at the very notion of friendship between a man and a woman, and used his blond, tanned good looks to immediately pursue some other quarry. Their intense, superficial courtship hadn't given her time to discover this fact *before* the wedding, unfortunately.

Adam though. . .

'Don't say "insipid". I know what you mean. It's usually a woman's polite way of saying, I wouldn't get steamy over you if you were the last man on earth, but. . .can I take it you don't mean that? My ego doesn't need that sort of face-saving, Louise, so give me the straight answer, please!'

'I'm. . .steamy over you already,' she admitted in a low voice. 'That's not the problem. That's the physical part. It's the emotional part that——'

'OK. Friends it is, then.' His voice was well-controlled, nice and light. 'Keep me apprised of any new developments, won't you?'

'I——' She spread her hands helplessly. 'I will, then.'

'And thanks for dinner,' he drawled, smiling a little.

'Thank *you*!'

His dark eyes were raking her with a mixture of impatience and wry amusement at the whole situation as he leaned against the doorway. The lazy lines of his body disturbed her nerve-endings and 'friendship' had never seemed like a more stupid and meaningless word. He sighed between his white teeth, as if he was feeling the same, clicked his tongue and said as he straightened lazily and crossed to the far door, 'You on nights next week?'

'Yep.'

'See you at some ungodly hour, no doubt.'

'Expect so. 'Night, then.'

'Night, landlady. . .'

CHAPTER SIX

IN THE nursery, on a flat white mattress that lay within its protective plastic sides atop a wheeled trolley, there came the angry mewing sound of a newborn's cry. Louise went over and looked at the tiny, swaddled thing. Red-faced, one fist balled and escaping from the confines of its flannelette blanket. . .quite a dark, downy head of hair, this one, shading to the remnants of foetal body hair on his shoulders and in the small of his back. She'd noticed that earlier when she had changed his nappy.

They were all so different, the babies, although at first they looked like identical parcels of blankets and little round heads. There was the difference in hair, for example. Some were quite bald, others had wispy and golden hair, but most of them were dark, even the ones that would be quite fair in a few months' time.

Their faces were different, too. They all had the red or dusky skin and tiny white pimples, just dots, really, that were called milia. The vaginal deliveries nearly always had bumpy heads and bruised faces. Some of them looked as if they'd been in a serious pub fight the night before. The Caesareans were less physically marked by birth, and often tended to be either the biggest or the smallest babies in the group. Small, if they'd had to be got out early and quickly, big if they'd refused to proceed as required down through the narrow birth canal.

This little kitten now, mewing for his mother's milk, was a Caesarean, and wasn't actually so little at all. He had weighed in at nine pounds seven ounces, and his five-foot-two-inch mother just hadn't had the pelvis to match.

'Next time,' Melissa Hayes had said ruefully to Louise last night, 'I won't take my pre-natal nutrition quite so seriously!'

She was still pretty sore, but this was her fifth post-op day now, and she would be going home tomorrow. Little Max was the kind of baby Louise had no qualms about saying goodbye to. Already he was beloved, and she knew that Mrs Hayes face would light up in a few minutes when she was awakened to find him wheeled up beside her bed and ready for his feed.

At Morleyvale, babies were mostly brought for feeding on demand at night, which kept the staff busy in the nursery but set up a good pattern for breast-feeding and still gave the mums some needed rest, although some did prefer to have their babies with them all night. At the moment, there were just four in here under Louise's care, part of a constantly changing stream which meant that she couldn't possibly begin to remember them all.

But she remembered some. Usually, of course, the ones that had made the most dramatic entry into the world. The Peterson triplets, for example. Two of them were safely home. The third was still across in NICU making heavy weather of it after some set-backs, but beginning to grow nicely now.

Louise wheeled baby Hayes's crib out of the nursery, and almost mowed down Judy Smith.

'Leave that!' she ordered abruptly, breaking the quiet routine of night-time baby care that Louise had been enjoying vastly all this week, with a very physical, maternal hunger. 'You're going out with a flying squad.'

'Now?' She realised it was a silly question as soon as the word escaped her; it had been an instinctive exclamation.

'Of course now!' Judy snapped. 'With Henslow. He's on his way and I know he'll throw a fit if he has to take Maria.'

'OK, so you'll——'

'She'll do the babies. Here she comes now. I'll tackle that horrible little cow in Room Eight for her. Third child and she's eighteen. God!'

'What's going on, Judy?'

It was Adam. Louise's heart immediately jumped, and her senses tingled. He'd appeared out of nowhere, it seemed, though in fact he must have come from Theatre where he'd just finished an emergency Caesarean on a diabetic mother.

'We need to send a flying squad.'

'What? Post-partum haemorrhage?'

'No.' Judy summarised quickly, and her face began to lose some of the bitterness it had held as she'd spoken of the teenage mother in Room Eight. 'Independent midwife. Arrested labour. Husband made the phone call, wife is refusing to come in, and midwife supports her. Over thirty-six hours, though. . .'

'Thirty-six hours?' His eyes had narrowed.

'The ambulance men have the details, and the address.'

'Who's the midwife?' Adam wanted to know. 'Know her name?'

'Penney?' Judy hazarded. 'Deirdre Penney, I think. . .'

'I'll go.'

'John's already on his way over.'

'Tell him to go back to bed.'

'But——'

'I've had trouble with this one before, and this time I want to be there first-hand!'

'Do *you* want Maria, then, or——?'

'I'll take Louise, thanks, since she's right here.'

And so Louise was pulled along in Adam's wake,

loving his dark bulk, his angry speed, his total focus, and minutes later they were on their way by ambulance, fully kitted up and going over the slender detail that had come in over the phone.

'The mother is twenty-two.' Adam was shaking his dark head. 'For a primip of forty, thirty-six hours is a long labour, but for a twenty-two-year-old. . .? I hate to think what we're going to find.'

'You seemed to know this midwife,' Louise said, caught up in the aura of his foreboding.

It was two in the morning. After the hallowed quiet of the nursery, the October streets were dismal in a wash of cold rain, and little traffic was about to impede the progress of the ambulance. Adam looked exhausted, as well he might. He'd been up half the night before, Louise knew, with a difficult delivery, and he had a full load of surgery on Thursdays, as well as a lecture to nursing students. Not for him the luxury of half the day in bed as she had had, and now he'd had surgery again tonight, and this. . .whatever it turned out to be. It certainly didn't sound good.

'I came across her indirectly last year,' he said. 'A woman came in to Casualty, ten days post-partum, with bleeding she thought was too heavy. Got seen by an inexperienced houseman—first week on the job— and he dithered around, gave her TV fluids and sent her home on bed-rest. Two days later, she turns up at one of my clinics, brought in by her husband, and by then it was one of the worst post-partum haemorrhages I've ever seen. She was fine with the right treatment and two units of blood, but when I first saw her her uterus was as boggy as a swamp and when I asked about post-partum care from her midwife—she'd delivered at home with the help of this Penney woman—I was told Mrs Penney had pronounced it quite normal and gone off on holiday.'

'So why is she still practising?'

HARLEQUIN MILLS & BOON

FREEPOST

P.O. BOX 70

CROYDON

SURREY

CR9 9EL

FREE BOOKS CERTIFICATE

YES! Please send me the free books and gifts to which I am entitled and no obligation, as explained overleaf, and that I am under writing to you. enter me in the £600,000 Prize Draw. I understand that I am under and that I may cancel at anytime simply by writing to you.

If you would like to enter the £600,000 prize draw but would prefer not to receive books please tick box. ☐

8A5D

Ms / Mrs / Miss / Mr _____

Address _____

_____

_____

_____ Postcode _____

You are invited to play

£600,000 LOTTO!

LOTTO CARD No: PA281 750

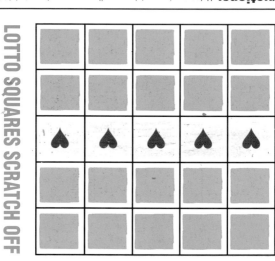

LOTTO SQUARES SCRATCH OFF

Instructions: Using a coin, scratch away silver squares, in a straight line (across, down or diagonal) until 5 hearts are revealed. Doing this makes you eligible for a chance to win one of the following prizes: Grand Prize, £600,000; First prize £30,000; Second Prize £6,000; Third Prize £3,000; Fourth Prize £600. VOID IF MORE THAN 5 SILVER SQUARES ARE SCRATCHED AWAY.

AND... YOU CAN CLAIM UP TO 4 FREE BOOKS, AN AUSTRIAN CRYSTAL NECKLACE AND A MYSTERY GIFT ABSOLUTELY FREE.

To register your entry in the £600,000 Prize Draw and to claim your **free books and gifts simply return this card. See the coupon overleaf.**

DON'T HESITATE REPLY TODAY!

OFFICIAL RULES
NO PURCHASE NECESSARY TO ENTER
MILLION DOLLAR SWEEPSTAKES (III)

To enter, follow the directions published. Method of entry may vary. For eligibility, entries m be received no later than March 31, 1996. No liability is assumed for printing errors, lost, or misdirected entries.

To determine winners, the sweepstakes numbers on submitted entries will be compa against a list of randomly, pre-selected prizewinning numbers. In the event all prizes claimed via the return of prizewinning numbers, random drawings will be held from among other entries received to award unclaimed prizes.

Prizewinners will be determined no later than June 30, 1996. Selection of winning numb and random drawings are under the supervision of D. L. Blair, Inc., an independent judg organisation whose decisions are final. Limit: one prize to a family or organisation. substitution will be made for any prize, except as offered. Taxes and duties on all prizes the sole responsibility of winners. Winners will be notified by mail. Odds of winning determined by the number of eligible entries distributed and received.

Sweepstakes open to residents of the U.S. (except Puerto Rico), Canada, Europe Taiwan who are 18 years of age or older, except employees and immediate family memb of Torstar Corp., D.L. Blair, Inc., their affiliates, subsidiaries, and all other agencies, enti and persons connected with the use, marketing or conduct of this sweepstakes. applicable laws and regulations apply. Sweepstakes offer void wherever prohibited by Any litigation within the province of Quebec respecting the conduct and awarding of a p in this sweepstakes must be submitted to the Regies des Loteries et Courses du Quebec order to win a prize, residents of Canada will be required to answer a time-limi arithmetical skill-testing question to be administered by mail.

Winners of major prizes (Grand through Fourth) will be obligated to sign and return an affidav Eligibility and Release of Liability within 30 days of notification. In the event of non-compli within this time period or if a prize is returned as undeliverable, D.L. Blair, Inc. may at its discretion, award that prize to an alternate winner. By acceptance of their prize, winr consent to use of their names, photographs or other likeness for purposes of advertising, t and promotion on behalf of Torstar Corp., its affiliates and subsidiaries, without fur compensation unless prohibited by law. Torstar Corp. and D.L. Blair, Inc., their affiliates subsidiaries not responsible for errors in printing of sweepstakes and prize winning numbers the event a duplication of a prize winning number occurs, a random drawing will be held f among all entries received with that prize winning number to award that prize.

This sweepstakes is presented by Torstar Corp., their subsidiaries, and affiliate conjunction with book, merchandise and/or product offerings. *The number of prizes to awarded and their value are as follows: Grand Prize - $1,000,000 (payable at $33,333, year for 30 years): First Prize - $50,000; Second Prize - $10,000; Third Prize - $5,00 Fourth Prizes - $1,000 each; 10 Fifth Prizes - $250 each; 1000 Sixth Prizes - $100 ea Values of all prizes are in U.S. currency. Prizes in each level will be presented in diffe creative executions, including various currencies, vehicles, merchandise and travel. presentation of a prize winning in a currency other than U.S. currency represents an approxin equivalent to the U.S. currency prize for that level, at that time. Prize winners will have opportunity of selecting a prize offered for that level; however, the actual non U.S. curre equivalent prize, if offered and selected, shall be awarded at the exchange rate existin 3:00 P.M. New York time on March 31, 1996. A travel prize option, if offered and selecte the winner, must be completed within 12 months of selection and is subject to: trave companion (s) completing and returning of a Release of Liability prior to travel; and hotel flight accommodations availability. For current list of all prize options offered within p levels, send a self-addressed, stamped envelope to MILLION DOLLAR SWEEPSTAKES Prize Options, Harlequin Mills & Boon, UK: PO Box 236, Croydon, Surrey, CR9 3 IRELAND: PO Box 4546, Dublin 24. For a list of prize winners (available after July 31, 1 send a separate, stamped self-addressed envelope to: Million Dollar Sweepstakes Winners, Harlequin Mills & Boon, UK: PO Box 236, Croydon, Surrey, CR9 3RU. IRELA PO Box 4546, Dublin 24.

*U.K. equivalent prize values at the time of printing. Grand Prize - £600,000; First Prize - £30, Second Prize - £6,000; Third Prize - £3,000; 3 Fourth Prizes - £600 each; 10 Fifth Prizes - £ each; 1,000 Sixth Prizes - £60 each.

ALTERNATE MEANS OF ENTRY
NO PURCHASE NECESSARY

To enter the Prize Draw without requesting books and gifts, tick box on coupon. Or you may print "£600,000 Lotto" plus your name and address on a postcard and send it to:- £600,000 L Harlequin Mills & Boon, P.O. Box 70, Croydon, Surrey CR93JE, and we'll assign a Prize number to you.

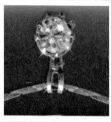

'The casualty visit. Couldn't pin down the responsibility between the midwife and the houseman. *She* claimed it must have got worse *after* she'd last seen the patient, and *he* was the one who hadn't spotted it. She wouldn't even consider that her own judgement might have been at fault. This time there'll be no such scapegoat!'

His face, in the moving light and shadow cast by a street-lamp as they passed beneath it, was grim, and Louise felt again this foreboding. Thirty-six hours was horribly long for a young woman's labour, and she wondered why on earth the woman was refusing to come to hospital. Surely that couldn't be right?

The husband met them at the door, deathly pale. He gave a dry sob as he opened it and pulled them in, confirming the story they had been given with his first words. 'They don't want you here,' he said. 'I didn't tell them till after I'd called. They still think everything's fine but. . .' another dry sob '. . .I know it isn't.' He swore in a cracked voice. 'Deirdre's got my wife *hypnotised*, I think. Get the baby out, that's all that matters—just get it out!'

He dragged them into a darkened bedroom that smelled of incense and fragrant massage oil. Soothing music played and the bed was fat with clean, comfortable pillows. An ideal set-up for a wonderful home birth, but this one was going wrong. The young first-time mum, Lisa Lewis, was half moaning, half breathing her way through a contraction as they entered. The midwife, an intense, angular woman with long straight greying hair, was coaching her forcefully. Louise could see that the uterus was bunching and tightening, but below there was no sign of crowning at all.

'Keep going. You can do it,' the midwife said. 'Not too much longer now. Keep on with your nipple stimulation between contractions, to release more oxytocin into your system. That'll speed things up. Keep your confidence up!'

'Yes, I'm confident,' Lisa Lewis intoned as the contraction left her. 'I can do this. It's my right to have the birth experience that I want! I can do this!'

She was shaking, wet with perspiration and grey with exhaustion, but her face was set grimly with her determination. 'I *can* do this,' she sobbed, breaking for a moment, then pulling herself together again.

Only now did the midwife notice the newcomers, and Mrs Lewis was still oblivious as she closed her eyes. 'What are you doing here?' Deirdre Penney said, recognising the nature of the interruption. 'You're invading this woman's privacy.'

'How long has she been in labour?' Adam asked abruptly.

'A bit over a day.'

'Nearly thirty-seven hours, Deirdre,' Mr Lewis said harshly.

'Dilated?'

'Seven centimetres. Almost eight.'

'She got to seven four hours ago,' Mr Lewis again.

'Foetal heart-rate?'

'I was just about to listen again when you interrupted!'

'Well-descended?'

'Oh, not yet quite fully engaged. The head is slow to mould, but with the nipple stimulation she's doing now the contractions should——'

'Let's have a look.'

'No! She hasn't given permission for——'

'I have, though,' Mr Lewis said. 'Shut up, Deirdre.'

'I'm in control, Mark, I'm in control,' Lisa said. 'Normal labour has many patterns.'

Adam was snapping on his gloves, ignoring the other voices in the room. 'Check the heart-rate, Louise. . .

Barely five centimetres dilated,' he barked a moment later.

'Heart-rate about eighty. Erratic.'

'Head still sky-high. She needs surgery *now*!'

'No! This is my patient! She's progressing.'

'She's in arrested labour with every indication of cephalo-pelvic disproportion *and* foetal distress,' he rasped.

'You told her she was almost eight centimetres, Deirdre,' Mark Lewis accused.

'To encourage her to keep working.'

'The baby's in distress? In *distress*?' At last Lisa Lewis seemed to come out of her trance. She struggled to get up, but the ambulance officers were ready with their stretcher and she was soon laid on it, not protesting now, only moaning as another contraction came, and then repeating over and over, 'The baby's in *distress*?'

'The heart-rate was coming up perfectly between contractions. It *was*,' Deirdre Penney was saying in the background. Adam didn't even bother to reply.

The ambulance journey back to the hospital seemed agonisingly slow. Adam gave a drug intravenously to try and strengthen the contractions in case a miracle happened and the baby began to descend as it should. But the real hope now lay in an emergency Caesarean. With Mrs Lewis hooked up to a monitor, the unborn baby's heartbeat was audible to Louise and Adam, and they could hear that it was slowing and weakening without needing to look at the digital read-out. Sixty beats per minute. Forty-eight. Adam had a drip in her hand already, and Louise was asking Mr Lewis about his wife's surgical history. No known problems. They'd be able to go straight in. . .

If Louise had thought that John Henslow was fast and efficient under pressure four weeks ago, then Adam was like lightning, and the team pelted down the corridor into the obstetrics theatre suite at a pace that had her panting. The theatre team had been alerted and the patient was prepped and put under general anaesthesia while Adam and Louise were still frantically scrubbing.

He had made the first incision almost before she reached the table, and they all saw the disturbing amount of meconium staining in the amniotic fluid released by his action, and then, seconds later, the baby was out, just as Louise picked up the suction catheter ready to clear out nose and throat. But in those last few minutes between ambulance and theatre, they'd lost the ability to monitor the heartbeat and now there was only silence, no outraged cry of indignation from the blue, inert infant.

For minutes on end, Adam and the paediatrician, Tanya Lawlor, worked over the meconium-stained baby, trying to coax a response, but it was no use, no use at all. . .

Adam swore with suppressed violence, half under his breath, and if Louise had not been fighting tears and a queasy rebellion against fate in her stomach she would have sworn too. The anaesthetist, Peter Craven, intent on his monitoring equipment, said wearily, 'What happened?'

'The cord's knotted twice,' the SHO reported as he delivered the placenta.

'That certainly didn't help, then,' Adam responded in a wooden tone. 'The cord must have been positioned so that it was getting compressed repeatedly by those endless, useless contractions. Louise?'

'Yes. . .' Her eyes met his over her mask.

'Could you bear to go out to the dad?'

'Of course.' Though she dreaded the idea.

'I don't want him kept in suspense while we stitch her up.'

'He may want to see the baby,' Tanya Lawlor said.

'We'll clean her up and——Oh, *hell*!' They all felt the same anger and powerlessness expressed in her angry syllable.

'If the midwife's around, get rid of her,' Adam rasped. I'm going to ask the director of Midwifery Services to get on the phone to the Professional Conduct Committee of the UKCC first thing tomorrow morning and have her suspended as soon as possible. She shouldn't be practising, and she won't be from now on if I have anything to do with it.'

'Should be no problem with that, should there?' the SHO asked. 'It seems a pretty clear case.'

'Yes, that's how I see it,' Adam agreed grimly. 'Tell the dad that, Louise, if you think it'll help.'

'OK.'

Louise stripped off her mask and cap and gloves, her stomach sinking at the thought of what she had to tell Mark Lewis. The baby girl had been perfectly formed and about nine pounds. . . Oh *hell*! Mentally, she echoed Tanya Lawlor's helpless profanity.

Out in the corridor, there was no sign of Deirdre Penney, but Mr Lewis was further down, pacing restlessly and grey-faced. Louise hadn't seen him watching through the glass during the frantic minutes of surgery. Too nervous, perhaps. For the best, as it meant that he hadn't seen those desperate, hopeless efforts over the lifeless infant. But it made her task harder now.

When he turned and saw her, he came towards her, his face alight with tremulous hope. The thing had gone so fast. He thought it was going to be fine.

'I'm sorry.' She had to fight not to cry herself. He didn't need to see her emotion when his own was so much worse.

'You mean. . .?' His face twisted.

'I'm afraid so. The oxygen and blood supply just weren't getting through that cord in the end.'

'Does Lisa know yet?'

'No, she's still under anaesthetic.'

'Let me tell her.'

'Of course, and in a while, if you want to—both of you—you can see the baby, spend a bit of time with her. Mr Van Curen is suturing the incision now. It'll be a little while before your wife is awake. Would you like a cup of tea?'

'Oh. . .yes. . .if you like. I don't care.'

'There's a little lounge in here, if you want to sit down.'

'No. . .'

She left him to his pacing, now erratic and agonised, and went to the unit kitchen. Deirdre Penney was there, hovering over the kettle. She looked up and gave a bright, tight smile. 'Right as rain?'

'No.' Louise was too angry to mince her words. 'She was dead before we could get her out.'

'Oh. . .a congenital defect?'

'The baby was perfect.'

'No, I think you'll find that there must have been something wrong that couldn't have been foreseen. I've managed plenty of labours that long with no problem at all.'

'I think you'd better go, Mrs Penney.' If the woman showed any remorse, any sense of culpability, or any of the grief that the entire theatre team was feeling, Louise might have had some sympathy to spare for her, but all that seemed to concern her was justifying her own course of action.

She was still talking, in fact. 'Mrs Lewis wasn't working hard enough, and her husband was no support. She should have been walking between contractions but she wouldn't. She stopped that after about sixteen hours, so of course she slowed down. She just couldn't summon the stamina, and that's scarcely my fault! But, in any case, the heart-rate was bouncing right back up after every contraction, right up until——'

'Do I have to phone hospital security?' Louise interrupted.

'Yes, that's right!' Mrs Penney hissed. 'Your attitude is typical of someone in one of these megalithic institutions. No human concern, no concept that birth and death are normal, natural processes. I'll go, but I think that the National Childbirth Trust will be on my——'

'Do you? I don't!' Louise snapped with letting her finish. 'I think they'll know exactly who's at fault in this. And now, if you'll excuse me, I'm trying to make a cup of tea for the father who's just lost his first-born child!'

Mrs Penney left, still untouched by any evidence of grief or regret. Louise made the tea, anger giving an uncontrollable palsy to her fingers so that she spilt a puddle of boiling water all over the bench. Finally the tea was made, and she found Mr Lewis sitting in the lounge flipping blindly through a sports magazine. He took the tea from her and gulped a scalding mouthful, then said hoarsely, 'Can something be done to her? To that woman who brainwashed my wife?'

'Yes.' Louise touched his arm. 'Something *will* be done, and she won't be able to practise again. I know that's small consolation.'

'We both liked her at first, especially Lisa. Deirdre talked so much about birth being natural and beautiful, and the body having an instinct for it that gets masked by the way we live these days. It seemed to make sense. She spent hours with Lisa, had her in classes for months. . . That's when I began to get a bad feeling. Lisa only ever talked about the birth. I had to be the one to say, Hey, the birth, brilliant, OK, what about afterwards? Hadn't we better think about what we're going to do with the *baby*, whether you're going to breast-feed, when we're going to take it down to Devon to see your parents?

'So, OK, we decided about that, then it was back to

the birth again. How amazing it was going to be, how she knew she was strong enough no matter what her labour was like. Lisa had a friend who's about six or seven months gone now—because she decided to go for a hospital birth, Lisa's just cut her off. Can't bear to even speak to her. That's obsession, isn't it? And Deirdre encouraged it, I thought.'

He talked on, and Louise let him, knowing how important it was. Adam slipped quietly into the room, and she acknowledged his presence with a tiny nod. Neither of them felt like smiling. Finally, Mr Lewis had talked out the first wave of shock and finished his tea.

'Your wife should be waking up any minute, if you'd like to go to her,' Adam said quietly.

'He'd like to be the first to tell her what's happened,' Louise explained.

'Good, yes. Here's Nurse Taylor to take you along. Do you have any questions first, Mr Lewis?'

'No, not at the moment, thanks.' He left with the trainee midwife, and Adam let out a tired, controlled sigh.

'God, Louise. . .'

'I know,' she nodded, finding her own emotion mirrored in him, and drawing a tremulous comfort from it. 'Sometimes when they're born dead you know it's for the best, because there was something so badly wrong. But this time. . . Want some tea?'

'No. I'm heading off soon. I'll see the parents again first, of course.'

'Home to bed?'

'Should do, but I won't sleep. No, I'm going to push boxes around in your house, let off some steam, since you're not there to be distracted.'

'OK.'

He paced the room. 'You know, I keep thinking of what you said, just last Saturday—about the baby being more important than the birth experience. You could have been talking about tonight.'

'I know.'

'I *believe* in home birth!' he rasped. Louise could hear the anger he felt about how powerless he had been tonight. 'And I believe in breathing techniques and birthing stools and whatever position the woman wants. I believe in a woman's instinct being correct, sometimes, even when an examination or a monitor says she's wrong. But that whole ideal of a natural birth *has* to be balanced against the real goal, which is a healthy mother and child, *not* some mystical bonding with the earth-mother spirit.'

'Ideally, if a couple want it, there can be both.'

'Ideally, there can be both but, if you have to choose, for God's sake choose a healthy baby! Birth's *not* a completely natural event for human beings any more. How can it be, when our spine and pelvis still haven't fully made the transition to walking on two legs, and when our diets and sitting and sleeping positions are so alien to anything we'd be doing if we'd stuck to our primate origins? If we're going to live the way we do, eating all that protein, standing in high heels on the tube, or sitting in front of television with slouching spines, we need technology to help women give birth safely——' He broke off and gave a brief, rueful smile. 'Sorry, I've got up on to my soap-box.'

'You're only saying what I think. He was talking about it, did you hear?' Louise said.

'Came in at the tail-end of it, I think.'

'He was saying how Lisa got obsessed with having a completely natural birth, egged on by Mrs Penney, to the point where she couldn't even consider anything else.'

'There's no way she'll keep practising!'

'I told Mr Lewis and I think that helped a bit.' She spread her hands and he nodded. Nothing could really help either of the Lewises, except time and eventually another pregnancy.

'Well. . . I'm going, Louise.'

'Go ahead. Get lots done.'

They smiled at each other and she had a sudden overpowering longing to be able to go to him, kick the door shut behind her so that they were alone in here and shelter in his arms for a very long time, feeling his cheek nuzzle against her hair and his lips touch hers in a kiss that would help both of them forget. His jaw was dark and unshaven now. He looked haggard with exhaustion and his eyes were bloodshot. He *ought* to sleep, but she had understood when he had said he wouldn't be able to. She wanted to smooth out the skin around those fatigue-bruised eyes. . .

But it was her own decision last Saturday that meant she couldn't do it. She had asked for friendship, nothing more than that, and he had agreed with a gentleness and generosity that was very new to her in her dealings with a man. She firmed her resolve and said, 'See you later on, maybe.'

'Yeah. . .'

And he had gone.

She found Judy at the nurses' station busy with paperwork and asked, 'Could I go back to the babies now? I know it's disruptive to chop and change, but I *need* a healthy, beautiful baby or two to hold after tonight. Know what I mean?'

There was no answer for a moment, and Judy's face was set hard as her pen dug into the paper in front of her.

'Judy?' Louise tried again.

'Oh. Yes. If you like. Tell Maria she might as well stay too. There's nothing much going on here tonight.'

'Quite enough for me. It's been so horrible!'

'Mm.'

Louise gave up and left. Everyone agreed that Judy

was getting worse. Gaby Driver and Maria Thomas had confessed, during a recent shopping trip with Louise, that they avoided her whenever possible these days, and Louise had to school herself not to do the same. It didn't make for a smooth-running unit on the shifts that Judy oversaw, and Louise wondered if the director of Midwifery Services needed to be brought in. But what could be done? That sort of confrontation could be so destructive if there wasn't an obvious solution. Still feeling fairly new, after less than two months in the job, Louise decided it wasn't her place to rock the boat.

The babies helped. They always did. Except that there should be a little baby Lewis in here, slumbering through its first few hours of life, and there wasn't. Two empty cribs wheeled into the corner seemed to emphasise this, and Louise tried not to look at them.

'I heard,' Maria said, shaking her halo of tight black plaits. 'How ghastly!'

'You doing nappy changes?'

'Yes, love. That's the usual reason for a bare bottom in this department.'

'Can I do them? Go and grab some coffee. . .and bring me one! I need something to do.'

'Love a coffee. And there's five babies still to do, so you'll be busy. They've all woken up at once, and little baby Hayes is busting for his mum again, aren't you, sugar-pie?'

Baby Hayes. The one she'd been about to wheel to his mother before she'd gone out on that flying squad trip. Half the night had gone by since then. Louise got to work on the babies, finding a healing in their lusty little bodies that she knew the Lewises would have to wait a long time for.

And so the last few hours of the night passed. It was a relief towards seven-fifteen when she heard the morning shift start to come on and realised that it would be time to report in a few minutes.

Suddenly, she felt a terrible need to see Adam again. All the babies were with their mums now, except little Kelly Simpson, one of last night's two safe new arrivals, and she was mewing now too. Mrs Simpson had been asleep since about two, having given birth at midnight. Louise wheeled the crib into Room Eleven, saw the new mother stir and smile with love, and left again, hell-bent on finding Adam to. . .to. . . Well, she didn't know what. Just say hello. Pass the time of day for a few minutes before giving her report on the night to the incoming midwives, that was all. Part of this friendship she had asked for.

But he wasn't in the midwifery sister's office, wasn't in Theatre, wasn't with any of the mums. Perhaps he hadn't got back yet. She wandered into the kitchen, and there he was—with Judy Smith, her head pillowed on his shoulder. The spiky midwifery sister was in tears, Louise soon saw, and she would have guessed anyway, even if she hadn't seen the red eyes, puffy nose and blotchy cheeks, from Adam's soothing murmurs.

'It's OK, Judy. . . Of course you want to cry about it. It's OK.'

That was all Louise heard. She blurted a needless, 'Oops, sorry!' and made a quick retreat, face burning.

It was crazy, illogical, *infuriating* to feel so jealous, but she recognised at once that it was indeed jealousy. Distrust, too.

That's what *I* wanted, she realised. To be in his arms, having him comfort me. What's Judy got to cry about? And why Adam? She's married—can't she cry on her husband's shoulder?

Adam in another woman's arms, apparently inno-cent. Brett in the arms of other women. . .a fellow teacher, an old schoolfriend, his insurance agent. She had thought those moments were innocent, too, for such a long time, and she had been wrong. The sense of betrayal was a body-memory that returned in her tightened throat and queasy stomach.

'Once bitten, twice shy,' she told herself. 'It's nothing. I've got no reason to distrust him.'

She wondered about confessing the feeling to him later, then decided against it. She had asked for friendship. She couldn't now start demanding effusive reassurance every time he touched another woman. It was nothing. Far better, then, to *say* nothing and push the unpleasant feelings aside. If she could. . .

CHAPTER SEVEN

A WET slick of old autumn leaves clogged Louise's garden rake for the umpteenth time and she lifted it to pull the mass off the rake's tines with her gloved hands. It was the end of November now, and high time she tidied up the garden ready for winter. She had to take her new role as property owner seriously and keep the place looking as Adam would want it to. That meant dead-heading the roses and raking up the wind-driven leaves that made soggy drifts in the front yard where his patients parked their cars.

It was nearly six in the evening, and Adam's new receptionist, Tracey Paul, had left several minutes ago, but there was still an unfamiliar car parked outside, as well as Adam's new and very prosaic cream Toyota, so he must still be with a patient. Today was Wednesday, the day he now held a weekly infertility clinic. The slow turn-over of anxious couples on Wednesday afternoons was very different from his Monday afternoon pre-natal and post-partum session, when happily pregnant or newly delivered mums could be whisked through a check-up in a matter of minutes.

Louise added another damp bundle of leaves to her barrow, then crossed the front yard to where Adam's car stood. She knew there were more heaps of leaves behind it as well. Stooping, she heard voices behind her and then as she turned to her barrow she recognised Mark and Lisa Lewis. Her six weeks post-partum check-up, of course, and Adam had shown his usual sensitivity in scheduling it at the end of an infertility session, not in the midst of Monday's parade of big bellies and brand-new babies brought in to be shown off.

Was it already six weeks since that ghastly night, though? Yes, it had to be. That had been the middle of October.

Adam had come out with the Lewises, and he was patting Lisa's shoulder. She was in tears, poor love. It must still be so hard. Louise bent over her rake again, not wanting to intrude, and the Lewises drove away a minute later.

Adam had caught sight of her and came over, and she knew a very silly Cinderella-like wish to have her garden-stained work-clothes instantly transformed into, say, something with sequins. 'Hi,' she said inanely.

'Hi.' He looked casually clean and very male in a charcoal-grey pullover, paler grey trousers and a white shirt.

'That was the Lewises?'

'Mm, yes.'

'Doing all right now?'

'As well as you'd expect. We went through the whole thing several times, but it's hard to convince Lisa that it's not her fault. I've told her again and again that she was in professional hands and that she was right to assume that she was getting competent decision-making from her midwife. Mark feels to blame too, for not sounding the alarm sooner. When I can help them to focus their anger on Mrs Penney instead of themselves, it'll be better.'

'Are they talking about the baby much?'

'Yes, quite a bit, and calling her by her name, which is good.'

'Paula, wasn't it?'

He nodded.

'Lisa's mother came in and saw the baby and held her—did you know?' Louise asked him now.

'No, I didn't.'

'Mary Rigmore said that had helped a bit too, given them some memories and a knowledge that she was real to other people as well. I think they took a few photographs.'

'I've told them there's every reason she'll conceive again soon.'

'They want to?'

'Yes, and in this case it may be the best form of healing. I did suggest they use contraception for about four cycles.'

'To give her body time to recover.'

'And give their grief some time to resolve itself. They want me, this time, and a fully monitored hospital birth.'

'Is that what you advised?'

'I did. Cephalo-pelvic disproportion can repeat itself, and second babies are usually bigger than first ones. She's a bit narrow at the back, from what I could feel. But at the same time, as I told them, I wouldn't rule out a vaginal delivery, and we'd do a scan late in the pregnancy to give us an idea of her chances.'

'Any news on what's happening with the Penney woman?'

'Well, these things move slowly, as you know. I'm pushing to get the UKCC hearing moved up. It's ridiculous that it takes so long, and meanwhile, since she works independently, there's no one to sack her and she's still practising.'

'If I felt she'd accepted some blame. . .'

'Just bravado, perhaps. I've alerted other hospitals in the area to watch out for any of her patients. Meanwhile, I hope she's being very cautious. . . But hey!' His face suddenly lost its gravity and he looked absurdly boyish and startlingly handsome. 'Want to come and see my new toy?'

'Your scanner?' She followed his cue and shook off

the angry memories of Deirdre Penney's tragic over-confidence.

'Yep,' Adam said. 'She's a beauty!'

'Really? And what's her name?' Louise laughed.

'Ulrika. Ulrika the ultrasound. No, just joking. I haven't endowed the thing with a personality. It's a bit too closely studded with intimidating buttons for that. But I'll show you some of the image printouts if you're interested.'

'Oh, I am!'

She flung her gardening gloves into the leaf-filled wheelbarrow and followed him through the front door, kicking off her dirty shoes and leaving them by the entrance to her own stairs. She felt a ridiculous surge of pleasure at his invitation, and when he suggested coffee a moment later—'Made with the help of my *other* new toy'—an electric drip percolator—she said yes to that too.

A moment later, there she was, inside his rooms. They were almost unrecognisable as the dark, cluttered environment where her father had spent his last years. The new paint—palest peach and cream—had added light, as had the removal of her mother's heavy velvet drapes, and most of the dark furniture. He had put a mirror and a side-table in the wide hall, and always kept fresh flowers there. She could smell their faint, cool perfume now. The waiting-room had some bright framed prints as well as the obligatory health charts and posters, and his office was a reassuring blend of formality and comfort, with all his degrees framed in a row along the south wall between the pair of windows.

This wasn't the first time she had seen what he had done. He'd invited her in to lunch twice, casual picnic-style meals of bread and cheese, cold meat and super-market salad, followed by buns and tea. Another time they had gone for coffee at the Four Seasons. Friend-ship. The thing she had asked for. Doled out in very careful doses, like some potent, addictive medicine. Each time, she had been so aware of him that she'd ached with it, while he had been scrupulously distant physically, as distant as if she had been a patient. His respect for what she had asked of him was so completely new to her experience after Brett that at times she thought, He's just lost interest. I've lost him. He wasn't prepared to wait.

And then, just as she was becoming painfully and fully convinced of this, a casual invitation, like today's.

He led her through to where the new ultrasound scanner reposed in all its expensive glory and took out a folder. 'Here are the printouts I've kept,' he said. 'Look, this one from last Friday documents a breech presentation that I wanted to turn from the outside.'

'Successful?'

'Yes. The mother felt a bit pushed about at the time, but she was glad once it was done and she should be in for a much easier delivery now.'

'Mm; this is the head, then?'

'Yes. And here's another picture that shows the posterior fontanelle extra-clearly.'

'Mm, yes, I see it.' She had to lean over to look inside the folder, and was aware of the soft brush of the pullover on his upper arm, just beyond her cheek. It would be so nice just to lean a little and rest her head there. . .'What's this one?' she asked quickly. Why did he always smell so nice? Some doctors only ever smelled of chemicals, but Adam. . .never!

'This? Oh. . .it was bad news, I'm afraid. Look, can you see it? A hydatid mole.'

'A molar pregnancy? I've never come across one.'

'Of course the pregnancy wasn't viable any longer, which I'd suspected. She was pretty upset, but it's extremely unlikely to happen next time round.' He flipped the pages quickly. 'Something more cheerful

here. Twins! Just eight weeks gestation, but you can
see the two sacs clearly.'

'Yes, like dark crescents. . .'

Louise looked at the grainy black and white photo
printout briefly, then stared down at her fingers for a
moment instead. Suddenly, it had stopped being a
matter of simple professional interest.

Odd pictures, they were, these fan-shaped ultrasound images, like pictures from the moon, taken with
some automated camera in a space-ship, not really like
ordinary photographs at all. This particular image was
a classic sample and she felt very much as if she'd seen
it before. . . Funny, she hadn't even thought that these
pictures might move and distress her. After all, she
worked with babies every day.

'And here are the placentas,' he was saying. 'Most
people think that's the foetus itself. And in real time
on the monitor we could see the two heartbeats quite
clearly. Grey and grainy, but the movement quite
distinct. Both parents were ecstatic, because they'd had
a long road to this point, with their infertility problems,
and now they'll get two for the price of one. They
wanted to know whether miscarriage was still a risk,
but I told them once there's a strong heartbeat like this
it's most unlikely.'

'I know.' Louise turned away for a moment. Sometimes at eight weeks there weren't heartbeats, and
effectively the miscarriage had already taken place,
even when there was no bleeding, no sign at all, and
you still felt queasy to the pit of your stomach every
time you drank tea or smelled toothpaste.

Not wanting Adam to see how she was feeling, she
squeezed her face into a painted smile and must have
masked her unexpected emotion well, as he was
already flipping to the next page and had noticed
nothing. 'Now, these are just some routine scans. Ten

weeks gestation, fourteen weeks gestation, nine weeks gestation. Have you seen enough?'

'I—I think so. Thanks, it was interesting.'

Now he *had* noticed something. 'You OK?' There were lines of concern scored into his handsome face, emphasising its bold planes.

'Just a bit tired,' she answered, shaking off the past.

'Mm, and I promised you coffee. It should be ready by now.'

'I'm dying for a cup, actually. . .'

He put his folder of pictures away and they went through to the big kitchen at the back, which looked rather bare these days in spite of Adam's attempt to fill it with prints and plants and quirky ornaments. The conservatory just beyond it, bright even on this grey day, was a much nicer place to sit and sip the rich, milky brew he had made.

She saw that he was watching her, and smiled, wondering as she had wondered before, How do I get there from here? He was smiling too, and she wanted to kiss those curving lips, go over and sit in his lap and wind her arms around his neck, feel him and taste him. . .

And that wasn't friendship.

'Better now?' he asked.

'Yes. . .'

'It's decaff, but it still gives a nice illusion of pepping you up!'

There was another silence as they drank, and after a little while she couldn't stand it any longer and got up to roam the small but airy space, aware that he was watching her restless motion. A minute later, he had stood up himself, come over and blocked her motion with his body, standing in front of her and demanding quietly, 'How are we going with this, Lou?'

'Fine, aren't we?'

'No, not fine. It's bloody hard! I don't know what to

do. I've tried to think of things. Like lunch, and showing you those scanner printouts. . .'

'They were interesting.'

He waved that aside. 'Sure, and it's nice to have lunch, and we talk, but in the air there's always the fact that we want to. . .' He touched her—a hand brushing upwards from her waist, a feather of a kiss grazing her mouth, fingers coaxing the wayward hair back from her cheek. 'Only we don't. We don't touch, and we're like magnets being forced apart. It goes against the grain. How can I concentrate on friendship when I really want—hell, just to have you in my arms, to touch when it feels right—which right now feels like it should be all the time?'

She struggled to speak, but he interrupted. 'Don't deny it, Lou! Because it's coming from you too. If it wasn't, I wouldn't be saying this. And doesn't that mean we're at the point where we should reconsider this friendship idea?'

He was touching her again, more closely now, his hands hot against her back, his thighs pressed against the length of hers, his lips on her hair and then darting into her mouth to demand her willing kiss. He was arguing so persuasively with his body, and she wanted to say, Unfair! Of course, when you put it like that. . .

She turned her head aside, lolling it back, but he only used this as a chance to trail his mouth hotly down her neck to the tender hollow just above her collarbone. 'Louise? Lou. . .?'

She tore herself away. 'Give me a chance, Adam! How can I answer you when——?'

'This *is* an answer, isn't it?' He held her shoulders, chafing at them, then ran his hands in to scoop up her chin and pull her face to him so that she couldn't turn from his cajoling, sensuous mouth. 'You want this. As much as I do. God, am I being unfair here?'

'Using. . .these tactics. . .?' she said against his lips.

'Yes.'

'Yes. You are. But——' She tore herself from him once more and said desperately, 'Adam, I've never denied I wanted this! I just need time to know if I want *more*!'

'Isn't there any sort of an instinct between a man and a woman that——?' he began hotly.

'No! Yes!' She was near to tears. 'But you *are* unfair. It *is* unfair to ask me to go on instinct alone. These things aren't that simple, Adam! What I felt for Brett——'

'I'm not Brett,' he growled.

'No, I know. . .'

'And you're not Sandra.' He'd told her a little about Sandra. 'We're each looking for something different this time, aren't we?'

'Yes. Yes. . .' She was trembling now, and she knew he had felt it.

He stiffened suddenly and released her, his eyes narrowed. 'God, I *am* being unfair. I'm sorry.'

'You're very good at it. . .' She managed the sly tease and it lightened the atmosphere between them a little.

'So are you.'

'I keep thinking of steps, Adam,' she said, serious again, trying to make him understand. 'And a journey. One step at a time. I don't know how many steps there are. I do know quite a bit about the end point of the journey.'

'Which is?'

'Love. The *right* relationship. All the rest of it. A marriage. A family. So if that's not somewhere down the line, the end point you'd like to get to as well. . .'

'Then get out now?'

'Yes. Look, I'm not saying there isn't room for honest mistakes. . .'

'Well, I like your end point. Space for a dog there too?'

'A dog?' she laughed. 'Sure. . .'

'Sorry. Irrelevant. But you're saying the next step——'

'The next step. . . You see, I'm not sure. Brett and I rushed into marriage. I won't do that again! What's the next step, Adam? *Step*, not headlong flight!'

He watched her, seeing the genuine trouble muddying the dark water of her lovely eyes. He was jealous of this Brett, there was no doubt about that. Might be tempted to sock him in the jaw if they ever met! The man had had her and had spoilt it somehow—oh, yes, it was all *definitely* Brett's fault!—and now she was finding it so hard.

He still wanted to seize her by the shoulders and *command* that she forget her past, start again. Did she need that, perhaps—someone to take command? Were her fears wishy-washy and unfounded? No. . . She wasn't a rabbit of a being, to make mountains out of emotional molehills. Somehow he knew that. And he respected her attitude to divorce. What did someone say once? That getting divorced should be made easier, but getting married should be made much harder.

Would he and Sandra have been divorced by now if they had married, as they so easily might have done if career goals hadn't got in the way? Possibly. They would certainly have been miserable together. . .

But Louise was waiting, frowning, for his answer.

'The next step? For us?' he said rather huskily. 'How about a movie?'

'A *movie*?'

'Maybe next week. And perhaps I could kiss you when I pick you up, just for half a minute, and kiss you again when I drop you home. A bit longer that time. Say, two minutes. . .'

'Adam. . .'

'Yes, I'm teasing. But I'm serious, too. Perhaps the next step simply has to be a very small one.'

'A movie,' she laughed. 'OK.'

'And a kiss?'

'No longer than two minutes.' She drew a careful breath, seeing how much he wanted to kiss her right now. As much as she wanted to kiss him, evidently.

They moved apart a little, acknowledging it with their eyes, and he growled throatily, 'Two minutes it is. For now, though, can you please go up to your flat and keep well out of my way for the rest of the day?'

'I'm going, Adam. I'm going this very minute!'

So they had their movie. And they had their kiss. It was longer than two minutes, of course, but shorter than it might have been. Shorter than both of them would have liked. Then Adam was away for nearly a week at a conference and she didn't see him—he rang just once—and she knew this was good. A breathing space, a chance to think, and to try *not* to think about him too much.

She started nights again, knowing he had been due back that morning and wondering, as she locked her little flat, whether he would be called into the unit tonight.

She loped down the carpeted stairs, pulling her warm coat around her as it was December now, then stopped for a moment in the little entranceway to water the plants. Looking out, down the street, there was as yet no sign of the bus labouring its way up Mountjoy Road, so she had the time. . .except that she had forgotten about the new timed light, which she had pressed upstairs, and which clicked off after its usual minute, leaving her in darkness.

Before she could switch it on again from this end, she heard voices in the main entranceway, just outside the glass-panelled door that marked her own entrance, leading to these stairs, and so stayed where she was, not wanting to intrude on Adam. He was back as planned, then, and he must have had surgery hours, though it was a bit late for a patient, surely?

'Oh, Adam, it's so wonderful to know, at last!' The female voice through the glass door sounded familiar, but she couldn't place it at the moment.

Adam's voice in reply was easily recognisable, of course. 'I'm very glad, Judy, you know that. . .' Judy? It couldn't be Judy Smith! But it was, and she actually sounded *happy*! '. . .but don't count on me for too much.'

'Oh, I'll try not to. I will. . . There's still Graham's. . .'

They were out in the front yard now, and Louise couldn't hear any more. She felt very guilty about what she had heard, though. Should she have declared her presence? There really hadn't been time. And she was left wondering over the significance of the exchange. So much emotion in Judy's voice. Such warmth in Adam's. Yet surely he must only be seeing Judy as a patient? Louise couldn't help speculating about what the problem could be. . .

Waiting, still in the darkness, she heard a small car start up and leave the driveway, then heard Adam come back inside and shut the door. Pity she didn't have time to see him. . . Did she, perhaps? No, in fact. . . Leaving hurriedly now, Louise saw the bus pull away from her stop and roar up the hill. There was little hope of catching it, as it made few stops at this time of night, so she had no choice but to walk up to the hospital, which always made her a little nervous after dark. She went as fast as she could and was breathless by the time she arrived. Add this to her surprise at what she had overheard between Adam and Judy. . . Judy, sounding so happy! Adam, who she so badly wanted to see for her own reasons. . . She was pretty dithery during report, and Nicola Hughes had to repeat some of the information about the woman in early labour who was now being handed over into Louise's charge.

She thought about mentioning the overheard conversation to Nicola, but decided against it. If Judy was Adam's patient, then it was confidential. And she *had* to be his patient. What other explanation was there for the two of them being alone in his office, well after dark? Brett could have thought of one or two, but Adam wasn't Brett!

Tonight had been quiet so far, but the day had been a busy one and the rooms were full of post-partum patients. Encouraging her labouring first-time mum, Mrs Appleby, to walk around the corridors as much as she could between contractions, Louise then checked the newly delivered women in her care, admired several healthy little babes, and chivvied a tardy dad off home at half-past ten. After this there was a short lull, but plenty of paperwork to fill in. Gaby Driver, too, in a talkative mood.

'What's got into our Judy tonight?' she said softly. The midwifery sister was in the office just across the corridor. Gaby's eyebrows were raised in her square, no-nonsense face.

'I don't know,' Louise answered quite truthfully.

'Can't remember when I last saw her so cheerful.'

'I don't think I ever have,' Louise admitted with a wry smile.

'Actually, she used to be quite pleasant, up until a couple of years ago, then she gradually got sourer and sourer. I mean, she's always been reserved, never has said much about her private life or shown much interest in anyone else's, but at least she'd be cheerful and pleasant, none of those tight-lipped asides—which, thank goodness, I don't think the patients ever hear.'

'If she has a problem, I do wish she'd be a bit *less* reserved,' Louise came in.

Gaby nodded. 'I know. It's hard, isn't it? If there is something, and she at least hinted, then we might all have more sympathy. But tonight, anyway, you wouldn't think she had a care in the world. Oops, that's my dad-to-be calling down the corridor, I think. Mrs Khan must be getting close.'

She left quickly, and Louise was soon busy again as well. John Henslow was called in to do an emergency Caesarean on a woman with placenta praevia, and Louise and Judy ended up assisting in Theatre. Normally, this would be an occasion for sizzling tension in the air, as Judy made little attempt to conceal her dislike of the senior registrar. Tonight, though. . .

'I'll tell the mum what a good job you did, as soon as she's awake,' Judy told him. 'This little boy's just beautiful, aren't you, darling?'

And she cuddled the little newborn, though it hadn't even been properly wiped yet.

After the surgery was successfully completed, Louise went back to the labouring first-time mum whom she had taken over from Nicola Hughes, and just before morning a healthy girl took her first oddly alert look at the world.

'She's staring right at me. I thought I wouldn't even see her eyes for the first week or two!' the thirty-two-year-old mother exclaimed.

And there was Judy again, poking her head around the door to say, 'May I see? Oh, isn't she heavenly? Yes, they're often wonderfully alert after a natural delivery like yours. Not like when our generation were babies and we were groggy with all those sedatives and what-not crossing the placenta.'

She bobbed out again, leaving Louise practically open-mouthed. If she was Adam's patient, then he must certainly have had good news for her tonight.

Could she be pregnant? Louise wondered, with a tiny, familiar twinge of wistful envy. But no, Judy very definitely didn't want children. She had said so, outright, more than once. Forget it, Louise told herself. It's Judy's business, after all.

The December dawn was a faint hint on the horizon outside now, and another night shift was almost over. Tired now she could hear the unit starting to wake up, and breakfast trolleys were already clattering out of the lift and through the carefully controlled security doors. In came one trolley, nosed ahead of an irritable diet maid.

'Why we have to have these daft key-cards. . .' she grumbled.

'Wouldn't want anyone stealing the babies, would you?' Louise answered her lightly.

The woman snorted. Her figure spoke of numerous pregnancies, so perhaps she no longer thought that babies were a very valuable commodity, but Louise knew that the danger was sadly real these days. Unlikely, to be sure, and the security precautions *were* a nuisance sometimes, but if just one baby ever vanished from the nursery. . . It didn't even bear thinking of.

She shuddered, and wondered why the hours of darkness always gave thoughts their most morbid cast. Time for a cup of coffee. . . And there in the kitchen were Judy and Adam, the latter evidently here for an early round.

'Do be careful,' he was saying.

'Oh, I know,' came Judy's fervent reply. 'I know we're not home free yet, but there's been so little to celebrate until now. Let me, Adam, just for today,' she beseeched, her voice failing a little now.

They saw Louise, and there was a sudden silence. Judy stared down into the sink for a moment then abruptly began to clatter the dirty cups around. Adam cleared his throat, muttered a husky, 'Excuse me,' and brushed swiftly past Louise—she felt the brief warmth of his body like an aura, and hoped his touch was deliberate—and on out of the room.

Judy began spooning coffee into a cup, while Louise filled the electric kettle. The silence was distinctly uncomfortable, then Judy said suddenly, 'You have a lovely house, and Adam is very much enjoying having such pleasant rooms so close to the hospital.' She crossed to the fridge and got out the milk as she spoke.

'Yes, it's working out well for me too,' Louise answered.

There was a small pause, then, 'But would you mind not mentioning to anyone that I was there this evening?' Now she was aimlessly stirring the powdered coffee in the bottom of her cup.

'I wouldn't dream of mentioning it, Judy,' Louise responded seriously. 'That was something Ad—Mr Van Curen and I discussed quite carefully: that being his landlady as well as a midwife here gave me a double duty to respect patient confidentiality.'

'What makes you assume I was there as a patient?' Judy demanded stiffly.

'Oh! Well! I just thought. . . But of course——'

'Don't leap to conclusions please, Staff.'

'I didn't mean——'

'Just do as I've asked and say nothing.'

'Of course.'

'I don't know why it's so hard for everyone in this unit to refrain from speculations about each other's private lives that are none of their business!'

Judy abandoned her unmade coffee and hurried from the kitchen, and Louise was left alone to contemplate her part in the uncomfortable conversation. She really hadn't intended to pry! The opposite! She'd been trying to be as careful and as tactful as she could, but Judy had dashed that in her face. And she couldn't plug the chill little trickle of mistrust that was seeping into her. If Judy wasn't his patient, then what *was* Adam's involvement? If it had been Brett in the same position, the answer would have been easy. . .

By eight o'clock on the Saturday night before Christmas, John Henslow's motives for having a party at his spacious town house were obvious. Louise was no longer the newest midwife in Morleyvale's maternity unit. A rather attractive and boisterous redhead named Alison Donnelly had started three weeks ago, replacing an older woman who was leaving nursing, and the senior registrar had been so exclusively attentive to her all evening that so far no one else had been able to speak to either of them.

Everyone had profited from John's hidden agenda, however, as he had catered lavishly for the evening, provided intoxicating dance music, and invited virtually everyone at the hospital with whom he came into contact. As Louise had volunteered to work over Christmas and New Year, she anticipated a very quiet holiday season, and was determined to enjoy what was likely to be, for her, its highlight.

'I can't think when I was last at this sort of a party!' Mary Rigmore shouted to her above the noise of music and conversation.

'Neither can I!'

'You look quite hot. Have you been dancing?' Mary had just arrived after an afternoon shift.

'I haven't stopped.' It had been joyous and sensous and exhilarating, in her stretchy black silk jersey dress, her body loosened and inspired by her awareness of Adam, who should be here any minute. She was longing to dance with him. . .'But I'm going to now, to catch my breath, and grab a drink.'

The punch looked thirst-quenching and inviting, but there were no cups left, so she went into the kitchen, found a big glass beer mug, rinsed it out then filled it to the brim with punch. She gulped the lot, poured another half-glass and only then realised, when it was very much too late, that the flavours of fruit juice, iced tea and soda water masked a heavy lacing of alcohol. It was going to her head already.

At the same moment, she saw Adam in the doorway at last, looking a little at sea in the face of such a crowd. He had come from the hospital, she knew, having been called in for a difficult birth just as Mary was coming off. They hadn't been able to see much of each other since his return from the conference, as he had had work to catch up on, and she had been rostered for her week of nights, then mainly afternoons.

This past Wednesday, they had passed so often in corridors or at the nurses' station, without the slightest opportunity to talk, that he had been heard to mutter darkly about ships in the night, and working together successfully to control a post-partum haemorrhage at eight the following morning hadn't, of course, afforded much chance for the kind of closeness she yearned for. As a result, the tension within her had been building, and it was so good to see him in this festive atmosphere.

She knew that her face lit up at the sight of him, and now they were both trying, without much success, to navigate towards each other through the crush. He ducked a bottle of beer that was waving wildly in someone's hand, while she sashayed in time to the dance music, a sinuous series of movements that just managed to steer her past two more pairs of dancers without her colliding into them to form a rather too intimate threesome.

He saw a space opening up, darted to fill it and ended up in Mary Rigmore's arms, giving her a hug that took her greatly by surprise until she recovered her balance and returned the gesture with a seasonal goodwill that might have seriously alarmed her husband of seventeen years, if he had been present. Adam was shrugging and turning down his mobile mouth in mimed apology to Louise across the room, and she was giggling helplessly as the music crashed in her ears and the room tilted and rocked a little.

Then she trod on a mince pie that someone had dropped, and felt it clinging stickily to the heel of her black shoe as she took several rickety steps. Bending down with a paper napkin grabbed from a nearby coffee-table, she took several minutes to clear up the mess, and when she straightened again she had completely lost sight of Adam. She found him again three minutes later, but now, suddenly, it wasn't funny any more.

He seemed to have forgotten about her completely, and was locked in a very lively conversation with, of all people, the new midwife, Alison Donnelly, and strangely John Henslow was now nowhere to be seen. The rolicking redhead had her mouth wide with laughter and she was gesturing so freely that her glass of punch splashed on to Adam's navy blue shirt-sleeve. He didn't seem to mind, holding it out so that Alison could make quite a gushing performance of apologising and wiping it off.

It was a familiar sort of picture, and, remembering the uncomfortable little mystery of Judy visiting Adam in his rooms, Louise couldn't help wondering miserably, I haven't picked another ladies' man, have I?

Suspicion rose like bile in her throat. Brett, too, had been a master at making his moves on other women in a way that looked casual and innocent—as casual and innocent as she had believed him to be for so long. Now, while a part of her insisted, Adam's different. This *is* innocent, the rest of her said, I'm not going to be duped so easily this time! And the two feelings warred within her, defying her power to determine which was the truth.

I *must* give him the benefit of the doubt, she decided. I won't let Brett ruin this!

Adam had caught sight of her again now, and she barged the last distance towards him, not caring that she bumped other people. It was too crowded. She couldn't help it. Everyone else was colliding and crushing together, too. Alison gave a last laugh at some comment of Adam's that Louise couldn't catch, and then moved away.

She grabbed Adam's arm, aware that she was gripping it too tightly, and that her eyes glittered, in spite of herself, with the suspicion she couldn't argue away.

'Hi!' she said briefly and a little unsteadily. That punch was still dizzying her head.

'Whew!' he frowned, twisting his arm to free it of her grip then taking her hands for a moment. His touch sang in her veins, but then his hands dropped again. 'What happened to you?'

'What happened to *me*?'

'One moment you were there, and then you weren't.'

'Oh. . . I trod on a mince pie. I was on the floor, cleaning it up, and when I surfaced there *you* were, with Alison Donnelly making love to your shirt-sleeve!' She had meant it to be funny, but it came out too crudely, and like an accusation, not a joke.

He was still frowning. 'You OK?'

'I'm fine.'

'No, you're not. Are you really angry with me for talking to Alison?'

She bristled against the amazement and disbelief in his tone, and her words came out loose and wild, coloured by her deep-running doubts. 'You can *talk* to whomever you like, Adam!' It was a clear threat, although her voice trembled. 'But make sure that's all it is!'

His dark eyes had narrowed, and he drew in a hissing breath, but said, making a clear effort at lightness,

'This is pretty heavy stuff for the middle of a party, isn't it? Is this really the place for redefining the parameters of our relationship? I thought we'd only just decided to heat up the friendship thing a bit, and now you're talking as if I've breached a sealed contract.'

And all at once she crumbled inside. The noise of the party sang in her ears and her throat burned. Oh, God, just look at me! Just listen to me! I'm obviously not ready for this yet!

'I'm not ready.' The last three words were blurted aloud, their desperation masked from the other party-goers by the noise of the music. 'I'm not ready for any kind of relationship yet, Adam.' It was an anguished realisation. 'I'm sorry.'

'Hey. . .'

He was reaching out for her, his hands enclosing hers in a hot, muscled grip that flooded desire up her arms and through her whole body. He was trying to kiss away her words, not caring who saw. But she dodged the onslaught of his tantalising mouth, angling her head and turning her face away.

'I want to be ready. . .' she mumbled fiercely. 'I wish I were. . . But I can't get rid of Brett. He's there. . .an image. . .moving between us whenever I start to think I've put him into the past and——It isn't fair to you, Adam! It isn't fair to me, because I hear myself saying things and putting things on you that. . .just don't belong. . .and I'm not prepared to do that to either of us!'

'Louise. . .'

'No! No!' Calming her wild tone, she went on in a low voice, 'Don't try to argue me out of it. This is too emotional for argument. Just accept it, please. We should have met three years from now!'

She meant it, and he must have seen that she did, felt it in the way she squeezed his hands with burning palms and rigid fingers, because he didn't argue, just nodded, his dark eyes glittering and his mouth a tight line. 'OK, Lou, I accept it.' He let out a controlled sigh. 'And I don't know that I can wait three years out of some half-promised hope that——'

'I wasn't asking you to wait,' she told him miserably. 'That's not what I mean. Of course it's not. I'm just saying. . .it wasn't meant to be, that's all.'

He nodded tersely. 'Seems that way. We've both tried, I think. We both saw. . .what might have been.'

'I hate this. . .' She closed her eyes.

'Let's not prolong it, then,' he said. 'This is Christmas. A party. We should be kissing under the mistletoe.'

'Remind me to avoid that this year!' She managed a laugh.

'Don't worry, I'll be doing the same. . .'

They parted—like ships, carried by the current of people into different corners of the room—and, though Louise stuck it out at the party for another half an hour, she didn't dance another step.

CHAPTER EIGHT

THOSE rent cheques of his kept coming every month. Adam had a bold scrawl, and he used a very black ink. Invariably, the cheques was dated the first of the month in that distinctive hand. The first of January, the first of February, the first of March. . . And with each month that passed the distance between them seemed to grow greater, as if they were both building a thick wall around themselves to block out too much awareness of what might have been.

The first hint of spring came, and with it another of Judy Smith's unexplained visits to Adam's surgery. Louise was in the front yard, tardily pruning the roses Adam had admired last autumn. Judy must have seen her there with her secateurs in hand, but she gave no acknowledgement, just ducked quickly inside.

It was nearly half an hour before she came out again, just as Louise had finished the pruning and was on her way upstairs. The three of them met in the entrance; Judy muttered something unintelligible and left, and Adam, wooden-faced, said a very bland, 'Hello, Louise.'

'Hello.' She fled up the stairs. It was always so much easier when she saw him at the hospital. Their meetings here tended to be very fraught with things unspoken, perhaps because they often took place when no one else was around.

The other first-floor flat was finished now, and rented out to a quiet older couple who spent much of their time visiting their children and grandchildren in other parts of the country, and she was starting to wish that she could have cloned them and put their duplicate in on the ground floor, instead of her professional tenant.

Her doorbell pealed just as she finished washing her hands of garden dirt and changing into clean cream twill trousers and a matching cotton sweater, and when she went to answer it she found Adam himself standing there, leaning his elbow on the door-frame at a level with his head.

There was no messing about with small talk. 'Look, I've been meaning to say this for a while. Would you mind not mentioning at the hospital that you see Judy here occasionally?' His dark gaze was a little wary and sceptical, mirroring her own.

'Of course I won't, Adam,' she answered him at once. 'Judy's already asked me the same thing.'

'She has? Good.' His brow cleared. 'You probably realise that this is a difficult situation for her, and I wouldn't want hospital gossip to make it any more so.'

'She didn't actually explain——'

'No,' he cut in quickly. 'She wouldn't. This. . .goes very much against the grain for her. I really can't say any more.'

'Then don't, please,' she insisted seriously. 'I'm not asking for details.'

Although the whole thing remained a mystery, Judy herself had said that she wasn't here as a patient, and she certainly didn't come during regular surgery hours. But if it was ever my business it certainly isn't now, Louise knew.

Adam hesitated, as if not quite wanting to go, but she wished he would. He was so very male in the way he seemed to fill her doorway, and he was close enough for her to see the little whorl of dark hair that curled at the open neck of his blue shirt. Her body's response to him remained relentless, even after more than three months of polite and well-meaning distance between them.

But he was speaking again. 'You might be interested in some good news, while I'm here. Lisa Lewis is pregnant again.'

Real pleasure broke through her painfully determined barrier against him. 'Oh, she is? I'm so pleased!'

'A little sooner than I'd have liked in some ways. They still have a lot of guilt and anger about what happened.'

'But that may take years to fully resolve itself.'

'Yes, so we'll hope this new baby helps rather than hinders it. They came in together on Monday and were able to see a good heartbeat on the scanner. Due the end of November.'

'And the question of Deirdre Penney?'

'The UKCC's Professional Conduct Committee has assessed the written depositions and agreed there needs to be a hearing. That's taking place in three months, and they may want your evidence.'

'They can have it! But. . .three months?'

'I know. Their backlog of cases is horrific, but what can they do? The Penney case isn't the only one of a serious nature. They couldn't move it any further forward without being unfair to other people with nursing careers hanging in the balance as they wait for their own hearings. The Lewises would have a good case for a malpractice suit, but they don't want to go that route and be forced to dwell on the thing.'

'Thanks for letting me know, then, Adam.'

'I knew you'd want to hear.'

They smiled at each other and she almost. . . almost. . .asked him if he had time to come in for a coffee, but before she could do so he broke the moment of contact, clicked his tongue in farewell and loped off down the stairs. She couldn't help watching him until he disappeared, wondering if there was any way that things could have worked out differently, and hating her past—her marriage and divorce—just *hating* it, all over again, for what it was doing to her life now, almost five years later.

After his car was safely out of earshot, she let herself out of the flat and went down to the Broadway for a late and very slow and leisurely morning coffee and scone at the Four Seasons Café, followed by some shopping to restock fridge and pantry.

At half-past two, as she entered the front yard weighed down with shopping bags, Louise didn't register the unfamiliar car parked there at first. She only noticed it as she put down her shopping to retrieve her keys, and then she took a good second look, as ther was someone still inside.

Slumped down in the driver's seat, with her legs resting high on the dashboard over on the passenger's side, the woman looked very uncomfortable, and she was crying.

'Look, can I help? What's wrong?' Louise had thrust her shopping bags quickly inside the door, hurried over and bent down to the open car window.

'I'm having a miscarriage, and Mr Van Curen's not there.' The stark words came after an abrupt halt to the sobs that had been shaking the slim brunette's shoulders.

'No, he doesn't have hours here on Thursday afternoons,' Louise said gently. 'Why? Did you think you had an appointment?'

'No, but I just assumed. . . I should have thought. I was driving to the shops, you see, and I felt a warmth between my legs. . . Look!' Louise followed the gesture and had to suppress a hiss between her teeth. The woman's pale green trousers were stained red in a wide, dramatic circle round her crotch. 'So I just changed direction and drove straight here. I thought he might be able to do something if I was quick enough, and now he's not here.'

'I'm going to drive you up to the hospital,' Louise

said. 'I work there. I'm a midwife. And you definitely need to be seen.'

The woman didn't hesitate, but slid quickly over to the passenger side, her legs still elevated to the dash-board, as if by working against gravity she could hold the baby in. Louise took the wheel. Not having driven since her years in Australia, she was a little rusty, but the journey was short and she pulled into the casualty entrance without incident.

She had questioned the woman as they drove. 'Did you have any spotting before this?'

'Just a tiny bit, over the past two days. A lot of women do, don't they?'

'Yes, as many as three in ten. How many weeks are you?'

'Eight. I was due for my first pre-natal visit next Monday. I've been seeing Mr Van Curen since November for infertility. We'd been trying for two years before that. . .'

'And you got pregnant, so that's good.'

'But this morning I thought I felt a bit of cramping. I thought that might be normal too, and it was so mild, I told myself not to worry. Maybe it was just a gastric upset.'

'How is it now?'

'Oh. . .getting worse, and I'm still bleeding, even with my legs like this. . .'

'Wait here; I'm going to get you a wheelchair.'

It didn't look good, so much blood, and cramping too. Louise handed the patient over to the casualty staff, then parked the car and came back to the building.

'Cathy Crosbie's her name,' said the admitting clerk. 'We've put her in a cubicle. She said her doctor's Van Curen. Should I page him?'

'Yes,' Louise nodded. 'He should be about finished

day surgery. Not that there's anything he'll be able to do. It seems pretty clear now.'

'Do you want to look at her, then? I was going to send in our SHO but he'll be tied up for another half-hour. Or I could page up to the maternity unit for a midwife on duty.'

'No, I'm happy to see her. And if you can't get Van Curen, send in the SHO when he's free. This is going to be hard for her and she might want another opinion, since I'm more or less a passer-by in her eyes. She's been trying for a baby for two years, she said.'

'Oh, no! She wanted the husband telephoned. . .'

'I'll do that too.'

Louise made the quick, difficult call, then found Mrs Crosbie in a curtained cubicle that wasn't nearly as private as their own wonderful new rooms up in Maternity. She washed carefully and put on gloves, feeling odd not to be in uniform or wearing her cap and badge. Finding green theatre gowns in a pile on a shelf, she took one and put that on instead, sensing that Mrs Crosbie might need some visible assurance of her competence and authority.

The woman, in her early thirties, was calm now, but she shook a little at Louise's gentle touch. Beneath the white drape that covered her lower limbs, the incontinence pad on the bed was already soaked with both clots and liquid blood, and when she made the internal examination Louise wasn't surprised to find that the cervix had opened.

'I'm sorry,' she said. 'It's not looking good. I'm really sorry.'

Mrs Crosbie began to cry again. 'I knew it. How could there still be a baby in there, with that much blood?'

There was a movement in the doorway and a green-eyed man with a bushy moustache and pale, miserable lips came in. 'Cathy?'

'Oh, Gary. . .'

Louise crept out for a minute to leave them alone, and was waiting in the noisy central area of the casualty department, hoping Adam would appear soon, when Gary Crosbie sought her out again, all his emotion in his eyes.

'What happens now?' he said. 'When do we see the doctor? Is there any chance?'

'Realistically, no,' she told him gently. 'Mr Van Curen will be here soon, I hope, to explain things more fully, but what will happen is that we'll do a scan to make absolutely sure there's no foetal sac, then unless Mr Van Curen feels that a D and C—dilation and curettage— is necessary, and he probably won't, your wife will be given a drug that will help the uterus to contract again and clean itself out.'

'And that's it?'

'That's it,' she echoed.

'God, I never even thought. . . We'd started talking about names. I should go in to her, but I don't know what to say. This has——' He broke off and had to struggle against some dry sobs that had Louise's own throat tightening in hard, painful sympathy. He was pressing the back of his hand tightly against his mouth, but then mastered himself and took it away. 'But I've got to be strong, haven't I?' He didn't notice that Adam had come up behind him. 'I've got to jolly her out of it, be the one who doesn't go to pieces, tell her it'll all be fine next time. I want to go in to her, but she mustn't see me like this!'

'No!' Suddenly Louise was gripping Gary Crosbie's arms urgently, forgetting Adam's presence totally. Her well-schooled and habitual professionalism had been overtaken by a far more emotional response. 'That's wrong! That's *not* what you have to do. Mr Crosbie, please! What your wife needs most of all now is to see that this is just as hard for you. You *must* let her see it so that you can grieve together.'

'You think so?'

'Yes!' Her own voice was almost breaking. 'The worst thing you could possibly do is to let her think she's the only one that minds. She has to know that you're both equal in this. The pain belongs to both of you. Show it to her!'

'I want to. . . At least, I'm not sure that I can hold it in.' His voice cracked again. 'But I thought I had to be strong.'

'No! Please, go to her now!' She pushed him towards the cubicle, and he went. Then, as she stood there, biting her lip and with tear-filled eyes, wondering if she'd gone way over the boundary that separated professionalism from over-involvement, she remembered that Adam was there and waiting to speak to Mr Crosbie, still unnoticed by the grieving man.

'Oh. . .! Damn! I'm sorry,' she said to the consultant.

'It's all right. I can wait. They need time alone together, clearly.'

There was a silence, and Louise realised that she was shaking. He had noticed, of course, but he didn't comment on it directly, just said in a careful voice, 'What you were telling them just then—that he must show his wife that he's grieving too. . .'

'Yes?'

'You seemed. . .very sure that it was the right advice.'

'I am sure,' she told him quietly.

And suddenly their eyes met, three months of careful distance dropped away, and there was a connection between them that was both familiar and frightening.

'Why?' he asked.

And she knew that she should tell him. She let out a

controlled sigh, then began carefully, 'Because I've been through it myself.'

'Like this?'

'Not exactly like this. It was twins, and a routine scan at eight weeks showed that there were no heartbeats when there should have been. Like Mr Crosbie, I hadn't had an inkling that anything was wrong. The picture on the ultrasound looked just like one of the ones you showed me a few months ago—two dark little crescents on a grey, grainy background, only mine were dead. People think that something so abstract. . . can't be much of a loss. But it is! Oh, it is!'

'Louise. . .' He held her hands for a moment, and she swayed towards him, feeling his hair feather against her cheek as he bent his head.

'They told me it was. . .just one of those things,' she said.

'A blighted ovum or a chromosomal defect?'

'Yes. There's no reason why I shouldn't conceive again one day and have a perfectly normal pregnancy. Only, of course, my life hasn't gone that way and there hasn't been the chance. . .yet. . .to find out if they're right. Mostly I'm sensible about it, but sometimes I still rebel. . .'

'But back when it happened Brett's sharing your grief got you through it?' His dark eyes were still fixed on her.

'No!' She was jolted abruptly into this denial by his unexpected question, and Brett's insensitivity was a vivid memory again. 'No! He *didn't* grieve, and that was the thing which put the final nail in the coffin of our awful marriage. If he'd grieved, as I needed him to, I might have had the incentive to forgive his infidelity and give us one more chance together. As it was. . . God, I hated him that day!' She felt her muscles tense uncontrollably.

'You *hated* him?' Adam rasped. 'Louise, I thought you still loved him!'

Her attention caught, she stared at him in amazement. 'But. . .*still*? I *never* loved him! That was the whole point, Adam! Surely you understand that? That's why I blame myself so much and feel such a failure—that I could have been so wrong about love and married a man like Brett. That's why I'm so afraid to get involved again, in case I make another mistake. My God, what have you been thinking?'

He spread his hands. 'What I thought you'd told me: that you felt your divorce was a failure because you still loved him and yet in spite of that you hadn't been able to hold him, and it didn't work.'

They stared at each other.

'We need to talk,' Adam said finally, his voice not quite steady. 'And now's not the time. Can I come up to you as soon as I'm finished for the day? Hell! No! I'm not *asking*, I'm just coming, OK?'

'OK. . .' she managed.

He looked grimly satisfied. 'From now on, Louise, when there's something that needs talking about between us——' The threatening sentence was left deliberately unfinished.

Gary Crosbie was coming towards them, and he addressed Adam at once, 'Can you see her now?'

'Of course.'

He began to walk towards the cubicle, while Mr Crosbie said to Louise, 'You were right. Thank you. We *are* both in this together. Once I stopped trying to pretend I was OK, we could just. . .' He couldn't find the words to finish, but Louise understood. Far too well. She patted his arm with constricted sympathy.

The two of them stood at the curtained cubicle entrance while Adam examined Mrs Crosbie just as Louise had done. Like Louise, he shook his head.

'You're losing some tissue now,' he said. 'There's no

need for you to stay here. Why don't you come down to the surgery? I'll give you a scan on the spot and write out a prescription for you. What you need is to be at home and to rest for a day or two. The pills I'll give you will make your thighs cramp, so don't try to walk much. In any case, you need to take things easy for a while. I'll give you something for the pain as well.'

'But why has this happened, Doctor?' Cathy Crosbie sounded anguished. 'It means I'll never have a child now, doesn't it? Something's just too badly wrong with my body.'

'Mrs Crosbie, as much as a third of first pregnancies end in miscarriage,' he told her, and, hearing the tenderness in his tone, Louise knew that the words were meant for herself as well. 'If we analyse tissue samples, we often find chromosomal defects that prevent these early-loss pregnancies from being viable, and I'm sure that's what has happened here. Nature knows what she's doing. This is very hard for you, I know, but there's every chance that your next pregnancy——'

'My *next* pregnancy?'

'Your next pregnancy,' he repeated firmly, 'will be smooth sailing from day one.'

'So, all those hormones again, and having intercourse on a timetable. . .'

'Not straight away. We'll take a few months' break before we begin that again.'

'Break? But I want to be pregnant again as soon as I can!'

'I know,' Adam nodded. 'Of course you do. But if you can be patient your body will have all its resources ready again. When the right baby starts growing inside you, you want it to have the best chance.'

'The right baby.' She patted her lower stomach.

'This little one was never meant to be. . .' She began to cry again.

'It seems not,' he agreed quietly. 'I've finished here at the hospital for now, so why don't I head down to the surgery, and I'll see you both there whenever you're ready?'

'Thanks, Doctor. . .and you, Nurse. If you hadn't been there. . .'

'I'm glad I could help.'

Louise took off her gown, put it in a linen bin and said goodbye to the grieving couple, then left the cubicle, wanting only to get away.

Still thinking of her own miscarriage, she said to herself what she had said before, many times, over the past few years. It was for the best. It wasn't the right time for a child to come into my life. One day, perhaps, there will be a right time. It was for the best.

The rightness of this knowledge didn't always quiet the rebellion, though—the sadness, the images of what might have been—and she knew that the Crosbies would probably have many more days of rebellion too. Her blind flight had already taken her from the hospital, but she couldn't quite face going home. Instead, she walked the streets until she came to Mountjoy Park, and sat there in the late sunshine of the April day, watching the children in the playground.

Her own twins would have been over four years old by now. And her marriage? She knew now that children, her unborn twins, would only have thrown her problems with Brett into even starker relief. Ugly images came to her: standing in some messy kitchen in the middle of the night, with two crying babies in her arms, shouting at Brett because he'd stayed out till all hours yet again, and was giving her no help with their children. . . An all too believable scene. She could imagine many more.

She left the playground, still disturbed by memories,

and walked back down Mountjoy Road, quietly let herself into the house, picked up her forgotten shopping bags and went with them up the stairs to wait for Adam.

'Hi.' He simply stood there, half an hour later. His cream shirt was unbuttoned at the neck, and his sleeves were rolled to the elbows, exposing the muscled forearms with their dusting of dark hair.

She let him in, holding the door as he brushed past so that she felt his warmth and caught a subtle drift of his musky male scent.

'How are the Crosbies?'

'As we thought,' he told her heavily. 'No sac visible on the scan. They've gone home. They're in for a difficult few months, but their infertility problems aren't too serious and I'm sure they'll conceive again. But I don't want——'

'I know.' She cut him off. 'You don't want to talk about the Crosbies. Neither do I. I just wanted to hear what happened.'

She paced through to the bright living-room and he followed her. She gestured to an armchair with a vague motion of her hand, and wasn't really surprised that he didn't sit down. She had no desire to do so, either, incredibly aware of his presence in the room, of the lazy grace of him, the darkness of his hair and eyes and the light tan of his skin, emphasised by the pale cream of his shirt.

And he was moving closer. His hands came out to trap her fingers. The balls of his thumbs ran over her knuckles and she stared down at the two sets of fingers so tightly entwined.

'So you had a bad marriage,' he said softly. 'A really rotten marriage. He was unfaithful and insensitive and wrong for you. Does that mean you're never going to trust a man again?'

'It's myself that I don't trust,' she blurted.

'Why?'

'Because I don't trust myself not to make the same mistake again!'

'It was all your fault, then? Including his infidelity? He was a paragon of a husband and you were a selfish, demanding shrew who drove him into the arms of other women?' The teasing brought a slight tilt to his firm lips.

'Of course not!'

'Of course not. So. . .'

'I should never have married him in the first place. I should have seen how little there was going for us. It was purely physical and I kidded myself like an infatuated teenager that it was the passion of the century. Marriage! It's a huge thing, a huge *task* to make a good marriage, and because I was too immature to see that I have a divorce hanging from my belt like a scalp. . . or like a notch on a gun, or something, and I've made my own contribution to those ghastly statistics about three out of every five marriages failing. And if I thought I could end up one of those people who bounce from one man to another, thinking every time, This is *the one*. . .'

She ground to a halt and looked up at him at last. He was still holding her hands and staring at her very seriously, his eyes seeming even darker and deeper than usual.

'You're being too hard on yourself.'

'No, I'm not!'

'Don't you think you've matured?'

'I hope I have. How can I know?'

'And us. What do you feel? There's something, isn't there?' Now he was holding her, lightly but very closely, and she could feel his warmth and weight all the way from his thighs to his shoulders. 'There *is* something!'

'Yes,' she answered him in a low voice. 'You know

that. It's been there for months, almost from the beginning.'

'And is it really just physical? Don't you remember those times we've laughed, the idiotic mixture of things we've been able to talk about, the way we work together? Do I have to *list* it all? And if there's a physical attraction between us too. . .' His voice grew suddenly low and throaty '. . .is that wrong? You're a sensual woman, Louise. Don't deny that!'

'No. . .'

She relaxed against him and it felt so good to be in his arms. It wasn't like Brett, when their moments of passion had always risen out of a hard-edged hunger or a need to prove something. This was far more gentle, in spite of the mounting urgency in both of them. He was touching her lips now, with tiny coaxing kisses that came and went as he still watched her.

'Louise. . . Louise. . .'

She said helplessly, 'What are you asking of me, Adam?' She pulled back and forced him to meet her gaze.

'I'm asking for a chance to know you. . .and to know the two of us together. . . Don't hang back. Don't talk about friendship as we tried to before. It *is* an insipid word when we're talking about. . .this.' His mouth searched hers. 'Trust me, Louise, since I hope I've never given you a reason not to. Talk to me this time, so that I know what's boiling away inside that bright, self-critical mind of yours. And let me. . .make love to you.' His voice was very husky now, and his words were whispered against her mouth. 'That's not wrong, is it? How else can we find out how deep this thing can go?'

She was helpless against the onslaught of his touch and his words. 'Promise me. . .' she began, then stopped.

'Promise you what, love?'

'Nothing. There's nothing either of us can promise yet, is there? It's wrong of me to ask. We have to give ourselves time to find out. . .'

A smile of satisfaction spread across his face, making the depths of his dark eyes very liquid, and suddenly neither of them wanted to talk any more. His mouth covered hers completely this time, drawing the sweetness from her with exquisite subtlety. Her own lips parted in response and she felt the teasing dart of his tongue, then the nipping of his teeth, with incredible gentleness and finesse, and then the full pressure of his hungry mouth again.

His fingers were running through her thick, soft mass of hair, then plaiting tendrils of sensation at her neck and shoulders. She closed her eyes and stood there in the maelstrom of his touch, loving his hands as they seared down her body, finding the slender firmness of her back, the soft curve of her stomach, the taut fullness of her buttocks and then, finally, the neat mounds of her breasts.

'Mm. . .' He echoed her sound, nuzzled her nose with his, and they laughed. 'Nice?'

'Nice.' She was touching him too, feeling the way the soft cotton of his shirt slipped beneath her palms against the tight, warm muscles of his back.

'More than nice, Lou. . .' The shortening of her name was a liquid caress.

She was trembling now, feeling his need and wanting to answer it so badly with her own complete response. The soft core of her was melting and swelling with desire and every nerve-ending clamoured to know more of him. His fingers were whispering at the neck of her cardigan now, and she felt the first button give way. He ran a soft forefinger down the opened space towards the slight valley between her breasts, then found another button to unfasten.

She wanted very badly to let him finish the loving

task. Her nipples tingled with anticipation and she knew just how right his touch there would be. But then he slowed and stopped, brushed her breasts one last time with his hands and cocked his head a little to one side as he swayed back just the few inches needed to put some space between them.

'This is still too soon,' he said. Then he laughed. 'I must be nutty, saying this when I want it so badly, and when it's been six months, I think, since I started wanting it. But we need to save it a little longer, don't we, if you're to feel really safe?'

'I—I think so.' She was amazed at his perception. He had said it almost before she had realised it herself.

'So what shall we do?' He was grinning at her. 'We can't just stay here or I'll be fighting to keep my hands off you all night. It's early. Maybe there's a movie. That was fun, wasn't it, when we did it before? Then dinner somewhere. Somewhere not too elegant tonight, I think, as I may want to kiss you across the table. A pub meal, maybe, or something completely exotic, like a little hole in the wall serving Turkish kebabs. What do you say? Then a late drink. . .'

'Adam! Stop! You haven't given me the chance to reply!' She was grinning too.

'So, modify the plan. I'm open to suggestions, you know.'

'But it all sounds just right, actually. I'd love a movie.'

'Silly or serious? What language?'

'Oh, definitely silly. American. One of their idiotic comedies, and then, yes, the Turkish hole in the wall.'

'And a walk by the river?'

'How long *is* this evening?'

'Well, it's only just after five. . .'

They went as they were and did as they had planned, and it was all perfect, from the chocolate and kisses shared in the darkened cinema and the warmth of him pressed against her above the arm-rest between them, to the spicy, filling meal in the restaurant they found near by. There *was* time for a walk afterwards, down by Westminster, and the tide was high and the water silvered by a moon dodging between the clouds.

He held her closely and she was warmed and sheltered by his strong body so that she began to crave his kiss with every pore in her skin, and he must have sensed it because he stopped and turned her towards him and took her into his arms right there. She forgot the chilly wind by the river and felt only his warmth. . . or was the sudden heat sourced within herself?

He was melting her again, and he knew it. She could almost feel the grin on his face as he paused for tiny moments between his swooping, plundering kisses. It felt so good and so right and her happiness filled her like a bubble, so tight in her chest that at times she could barely breathe. If this was really happening. . . If it could really work. . .

'Do you know,' he whispered, his lips feathering her ear, 'I've gone off the idea of a late drink? Can I take you home? I'd like. . .' he nuzzled her '. . .to be able to do more of this. . .in private.'

So they found the nearest Tube station and clattered down the echoing stairs to the platform, both impatient and exhilarated. It was hard not to reveal to the whole train what they felt, and when she kept catching him out in a secret, exultant smile she knew that her own face must look the same. On the way up from the station to Mountjoy Road, he pulled her with him and held her so tightly that, again, she was breathless, and then he took her hand and began to race with her so that they fell through her front door and climbed the stairs helpless with laughter.

The silent stillness of her flat came as a sudden contrast, and if they had had to struggle several hours ago to damp down their increasing need for each other, in the magic of the night it now seemed impossible. She stood holding her breath after the door had clicked shut behind them, and neither of them even remembered to switch on a light, although she was blinking and half-blind in the dimness.

She felt and heard, rather than saw, his inevitable movement towards her, and his kiss, when it came, was cold from their rapid walk up from the station. His cheek, too, as he rubbed it against the smoothness of her face. She wound her arms around him and sighed against his shoulder, unable even to think of sending him away, although a few hours ago she hadn't intended this at all.

His whispered question didn't come as a surprise. 'Can I stay after all?'

'Yes. . .'

'Oh, God, Louise, you don't know how much I hoped you'd say that!'

'Yes, I do. . .'

After this, there was little need for words. They tumbled on to the couch, fought their way out of confining jackets, settled the question of protection in two sketched phrases—because that baby she wanted so badly one day definitely shouldn't get started yet— then they moved to the bed. His removal of her clothes was a ritual and he did it perfectly, making her lie still, refusing to let her help and laughing at her impatient mewing protest. Then it was her turn, and she found that his skin felt as good as she had known it would— silky and supple and smooth, and buffed lightly with springy, fragrant hair just where it should be.

His kisses grew deeper and more urgent, and he touched her in places that made her shudder with ecstasy and need, and when her swollen softness and cat-like cries told him she was ready they came together with an intensity and a sense of rightness that became a triumphant, rhythmic eternity of release and completion.

She hadn't intended to fall asleep, but her body was so relaxed and replete against his that sleep stole over both of them as they were still entwined and panting. During the night, when she stirred, she was aware of him still touching her—sometimes a hand curved against her hip, sometimes more intimately cradling her breast as he pressed his torso against her back—and there was no reason to wake or talk or send him home, so she simply smiled and drifted into sleep once again.

When the alarm gave its strident announcement of morning, the sound jolted both of them out of dreaming and she felt him struggle and sit up groggily before she had the slightly ability to move herself.

'Hell! What's the time?' His voice was creaky with sleep.

'Six, must be. I've got a morning.' She remembered it only as she spoke the words.

'And I have general rounds in Gynae at seven, then on to you lot. I've got notes downstairs. . .'

He was already half into his clothes. Louise woke up enough to watch him, torn between her fascination at the sight of those muscles working in his shoulders then disappearing beneath his cream shirt, and the morning-after regret that was leaving a sour taste in her mouth far stronger than that of the spicy food they had eaten.

He needs to say something, so I'll know it's all right, she thought, but he didn't, and she could see from the look of concentration on his face that he was already thinking of his patients and the things he had to do today.

'Breakfast?' Her offer came out as a squeak.

'No time. I've got to go through some test results,

and there's a paper I planned to photocopy for the students on their gynae stint at the moment.'

'I'll make sure there's coffee waiting for you when you get to us, then,' she ventured boldly, and at last he turned and tossed her a smile.

'Biscuits, too, if you can manage it, or I won't eat till lunchtime.'

'I may even manage a scone or a sandwich.' She had to fight to keep the warmth in her voice.

But he heard the tight tone and was across the room in two strides, fully dressed now, although she still lay against the pillows with the duvet held protectively up to her shoulders. Beneath it, she was still quite unclothed. 'Hey. . .' he said.

'Mm?'

'I'm a doctor, remember? A consultant?'

'I know.'

'So I have to go.'

'I know.'

'This doesn't mean. . .'

'I *know*!'

The duvet had slipped down and his hand came to touch the pink tip of her breast, already tightly furled, then cup it with gentle heat and pressure. He kissed her softly on her slightly parted lips, then drew away, his eyes giving her a last caress of their own.

'See you later, then,' she managed, and this time she must have fooled him—either that or he simply didn't have the time, because a moment later he was gone, closing the door of her flat behind him loudly, and she could hear his feet thudding hurriedly down the carpeted stairs.

'So, Louise, you've done it,' she said aloud to the empty room. 'You've slept with a man again. The first time since Brett. And Brett was the first of all, so is that so bad?'

But she knew this wasn't the issue. She wasn't afraid

of being promiscuous. She knew she was not that and never could be. It had been wonderful last night with Adam. So wonderful that she had to struggle now even to remember how it had felt with Brett, if it had been anything like this. She didn't think so. Brett had been a sensuous man, but selfishly so, and Adam had been so very generous.

But I want promises, she realised. I want a huge, iron-clad promise from him that this is right and nothing can ever, ever go wrong with it, and I can't have that. Not yet, anyway. And I have to be patient, and that's all there is to it!

Patient, on tenterhooks, and madly in love. . .

CHAPTER NINE

THEY spent every spare moment of the next week together, day and night.

Twice, when Louise had afternoon shifts, Adam came up to her flat for lunch before a clinic, and what began with salad or sandwiches and tea ended in lovemaking, followed by a hasty dive into her uniform ready for work at half-past one. The pleasure they took in it seemed to be stolen from the spring sunshine outside, and from their guilty awareness that the rest of the world was doing shopping and laundry, accounting and conferencing.

Twice, he came to her bed in the middle of the night, straight from the hospital, telling her at first that he was too tired even to talk but then ending up making love to her all the same as they lay together in the darkness of her room.

Adam was a magnificent lover, tender and inventive, at ease with his body and with hers, patient and teasing and hungry and flamboyant all at once. Louise's skin crawled now when he so much as looked at her, and when they touched she wanted him at once with an intensity that would have embarrassed her except that he obviously felt the same. She could see it in his dark eyes and his creamy, teasing smile, in his silence and in his husky voice.

And yet in many ways their lovemaking was the least important thing. With the doubts and fears about the future that still roiled within her, Louise took a constant, passionate inventory of all the moments they shared: the laconic snatches of conversation as they made tea together in her little kitchen overlooking the back garden, nutty exchanges in the shower as they soaped each other then came together in a glue of perfumed lather to kiss, a night when he had so much work to do that they just sat there in her living-room for two hours with music in the background while he pored over papers and she read a book.

And all of it was good. That was the only thing that allowed her to start to feel safe, and her sense of safety grew as the days passed so that nine days later, when her next week of night duty came, she *almost* didn't mind that for the next seven days she would be sleeping in her bed alone, groggily, in the daylight hours, while he worked. Entering the unit at ten past nine, she wondered if any of her fellow midwives had guessed yet. Surely there was a glow to her? She felt it inside, felt it escaping, as unconfinable as the scent of roses in a June breeze.

Today, a Saturday, they had started to have lunch together at his place, then he'd been called out, and had been gone for so long that she'd ended up eating plain buttered toast and turning their lunch into dinner, loving the feeling of puttering in his kitchen while he wasn't there. He had arrived back at his flat at five, amazed at the beautifully laid table, the tray of hors-d'oeuvres, the wine and the soft music. It had been almost a pity when his kiss of thanks had gone out of control, and their lovemaking had taken so long that in the end their eating of the meal was rushed.

But she was here in the maternity unit on time, and listened attentively as Judy snapped out her report. Covertly, Gaby Driver, who was about to go off as well, gave a thumbs-down sign and the other midwives knew that the shift with Judy in charge must have gone badly. Adam hadn't mentioned it, after his return from the hospital either, but then the consultant obstetrician was often protected by his position from tension between the midwifery staff.

Judy's mood swings had been quite wild lately, and none of them ever knew in advance what to expect. She could be strangely tense with a reined-in exultation on odd days, and on most others more bitter and caustic then ever. Now the night-shift midwives were all thankful that she was going off duty, not coming on.

After Judy had left, Gaby Driver stayed behind to talk to Mary Rigmore.

'Do you want me to leave?' Louise offered, looking up from the backlog of paperwork she had started on at the nurses' station. 'I could go and pack away those new supplies.'

'No, stay,' Gaby said. 'It's just about Judy.'

'What happened?' Mary was sympathetic, yet a little reserved as well. Clearly, she didn't want to hear any petty complaints, although, like all of them, she acknowledged that there was a problem.

'She was really tough with one of the mums. I couldn't believe it!' Gaby's voice squeaked in her plump chest. 'It was deliberate, Mary, it really was, like a toddler in a temper. She was giving a pain-killing injection. . .you know, it was Andrea Wilson, and this is her seventh child so her post-partum contractions are quite painful, the way her uterus has been stretched. . . and she just rammed it home like spearing a piece of meat. I couldn't believe it!' she repeated.

'Are you sure it was deliberate?' Mary asked. 'She looked very tired, and her face was quite puffy, perhaps she's not well and she slipped a bit.'

'It was deliberate! I saw her face! Andrea screamed.'

'Well, Andrea screams at anything,' Mary pointed out drily.

'I know, I admit none of us is a big fan of Andrea Wilson—she *doesn't* want that baby, you can tell, and it's appalling the way she keeps on having them, a different father each time, and just sends them off to foster care whenever she's sick of them. . .'

'That's the key, though, with Judy, isn't it?' Louise came in suddenly. Till now, she had just listened as she filled in some forms, but this comment of practical Gaby's had caught her attention. She liked the other nurse, and they'd spent quite a bit of off-duty time together lately. A first-time mum in early labour shuffled past along the corridor with her anxious husband in tow, and Louise lowered her voice. 'She just can't cope at all with the half-hearted mums. She's always making asides about them, any mum who she doesn't think has the right attitude, and now perhaps she's actually taking out her hostility on them during treatment.'

'Oh, surely not! I've known Judy for years!' Mary protested. 'Of course she has a problem with people like Andrea Wilson. We all do, don't we? Seeing her produce another baby for the welfare system to support. But to suggest that Judy is being deliberately, physically *cruel* to such patients. . .'

'Mary, I'm only telling you what I saw,' Gaby said. 'And I think it's got to the point where something has to be done. I think she's breaking the nurses' code of conduct they've been reminding us about lately.'

Mary sighed. 'Do you want to file a report, then? Bring management into it?'

'No, not yet, I——'

'Then what? She's an exceptional midwife. We had a shoulder dystocia last week just as I was coming on, and she did a Wood's manoeuvre and got it out vaginally before Henslow even responded to his bleeper. I don't think the parents ever realised anything was wrong.'

'Was that the Eliases?'

'Yes.'

'Caring parents and a much wanted second baby. I really think if that had happened to Andrea Wilson Judy *wouldn't* have tried so hard. Look, I just wanted to tell you so that if anyone else notices any other incidents. . . I *know* it's a tough one!'

Poor Gaby! Her rather square face was tightened with worry, and Mary only looked helpless. 'I don't want Judy to think that we're all against her.'

'But we *have* to put the patients first.'

'Could someone talk to her privately?' Louise suggested.

'Who?' Gaby demanded spreading her hands. 'You know how protective she is of her privacy, Louise. Which of us would say that we're close enough to her personally to carry any weight?'

'She does seem to get on pretty well with Adam Van Curen,' Mary said slowly now. 'Perhaps that's the way to go. I've seen them talking together several times. I've even wondered. . .' She laughed. 'I'm sure I'm wrong. But Judy can be so pretty when she tries, and Adam is currently unattached, as far as we know. We know nothing about Judy's marriage. Perhaps it's in trouble and that's the reason for her moodiness,and Adam's going to come along like a knight in shining armour and——' She broke off and laughed again. 'That's silly, isn't it?'

Gaby shrugged. 'Maybe not.'

Louise said nothing and hoped that her face wasn't burning as she felt it was.

'Maybe there *is* something going on,' Gaby went on. 'But, in any case, yes, Mr Van Curen might be the person to talk to her.'

'Well, I won't suggest it *yet*,' Mary prevaricated, with an aura of judicious decision-making that hid uncertainty beneath. 'I'll wait a few days or so and try to observe myself. . .although of course we're never on the same shift.'

'Ask Barbara what she thinks, too, and Moira,' Gaby offered, referring to two more of the older and more senior midwives, whose opinions she obviously felt Mary would trust.

'I'll wait a few days on that too, Gaby,' Mary decided. 'I'd hate to jeopardise Judy's career in any way.'

She picked up her pen deliberately, signalling that the subject was closed, and Gaby went belatedly off home, clearly dissatisfied with what had happened.

Louse found it difficult to think about anything but the reference to Adam. Of course it wasn't true that he and Judy were involved! How could it be? With the heady aura of Adam's lovemaking filling her senses like a perfume all the past week and more, such an idea seemed laughable. And yet . . .

She remembered her passionate encounters with him at lunchtime, and their nuance of clandestine pleasure. He'd even said something. . .'Like it when it's a bit wicked like this, don't you? As if I was your lover, Black Jack Davey, and your tight-lipped husband, the Squire—the one your parents made you marry against your will when you were fifteen—might come home from hunting any minute.'

She had laughed at the time, but now she wondered. . . Had he ever been a woman's lover, listening for her husband's car in the drive? Could Judy's wildly swinging moods reflect ups and downs in an affair with Adam? Her mood had certainly been down this past week or so.

Looking at it this way, it almost made sense. She was plunged, beyond her control, into that same, all too familiar state of suspicious misery that Brett's repeated infidelity had placed her in, once she had belatedly learnt of it, looking at every woman as a potential threat, traitor, temptation. . .

And, though her instinct was to trust Adam, she still *couldn't* trust herself. Perhaps I'm wrong to trust him, as wrong about him as I was about Brett. . .she thought.

And so in the end she was left with miserable suspicions that wouldn't go away. It didn't help that the night was a quiet one so far. She would have welcomed a rush of healthy deliveries, but instead there were just three women in early labour and one, under Maria Thomas's care, who was about to give birth. Naomi Johnson was dealing with the babies, and Mary Rigmore and Joanne Lee were with the labouring mums, so that left Louise to do the routine post-partum checks on the mothers who had delivered over the past few days. Not surprisingly, they were drowsily absorbed in feeding their babies, or on the point of going to sleep themselves, so there was little opportunity even for some distracting conversation.

Andrea Wilson seemed the most wakeful. She shifted irritably in the bed when Louise came to take her observations, and hissed loudly and indignantly at the pressure of Louise's hands externally palpating her uterus. Its tone didn't feel too good, but Louise's experience with highly multiparous women wasn't extensive. Andrea had given birth only twelve hours ago. How long did the uterus take to contract again after its seventh stretching? She made a note to get Mary Rigmore's opinion if it didn't feel better four hours from now, checked that the amount of Mrs Wilson's bleeding was within normal limits, and was about to move on when the patient's scratchy voice recalled her.

'Isn't there nowhere I can go for a fag?'

'Outside?' Louise joked. Like many hospitals, Morleyvale's policy on smoking indoors was now very strict, reflecting the latest medical evidence on cigarettes.

'Bloody hell!' Andrea said disgustedly. 'That's discrimination, that is! Used to at least be able to smoke in the kitchen!'

She was struggling to a sitting position and easing herself out of the bed as she spoke, her words muffled by coughing.

'They've found out more about the dangers of passive smoking in the past few years,' Louise began. 'You wouldn't want the babies to have to breathe——' She broke off. Mrs Wilson wasn't even listening.

'Which door should I go out of?'

'I beg your pardon?'

'Which door? To get outside. For my fag.' Andrea was rummaging in her slick vinyl suitcase for a packet of cigarettes, and Louise was appalled.

'Oh, look, I was just joking about that. There really *isn't* anywhere. This is a no-smoking hospital now.'

'I'm going outside, OK? Call security if you like, but *you're* not stopping me! I'll be back when I've had me fag.'

She hobbled purposefully out, still too recently delivered to walk smoothly, and Louise shrugged helplessly. The unit was three floors up, but if Mrs Wilson was so desperate and belligerent, then let her brave the lifts and the chilly night in nothing but velour slippers and a chenille dressing-gown over her cheap pink satin nightdress.

The recalcitrant patient was back in ten minutes— she must have been puffing furiously out there—but Louise regretted that she hadn't been more forceful in stopping her four hours later when she palpated the uterus again. Still boggy, and Mrs Wilson was now bleeding more than was usual. Could that hobbling trip out into the night have aggravated the blood loss? She called Mary, who did her own exam, to a background of raucous protests from the patient.

'Would you like something more for the pain?' Louise asked, not without sympathy. She knew that in some highly multiparous women the after-birth pains could be more severe than the contractions during labour.

'Course I bloody would!'

'It is soft,' Mary agreed quietly, out in the corridor a few minutes later. 'There's no rupture, and no retained products of conception. Mr Van Curen prescribed some drugs to help contract the uterus if necessary, and I'll rub her up a bit—which she won't thank me for!'

'Who would?'

'Well, yes, but I can see why Judy finds this one difficult!'

Louise had to agree, as Mrs Wilson complained for the rest of the night. By the time the shift ended, her uterus had tightened slightly and the blood loss seemed to be decreasing, but at change-over report Mary stressed that the mother of seven needed to be carefully monitored. Wondering what she would find fourteen hours later. . .and wondering whether Adam would have time to visit her later today. . . Louise left the hospital and tumbled gratefully into bed.

Adam *did* come. He woke her at two in the afternoon, letting himself into her flat so quietly, with the key she had given him a few days ago, that she was unaware of him until he entered her room with a cooked breakfast on a tray.

'Don't expect this after every night shift,' he warned her at once, and she laughed.

'I should think not! Or *you'd* expect it after every call-out.' She sat up and stretched, enjoying the knowledge that he was eyeing her hungrily, his smile filled with lazy desire.

'I *was* called out, actually, this morning.'

'Oh, who? Maternity or Gynae?'

'Maternity. Andrea Wilson. I saw your writing on her notes.'

'The bleeding got worse?'

'Yes. I tried drug therapy, but that didn't work, and we ended up doing a uterine artery ligation.'

'So all's well now?'

'Well, it was dramatic, and she protested pretty loudly at first—thought I was suggesting a hysterectomy, and was afraid no man would ever want her again.'

'You'd have been forgiven for telling her that might be a good thing!'

'Not an easy patient to like, is she? You'll have her for a few extra days now.'

'We'll manage.'

It was said absently. Louise was on the point of saying something about Gaby's story last night—Judy and her vindictive aggression towards Andrea Wilson. It would have been natural to mention it, to get Adam's opinion, but somehow the words didn't come and a minute or two later, they had got on to other subjects, and she forgot all about it.

'Once you've got that into you,' he was saying, 'would you like to come riding in Richmond Park for a couple of hours?'

'Riding? I don't ride!' she protested.

'You told me you did, I'm sure.'

'Years ago! I had my horse-adoration phase like most pre-teenage girls, and Dad succumbed and took me for lessons for a couple of years.'

'Then you ride,' said the farm-bred Adam with a shrug, as if it were easy.

'I'm so rusty I'd probably squeak rising to the trot,' she told him. 'And anyway, aren't you on call?'

He shrugged and grinned. 'I got Tom Phelps to cover from noon on.'

'Adam!'

'I owe him eighteen hours now, which is generous of me really. It should only be seventeen, since I wasn't out of Theatre after Andrea Wilson's surgery until well after one.'

So he out-argued her and within an hour she was showered and dressed and ready, and they drove to meet his friends, Chris and Caroline Scott-Findlay, on the south side of the park, and had a wonderful late-afternoon ride. Thanks to the good-tempered and well-cared-for mount the Scott-Findlays had brought for her, Louise found that she was very much less rusty than she had expected, and felt exhilarated and alive for nearly two hours on the bridle-paths.

Chris and Caroline were clearly rather well off but surprisingly casual, with a book-crammed house and a garden surrounding the stables out the back that had flowers and herbs and vegetables hopelessly mixed. They were relaxed and friendly with Louise, and if all of them were aware that this was significant—Adam was introducing her to his friends—then nothing was said.

'This'll be my last ride for a while, Adam,' Caroline said as they walked the horses back to the stables.

'Really? Work pressure building up?'

'No! Honestly, I thought you'd guess straight away. We're expecting a little Scott-Findlay just before Christmas.'

'Caroline! Fantastic!'

'But I'm not coming to you as a customer; are you insulted?'

'Course not. Healthy mare like you.' He made to smack her smartly on the rump and she got out of the way just in time. 'You could have a midwife and a home birth, I should think.'

'Well, not sure about that, but I just don't fancy spoiling a beautiful friendship by having you pull something wriggly from my insides.'

'Understandable,' he agreed mildly. 'Although in

the heat of the moment I assure you it's no more intimate than removing a splinter, is it, Louise?'

'More like a log, but yes,' she agreed, and they all laughed.

There was time for a late tea, and Louise made a big pot in the kitchen, while Caroline spilled a packet of pre-made scones into the oven and opened some cans of soup. 'Don't you think it's a pity that people work in factories making this stuff *en masse* instead of doing it individually in nice big old kitchens like this?' she asked, just as the men came in.

'Are you on about the servant problem again, Caroline?' her husband groaned.

'Just seems a shame, that's all. Servants filled up these big houses so nicely. I gather you have one too, Louise? Adam told us.'

'Yes, about this size.' She couldn't help glowing at the knowledge that he'd talked about her to his friends.

'If Chris didn't have his office here. . .' Caroline went on as she darted from stove to pantry and back again. 'I mean, we love it, but we still don't use all the rooms.'

'Fill them with children,' Adam said. 'That's what I'd do. How many rooms aren't you using properly?'

'Five!'

'There you go, then. Four children and an au pair.'

'That'd tax the plumbing,' Chris growled.

But Louise wasn't really listening. She had seen the way Adam's eyes had flicked quickly to her own face when he'd talked about children, and the thought that he might be that serious about their relationship flooded her with such a mixture of gladness and sheer panic that she almost lost the ability to breathe.

The light meal was fun and threatened to make her late for work, so reluctantly she nudged Adam and got him to drive her home, then arrived at the maternity unit to find that Judy hadn't been on today and everyone was cheerful, although Andrea Wilson was a bit of a thorn in the side. Her incision was large and painful, and if she hadn't complained constantly about not being allowed to smoke in bed everyone might have had more sympathy for her.

'And she hasn't asked to see her baby *once!*' Maria Thomas told Louise after the latter's meal break at midnight.

The West Indian nurse was so good with the babies, her big hands patting and massaging each little form as she changed the nappies, and her hybrid Trinidad-London accent dropping to a musical coo as she talked to them. She picked up seven-pound Kylie Wilson now, unswaddled her and ripped open the adhesive tapes on the disposable nappy.

The baby was sturdy and fair-skinned, her hair the same cinnamon-brown that could be glimpsed at the roots of Andrea Wilson's untidy frizz of blonde. Her face was surprisingly unmarked by her passage through the birth canal, and she was already showing signs of an elfin prettiness.

'Little love, little darling!' Maria cooed. 'Bless you! May God bless you! You're going to need him.'

The baby woke and began to cry and Louise said, 'I'll take her in, shall I?'

'Yes, do. See if there's a response.'

'Is she breast-feeding?'

'Course not. Far too inconvenient, that is. Can't palm the baby off on anyone else, that way.'

Louise took the little girl in and Andrea Wilson grudgingly held a bottle to her mouth, then called to have Kylie taken back to the nursery the moment it was empty.

'Would you like her again later to spend a bit of special time with her?' Louise suggested gently.

'"Special time"?' the woman crowed derisively. 'This is my seventh. If Kylie wants "special time" I'll give her to Linda, my eldest. She's fourteen. *She* thinks she *likes* babies! Silly little cow, if she goes on like that she'll be up the duff herself by the time she's sixteen. . .'

And it was lucky that she didn't have a pain-killing injection due, or Louise might have been strongly tempted to do exactly as Judy had apparently done on Saturday afternoon. Not for the first time, her heart ached for an unwanted child.

The night got busy after this, and she was off late and tired the next morning, leaving a unit that was almost full with babies who were very much wanted indeed. Still down on sleep after so much time spent with Adam, she slept soundly after breakfast and the newspaper at the Four Seasons Café, all the way through until five-thirty, when she still felt groggy and disorientated, until a shower restored her enough to make salad and scrambled eggs on toast for her tea.

Adam had warned her that they would not see each other today, and possibly not much all week since he was busy and their schedules clashed. He had pre-natal clinic this afternoon, as it was Monday, and that sometimes went on late. It was horribly tempting to wander down to the front yard in the hope of seeing him when he left for the day, but she resisted.

Meanwhile, everyone else was just going home for a meal, and their day was winding down. Outside in the front yard, for instance, she heard through the open window a car door slam and its engine start, another slam and the sound of feet and tyres on gritty brick. Adam's receptionist, Tracey, leaving late, along with the last patient of the day. There was no doubt about it—night shifts were disorientating.

She couldn't concentrate on reading, and switched the television on, watched it for a while, then let a silly game show burble in the background as she paced restlessly to the bay window that overlooked the front yard.

And there was Judy Smith, her face tense, getting out of her car and disappearing inside. Hers was the only car now, apart from Adam's, presumably, parked down the side. This nagging mystery again. Tracey Paul's car had gone. Adam was definitely alone. So what was Judy doing here?

She's not a patient. . .yet she comes so often! Is this Brett all over again? Are all men the same? Or do I just choose the unfaithful kind?

Even now, she kept telling herself that she was wrong, and that she'd find an innocent answer, surely, if only she kept looking out of the window, but nothing happened. Judy was inside Adam's office now, and everything was very quiet. Then a taxi pulled into the semicircle of the driveway and out stepped a tired-looking man in his late forties, carrying a briefcase and a suit-bag as if he'd just come from the airport. He looked at his watch and looked at Judy's car, then strode so purposefully towards the front door that Louise wasn't surprised to hear the bell for the ground floor sound in a long, continuous peel.

What on earth was going on? It was nearly time for her to leave for work now. She paced the room, miserable, not knowing what to think or do. Claustrophobic and restless, she left the flat, planning to get an earlier bus although she knew it would get her to the hospital with many minutes to spare, and, suddenly, there in the front yard was a triangle comprising Adam and Judy and the unknown man who'd arrived in the taxi. Judy's husband, Louise suddenly realised.

Adam's eyes were big and dark and miserable, and his mouth was set in a tight line. Judy sobbed wildly and her husband—Graham, wasn't it?—tried to hold her even though she fought him off. 'With you away so much, how can it ever be any different?' she flung at him.

'If it's my job. . .'

'Of course it's not your job! Your job is a *minute* part of it!'

'. . .then we can do something about that. Judy, we mustn't let this destroy us, darling——'

But she broke away, still sobbing, flung her car keys to the ground, and fled out of the yard and down Mountjoy Road.

'Look, I don't know what I can say——' Adam began, but Graham cut him off.

'I'll go.' He spoke very stiffly. 'It's my place to, Adam, after all. I am her husband.'

And if that wasn't a scene between a woman, her husband and her lover, whether past or present, then Louise didn't know what it could be!

Mr Smith bent down, picked up the keys, then walked to the car, his gait made rigid by his fight for control, and drove away without another word. No one had even acknowledged Louise's presence, and now she resolutely continued across the yard, aching inside and her temples tight with a pounding headache that hadn't been there five minutes ago.

'Lou, wait! Why are you looking so angry?' Adam was coming after her and she rounded on him, having needed only those few words from him to unleash the flood of her emotion.

'Because—leaving aside any question of *us*——' her voice almost broke on the word '—I don't appreciate the fact that you're using the rooms I lease to you as a place for clandestine meetings, nor that you chose my front yard in which to confront your lover's husband!'

Adam stopped dead in his tracks, open-mouthed. 'What? You think that Judy and I are having an *affair*? After all that you and I——'

'What else am I to think?' she broke in, close to tears.

'I'd have thought it was obvious,' he answered her, gently now, 'given my profession. She's seeing me as a patient.'

'A patient? She said she wasn't! She told me outright that she wasn't!'

'Of course. Does that surprise you?' he demanded. 'This is agony for her, this infertility! You know how reserved she is, Louise. The only way to deal with it in front of other people—especially at work, surrounded by all those newborn babies and glowing couples—is to deny that it's happening, deny she wants any children at all!'

'But I didn't know that!'

'And you still can't act on faith when it comes to us, can you?' He sounded very tired suddenly, and there was a note of resignation in his voice, as if he was admitting defeat. 'You still can't trust what we feel.'

'No, I can't,' she said miserably. 'I've just proved that, haven't I? I've tried, Adam.'

'I know. So have I.' He paused, then added abruptly, 'To be honest, I'm not sure what to do next. . .'

'I—I don't blame you, Adam, in your position,' she acknowledged. 'I wish. . . If Judy. . .' But the misunderstanding over Judy wasn't the real issue, and they both knew it. It went deeper than that. If it hadn't been Judy, it would have been someone else. An obstetrician probably encountered more youthful, glowingly attractive women in his work than anyone short of a fashion photographer. . .

'Let's not discuss it now,' he said kindly, after her own attempt to speak had floundered into a strained silence. 'Give me some time, Louise. . .'

'Time?'

'Yes. I need to think. Maybe we both do.'

'OK. I—I have to get up to the hospital anyway.'

'See you some time, then. We'll talk. . .' But they had talked before. At some point, there was a limit to what talking could do.

'Yes, Adam.' She nodded very carefully. 'Bye. . .'

She crossed to the bus-stop, numb at first, and then began to think of Judy, whose problem was far more tragic than her own. Infertility! The secrecy made sense. Her mood swings made sense too—the elation when the cause of her infertility was discovered, anger and misery when the ensuing treatment failed to make a miracle happen, and of course there was the effect of the fertility drugs she must be taking, which could be horrendous. If Judy's ovaries were being fed hormonal therapies to stimulate egg production, she was probably experiencing headaches, bloating, nausea, mood alteration. . . And if her treatment had gone even further and she was on the emotional roller-coaster of an in vitro programme. . .

Poor Judy! she thought. And she has to see happy mothers and darling little newborns every day! As she got on the bus and took the five-minute ride up the hill, it was the other midwife's problems that concerned Louise most. Midwifery is too hard. It's been hard enough for me at times, and really what I've been through is nothing! If this keeps up, if she can't get pregnant even after all Adam's help, surely she should go into general nursing?

Adam's help. . . Adam had really been very kind tonight, after her quite uncalled-for outburst, she was starting to feel. And kindness was a very ominous thing, somehow, between two lovers newly embarked on a relationship. It was the response of someone who was beginning to realise he had made a mistake. . .

By the time she reached the maternity unit at ten past nine, she was wrapped in a blanket of miserable certainty about what Adam would tell her the next time they met.

CHAPTER TEN

THREE o'clock in the morning. Not a good time to be brooding on any subject at all. Louise's patient was in active labour and almost at the end of the first stage. Any moment now she would feel the urge to begin pushing, and she had done well up to this point, with the support of her husband, and Louise in the room as well whenever she could be. Now was not the time to be regretting her angry outburst to Adam. . .but she was regretting it all the same.

'Now. I'm ready now!' Mrs Beatty said.

She was a big woman—well, overweight, to be honest, as well as muscular, and her husband was bigger, and from the first push she worked hard and used her strength well so that visible progress was made with each contraction.

'The head's crowning, Sharon, I can see it! It's got wet black hair!'

And Louise came in, 'You're doing really well, Mrs Beatty. You'll have your baby in a few minutes!'

She was ready now to assist the head gently and then the natural rotation of the shoulders that usually occurred, so that they could be delivered one at a time, anterior then posterior. . . Yes, the head was out.

But the shoulders weren't coming. It took only a moment for Louise to be flooded with the chill realisation that she had a case of shoulder dystocia on her hands. Mrs Beatty was already straining to push through the next contraction.

'Just pant through this one, please.' She knew her voice had betrayed some panic, and was aware of the husband's sudden glance. 'I'm just going to manipulate. . .' She didn't finish, and was already trying to slide her fingers along the baby's back, still within the uterus, to perform a Wood's manoeuvre. She remembered that Judy Smith had done it successfully just recently, according to Mary Rigmore, and for once wished that the other midwife were in charge of this shift. . .

The baby wasn't coming. It was pointless to keep trying, and there was little time to waste. 'I'll have to get a bit of help here.' The baby's shoulder might have to be broken to get it out if nothing else worked.

Forcing herself to keep calm, she went into the corridor to summon Mary, and when it was Adam she nearly collided with she could have cried with relief. He looked exhausted. He must have just come from Theatre, and she wondered if he had caught any sleep since his difficult parting from her at nine. He didn't smile when he saw her, but she pushed that fact aside.

'Shoulder dystocia. I can't free it,' she said. 'Will we have to break it? Or try to push the head back and do a Caesarean?'

'Let's see.' He was in the room and snapping on a fresh set of gloves within seconds, and he greeted the patient and her anxious husband with a relaxed phrase or two, as if this were a mere hitch in the delivery, instead of the nightmare complication it could sometimes become. 'Now, Mrs. . .?'

'Beatty,' Louise supplied. She was profoundly relieved at having him here, in spite of the unresolved emotions between them at the moment, and knew her heart was racing.

'Mrs Beatty, I'm just going to take your feet now and stretch them down a bit.' He spoke calmly and steadily. 'Now, if you'll just let me move you. . . And Staff, give me some pressure above the pubic bone, could you? Obliquely. . .'

'OK. . .'

'Yes, that's good. Now, this is uncomfortable, Mrs Beatty, I know, but you've obviously got a little rugby player in there and——Ah!'

'Thank God!' Louise breathed.

The anterior shoulder was freed from behind the pubic bone, and now the posterior shoulder came easily. Seconds later, the baby was fully delivered, and it *was* a boy, a big one, just as Adam had predicted. The McRobert's manoeuvre—which Louise had quite forgotten to try—had straightened and rotated Mrs Beatty's pelvis, allowing the shoulder to slip free.

'No further problems, I should think,' Adam said.

His gloves were off and he had gone before either Louise or the Beattys even had time to thank him, and she knew that wasn't like him. Fortunately, the new parents were oblivious, concerned only with their baby, and Louise had little time to dwell on the matter either, with a new baby to examine and clean and a mother to take care of.

In the back of her mind, though, she knew what his abrupt departure meant. He couldn't face her yet, hadn't decided quite how to tell her that their relationship was over.

At home, after the shift was over, she slept badly, and telling herself that she *had* to sleep or she'd be miserably tired at work again tonight didn't help. It was an unpleasant day, unseasonably cold and very wet in a relentless sort of way that meant there weren't even any exhilarating clouds scudding across the sky, just low shreds of grey.

When she arrived for report that night, Maria Thomas was fighting off a cold and was fretting at Mary's suggestions for extra hygiene precautions to reduce the risk of mothers or babies catching it.

'And Judy's gone already,' Gaby Driver reported. 'Had a headache and asked me to give her report. Which is easy enough, as it's been a pretty quiet afternoon. Andrea Wilson is still her charming self, I'm afraid, and Judy really must have had a headache because she looked so grim, none of us dared to speak to her.'

Everyone made an appreciative face, and Louise stared down at her fingers, set apart by the knowledge she now had about poor Judy's troubles. It was so hard for the older woman, and so *unfair*! She almost said something to the other midwives, but knew that Judy would not thank her for it.

'We've got Mrs Braddon in pre-term labour with her twins. Not sure if we can hold her off. She's not due for another eight weeks. Mr Van Curen's on his way in. . .'

Gaby's summary went on. Louise was sent in to Mrs Braddon, which she *didn't* appreciate, as it meant she would soon be face to face with Adam again. She was upset but not surprised that he hadn't tried to contact her during the day, and knew she would have to fight to keep a professional mask over her feelings. She was brooding on this as she went to the Braddons in Room Four, and didn't think anything of seeing Judy Smith slip quietly out of the bathroom.

Adam arrived soon afterwards, and like yesterday he didn't stay longer than was strictly necessary, examining the patient and prescribing bed-rest, intravenous fluids and a drug which would hopefully arrest the contractions, infused at varying rates over the next twelve hours. He didn't meet Louise's eye at all. After he had gone, a worried Mrs Braddon said, 'Is he coming back? I had some questions, and normally he asks. He seemed tired today. Is he very busy? Perhaps I shouldn't bother him.'

'I'll call him back,' Louise said somewhat grimly. 'Evidently he didn't realise you had questions. I'm sorry.'

She went resolutely out of the room, intending to

confront him. If he was going to let the difficulties between them affect patient care, then they had to resolve this *now*, and he must realise that as well as she did. What he was preparing to say was going to hurt, but she could handle it!

But there was a commotion going on at the nurses' station—a quiet one, as no one wanted to alarm the patients, but easily perceptible to Louise. She saw slight, blonde Naomi Johnson, white-faced and shaking at the desk, and both Mary Rigmore and Adam were listening to her with concern etched on their faces.

'I took her in to Mrs Wilson as soon as I came on, because Judy had said she was due for a bottle, apparently,' Naomi was saying as Louise approached. 'Then I got busy with the other babies and didn't think anything of it until after ten, then I realised Mrs Wilson hadn't asked for Kylie to be brought back to the nursery, so I went to check because that's so unusual. I mean. . .' She spread her hands. 'We all know, don't we?'

Mary nodded.

'And the baby wasn't there. So I thought, OK, I'm going crackers, she *is* back in the nursery, and I went back and she wasn't, and I've looked. . . Oh, God, I've even checked the babies who are with their mothers, as if a mum wouldn't know she'd been given the wrong one! She's nowhere. She's not in the unit! She's been taken!'

Naomi was shaking so hard now that Louise saw Adam coax her into a chair, and a sense that something was going on had brought Maria and Joanne and Barbara away from their duties to ask, 'What's up?'

Mary was wringing her hands. 'Nothing. Andrea Wilson's baby is missing, that's all, and——'

'*Missing*?'

'You haven't seen her, have you? She's not just parked somewhere?'

'Mary, we would have noticed,' Adam said. The midwifery sister was going to pieces and somehow he had now taken quiet control. 'Naomi, go through your story again. Maybe there's something we're missing. Our security's pretty good here. Surely a stranger couldn't have come in? It must be someone we can put a finger on. Could the father have taken her?'

'The father?' Maria Thomas snorted. 'I doubt she knows who he is!'

'Another relative? Did she have visitors?'

'Earlier, I think,' Naomi said.

'Could someone have hidden in the bathroom and——?' Maria again.

Adam frowned. 'Let's follow this through.'

Louise was thinking. The bathroom. . . Now why does that click in my mind?

Naomi was still thinking about visitors. 'She must have had her daughter, the fourteen-year-old, because Andrea said she—the daughter—had given Kylie her eight o'clock bottle tonight.'

'Her eight o'clock bottle? Hang on, that doesn't add up.'

'No, it doesn't, because Judy told me she hadn't had it.'

Something clicked again in Louise's mind. Judy, wrong—or lying—about the bottle. Judy, coming out of the bathroom a good three quarters of an hour after she'd supposedly left early with a headache. Judy, delivering babies every day while she struggled with her own infertility, and getting so angry about a mother who didn't want her seventh child that she had stabbed in a pain-killing injection like using a dagger. Could Judy have——? Surely not? But Louise's spine crawled with an intuition that she couldn't just let go of.

'Adam,' she came in tentatively. Everyone looked at her, and she knew she couldn't just say it, betray Judy's problem and accuse her of kidnapping a newborn baby, on so little evidence.

'Yes, Staff Nurse Redding?'

She floundered for a moment, then seized on her original reason for seeking his attention. 'Um. . . Mrs Braddon had some questions.'

'Well, they can wait!' he answered impatiently. 'This is a serious situation!'

She met his dark gaze and put all the significance she could into her look. 'Quite urgent questions,' she said. 'If you could come now? It's really very necessary.'

He still looked very much at sea, but answered slowly, 'All right. If it's that important. Excuse me for a minute, everyone. I should only be a short time, I hope.' He emphasised the last words. 'Meanwhile, if you could all think it all through again. . . There's this discrepancy over the second bottle, for example.'

The other midwives were left to think and talk or to make hasty checks on patients who were fortunately not in urgent need of care. Adam and Louise had no choice but to stand just outside Mrs Braddon's door, and the latter was losing out in this, her fears about a premature delivery taking second place to the drama of the missing child.

'What *is* this, Louise?' Adam demanded, the sculpted torso that was so dangerously familiar to her bending quite threateningly towards her.

She wasted no time. 'Judy. I think Judy's taken the baby.'

'*Judy*?'

In a few short phrases, she sketched the reason for her suspicions, then spread her hands. It sounded pretty thin. But he nodded slowly. 'She reached a crisis yesterday. We harvested her eggs for the third time, hoping for an in vitro fertilisation, but once again there was nothing we could use, although we've had her on a horrific regime of hormones. I told her it was time to stop trying. She wouldn't accept it. All sorts of stuff came out, and she did mention Andrea Wilson and other women like her. Oh, God!'

'She wouldn't harm little Kylie, surely?'

'No, that's the last thing she'd do. She'd just take her somewhere and——'

'And *love* her. Oh, poor Judy!' Louise knew that yearning herself.

'But where?' Adam was saying. 'Would she go home.'

'If her husband's away. . . Isn't he away a lot?'

'Yes, and I think he was flying to New York today.'

They looked at each other. 'That's it, then,' he said heavily. 'She's taken Kylie Wilson home.'

After this, things moved very fast. In a few crisp phrases, which Mary Rigmore didn't dare to question, Adam directed her to arrange someone to cover for Louise and himself, telling her that Mrs Braddon needed particular care. He explained nothing about Judy and only the fact that he was the consultant kept the other midwives from demanding an explanation.

'Don't ring the police yet,' he said. 'I think I know where this baby is, and I'd like to have a midwife with me.'

Moments later, he and Louise were on their way out of the unit, saying nothing, their footsteps rapping like gunshots as they raced down the corridor to the lift. It wasn't until they reached his car that Louise spoke.

'You know where she lives?'

'I've never been there, but I remember the address. Look up on the map, would you, and direct me there?'

Louise got the *A to Z* from the glove-box, glad that her father had educated her in his enjoyment of maps and navigation. She was already churned up enough, and so was Adam. If she got them lost in an unfamiliar part of London. . .

She didn't, and within minutes they had arrived

outside the pleasant detached house that belonged to Judy and her husband.

'Louise?' Adam said as he switched off the engine.

'Yes?'

'I'm glad it's you here.'

Their eyes met. 'Thanks,' she answered him briefly, and saw that he was watching her mouth. His kiss came before she had a chance to decide whether she wanted it, and her response was as instinctive as the need to eat when she felt hunger. But he drew away after the briefest searing of his lips on hers.

'We have a lot to talk about later.'

'Do we?'

'You *know* we do, Lou!' And his dark look had such power to move her that for a moment, as he left the car, she couldn't summon the strength to follow.

It returned to her just as he had turned as if to question her frozen immobility, and then they were walking side by side up the bricked walk that led to the front door.

'There's. . .no bell,' she said, hearing the trembling in her own voice.

The house was very quiet. What if they were wrong? Or would it be worse if they were right? What state would they find Judy in? Would she willingly give the baby back? Louise saw the deep breath Adam took to master himself, then his hand formed a fist and sharp knuckles rapped on the clouded glass. A shadow appeared, silhouetted against the light that stretched in a yellow shaft down the passage.

The door opened slowly, and there was Judy, with Kylie Wilson bundled softly in her arms, sound asleep. For a long moment, she looked at them in silence, and Louise felt Adam sway subtly closer so that his hand brushed her arm in a gesture of unity. Then, 'Come in,' Judy said.

They followed her into the softly lamplit drawing-room.

'You know you'll have to give her back, Judy,' Adam said, very gently.

'Of course I know that.' Judy looked very tired. 'All I wanted was a day. Just one day to pretend she was mine. Mm, I can feel her breathing on my neck. We tried for so long, thinking it was Graham at first with his poor sperm motility, then realising I had problems too, the endometriosis and fibroids. We solved that, and I *still* didn't get pregnant. Then when I started coming to you and you found that my tubes were completely blocked, Adam, I was so ecstatic that day. I was so sure that that was the answer and my eggs would be perfect and we'd succeed with in vitro. Then to find that even with hormone therapy all I could produce each month were two or three damaged eggs. . . I just couldn't bear it any longer. My childless arms felt so *empty*. . . But you're here sooner than I thought. Does everyone know?'

'Just us,' he told her. 'We weren't sure, you see, so we didn't tell anyone else.'

'The police?'

'No.'

'Naomi was working with the babies tonight, wasn't she? I expect she's beside herself. That was. . .unfair of me. I'll be taken off the register, won't I?'

'I'm afraid so.'

'It doesn't matter. I'd decided to give up nursing anyway. It's just been getting too hard.'

'That's probably best, Judy,' Adam agreed.

She was crying quietly now. 'I knew I shouldn't have done it, but I knew Andrea Wilson wouldn't care. I wouldn't have dreamed of taking one of the ones that was wanted, but this little thing. . .'

'Her sister wants her, Judy,' Adam said. 'I've been talking to Isabel Knight about the Wilson family.'

Louise recognised the name of one of the hospital's social workers. 'She says that it's Linda who keeps the family together these days.'

'But she's only fourteen. . .'

'I know, and being forced to grow up before her time, but now that the welfare people know about Linda they can make sure she gets the support she needs, and the rest of the children have a real chance under her influence. A sister's love isn't the same as a mother's, but a baby can thrive under all kinds of love, not just the love that nurtured it in the womb.'

'What are you trying to say, Adam?'

'Adoption. . .?'

Judy sighed. 'Yes, that's the obvious step. I expect we will. A dear little black-haired baby from China or South America. At the moment I'm so lost. If Graham wasn't away so often. . .but I've had to go through so much of this alone, when I count on him and his love so completely. We haven't even really talked about adoption.'

Out in the street, Louise heard a car pull up and then drive away, and a minute later there were footsteps coming up the front walk. The door opened and Judy gasped as her husband entered. 'You're supposed to be on your way to New York!'

He stood in stunned silence for a moment, taking in the scene, then, 'A baby! Judy. . .?'

She began to cry again, and Louise came in, 'Judy just borrowed this one for a little while, didn't you Judy?'

'I *stole* her, Graham. You're supposed to be away. I didn't want you to know. To see me. . .give way. . . like this.'

'Oh, hell, Judy. . .' Graham held her and the baby. 'I couldn't go. I waited right up until they called us for boarding, then I knew I couldn't go. I rang Steve Patterson from the airport, and he's catching a flight first thing tomorrow. He's young and single and he's a good hard worker, wants to get ahead. I'll send him from now on whenever I can. You were right when we talked on Monday about how hard this travelling has been on our marriage. I love you so much, and when I realised that by being away I was risking letting this infertility thing destroy everything we had. . .'

He couldn't go on, and Adam said gently, 'Louise and I should take Kylie back to the hospital, Judy, if that's all right.'

For a moment there was only stark, keen sorrow in Judy's face, then she smiled very carefully. 'Of course you should. I just brought her in a basket in the back of the car, not a proper carrier. Here it is, in here.' She passed the baby to Louise. 'Hold her head. . . Oh, of course, I don't have to tell you that.' Then she went to bring the basket.

Louise held the tiny bundle and kissed the top of its downy, baby-scented little head. Baby Kylie was safe. She'd never been in any danger, and Louise couldn't help wishing, against all logic, that Judy had been able to have her for a little longer. But perhaps Kylie had done the work Judy needed her to do. Graham Smith was holding his wife now.

'We don't need your salary, darling, if you'd like not to work at all for a while. You could travel with me sometimes. I have to go to China next month.'

'China? I was just talking about adopting a little Chinese baby. . .'

'Adoption?' His face lit up. 'I didn't think you'd want to. You always used to say how much you wanted to experience pregnancy for yourself, experience giving birth, after helping so many other women do it.'

'Well, you know, Graham, anyone can do that part!' Judy smiled. 'It's the love later on that takes talent. . .'

A few minutes later, Adam and Louise left, taking little Kylie with them in her makeshift bed. The tiny girl was still sleeping, and the car was very quiet as they drove, so quiet that Louise got lost in thoughts about Judy, and about the Wilson family, and didn't notice that Adam wasn't stopping in the hospital car park, but in a quiet side-street a few blocks away from it. When she did realise, she looked up, startled, to meet his watchful gaze.

'Why here?' she asked.

'We should get back with the baby,' he agreed. 'But if we do that you're bound to have a delivery approaching and I won't get to talk to you for the rest of the night, and suddenly, after what's happened, I just can't wait any longer. I know at last, you see, what I need to say. . .'

'What you need to say. . .' Her heart was pounding and she felt miserable. Was he going to tell her, kindly, that this wasn't working and they had better forget it? She could scarcely blame him. . .

'I want to ask you to marry me.' He said it so calmly and simply that it took her a moment to realise what the words meant.

'*Marry* you?' She could scarcely breathe. She had leapt at that word, that opportunity, nearly eight years ago. Now the very idea terrified her, and yet. . . 'Adam, on Monday night I gave you a jealous scene straight out of a television soap opera. All along I've made things impossible for us——'

He put a finger to her lips, stemming the tide of words, and whispered, 'One question, Lou.'

'Adam——'

'Just one. Do you love me?'

'Yes.'

'And does it—OK, *two* questions—does it bear any resemblance now to anything you've ever felt before?'

'No. But marriage is hard work, Adam.'

'Do you think I don't know that?'

'Judy and Graham, tonight, clearly with all the love

in the world, but with Judy's infertility even their marriage was threatened. . .'

'You don't think I'm capable of hard work?'

'Of course I do. It's me, Adam. All along it's been me! I've been married, and I failed at it! How can you just sit there and say——?'

'Point number one, you *didn't* fail,' he cut in urgently, almost angrily. '*He* failed *you*! Your greatest sins were naïveté and impetuousness, Louise, and you have to start forgiving yourself for those. *I* do! Point number two, I am never, ever going to be unfaithful to you. OK? Got that? Shall I say it again? I am never, ever, ever going to be unfaithful! It's just not what I believe marriage is about. And if you can't take that on trust by the time we exchange our vows, then yes, we'd better *not* exchange them. Am I bulldozing you into this?'

'Yes. . .'

'Good! It's what you need! I realised it tonight, still mulling over it, as we drove to Judy's.'

'Adam——'

'You're terrified, aren't you?' He had pulled her close to him now, and his lips whispered against her mouth in a phantom kiss that deepened almost at once into a hungry plundering, answered fully by the feverish exploration of her own parted mouth. 'Don't be. . .'

His hands seared down her back to pull her closely to him and the heat in both of them was so powerful and unmistakable that it made her breathing fast and tight and dizzy.

They knew each other, after the passion of the past week and more, with an intimacy that had her blushing when she thought of it, and she wanted so badly to simply take what he was offering her as if it were the pot of gold at the end of the rainbow, but she knew it wasn't. Angrily, she twisted free of him, and in the back of the car baby Kylie stirred a little and then settled again.

'I don't want another divorce.' Her voice was deliberately harsh, and he frowned at the blunt words, but she didn't care. When he began to speak—cajoling, reasoning—she cut him off. 'And *don't* tell me that it's impossible. These days it's *always* possible!'

'OK,' he nodded. She was surprised at the instant agreement, and he laughed. 'Hey, I'm not going to give you feverish promises.'

'You're not?'

'No, I'm not. I've thought about it a lot since Monday. It rocked me, I admit, that you could think I was involved with Judy after all that's been happening between us lately, then I put myself in your position and realised I'd probably feel the same, and that your doubts are only a tribute to how seriously you take the idea of marriage and commitment. And I love that in you.' He touched her mouth again. 'I love it that you can't take it lightly. But I couldn't think, at first, how we could get through it, get out the other side to a place where you could trust. . . And then tonight I found the answer.' Again, his lips were against hers as he spoke. 'If it's acceptable. . .' There came a wicked little smile.

'What, Adam?' She was aching to know, desperate for him to offer the one thing that could make her trust this, only she didn't know what that one miraculous thing could possibly be. Was he a magician?

'A long engagement. . .'

'*What*?'

He was kissing her again, his tongue lapping at the corners of her mouth and then his lips covering hers with languorous command. 'A very busy, very romantic, very long, *long* engagement. Two years, if you want it. Three,' he amended teasingly. 'After all, we've got so much to fit in. A cruise, I think, and som

skiing. Meeting my friends, and staying with my
parents on their farm. My sister has a wonderful place
too, up near Buxton. Meeting those friends of yours
and your father's that sound so fascinating. I expect
that would entail some more travelling together,
wouldn't it? Then there's deciding where we're going
to live, and how many children we'd like. After all, we
already know you can get pregnant. . .'

'And stay pregnant?'

'And *stay* pregnant!' he echoed firmly. 'I'm an obstetrician, remember? And your house would make a
great place for a big family, with my surgery kept as it
is in the front. Anyway, where was I? Oh, yes—
perhaps we need to spend some time choosing a dog
together. Next Christmas, I think I'd like to give you a
dog, as well as some jewellery, of course. . .'

And she was laughing. He had done it! He was
laughing now too, a throaty, triumphant sound, as he
recognised her capitulation. 'Won't that make you feel
safe?' he whispered. 'That you won't be repeating an
old mistake?'

Her consent didn't come in words, and their kiss
lasted for a very long time. Back at the hospital, they
were still in a glow as he parked the car, and as they
opened the back door ready to bring out baby Kylie in
her basket it took them a moment to realise that a man
parked near by, also with his doors open, was hailing
them madly.

'You've got to go in and get a doctor for me quickly,'
he called desperately as he ran towards them. 'My
wife's having a baby. It's. . .it's coming out already,
right here in the car, and I don't know what to do!'

'You're in luck, actually,' Adam said with a dry
smile. 'No need to go inside. You've got an obstetrical
team right here.' He pulled Louise closely against him,
and she felt so *right* at his side that she couldn't speak
at all. 'A world-class obstetric team, I think I can say.'

'Oh, thank God!' He called to his wife. 'Maggie, sweetheart, there's a doctor and a midwife coming now. Hold on, darling.'

'Ready, Staff?' Adam asked Louise, a broad grin on his face.

'Ready. . . And Adam?' she said, finding voice at last.

'Yes, my darling Lou?'

'If. . .if our engagement didn't end up to be quite as long as you were suggesting. . .?'

He spread his hands, still grinning. 'We'll just do all those things *after* we're married. . . We'll set the date when *you're* ready, my love!'

'It's quite a decision. A long engagement, or a short one. Both choices sound so nice. . .'

Five minutes later, at precisely one in the morning, a new baby boy, perfectly made, took his first look at what was probably, at the moment, the happiest obstetrical team on the face of the planet.

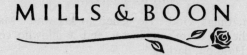

MILLS & BOON

LOVE CALL

The books for enjoyment this month are:

MIDWIFE'S DILEMMA	Lilian Darcy
MADE FOR EACH OTHER	Elizabeth Harrison
HOSPITAL AT RISK	Clare Lavenham
SEEING EYE TO EYE	Josie Metcalfe

Treats in store!

Watch next month for the following absorbing stories:

NEVER SAY NEVER	Margaret Barker
DANGEROUS PHYSICIAN	Marion Lennox
THE CALL OF DUTY	Jessica Matthews
FLIGHT INTO LOVE	Meredith Webber

WIN

A years supply of Mills & Boon romances — absolutely free!

Would you like to win a years supply of heartwarming and passionate romances? Well, you can and they're FREE! All you have to do is complete the word puzzle below and send it to us by 29th February 1996. The first 5 correct entries picked out of the bag after that date will win a years supply of Mills & Boon romances (six books every month—worth over £100). What could be easier?

GMWIMSIN

NNSAUT

ACEHB

EMSMUR

ANCOE

DNSA

RTOISTU

THEOL

ATYCH

NSU

MYSTERY DESTINATION

Please turn over for details on how to enter

David Farrar BA

Brodie's Notes on J. G. Farrell's

The Siege of Krishnapur

Pan Books London and Sydney

First published 1981 by Pan Books Ltd
Cavaye Place, London SW10 9PG
2   3   4   5   6   7   8   9
© David Farrar 1981
ISBN 0 330 50178 X
Filmset in Great Britain by
Northumberland Press Ltd, Gateshead, Tyne and Wear
Printed and bound by
Richard Clay (The Chaucer Press) Ltd, Bungay, Suffolk

Contents

Page references in these Notes are to the Penguin edition of
The Siege of Krishnapur, but as each chapter is analysed separately,
the Notes may be used with any edition of the book

To the student

A close reading of the set book is the student's primary task.
These Notes will help to increase your understanding and
appreciation of the novel, and to stimulate *your own* thinking
about it. *The Notes are in no way intended as a substitute* for a
thorough knowledge of the book.

The author and his work

James Farrell was born in Liverpool on 23 January 1935 though he was to spend most of his childhood in Ireland. He went on to Brasenose College, Oxford where his chief interest was football. Both his university and football careers were interrupted when he was stricken with polio. Six months later he emerged from an iron lung transformed from a healthy young sportsman into a comparatively frail novelist. It seems likely that this experience influenced the themes of disease and decay which run through his books.

Though Farrell travelled widely in pursuit of material for his novels, he made his home in a tiny flat in London's Hampstead where he led the quiet, disciplined, moderate life of a bachelor writer. He remained in Hampstead until the spring of 1979 when he moved to a cottage in Bantry, Ireland. Here Farrell developed the passion for fishing that was to lead to his tragically early death in August 1979 at the age of 44. In the high seas which led to the disaster which overtook the Fastnet Race, Farrell was washed off the rock from which he was fishing and drowned. Some literary critics considered that he had only just begun to produce his best work.

J. G. Farrell wrote six novels, (the first three of which he came to dislike): *A Man from Elsewhere* (1963), *The Lung* (1965) and *A Girl in the Head* (1967). It is on the remaining three, the so-called 'Empire' trilogy, that his reputation rests: *Troubles* (1970) *The Siege of Krishnapur* (1973) and *The Singapore Grip* (1978).

Each novel in the Empire trilogy has the common theme of the decay and destruction of civilization. Each is set in areas of the world (Ireland, India and Singapore) onto which the British way of life, its standards etc., had been grafted and which was eventually to be destroyed by either internal or external forces. It is as though Farrell sees the health of civilization as being as frail and vulnerable as the health of the individual. Civilization is engaged in a constant battle with the forces of destruction and Nature is alarmingly swift, particularly in tropical areas, to overrun and engulf it.

Farrell seems curiously conscious of both the necessity for human endeavour and of its futility. His lesser characters engage in furious effort guided by their particular ideas or ideologies but his principal characters, who tend to have or to develop a sharper vision and insight, wage constant battles against lethargy and a sense of hopelessness. To this extent his view of human existence is deeply pessimistic, yet he is neither contemptuous nor disapproving of his fellow man. Though his characters inflict terrible wounds on each other, the author views them with charitable good humour.

Farrell's skilful combination of humour and concern in his treatment of major political and social themes, is, in fact, one of his finest achievements. In a review of *Troubles* the literary critic Stephen Wall commented on Farrell's talent for substantiating the bizarre milieu. 'Through the eyes of his heroes, isolated, sometimes eccentric figures, we view Mr Farrell's strange world, while satirical reflections on other people are matched by even more ironic treatment of the hero himself. In style and outlook he has affinities with Beckett and Nabokov – as with them we can never be unaware that he is an exile – but Farrell's comic style is more closely and richly textured than the former's and the view of humanity less chilling than Nabokov's.'

It may have been a desire to cover major (and controversial) subjects which led Farrell to the historical novel form, and the period of the decay of the British Empire. Characteristically, he condemned the English in the 1960s and '70s for their preoccupation with small-scale trivia. One does not have to look far for the influence of the Russian novelists on his work: he was an admirer of both Tolstoy and Dostoevsky. His interest in adventure stories (of which *The Siege of Krishnapur* is certainly one) was stimulated by Joseph Conrad and Richard Hughes and again in *The Siege* there are echoes of the French novelist, Albert Camus, and his book *La Peste*, the story of a town cut off by bubonic plague.

All Farrell's works consist of a mixture of styles and themes from which it is difficult to derive a single, coherent philosophy. He is by turn profoundly pessimistic, obsessed by the decay and destruction of all Man's highest ideas and achievements and tolerantly clear-sighted: human effort may ultimately be pointless, yet there remain charity, humour and compassion.

Further reading

Troubles, J. G. Farrell (Penguin)
The Singapore Grip, J. G. Farrell (Fontana)

Background

Farrell takes, as the setting for his novel, the India of 1856–7. The name of the particular location, Krishnapur, is invented by him though it is clearly based upon at least two and possibly more real Indian towns. These towns, military bases for the European troops, were Kanpur, Cawnpore and Lucknow. The siege of Krishnapur contains features of both the Cawnpore and Lucknow sieges. Barrackpore, mentioned in the book, actually existed as another major British military centre, as did Meerut.

As the author explains in the 'Afterword', the characters, though fictional, are based heavily on fact. Sections of dialogue are taken almost unchanged from diaries and records. Thus, though we are dealing with a work of fiction, historical fact plays an enormously important part, and it is clear that the reader should have some understanding of the nature of the British East India Company (referred to as 'The Company' in the novel), of its role in the development of the British rule and of the great revolt in 1857 known as the Indian Mutiny which was to lead in 1858 to the British government taking over the political and military powers previously enjoyed by the Company.

The British East India Co.

On 31 December 1600, Queen Elizabeth I granted a royal charter to a small group of private traders, licensing them to trade with India and the Far East. Numbers of other European countries set up similar trading companies, some of which became bitter rivals of the British Company. The French, Dutch and Portuguese were foremost amongst these competitors on the Indian mainland. Heavily armed ships (East Indiamen) and small armies were employed by the British Company to protect and expand trading routes and territories. Under Charles II the Company gained the right to acquire territory, coin money, command troops, make war and peace and exercise both civil and criminal law. From 1689 the history of EIC is the history of British rule in India.

The original trading company was run by a Court of Directors in

London which was quite independent of the government. However, by the mid 18th-century the Company had become so powerful and wealthy after Clive's brilliant victory at Plassey that the British Government decided to raise the governor of Bengal (a Company appointment), a position then occupied by Warren Hastings, to the rank of governor general, and made this appointment subject to the approval of the Crown. In 1784 Pitt's India Bill created a board of control, as a department of the British government, to exercise political, military and financial superintendance over the British possessions in India. After a series of bills in the early 19th-century the EIC ceased to be a trading concern and exercised only administrative functions. Following the Indian Mutiny of 1857, Indian administration was taken over by the Crown.

The Indian Mutiny

The Indian Mutiny refers to the great revolt of the Bengal native army in 1857. Its causes were many though some are still a source of controversy. One obvious factor which made it possible was the degree to which native soldiers outnumbered the European units whose ranks had been depleted by wars elsewhere. Over the previous 100 years, the British armies had been spectacularly successful and the warlike races of India had been eager to enlist, which they did in huge numbers. Their officers were Europeans, usually British.

Prior to 1857 there had been several small outbreaks of revolt amongst the native soldiers (sepoys) over such issues as the over-introduction of European clothing and equipment, low pay, and social reforms which struck at ancient social and religious privileges. Defeats suffered by the British armies in the 1840s shook morale. Such grievances provided the background to the great mutiny.

The final incident, mentioned in Farrell's book, which sparked off the revolt was the introduction of the greased cartridge for use in the Enfield rifle. One end of this cartridge had to be bitten off in order to pour out the powder. The grease used was made of a type of animal fat deeply offensive to the religious feeling of the native soldiers who were mainly Muslims. Though the grease was rapidly replaced by clarified butter the damage was done. There can be no doubt that the sepoys genuinely feared that they would be defiled by the use of the unclean cartridges.

Then followed the strange episode of the chapatis. These were (and are) small cakes of unleavened bread. A village watchman would arrive at a village telling those inhabitants who received one chapati to bake four more and pass them on. Like an early version of the chain letter, nobody knew where the strange order originated. A tense India received them as portents – they were known to have circulated before at times of trouble. Another sign of impending trouble was the outbreak of incendiary fires in the lines of native troops.

In February 1857 native troops at Berhampore refused to use the new cartridges. They were ordered to march to Barrackpore for disbandment but on the way a sepoy named Mangal Pandi shot his adjutant and cut down the European sergeant major of the battalion. From this moment the mutineers became known as 'Pandies'. It was General Hearsey (mentioned in Chapter 2 on pages 36 and 44 of *The Siege of Krishnapur*) who personally tackled the rebel Mangal Pandi.

A number of prominent men, among them Lord Ellenborough, Sir Charles Napier, General John Jacob and particularly Sir Henry Lawrence had warned of the possibility of the disaster. From the reader's point of view it is interesting to note that Sir Henry Lawrence of Lucknow bears a number of resemblances to Mr Hopkins the Collector of *The Siege of Krishnapur*.

The first major outbreak of the Mutiny occurred at Meerut, the events of which are accurately recorded in Chapter 3, p.63 of the novel. In fact the mutinous troops from Meerut marched on Delhi where there was an appalling massacre of Europeans, including women and children. It was here that a group of young British officers, no longer able to hold out against the native troops, exploded their own powder magazine, causing immense damage to the enemy. It may have been this act which inspired Farrell's description of Harry Dunstaple's destruction at the sepoy powder dump.

Meanwhile, terrible events had been taking place at Cawnpore and Lucknow. The siege at Cawnpore, where about 330 women and children had taken refuge, lasted only about three weeks, when the besieged Europeans, much weakened by heat and sickness, negotiated a safe passage by boat. The sepoys, however, massacred the men at the boats and rounded up the women and children. A relieving British force arrived a month later to find that the women and children had been hacked to death the night before and their bodies thrown down a well shaft. No action throughout the mutiny caused greater outrage than this.

At Lucknow, the Residency was to provide refuge for a mixed contingent of loyal sepoys, European soldiers and civilian volunteers, totalling about 1720 men. The besieging force numbered about 60 000. After a bitter battle the helpless inmates of the Residency were conveyed safely to Cawnpore but Lucknow was only fully recovered after a second engagement some time later.

The Great Exhibition, 1851

Only five years before the events of the Mutiny a great exhibition was mounted in London. It was designed to project an image of Great Britain as 'the workshop of the world'. The man responsible for the idea and much of the work was the German husband of Queen Victoria, Prince Albert. The exhibition was housed in a massive building of steel and glass called the Crystal Palace, specially designed for the occasion. The thousands of exhibits were selected as examples of man's ingenuity in applying the arts and sciences in the service of industry.

The entire nation enjoyed the atmosphere of carnival and success which surrounded the exhibition and it became a symbol of national pride and confidence. It embodied the mid-Victorian idea of human progress. The surplus proceeds from the exhibition were used to found what is now known as the Victoria and Albert museum. The Crystal Palace was moved from Hyde Park to Sydenham where it was finally destroyed by fire in 1936.

Plot and themes

Plot

Since 'what happens' is clearly of secondary importance to the author, the plot itself is simple. Chapatis (small cakes of unleavened bread) begin to turn up in unexpected places in Krishnapur, an administrative centre in that area of India controlled by the British East India Company in 1857. Their sudden appearance, seemingly of no particular significance, is interpreted by Mr Hopkins, the Collector (the administrative head of the British cantonment) as an ominous signal of an impending Indian attack. He gives orders for defensive ditches and ramparts to be dug round the Residency under the pretext that they are required for drainage purposes. He also attempts to warn other highly placed residents in Calcutta but they refuse to take him seriously.

From distant areas of British India there are rumours of uprisings among the native soldiers (the sepoys) but these are shrugged off until an uprising actually takes place at Captainganj, the neighbouring military headquarters. Here many of the senior British officers are shot; those who escape take refuge in Krishnapur. News of the massacre spreads through the countryside and the Residency is quickly engulfed by large numbers of terrified Europeans, who are for the most part British. From this point begins the siege which decimates their numbers through disease, starvation, enemy fire, sunstroke and suicide.

At first, though shocked and overcrowded, the British residents attempt to uphold the social norms, divisions and etiquettes which had hitherto dominated their autocratic occupation of the cantonment. Then petty disputes break out, particularly among the women. At the centre of one of these is Lucy Hughes, who has been threatening to kill herself because she has been 'ruined' by a young soldier. Thanks to the efforts of George Fleury, Harry Dunstaple and his sister Louise, Lucy has been persuaded to leave the '*dak* bungalow' and to take refuge in the Residency, much to the mortification of the other ladies.

Numbers of Eurasians and native Christians attempt to find shelter in the Residency but only the Eurasians are accepted. The native

Christians are, however, given certificates of loyalty which they promptly sell. Hari, the Maharajah's son who is also a friend of the Collector, arrives with his Prime Minister to receive his certificate and is taken a virtual hostage by the Collector who feels his presence in the Residency may secure some small advantages for the besieged.

Many are killed during the first attack on the Residency, but because of the sepoys' failure to follow up immediately with a charge, the British manage to hold on to what has now become virtually a fort. When the charge eventually takes place Harry and Fleury inflict heavy casualties on the enemy with their cannon and these two also involve themselves in heroic hand-to-hand fighting with the sepoys.

A period of relative calm follows though conditions are wretched, particularly in the hospital. During the lull the Collector approves a plan to dig mines under the sepoy lines in order to fire explosives. The charge is detonated and during the ensuing confusion Harry, Fleury and others ride into the enemy, killing sepoys and spiking guns. On their return to the Residency, they are acclaimed as heroes.

A lengthy period of increasing misery follows, with many dying from a variety of causes; quarrels erupt over medicine, religion, progress, resulting in sharp divisions among the besieged. The rains threaten, conditions worsen, and the Collector decides there is nothing further to be gained from holding Hari and releases him.

The Collector decides to reduce the physical size of the garrison in order to make defence easier with far fewer men. At the moment of the retreat the Collector finally collapses from a developing illness. The sepoys attack but are driven back by cannon fire and an explosion in the Cutchery which envelops them in a snowstorm of falling papers – the accumulated records of the British rule in India.

The monsoon season begins and the rains threaten to wash away the defences. The garrison are powerless to halt the steady erosion, though the downpour also prevents sepoy attacks. There are more deaths, one or two births, of these one survives and, in depressing surroundings is baptized.

The food stores of the dead are auctioned and this serves to uncover fraud, deception and profiteering. The auction is cancelled. The bitter dispute over cholera between the doctors comes to a head when Dr Dunstaple drinks off a quantity of a clear fluid which he allows people to think is the so-called 'rice water' claimed by Dr McNab to be deadly in transmitting the disease. Dr Dunstaple does contract cholera, but dies of a heart attack after revealing the fluid was, in fact, ordinary water.

The garrison declines still further into starvation and disease; eventually the sepoys mount another attack. The garrison is in a state of acute despair when there is a tremendous explosion. Harry Dunstaple has succeeded in extending the range of his cannon and has blown up the sepoy ammunition magazine. The attack is again repulsed.

As the few survivors cling to life, with food and ammunition supplies exhausted, a relieving British force arrives. The siege is over.

Themes

There are several interlocking themes in *The Siege of Krishnapur*, operating at different levels. Each of the main themes is epitomized by a central symbol. The most abstract, timeless and all-embracing of these is the image of the two men and their bullocks, toiling every day of their lives to draw water in the midst of the vast and hostile terrain of India. We meet this image at the very beginning of the book and it is the final image carried away by the Collector when he leaves India for the last time. It is Farrell's image, not just of Indian life, but of the reality of all life when it is stripped bare of the trappings of civilization and culture which the Collector sees as 'a cosmetic painted on life by rich people to conceal its ugliness' (Chapter 32, p.345). According to this view, life is harsh, unremitting, repetitive, and pointless. This image acts as a frame within which everything else is set and against which everything else must be measured. It provides an ironic perspective for all the preoccupations of the characters. How for example, are we to regard the Collector's enthusiasm for progress and civilization, the Padre's concern with religion and sin and Fleury's passion for feelings in the light of such a stern and empty realism? They are reduced to the level of the unimportant, even to the trivial.

A second, much more concrete image is located in a particular historical period; this is the siege itself. The importance of this image is emphasized by the fact that it forms the title of the book. In a perfectly obvious sense the book is about a physical siege but at another level it has much wider implications.

Victorian, mid 19th-century Britain was economically hugely successful, militarily very strong and morally massively confident. In every sphere ideas and progress were felt to be on the move towards perfection. Other peoples, other religions, other systems of ideas were regarded as inferior, either with the benevolent goodwill we find in the Collector or the ignorant and insensitive contempt of a Rayne or Burlton.

It was this confidence, these ideas and systems that Britain took out into the rest of the world with either missionary zeal and a desire to raise the level of less fortunate peoples or a ruthless determination to make the maximum profit out of the natives. Wherever the British went they took with them the ideas, beliefs, and behaviour as a justification for their presence in that part of the world and as standards both for themselves and for those they were busy colonizing. Their ideals, however, were the product of their own particular branch of society in England – and this the British frequently chose to ignore. Such systems were entirely inappropriate for other lands with different cultural roots, climates, aspirations; time and time again the natives of the new colonies rose up and rebelled against the alien life-style imposed on them.

By treating the siege as the central situation Farrell is able to use it to bring the Victorian concepts of civilization and progress under attack thus demonstrating their fragility and vulnerability. It is a further irony that despite the fact their ideas are tested to destruction and made to appear ridiculous, the characters in the main fail to learn the obvious lessons; the reader is left with the suspicion that exactly the same mistakes will be made all over again. The Collector is driven into empty withdrawal, Fleury from one fashionable pose into another, the Padre, the Magistrate and Harry remain as far as we know, much as they were.

The Great Exhibition of 1856, a further symbol, the great showcase of the British way of life demonstrates more specifically the Victorian notion of progress. Many of the inventions proudly exhibited and mentioned in Farrell's book are now, to us, little more than novelties, the floating church for seamen; the expanding pianoforte for yachts; artificial teeth carved in hippopotamus ivory, but to the Collector this exhibition was a 'collective prayer' (p.59). If God is seen as the Great Inventor or Designer then man is obeying God's will if he invents and designs. What more perfect justification could there be for an Industrial Revolution or for exporting such a revolution to other lands and other peoples? The Collector however, does attempt to draw together a number of strands in his efforts to discover the purpose of man's life on earth. He tries to see man's creative and industrial efforts, his intellectual endeavours and his religious beliefs coming together as one powerful force to thrust him onward and upward. Other characters tend to concentrate on a single aspect of man's search for reason and purpose in his existence. Fleury on the cultivation of feelings; the Padre on seeking out and following God's will and the Magistrate on phrenology. (Phrenology is in a different category, of course. Since the Magistrate has lost all faith in life and people he spends his time trying to prove that man's life is determined by the bumps on his head and so emphasizes its futility.)

At a more general level again Farrell is pointing out the danger of adopting a single point of view and trying to impose it on others. Just as the British were imposing their own rules on the Indians, so Fleury, the Padre and Dr Dunstaple render themselves ridiculous by constantly trying to dominate those around them, and so reveal their acute narrowness of vision and arrogance in presuming that they are the sole possessors of the truth.

Structure and style

Structure

Historical events inevitably influence the structure of this novel. Though Krishnapur never existed and its siege is therefore imaginary, the course of events in the book is closely related to attacks which did in fact take place in Lucknow, Cawnpore and Delhi. Since the novelist is not bound by historical fact he is free to allow other considerations to influence the shape of his work.

The division of the book into four parts and thirty-two chapters is of little help to the reader. None of them carries a title, they are of enormously differing lengths, there seems to be little concern for unity of content and even the major divisions appear largely arbitrary. Sometimes the passage of time is indicated by these divisions – often it is not. Frequently the action is interrupted so that some aspect of an idea can be developed, sometimes in dialogue, more often in the thoughts of one of the principal characters – usually the Collector.

And here we come upon the central point which the reader must constantly keep in mind. *The Siege of Krishnapur* examines ideas and issues; it is not primarily about India or the Indians, any particular character, nor even the siege. These are merely vehicles for the author's main purpose which is twofold. First he sets out to provide an (ironic) panorama of the major ideas, prejudices, beliefs, ideas, fantasies, myths, controversies and stupidities which motivated the Victorian establishment in its attempt to forge an Empire based on its own standards of civilization; secondly – and more basically – he examines the true reasons for existence on earth. These issues have been referred to in more detail in the section on 'Themes' but it is necessary to mention them here also because it sometimes appears that the structure of the novel is heavily influenced by the author's desire to make one of his points about religion, or medicine, or science or progress or the position of women.

Instances of this are not hard to find but one should look closely for example, at the visit of Fleury and Harry to the Maharajah's palace (Part 1, Chapter 5). The plot is not in any way advanced by this visit which does, however, provide some curious local colour and more importantly, illustrates the ludicrous effects of any attempt to graft Victorian English manners, habits, science and technology onto an alien culture. The incident when Dr Dunstaple breaks the vase and immediately blames Fleury for it (Part 1, Chapter 2), is later revealed as having again two functions: the first, as a character note on Dr Dunstaple, the second to discredit in advance the supporter of retrograde methods in medicine (it could have been any science) and to illustrate his lack of regard for truth and honesty.

One should consider too the role of the Padre. That such a British community in India would have a minister of religion who would comfort and guide his flock in times of trouble is understandable but here the Padre's contributions are usually so exaggerated and absurdly ill-timed. A fine example of this is given in Part 2, Chapter 12 when in the midst of a raging battle with the sepoys the Padre tries to prove to Fleury the existence of God by pursuing him with examples of the marvels of Nature. Again we can see this, not only as a portrayal of a particularly crazy, even lunatic individual but as the author's way of mocking certain aspects of religious belief which blind their adherents to even the most desperate and obvious practical situations – often to reality itself.

Farrell frequently inserts incidents, episodes, even characters which have little purpose in the plot as a means of illustrating a point, and the timing and the nature of these episodes is often contrived to produce a comic effect.

In terms of time and place, the novel is tightly structured. Apart from the epilogue when we are given a brief, even perfunctory glimpse of the fate of some of the characters, the action spans a few months only, perhaps six or seven. The action is entirely confined to the Residency and its near environs apart from a brief excursion into Calcutta during the cool season. The effect, however, is never claustrophobic, rather the reverse. Though time and place are confined and the number of characters who take a central part is small, the range of ideas is vast. Farrell manages to convey to us an entire and complex civilization and in doing so he moves freely among the major topics of the day – religion, science, moral values and art – but at the same time he is prepared to discourse at length on such apparent trivia as a champion file, a gorse bruiser, electro-plating and the making of daguerreotypes. These are precisely the kinds of thing which Fleury describes as 'irrelevant rubbish' but the author is clearly fascinated by them.

The Victorians were always intrigued by technology and inventions and had enormous faith in their effectiveness in promoting human progress and happiness. Everything had its purpose and place in the grand scheme of things. Farrell mocks this confidence by having these treasured inventions put to unexpected and often ludicrous use, as, for example, when the administrative records stored in the Cutchery are blown sky high and flutter down as a blinding snowstorm, helping to repel the sepoys, or when Harry uses the electro-plated heads of poets as cannon balls with improbable and comic results.

The author is then frequently working on two or three levels: first, he is describing an event e.g. Hari makes a daguerreotype; second he is providing an example of a curious and now almost forgotten technique; and third, since the whole episode culminates in near farce with the series of misunderstandings between Hari and Fleury ending with the latter abandoned with his head firmly gripped in a clamp Farrell is making ironic fun of Hari's exaggerated respect for technology and Fleury's equally exaggerated rejection of it. In this case a fourth level can be identified in that this episode takes place in the most improbable surroundings imaginable and illustrates the folly of attempting to 'convert' Indian culture to Western patterns – the gulf is unbridgeable. In this sense he is making a somewhat similar point to that made by E. M. Forster in *A Passage to India*.

Finally we must consider the question of 'point of view' and 'voice'. Farrell uses the conventional story-teller's technique of mixing the 'omniscient observer' style with direct speech or dialogue. Though he often speaks 'about' characters from the outside in his persona as story-teller, he also assumes the power to enter the minds of some of them and to write as though they were recording their own thoughts.

Style

There is no one term which will suffice to characterize Farrell's style since he does not even attempt stylistic unity. He himself acknowledges in the 'Afterword' that he has taken extracts virtually word for word, from letters, diaries and notebooks of the time. Though in one sense there is a high degree of authenticity to be gained from this technique in another it must be clear that the sources themselves, as the products of many hands, vary in style. In fact it is true to say that many passages in the book carry the strong stamp of the research notebook. Both the disputes between Dr McNab and Dr Dunstaple on the subject of cholera carry a wealth of technical detail which it is hard to imagine being spontaneously produced in the heat of bitter public debate. Other examples of the fruits of the research notebook are to be found in the lengthy descriptions of the techniques involved in the making of daguerreotypes; Harry's instructions on firing cannons; details of military mining, a number of the Padre's sermons and harangues; and various references to the contents of the Great Exhibition. Of course, all these are taken from written sources whilst Farrell often includes them in passages of speech. Since written language always tends to be more formal than spoken this is what gives some of the dialogue its rather stiff and mannered features.

It is interesting to note that there is relatively little dialogue in this novel in the form of true conversation. There is much debate and characters often make speeches. The Collector, the Padre and the two doctors are much given to these kinds of utterance. In the case of the Collector, the reader is often privy to his thoughts, so that in a way the Collector converses with the reader. Even those conversations which are more personal tend also to be more about ideas than about feelings. In this way Farrell distances the reader from the true pain and anguish that his characters must have felt in such appalling circumstances. He is not squeamish about showing us blood or describing in horrific detail events of wounding, killing, disease and the stench of death but he rarely allows us to become too involved by obliging us to share the participants deeper feelings.

In fact Farrell keeps the reader at an even greater distance by treating the most gory and dreadful scenes in a humorous vein. In this he uses the techniques of exaggeration and caricature. There are numerous examples throughout the book but two will suffice:

Now Hogan, having rallied himself, opened his mouth to give his first order; his brown teeth parted, but as they did so a musket ball vanished between them into his open mouth; his eyes bulged, he appeared to swallow it, then he dropped conveniently near to the other bodies, the back of his skull shattered. (Part 2, Chapter 10, p.155)

And again:

The sepoy seemed to swell as he drew back his sword; he grew larger and larger until it seemed that his tunic ... must burst; his face grew redder and redder, as he raised his sabre in both hands as if his motive were not merely to kill Fleury but to chop him in two lengthwise, with one stroke. But the stroke was never delivered. Instead, he removed his eyes from Fleury's terrified face and dropped them to his own stomach, for a bright tip of metal had suddenly sprung out of it, a little to the right of his belly button. Both he and Fleury stared at it in astonishment. And then the sepoy stopped swelling and began to shrivel. Soon he was normal size again. But he continued to shrivel until, suddenly, he dropped out of sight revealing Harry's rather earnest features peering to Fleury to see if he was all right. (2,12,167)

In fact both of these events, taken at face value are horrible and yet the treatment is in the style of popular cartoon films for children, in which acts of great violence occur but do not shock because they are treated with humour, exaggeration and a concentration of ludicrously inappropriate detail. All these features are to be found many times in the course of the book. The episode concerning Fleury's Cavalry Eradicator is another clear example though it is also an opportunity for Farrell to poke fun at the Victorian passion for gadgetry and the ridiculous misuse of technology.

Humour of one kind or another is a central technique used by Farrell, not only to entertain the reader but to achieve a variety of other purposes. In the early pages he is concerned to poke fun at the social attitudes of the British in India and his humour at such moments is very much in the tradition of Jane Austen. Here the wit is gentle but acid: 'The Season had been unusually successful ... There had been many splendid balls and an unusual number of weddings and other entertainments' (1,2,23). And again on the same page 'But the cold season was nearing its end by the time Fleury and his sister, Miriam, arrived and new faces like theirs were longed for in Calcutta drawing-rooms; (by this time all the old faces were so familiar that they could hardly be looked at any more).'

Here though it is the narrator who is speaking, Farrell is clearly mimicking the tone and language adopted by the society ladies who were in the habit of making such remarks. This is a frequent stylistic device of Farrell's. Another example appears on the previous page (22): 'being military he [Harry] tended these days to work with condescension upon civilians and Calcutta was undoubtedly riddled with the fellows'. Farrell uses these 'narrative voices' as vehicles for his comments and value judgements. Though it is the Collector more often than not who acts as the author's mouthpiece, Farrell uses his other characters as well. At the ball in Calcutta he uses Fleury for this purpose and to some extent Miriam's perceptions on her visit to the opium factory are those of the author. By using this device Farrell is able, as it were, to speak on more than one level at the same time and is so able to achieve a type of humour and comment otherwise impossible. We are invited to laugh at the observer as well as at the observed.

Violent contrast is another source of humour in the book. This can take many forms. There is something quite ludicrous about Fleury's clothing when one considers that he wears a smoking jacket and tasselled cap in battle, which he later exchanges for an outfit in Lincoln green, making him look like Robin Hood. Lucy's polite tea parties, conducted with the usual etiquettes whilst shells rain down on the building, are further examples. Perhaps one of the most sustained contrasts is to be found in the behaviour of the Padre who harangues Fleury in the midst of battle about the perfect appropriateness of all God's creation. Hari's eating of boiled eggs and reading 'Black-wood's Magazine' surrounded by the utterly contrasting trappings of an Oriental culture is amusing certainly, but also invites us to consider the futility and nonsense of attempting to graft a Western on to an Eastern culture.

At the other end of the scale Farrell uses black farce as a source of amusement. The dispute between the two priests about whether the longer or the shorter corpse is Catholic or Protestant has farcical elements though it clearly also has a bitter satirical purpose in expos-ing the folly of certain kinds of religious prejudice. The blowing up of the Cutcherry and the ensuing snowstorm of papers which so bewilders the sepoys is splendidly farcical but again pointedly exposes the futility of so much bureaucratic paperwork, which, at last, in its destruction finds a useful purpose. One final example illustrates Farrell's talents in this area. This occurs when the vain and silly Lucy is covered by a mass of flying beetles. The two young men, Fleury and Harry set about scraping her naked body with, of all things, the torn off covers of a bible. Their utter naivety concerning the hidden parts of the female anatomy strikes us as hilariously funny and their attempts to be resourcefully gallant serve only to expose yet another dimension of Victorian prudery and evasion concerning even the most elementary facts of life. That they should have desecrated a bible for such a purpose only to be caught in the act by the fanatical Padre adds another dimension to the humour.

Whilst it is true that large portions of the novel are funny and that many serious points are made through humour this is by no means true all the time. A couple of examples may be useful:

He [The Collector] was invaded by a great sadness, then. The sadness emanated from the three silent figures sewn up in bedding and he thought again of his death statistics, but was not comforted ... And as he dug, he wept. He saw Hari's animated face, and numberless dead men, and the hatred on the faces of the sepoys ... and it suddenly seemed to him that he could see clearly the basis of all conflict and misery, something mysterious which grows in men at the same time as hair and teeth and brains and which reveals its presence by the utter and atrocious inflexibility of all human habits and beliefs, even including his own. (2,14,198-9)

There is nothing humorous about this though interestingly nor is it as moving as might be expected. The figures wrapped in bedding are anonymous corpses and the Collector's grief is a generalized one for the whole of Man's condition. It is individualized, specific feeling which is more likely to touch us deeply. Such moments are almost non-existent in this book though one stands out:

On his [the Collector's] way upstairs he passed Miriam in the hall and without particularly meaning to he put his arm around her. She was on her hands and knees when this happened, searching the floor with a candle for some pearls she had dropped ... When the Collector touched her she did not faint or seem offended; she returned the pressure quite firmly and then sat back on her heels, brushing a lock of hair out of her eyes with her knuckles because her hands were dirty. She looked at him for a long time but did not say anything. After a while she went on looking for her pearls and he went on his way upstairs. (2,14,200)

In a world in which the feelings of men and women have to be filtered through a tight network of rules and conventions (to the point where they almost cease to have the capacity for natural feelings at all) such a moment of unaffected human contact and warmth is rare and previous. However, even here the novelist is concerned not to let us become too involved because he goes on to say: 'At that moment he had been feeling the need for some kind of comfort ... perhaps any kind could have done ... a good bottle of claret, for example, instead. Still, Mrs Lang was a sensible woman and he did not think she would mind. "Funny creatures, women, all the same", he mused, "One never knows quite what goes on in their minds."'

The episode is not followed up at all; man and woman go on not knowing quite what goes on in each other's minds. In just the same way the different races never understand each other. We hear of the hatred on the faces of the sepoys but we, like the characters in the book, are kept in complete ignorance of the causes of their hatred; we can neither feel with them in their hatred nor condemn them – we simply do not know enough about them.

Not only is Farrell's treatment of people either ironic or humorous but also his treatment of things. On several occasions objects like electro-plated statuettes or the mosaic marble busts of Greek philosophers are put to grotesquely inappropriate uses. The heads of poets are used as shot, Shakespeare's head flying the truest and therefore doing the greatest damage on account of his baldness. Keats's head, romantically festooned with curls killing only a fat moneylender and a camel, both off target. The statues of Plato and Aristotle, two of the founding fathers of Western civilization, stand guard over the whole scene of totally uncivilized destruction. Portions of the marble statue, named with terrible irony, 'The Spirit of Science Conquers Ignorance and Prejudice' are used as canister shot and shatter the spine of a sepoy. Teaspoons, forks and silver sugar tongs, the trappings of polite and respectable society, inflict terrible wounds. Even the Greek pillars of the Residency turn out not to be marble after all; they too are a fake.

The purpose behind all this is unmistakable: it is to expose Victorian civilization in its every aspect as a sham and a fraud. It follows then that every product of civilization, be it people or things, is a fraud and a deception too. Though the book is fundamentally about ideas they too, as a product of civilization, are a fraud and are ultimately only fit to be laughed at. The people who live by those ideas are also fit only to be objects of humour and satire. Few are spared. The Collector, Miriam and Dr McNab, being the least contaminated by the fraudulent aspects of civilization, are taken more seriously on the whole. However, in the case of the latter two their characters are not sufficiently developed to alter the focus of the book and the Collector is a complex mixture of the fraudulent and the genuine so that even he is often a figure of fun. Sadly the Collector's realization of these truths leads him to a kind of dazed inactivity and withdrawal.

Finally, though Farrell's treatment of his characters is full of irony it is also an affectionate treatment. One cannot believe that he hates them, in spite of everything. But also, they do not learn. He does not leave us with much hope. His view of the reality of existence seems to be embodied in the image with which he both begins and ends the book: '... more often, there is just a well to be worked from dawn till dusk by the same two men and two bullocks every single day of their lives.'

Even the most dramatic affairs of men's lives are significant in the overall scheme of things:

The Collector experienced more strongly than ever before the vastness of India; he realized then, because of the widening perspective, what a small affair the siege of Krishnapur had been, how unimportant, how devoid of significance. (4,32,343)

Men are not hateful, they are simply unimportant, so they may as well be laughed at. The business of trying to find out what life is about is exhausting and finally frustrating, since there seems to be no answers. Farrell seems throughout the book to be saying that on the whole it is pleasanter to laugh than to weep or to rage – and this is deeply embedded in his style.

Characters

the Collector

The Collector was a large and handsome man ... He dressed fastidiously ... He was a man of considerable dignity, too, with a keen, but erratic, sense of social proprieties. Not surprisingly, he was held in awe by the European community; no doubt this was partly because they could not see his faults very clearly.

The Collector, Mr Hopkins, is the central, focal character of the book. It is through his eyes and his perceptions that we see many events and other characters. Though he is much the most developed character in the novel it cannot be said that we really come close to him as a person; like all the others he is kept at a distance from us. This distance is underlined by the constant use of his title rather than his name. This formality is partly a consequence of the superior position of authority that he occupies but it is also part of the author's general technique. It is noticeable too that though we often see through his eyes (almost all of Part 2 for instance is built around a tour of the enclave undertaken by the Collector), are often a party to his thoughts, hear what he says and see what he does, we are rarely present when he engages in sustained conversation with another person.

The Collector frequently expounds his ideas or makes pronouncements but almost never does he interact at a personal level even with members of his own family. Genuine dialogue is rare. Doubtless Farrell intends this to reflect the well-known Victorian reticence towards exposing feelings but it is also a part of his deliberate policy of keeping the reader at arm's length from the characters. Too great an involvement at the level of personal identification with the characters might interfere with the reader's involvement with the ideas.

We are told little about the Collector's appearance except that his whiskers produce a cat-like effect. This is intriguing since his character is far from cat-like, apart from periods when he becomes remote and inscrutable. The Collector's manner of dressing and his attention to his toilet are meticulous and formal. He is the standard bearer for Victorian respectability and civilized behaviour in foreign parts. His actions and even his feelings are consistently guided by a keen sense of duty. Even his feelings for his children are repeatedly said to be dutiful. Since he has difficulty in remembering which is which, and is irritated when they show concern for his safety, we must assume that his fatherly feelings do not go deep. Similarly, he shows irritation at his wife's distress at losing her baby, packs her off to England and, as far as we are aware, never thinks or speaks of her again. Though his children remain with him throughout the siege, he has surprisingly little to do with them.

Such characteristics might be expected to render the Collector unpleasant, even repugnant to the reader, yet he is not. This is because he does possess other, more endearing human qualities. Though he clearly finds loving difficult, he nevertheless feels compassion for suffering humanity. He is terribly saddened by the deaths of children during the siege; he feels sympathy for the ladies of the Krishnapur Poetry Society whose work is being savaged by the Magistrate; he is guilt stricken and sorrowful over the flight of Hari whom he has imprisoned in the Residency. The Collector even goes so far as to be appalled by the destructive force of the cannon he lets off in the Residency in the closing stages of the siege – though both he and the remnants of his starving garrison are fighting desperately for their lives. In fact he is never motivated by hate or mean-spiritedness even against those who are inflicting terrible suffering on himself and his companions.

Nor is the Collector immune to other human feelings. He has quite a weakness for pretty women though he can never see them as the equals of men. He refers to them as 'the soft and milky rabble of womankind' (13,171) and later says 'They are made of softer substance. They arouse our desire, but they are not our equals' (13,175). It says much, however, for his capacity for insight that he wonders whether perhaps it is not the way of life which men compel women to follow which makes them what they are. In Chapter 23, p.262 he says 'Perhaps it is our fault that we keep them in so much idleness? . . . Perhaps it is us who have made them what they are?' He even likes women for their faults. He finds them feminine and he prefers it that way. 'But no. It's their nature.' He prefers his feelings of paternalism to feelings of equality.

His attitude towards the native Indian is much the same: he wishes them nothing but well. It is the Collector's great hope that the benefits of science, industry and technology can be brought to India to raise that civilization to the level of the superior British civilization. His confidence in that superiority seems initially to be unshakeable, hence his enthusiasm for the Great Exhibition and his collection of machines and technological curiosities. For him the products of science and industry, just as much as Art and Religion, embody and symbolize the search for spiritual and moral truth, and since science and industry have made such huge strides, bringing with them the prospect of unlimited wealth and comfort, is it not reasonable to suppose that spiritual and moral wealth are as readily attainable? Such was the logic of the Victorian and the Collector is the spokesman for those beliefs.

As the siege continues, however, horror is piled on horror. The Collector is brought face to face with reality in the form of death, pain, disease, filth, squalor, violence, treachery, intolerance, ignorance; everything dreadful in man's condition from the climate to human nature is there. His confidence certainly is shaken but neither bitterness nor hatred follow it.

Gradually his confidence is overtaken by caution. He is the only character with the breadth of vision and courage to see that enthusiasm for one set of beliefs and ideas, as though they alone embody all truth, is the truly destructive force in human affairs. This is the significance of the comic episode in Chapter 31, when the Collector sits on the three-legged throne. If he allows himself to become agitated by enthusiasm he tends to be tipped, painfully, onto the floor; he learns caution and balance.

His qualities of courage and vision, of course, are in evidence much earlier in the book. It is the Collector who recognizes the threat of rebellion; who has the courage to build the ramparts in the face of ridicule and taunts of cowardice; who risks looking foolish by voicing his fears to the powerful and influential in Calcutta and it is he who organizes plans and directs all the defences and strategies of the enclave, so much so that the others come to think that 'The siege, in a manner of speaking, was his idea.' (15,203).

Perhaps it is the Collector's sensitivity which finally destroys him for it makes him susceptible to the softness of women, the religious feelings of the Muslims, the suffering of children, the horrors of the hospital even the fate of the dogs and water buffalo. As he gets older, he becomes less and less able to cope in the face of the magnitude of the world's problems. He resorts to a bemused withdrawal from all action or involvement. He indiscriminately reads the newspapers and stares at the poor, having given up any kind of constructive career. He becomes a despairing spectator. Ideas, optimism, civilization, culture have all let him down. 'Culture is a sham. It's a cosmetic painted on life by rich people to conceal its ugliness' (32,345).

The Collector is one of only two characters in the book (the other is Fleury) who undergoes any real change. At the outset he is full of confidence in the unlimited power of the social institutions, industry, science, morality, ideas and art of the Western world, and particularly Britain. This confidence in the power of reason and Man's efforts to help himself is however balanced by his capacity for such feelings as compassion and sympathy; in his own terms he has a heart. From this confidence he begins to move towards loss of faith. His belief in religion disintegrates in the face of immense suffering. His faith in the others slowly crumbles. By the end of the siege he has become cautious and tentative. He is, however, unable to turn this kind of balance into action and spends the rest of his life in a state of withdrawal. Why inaction and paralysis are all he can resort to we are not told.

It is perhaps significant that the Collector, on the one occasion he suffers physically, contracts a disease affecting his sight. He suffers pain in one leg and loss of vision. When he recovers he sees the world very differently. His loss is only partial, but so is his recovery.

Fleury

He had no sensation of danger in the least. The result was that he tended by default, to find himself in the 'confident' camp ... though, at the same time, quite ready to leg it for the Residency at the first sign of trouble.

We learn a good deal about George Fleury prior to his arrival. There is even a suggestion that he is slightly mad since he is fond of playing the violin by moonlight in a ruined pagoda. He turns out to be a pale, plump, ineffectual young man, whom his sister unromantically nicknames Dobbin. Under the influence of the Oxford of his day he has assumed the role of the decadent, Gothic 'Romantic', heart, art and sensibility. The Romantic movement in literature and art had passed its peak by 1850; and poets like Wordsworth, Coleridge, Byron and Blake had allowed their passionately held views to degenerate into a self-righteous striking of attitudes.

Fleury is amiable but quite ridiculous. He affects to stand for the cultivation of feeling, love, sensitivity, idealism. He despises science, rationalism, industry, materialism, anything heartless and impersonal. In this he is the antithesis of the Magistrate. Yet Fleury's meeting with Hari, when the young Indian shows him his collection of cultural curiosities and insists on making a daguerreotype of him, ends ludicrously in disaster. Fleury is obsessed with his romantic ideals, but ironically, wholly insensitive to the feelings of his companion, whom he succeeds only in insulting and antagonizing. He is equally unsuccessful in his efforts to endear himself to Louise.

During the early stages of the siege Fleury finds the pressures of practical necessity altogether too fatiguing and frequently takes himself off to sit in the shade with a book of poetry, or simply daydream. As time passes, however, Fleury makes two interlinked discoveries: the first that survival depends on action, and the second that through action, Louise's approval which has hitherto eluded him is to be won. He is pushed into the first of these by Harry Dunstaple and stumbles on the second by accident.

Fleury's various encounters with the enemy sepoys are hilarious. His bumbling ineptitude, and downright silliness in battle and all matters practical are reminiscent of film characters like Charlie Chaplin or Stan Laurel. He is the little man, always on the verge of disaster who nevertheless manages to come out on top, vanquishing mightier opponents, and reducing each battle to a shambles of black farce. Unconscious of appalling dangers, Fleury is so detached from reality that he appears brave. In spite of himself, he survives.

As a result of his growing, if somewhat undeserved, reputation for valour and his consequent success with Louise Fleury gradually adopts a more positive approach. The first evidence of his new outlook comes in the form of the 'Eradicator', his invention designed to spear several men at once (no sillier incidentally than some of the inventions on display at the Great Exhibition and referred to earlier by the Collector). The results of these efforts are predictably ludicrous. His new found masculinity is next symbolized in the Lincoln green coat. This succeeds in making him an easier target for the enemy, and in making him appear even more incongruous than he had done in his fashionable but inappropriate Tweedside coat, and his smoking jacket. Comparison between Robin Hood and George Fleury is clearly unthinkable – no one could bear less resemblance to the legendary hero of the greenwood than Fleury. His hapless wooing of Louise is well in character: when his moments of ardour are at their peak he becomes drenched with sweat (9,132) and at the height of his excitement and ecstasy he reads her a tract on human progress. He follows this up by aiming a kick at a local dog.

Farrell consistently debunks Fleury and stresses the contrast between his words on the one hand and his behaviour on the other. The most effective example comes at the end of the novel, when Fleury and the Collector meet in London. Fleury is anxious to be off, explaining that he has an appointment with 'a young lady of passionate disposition'. Yet he is still talking of 'a higher life'. His infidelity gives the lie to his sanctimonious idealism and, were he fully aware of what he is doing, the cynicism and hypocrisy would be complete. As it is, Fleury epitomizes the many Victorians who were never able to make the connection between their public position (adopted in all sincerity) and their private lives over which a thick veil had, of necessity, to be drawn: the gulf between the two was unbridgeable.

Harry Dunstaple

Harry, finding himself unarmed, was suffering not from fear but from disappointment. Here was a possibility of some action at last and he was going to miss it!

In many respects Harry is the antithesis of George Fleury: whereas Fleury believes that the only way to discover truth and a reason for living is through discussion and argument, Harry can see no point in so much talk about nothing. He has no intellectual curiosity or subtlety. He is the traditional man of action, seeing shooting and killing as adventures not to be missed. Soldiering is the be all and end all of his life. He is notable exclusively for what he does and not what he says or thinks.

For Harry, dealing with the natives is a matter of thrashing them to keep them in line, though he draws the line at killing them. He considers that thrashing should also be meted out to cads who ruin young ladies.

Female unaccountable bursts of emotion are explained by Harry as something to do with their works; he has no idea what. This is the level of his understanding of human feelings, and of the feelings of women in particular. Harry is equally unfamiliar with the female anatomy as illustrated when he scrapes the flying bugs off Lucy (22,256).

Yet, of course, the irony is that without men such as Harry the siege would have been lost. The world depends on practical men of action. His function is dramatically epitomized by the superb piece of gunnery which blows up the sepoy ammunition store. Whatever Harry's weaknesses, he is good at his job. In terms of character development the siege has no effect on him. He goes on to get his promotion to the rank of General and the last we hear of him is that he is shooting tigers, the traditional occupation of the upper class British male in India.

Harry typifies those Victorians who cultivated 'not-thinking' as a way of life. They assumed the superiority of the white British male and from that all else followed. Women and foreigners alike were patronized and kept in their place. Life was thus rendered simple and that was how they preferred it.

Hari

Hari, like any reasonable person, found these desires (money, jewels, naked girls) incomprehensible. His father was prepared to connive at the destruction of the fount of knowledge ... the knowledge that had produced Shakespeare and would soon have railway trains galloping across the Indian continent!

Hari, the Indian prince, is the only non-British character in the book but he does not in any way represent an attempt on the author's part to offer us a serious picture of the native community. Hari is even more of a caricature than the Padre; rather than a character, he is endowed with a collection of exaggerated features.

We meet him first during the visit of Harry and Fleury to the old Maharajah's Palace and are struck by his absurd efforts at Westernization (even his name is a mis-spelling of the Western 'Harry'). In the grotesque surroundings of the palace Hari is reading Blackwood's Magazine (an upper-class British cultural journal) eating a boiled egg (that most English of breakfasts), and trying not to sit on the floor because to do so would be uncivilized. His dilemma in attempting to 'progress' towards Western ideas, at the same time occupying his traditional place in ancient Indian Society is epitomized in the strange mannerism he has developed of simulating the action of walking forward to greet his guests but, in fact, remaining on the spot. He is trapped between an exaggerated yet uncomprehending worship of Western ideas of progress through science and technology on the one hand and the religious, cultural and political beliefs he has been brought up with on the other. The difficulty is that these religious and cultural traditions actually contradict Western progress and Hari is left somewhere between the two in an impossible position.

Because he is ignorant of Western scientific thought Hari chooses as his particular interest the making of daguerreotypes, a process of photography so inefficient and even unpleasant that it was rapidly overtaken by fresh methods; it is now no more than a curious detail in the history of technology. For the same reason Hari is an easy and naive victim of the Magistrate's misplaced enthusiasm for phrenology and makes himself even more ridiculous by falling for it.

Hari's pathetic efforts to apply his English public school education to life in India are also shown in his designation of his chief assistant as 'Prime Minister'. Hari's Prime Minister is ludicrously dressed in a rag-bag of Western clothes; he trots after his master like an obedient dog, is sent on errands, never speaks and spends as much time as possible in an attitude of Eastern meditation; an astonishing example of the Indian idea of the status of a Prime Minister.

Hari has great personal charm. He is eager to please, even Harry Dunstaple whose blue eyes he finds obscene, and whom he finds 'stiff and punctilious' (5,84). He is a great favourite with the Collector. Hari's misuse of English, clearly employed for comic effect, is nevertheless endearing and there are many examples of a delightful personality, as in his description of his disreputable father, his affection for his old schoolmaster and his apologies for his backward country. In one respect, however, he is too subtle for his guest Fleury. Out of traditional courtesy to the visitor he belittles his own treasures: the disgraceful pictures, the uninteresting knives, guns and so on; however, Hari is upset to find the insensitive Fleury, even more ignorant of the East than Hari is of the West, taking him at his word and agreeing that the contents of the palace are rubbish.

Later on, Hari arrives at the Residency ready to collect his certificate of loyalty only to be taken hostage for political reasons by his friend the Collector. Hari complains bitterly to the Collector who, though conscience-stricken, abides by his decision. Hari goes into sulky decline until he is introduced to phrenology when in his enthusiasm he shaves and marks out the skull of his long-suffering Prime Minister. The Collector finally relents and sends Hari (and the Prime Minister)

back to his father's palace, a sad and shrunken figure, the unwitting
and helpless victim of the British he had for so long revered.

The Padre

Yet at the same time he could not understand why the Bible should have had
to be translated at all, even in the first place ... why it should have been
written in Hebrew and Greek when English was the obvious language ...
English was spoken in every corner of every continent.

In a gallery of caricatures, the Padre is the greatest of them all. He
is the creation of the author's satirical and comic art, not to be taken
seriously. He talks only about religion: he is entirely in the grip of
one set of ideas and beliefs, in fact one ideology. Though his wife and
mother are both involved in the siege we do not hear him speak to
either of them. He digs one grave but makes no further contribution
except to expound his own peculiar version of Christian dogma and
blind patriotism.

   The Padre first appears in the novel extolling the virtues of a fatuous
floating church for seamen: a 'consummate embodiment of Faith'. He
spends much of his time from then on (even in Sunday School to the
children whom, we gather, he often upsets) attempting to demonstrate
the existence and nature of God as the Great Architect or the First
Designer. For the Padre God is a kind of super-technologist who
has designed all creation with enormous cunning and foresight so that
it is perfectly adapted to its purpose.

   Just as Fleury's romantic philosophy prevents him from understanding and seeing Hari as he really is, the Padre views everything through
the distorting glass of his religious obsession. Every non-Christian is
'heathenish and idolatrous' (9,130). His one charitable gesture towards the native Christians in getting the children to give them
crystallized fruit is rendered useless: his understanding of the natives
is non-existent and it does not occur to him that they will throw the
fruits away.

   The Padre continually sees what is not there (e.g. he mistakes the
jars at the back of the Church for members of the congregation) and
fails to see what is there (e.g. the need to concentrate on defence in
battle, not on doctrine). People are not human beings to be seen in
all their aspects; they are sinners to be chided into repentance. A siege
is not a siege it is God's retribution for the sin of heresy. The battle,

therefore, is not to be won by fighting the enemy but by seeking out heresy amidst the cannon and rifle fire (see Chapter 12).

His bigotry extends to non-Protestants, resulting in an unseemly quarrel about the size of the graveyard to be devoted to Catholic corpses. His beliefs are obsessive, narrow and intolerant.

The Padre provides much of the comedy in the novel. His facility for choosing staggeringly inappropriate moments for raising earnest doctrinal issues is a constant source of hilarity. And yet ironically the Padre who considers his primary duty is to enlighten those around him, proves to be the most deluded of them all.

The Magistrate

The Magistrate was somewhat younger than the Collector and had the red hair and ginger whiskers of the born atheist; his face wore a constant expression of cynical surprise, one eyebrow raised and the corner of his mouth compressed.

Tom Willoughby, like the Collector, is usually referred to by his official title. In this case his habit of sitting magisterially and contemptuously in judgement on his fellow men would seem to account for this. The Magistrate is a rationalist atheist whose intellectual position has led him to reject all that is tender, romantic or mystical in life and to adopt an almost total cynicism.

His admiration for reason and cold logic in the absence of any set of beliefs or hopes which might give purpose to the process of life and his lack of any warm emotions for others which might render that life tolerable leaves him empty and negative. Men are fools, institutions a sham, generous or charitable actions are disguised hypocrisy and self-seeking, ideas are impotent. The beliefs of the Mohammedans are worthy only of contempt and irritation.

The Magistrate's one real interest is to demonstrate that human behaviour and feelings are determined by something so trivial as bumps on the head. The irony is of course that this supremely rational man should have put his faith in the most bogus, superstitious 'science' of them all, phrenology. His faith in bumps on the head exactly balances the faith of the Indian landowners in their sacrifices of black goats for which he has such unbounded contempt. How ironic too that it should be Lucy who finally explodes his theory by slapping his face when he is in the process of attempting to prove it by showing that she is entirely dominated by a propensity for amativeness! Both the bumps and the amativeness fail him.

Our first meeting with the Magistrate at the Krishnapur Poetry Society reveals his lack of human sympathy or sensitivity. Each subsequent encounter reinforces this impression. Even when weak and ill he scoffs at the efforts of the Sikhs to dig a well. He is not an evil man, more an object of ridicule. As a character he shows no sign of development or change. At the end of the book the Magistrate disappears, leaving us with no clues as to how he reacted to the explosion of his pet theory. One cannot however, imagine it having much effect.

Miriam

Miriam was tired of womanhood. She wanted simply to experience life as an anonymous human being of flesh and blood. She was tired of having to adjust to other people's ideas of what a woman should be.

In a book reflecting a society dominated by man, Miriam occupies an important position in spite of her relatively small part in the action. Her first action in disappearing into her room and thus displeasing her brother Fleury sets the tone for her independence of mind. Miriam's nickname for her brother, Dobbin, which so annoys him is another sign that she refuses to be taken in by his high minded, romantic pose.

Almost every circumstance we see Miriam in is a reinforcement of the down-to-earth realism that we associate with her. It is she who sees and discusses the naked Hindu with the Collector (5,89). Where other women might have fainted Miriam asks a sensible question. It is Miriam to whom Louise goes when in need of advice concerning her father, and it is she who has sensible things to say to the same young lady about men and love. When the Collector is ill it is Miriam who steadfastly nurses him (as she had the General) and looks after his natural functions without flinching (from the facts or the words). Her outspokenness is a source of shock to the more conventional and less intelligent, Louise, particularly when Miriam refers to the 'carnal conversation', (rape) as their probable fate if captured by the sepoys. Considering their desperate situation and the likelihood of Harry's death, Miriam is astonished to find Louise worrying over the possibility of her brother entering into an unsuitable marriage with Lucy. The siege over, Miriam marries Dr McNab who, in common with her, has preserved a calm and practical sanity throughout the horrors.

There are two other moments in the novel when the author gives us a unique insight into Miriam's character at a depth reserved only for herself and the Collector. The first is an apparently insignificant incident in Chapter 14, p.200. The Collector is on his way upstairs after an exhausting and discouraging day when he meets Miriam who is on her hands and knees searching for pearls she has lost from a necklace. Briefly the Collector puts his arm round her. She does not flinch or faint but calmly returns the pressure and looks at him in silence. Her action of brushing aside her hair with her knuckles because her hands are dirty adds to the poignancy of a moment of genuine human contact and feeling at a level of unaffected realism almost unique in the book. The second is not an event but a hint at the nature of her past life. In Chapter 20, p.241 we learn that Miriam's marriage had almost destroyed her, and that she compares it with the experience of drowning (we are not told specifically why). She no longer desires to be linked to a man and has rejected the usual aims of a woman's life as they then were, to capture a man and enjoy a lifetime's dependency and subservience. Miriam wants to be an independent person in her own right, a person rather than a woman.

Though modern in so many of her attitudes and aspirations nevertheless Miriam is in some respects a woman of her time with typical flaws and weaknesses. She is hopeless at cooking, she has no objection to being bossed about by Harry and she is shocked by the incident when Lucy becomes covered by insects and her naked body is scraped clean by her brother and Harry. Miriam is a complex character with a dimension of depth lacking in most of the others: she relates to others directly, not through the distorting glass of a particular set of beliefs or ideas. Miriam is the most sympathetic and human character in the book.

Louise and Lucy

> From this pale and anaemic-looking girl who had once thought only of
> turning the heads of young officers ... he now saw a young woman of
> inflexible will-power emerging.
> Lucy Hughes provided a problem which the Collector was unable to
> solve. She was ostracized even by the members of the lowest group, in
> fact by everyone except Louise.

Although dissimilar in character these two ladies epitomize the Victorian ideals of womanhood. Both are beautiful, spoiled, intent on securing a husband and indifferent to revolutionary ideas and the major issues being thrashed out by the menfolk around them. Events are observed strictly through their own eyes and even at moments of crisis they are easily distracted by the trivial, Lucy by a mosquito in the midst of discussing whether she should kill herself (8,125) and Louise by an unsightly boil at a time when dozens around her are dying of cholera, wounds and starvation.

The irony is, of course, that these apparently silly dependent creatures exercise subtle techniques to ensnare and overpower the men. Lucy's repeated references to her 'ruined' condition emphasize her sexuality and arouse male gallantry and protectiveness. Her interest in the mosquito directs attention to her undeniably lovely body. Significantly, it is Louise who recognizes what she is up to.

Louise is the more substantial character of the two. Our first impressions of her are that she is irritable, vain and trivial. She is indifferent to Fleury's attempts to express his opinion on a variety of subjects, much preferring the attentions and horseplay of young officers. However, Louise is one of the few characters who develop and mature. Like Miriam, she devotes herself to nursing the sick and wounded during the siege. On Fleury's birthday it is she who cooks his pudding. Louise shows genuine concern for her father and brother (misplaced though some of it may be) and for Fleury's safety. Though Miriam occasionally finds her 'sweetness and prudish innocence rather cloying' it is Louise whom Miriam makes her friend. By the end of the siege she has become a different person. She submerges her personal dislike for Dr McNab and spends her time helping him to tend the sick and dying. Her prudish modesty disappears as more important considerations present themselves. It is sadly ironic that years later, married to Fleury, Louise becomes a deceived wife.

Lucy, too, turns to more useful activities than giving tea parties.

She becomes adept at manufacturing cartridges – not a skill with which we associate her in the earlier pages of the book. However, this seems to be the extent of her improvement and we are left with an impression of a selfish schemer of little depth, integrity or principles. When she slaps the Magistrate's face for fondling her neck she does it out of an instinct that that is the socially decreed thing to do, not out of a personal response to an offensive approach. It is his look of disappointment which offends her.

Drs Dunstaple and McNab

His manner was formal and reticent; although still quite young he had a middle-aged and melancholy air and like many gloomy people, he looked discreet.

But recently his plump, good-humoured face had set into lines of bad temper and bitterness. His rosy complexion had taken on a deeper, unhealthy flush, and although clearly exhausted, he was, nevertheless, in a constant state of frenetic activity and fuss, talking now of one thing, now of another.

Dr Dunstaple (something of a ladies' man) reveals unexpected cunning deceit when he knocks a vase to the floor and 'forgives' Fleury for his clumsiness. Later when, under stress, all other considerations are abandoned he is 'consumed' by a lunatic obstinacy. Professional integrity, common sense, even regard for his own life, have no place in his bitter quarrel with Dr McNab.

Dr McNab is the antithesis of Dr Dunstaple. Dunstaple is hysterical, reckless of truth, backward looking, McNab is cool, concerned with facts and statistics and progressive. Dunstaple is intolerant, McNab is compassionate. It seems natural for McNab to marry Miriam – by far the most down-to-earth, forward-looking female in the novel.

Each in his own way McNab and Dunstaple work hard for the sick, but there any resemblance between them ends; in all else their attitudes are wholly diverse.

Minor characters

A number of characters – Burlton, Rayne, Ford and Lieutenant Cutler have their moment in Part 3 and though making later appearances play no further personal role (though they are involved in the action). They serve mainly to highlight the satire on Victorian colonial attitudes. Their treatment of the native Indians is one of brutal contempt. Assuming a lofty superiority, they are revealed to be foolish and ignorant. The elderly General who arrives to discuss cricket in Part 4 and dies in Part 5 is little better.

The minor women are either tearful, sentimental and conventional (Mrs Dunstaple and the Collector's wife) or petty, selfish and unfeeling (the ladies in the billiards room).

Chapter summaries, textual notes and revision questions

Part 1
Chapter 1

The reader is taken across the white-hot, featureless Indian plain towards Krishnapur. Reference is made to the relentless sun, decay and death: man is insignificant against this vast backcloth. The two men and two bullocks drawing water every day of their lives first encountered here will reappear throughout, symbolizing a certain futility in the affairs of man.

Two major characters, Mr Hopkins, the Collector, and Tom Willoughby, the Magistrate, are introduced and described briefly, as is the Residency. Chapatis have been appearing mysteriously in the Residency and in other places throughout British India. The Collector suspects that they are an ominous threat of trouble from the native population. Worried, he orders trenches to be dug round the Residency, supposedly for drainage but in fact as a defence in the event of attack.

Life in the Residency continues to run its normal course. Local European ladies, with the Magistrate as their Chairman, attend a meeting of the Krishnapur Poetry Society.

Krishnapur Invented name of an Indian town and centre of administration. Based on fact, however.

shale Clay rock.

one gets nowhere at all without them i.e. civilization rests upon solidity and continuity. Bricks appear to provide this foundation. By the end of the book we see this to be an illusion.

Company The British East India Company; see section on Background.

cantonment Permanent military town.

chapatis Thin cakes of unleavened bread.

the Collector Chief administrator of a district under the control of the Company.

khansamah Butler.

Joint Magistrate Senior legal executive of the Company.

Residency Official headquarters and home of a Collector.

the young Queen i.e. Victoria (1837–1901).

palliate Reduce the bad effects of.

hypothetical Theoretically possible.

insurrection Rising, or revolt.

transept Part of a church at right angles to the main building.

causality The relation of cause and effect.

Only the youngest ... excused attendance Even the smallest children (except babies) were treated as miniature adults by the Victorians.

phrenology A supposed science (in fact a fraud) which stated that human characteristics are composed of mental faculties which create bumps on the head. A person's character can, therefore, be established by feeling these bumps.

the red hair ... born atheist Red hair was supposed to be a sign of paganism.

ginger to cinnamon Two strong spices of sandy and reddish colour.

jackal Dog-like, wild animal with a reputation for greed and cowardice.

as if in the dock As if on trial.

erl-king King of the elves (Danish mythology).

ayah Nursemaid.

punkahs Fans made of palm leaf.

cretonne Printed cotton fabric.

Great Exhibition See section on Background.

furlough Leave, holiday.

Edmund Burke (1729–97) British statesman and political writer, author of *Reflections on the French Revolution*.

Newton Sir Isaac Newton (1642–1727). British physicist famous for his statement of the Laws of Gravity.

love of approbation Desire to be approved of.

the mutiny at Vellore An earlier uprising of sepoys in 1806.

the Collector's weakness i.e. cowardly fear of mutiny.

Chapter 2

There is little movement of the plot in this section. Some background information is provided, and a number of the chief characters (George Fleury, his sister Miriam and the Dunstaple family) are introduced.

The scene moves from Krishnapur to Calcutta for the cool season. This is the centre of fashion for the Europeans of the area. The main purpose of their seasonal visits is to pursue refined pleasures and to procure marriage partners for their young. The newcomer to India, George Fleury, is of particular interest to the Dunstaples, since his father is a director of the Company in London; thus George is invested with a high degree of eligibility – and the Dunstaples have a pretty daughter, Louise. While Fleury is at the Dunstaples' house the Collector arrives with his wife; having suffered the loss of a child, she is due to return to England, after which we hear no more of her.

A picnic is arranged by Dr Dunstaple to which Fleury is invited. He continues to make a rather poor impression on Louise, who shows more interest in the dashing young officers who join the party. They talk for a while of native unrest but no one shows much concern.

The Collector, on the other hand, is seriously disturbed and while in Calcutta attempts to warn a number of influential people of the approaching danger. They pay no attention, however, and come to regard him as a slightly ridiculous figure.

Finally, Fleury attends an end-of-season ball. The manners and attire are European, the heat wholly Indian – a combination destined to produce a good deal of discomfort and a very unpleasant smell.

This chapter provides a clear picture of the leisured, confidently-managed lives of the Europeans by comparison with the inferior status of the native Indians. The stir caused by Fleury's jacket and the soiling of the hems of the ladies' dresses is in finely ironic contrast to the horrors which are to come.

insipid Lacking in spirit, feeble.

flirting chastely Playing at love but not seriously.

the cold season Fashionable time to go to the city for the social life.

ensign Junior officer.

pig-sticking and ortolans Hunting wild boar and birds.

Sebastopol A major battle in the Crimean war, ending in disaster for the British.

beau Man of fashion.

the Chowringhee Principal avenue in Calcutta.

gharry Vehicle, coach, for hire.

It wasn't in the least your fault Dr Dunstaple is immediately discredited as a hypocrite capable of deception.

daguerreotype Early photograph.

Although he generally liked sad things An important element in Fleury's romantic, poetic temperament which is to undergo such complete change by the end of the book.

dak gharry Mail coach also used for carrying passengers.

Crimea In Southern Russia; the scene of a war between Britain and France on the one hand, and Russia on the other.

Tennyson Alfred, Lord Tennyson (1809–92), the great romantic poet.

the soft and milky rabble of womankind Women are seen as nurturing and kind but weak and disorganized. A typically superior and patronizing attitude taken by Victorian males.

misprised Scorned.

Chateaubriand (1768–1848) François René Vicomte de Chateaubriand. Great French writer and statesman, whose works include *Voyage en Amérique, Lettres sur l'Italie.*

ghat Landing stage.

Dravidian cut-throats Southern Indian race of threatening appearance and violent habits.

Hooghly River running through Calcutta.

sais Groom.

surreptitiously Stealthily.

the Great Banyan Fig tree with vast rooting branches.

new Enfield rifles Named after the town in England where they were manufactured.

sepoys Indian soldiers in European service.

Attah of roses Fragrant essence made in Bulgaria and elsewhere, chiefly from the damask rose.

Mendicity Society 'Mendicant': a beggar; thus 'mendicity': condition of a beggar.

maidan Open plain or space in India.

Howrah Bridge Cantilever bridge connecting Calcutta with Howrah, a city and district in West Bengal.

Mofussil Land outside the capital or the great towns; provincial, rural area.

great, broad-shouldered, genial Englishman Admired type of Englishman of the times – intellectual sensitivities omitted.

philistine Of material outlook, indifferent to culture.

galloppe A lively dance, or dance tune.

rice powder Pulverized rice, used as face-powder.

infanticide The killing of a new-born child as a social institution in some societies.

suttee The practice of Indian widows to burn themselves to death on their husbands' funeral pyres.

'nautch' girls Professional dancing girls in India.

chaperones Older women accompanying young girls for the sake either of protection or appearance.

nubile Marriageable.

prickly heat Skin irritation caused by heat.

wool-gathering Absent-minded dreaming.

Chapter 3

On the journey from Calcutta to Krishnapur, Harry Fleury and Miriam, who are travelling together, are informed that a 'ruined' English lady is attempting to kill herself. They are embarrassed and nonplussed.

The remainder of this section concentrates on illustrating two contrasting aspects of the British mentality in India. On the one hand these are the attitudes of the Collector, the Padre and Fleury and, on the other, those of people like Ford and Rayne. (These are dealt with more fully in the section on 'Themes'.) In their individual ways the first group is high-minded and well-intentioned (if misguided) in its pursuit of universal progress; the second group is cynical and stupidly contemptuous. The members of this latter group give their native servants names like Ant, Ram and Monkey, and treat them accordingly. At the end of the chapter, the mindless, destructive practical joke, when Lieutenant Cutter rides his horse into the drawing-room of the bungalow and sets about the furnishings with his sabre, dramatically highlights the contrasting schools of behaviour.

nabob's house i.e. a European who has become rich in the East.
incongruous Unsuitable.
dak Mail-post, mail; *dak* bungalow – house for travellers in India.
betel The leaf of the betel-pepper which is chewed in the East.
seidlitz powders Laxative powders.
apoplectic Lifeless looking.
trepidation Agitation, fear.
fallible Liable to error or mistake.
to be a general Caligula, the insane Roman emperor who made his horse a consul.
hierarchy Division of governing bodies into groups or classes which are successively subordinate.
croaking Foreboding evil, thus helping to bring it nearer.
portico Row of columns along front or side of building.
Maharajah Great Indian prince.
eccentric Odd.
libidinous Lustful.
herbivore Animal living on grass or herbage.
Humani generis progressus (Lat) progress of the human race.
garrulous Talkative.

Gibbon Edward Gibbon (1739–94). Author of *Decline and Fall of the Roman Empire.*

Keats John Keats (1795–1821). Great English poet.

Voltaire François Marie Arouet (1694–1778). French writer of wit and satire, critic of all institutions, the embodiment of 18th-century 'enlightenment'.

Lamartine Alphonse de Lamartine (1790–1869). French poet, historian and statesman.

The Collector had been behaving oddly … our scheme of things At this stage the Collector believes that moral and spiritual progress in Man must go hand in hand with material, scientific and technological progress. This belief is first overcome by doubt and then shattered by the end of the book.

imbues Permeates, fills.

phenomenon Something remarkable apprehended by the senses; the appearance of something wonderful.

Mr Brunel Isambard Kingdom Brunel (1806–59). Eminent engineer of bridges, ships and tunnels.

Tractarian *Tracts for the Times* published 1833–4 in Oxford. A system of religious opinion, mainly asserting the authority of the Anglican Church.

consummate embodiment Complete expression.

theological beagling Beagle: small hunting dog. Religious hunt for the truth, religious argument.

ram in a thicket Biblical allusion to the story of Abraham about to sacrifice Isaac when God presented a ram.

sophistry Skill in fallacious reasoning.

emulation Copy, imitation.

artefacts Products of human workmanship.

punkah-wallah Native employed to fan the air with a 'punkah'.

emaciated Very thin, wasted away.

sardonically Scornfully, heartlessly.

griff i.e. 'griffin' newly-arrived European.

his ilk i.e. his same crowd.

simian Ape-like.

mems Memsahib, a married European lady in India.

badmashes Evil-doers, thugs.

babus Babu, i.e. 'Mr' – used in parts of India. An Indian with superficial English education.

Mogul Empire An Indian empire founded by the Mahomedan conqueror, Badar (1483–1530).

lethargic Inactive, unnaturally sleepy.

milk-sop Soft, effeminate fellow.

brandy pawnee Brandy and water.
solar topee Sun helmet used in India, more correctly spelt sola topi.

Chapter 4

The Collector, troubled with sleeplessness, summons Dr McNab, newly arrived in Krishnapur. They have a brief discussion about children and religion.

As signs of unrest among the sepoys increase, the Collector receives a visit from General Jackson, commander of the Captainganj garrison. The General has come to talk about cricket. He dismisses with contempt the Collector's fears, and scorns the fortifications, announcing that he has the situation well under control. He is a caricature whose judgement the reader (like the Collector) is inclined to distrust.

The British in the cantonment are divided into two groups: the confident and the afraid. The Collector continues quietly to build up the defences.

charpoy Common Indian bed, sometimes attractively painted.
Arnold Thomas Arnold (1795–1842). Legendary headmaster of Rugby School.
Kingsley Charles Kingsley (1819–75). Author of children's stories, among them *The Water Babies*, poet and historian.
havildar Indian sergeant.
sowars Indian troopers, mounted police.
sanguine Confident, full of hope.
disaffection Alienation, unfriendliness.
pettifogging Arguing falsely.
insouciance Indifference, lack of concern.
implacably Without giving up or relenting.

Chapter 5

Fleury and Harry go to visit the local Maharajah (the senior Indian leader of the area) and his son Hari. This is the novel's only major excursion into the true Indian environment. Even here, however, we discover little of the real nature of native India since Hari, the only Indian character of the book, has been educated by the British. The visit has a political as well as a social purpose: although he cannot make a direct request, the Collector hopes to ensure at least the neutrality of the Maharajah's army (such as it is) if not its active support in the event of an attack by the sepoys.

On arrival, Harry feels suddenly ill and is obliged to rest. Fleury is given a tour of the 'palace' and Hari, who has learned how to make daguerreotypes (early photographs) offers to make one of Fleury. While this is in progress the two young men discuss various aspects of civilization and technology, but what begins as a promising friendship breaks down completely in a series of misunderstandings. Despite Hari's English education it is impossible for these two youthful representatives of Eastern and Western cultures to understand each other. The unbridgeable gulf between them is reflected in the picture we are given of the extraordinary palace, the servants and soldiers, and above all the slumbering, unclad Maharajah.

We gain similar insights into the strangeness of India from Miriam's journey to the opium factory, and her experience there.

zemindars Native proprietors and payers of community revenues.
landau A carriage with a folding top.
different kettle of fish Quite another matter.
pericardium Membranous sac round the heart.
peepul Bo-tree. The name given by the Buddhists in India to the sacred wild fig beneath which the Buddha attained perfect knowledge.
Zouaves French Infantry, originally Algerians, who wore Moorish-style uniforms.
himalayas of crystal Mountains of cut glass.
garnets Red, precious stones.
lapis lazuli A deep blue stone.
agate Variegated, banded, semi-precious stone.
simulated Pretended, seeming.
but also so perfect as utterly to destroy perspective Hari's trick of movement disorientated and threw off balance the observer.
in twinkling In a moment.
debility Weakness.
cholera A highly infectious, deadly fever.
dhoti Hindu loin cloth.
Namaste Term of greeting.
supine Lying motionless.
half hunter A pocket-watch with a circle of glass let into the case.
durzie Native tailor.
Savile Row Street in Mayfair, London, famous for high-class tailoring.
beatitude Heavenly happiness.

godowns Warehouses or storerooms.

Shrewsbury Famous English public school.

punctilious Scrupulous, exact.

there was something obscene about blue eyes All Indians have dark eyes; to Hari, therefore, blue eyes seem unnatural and very disagreeable.

pater Latin for 'father': a term of address widely used by the sons of middle and upper-class families in Victorian England.

Morpheus Ovid's name for the god of dreams, and son of Sleep; now associated with sleep-inducing drug, morphine.

abominable pictures Many Eastern works of art, religious and otherwise, are explicitly sexual. Hari felt the need to call them 'abominable' because he knew they offended against Western respectability.

lewd Lustful, sexual.

cow here, cow there, cow everywhere The cow is a sacred beast in India and has the right to wander where it likes.

astrological clock Composed of signs of the zodiac for predicting the future and telling fortunes.

ryot Indian peasant.

pomade Ointment for the hair.

trident Large, three-pronged fork.

renunciation The act of giving something up.

ascetic Of self-denial.

dissolute Debauched, immoral.

Faith, Science ... Rotation of Crops Here the Collector muddles together aspects of religious, scientific, moral, social and agricultural progress as though they all went forward together. He later learns that they do not.

mercury vapour The smell and fumes which are given off by the chemical mercury.

chlorine ... potassium cyanide Other chemicals needed to make daguerreotypes.

I can see you feel the same Fleury here shows a characteristic lack of understanding of the true feelings of another person, in this case one of another race. He is equally ignorant of women, and of men who hold views that differ from his own. This is a common trait of a number of characters in the novel.

howdah Seat fastened to elephant's back.

Observatory Hive Beehive cut away and cased in glass so that the activity of the bees can be watched.

quietly-employed ... industry and order The orderly activity and hardworking nature of the bees was much praised and held up as an example to man.

sensitized Made sensitive to light.

Plato Famous early Greek philosopher (b.427 BC). One of the founding fathers of Western civilization.

An engine has no heart i.e. it has no life or feelings.

Chapter 6

The first part of this chapter gives a further example of the gulf between Western and Eastern thinking. The Magistrate is frustrated in his attempt to persuade local landowners to protect themselves against flooding by strengthening the river banks, while they have more faith in the efficacy of sacrificing black goats. The Magistrate is incapable of comprehending the Indians' attitude and, unlike the Collector, he displays equal insensitivity over the proposed demolition of the Muslim mosque for tactical defence purposes.

General Jackson, who had derided the Collector's defence measures, is brought seriously wounded to the Residency.

Fleury and Harry (now recovered) leave the palace in haste, Harry having heard that the sepoys have mutinied and attacked their officers.

attrition Wearing down.
Brahmins Priestly caste of Hindu.
Sircar Indian clerk.
coercion Force.
feringhees Hindu name for Europeans.
bas-relief Type of sculpture.
gagging Choking.
sowars Indian troopers or mounted policemen.
malodorous Evil-smelling.
retina The lens of the eye.
introverted Turned in upon itself.

Chapter 7

News of the massacre of British officers at Captainganj spreads, and terrified refugees from the entire district crowd into the Residency for protection, bringing with them huge quantities of possessions. Even in this crisis Dr Dunstaple cannot resist the temptation to begin the feud with his new colleague, Dr McNab, which is later to erupt with such violence.

The Collector swiftly and efficiently sets about organizing the defences of the Residency while the first buildings outside the Residency compound are set on fire by the mutineers. Religious feeling on all sides is offended by the practical necessities: stores are put into the Church, there is a quarrel over the allocation of spaces in the graveyard and the Indian mosque is destroyed because it is blocking the cannons.

Fleury and Harry are despatched to fetch Miss Hughes, the 'fallen woman' of Chapter 3, into the Residency. She refuses to accompany them; she has, she insists, nothing to live for. Both young men try to think up some good reason to offer her but without success, and they are forced to leave without her.

monsoon Wind which brings heavy rain in India.

indigo Plant grown for its violet blue dye.

hackeries Bullock carts.

coolies Hired native labourer.

Sikhs Members of a north Indian religious sect.

ah, could he have brought ... his inventions At this stage the Collector still has a strong attachment to his material possessions.

nimbus Misty, bituminous cloud.

staunch To cut off bleeding.

Hae ye no ... ants Scottish dialect: 'Haven't you heard of burtunga ants?'

Och, then, lesten to this, laddie Scottish dialect: 'Oh, then, listen to this, my boy.'

Och, Dunstaple ... 'ere long Scottish dialect: 'I have found a nest of the little creatures and I shall see for myself soon.' Dr Dunstaple is, of course, mocking Dr McNab by imitating his accent.

abattoir Public slaughterhouse where animals are killed.

assuage To soften.

tamarind A kind of tropical tree.

sack Destroy.

Saint Petersburg Ancient Russian city, now known as Leningrad.

Cutcherry Indian magistrate's office.

rationalism Reliance upon reason alone.

battery A group of guns.

pickets Guards.

Thank heaven ... peculiar habits The Collector enjoys a complacent sense of his own rightness.

Greek and gothic Contrasting architectural styles.

its illustrious parent, East India House in Leadenhall Street The famous headquarters in London of the British East India Company.

baronial Heavily carved style, particularly favoured in Scottish country mansions.

impregnable Cannot be taken or attacked successfully.

taciturn Silent.

cascable Section behind the base ring of a cannon.

vernacular Native dialect.

arbitrate Decide, judge.

with asperity Sharply.

rudimentary Undeveloped.

atrophied Wasted away.

one powerful propensity only Dominant tendency.

cryptically Mysteriously.

comatose Sleepy.

ostentatiously Openly and as obviously as possible.

Chapter 8

A period of calm follows, giving those in the Residency time to organize themselves and prepare for the siege. A great crowd of native Christians and Eurasians (also in danger from the Hindu sepoys) attempts to gain the safety of the Residency. The Eurasians are admitted but the native Christians are only given a certificate of loyalty. The old General finally dies of his wounds.

The Padre preaches that the root cause of their trouble is 'Sin', and he begins to reveal signs of the half-mad fanaticism characteristic of his later behaviour.

Fleury and Harry make a further attempt to persuade Lucy Hughes to come into the Residency. Again their pleas fail, though they are both becoming increasingly charmed by Lucy's looks and femininity. They decide she is afraid of the other women, and resolve to recruit one of the ladies to persuade her to change her mind.

lâtees Sticks or truncheons.

khus tatties Mats of bamboo cuscus grass roots, kept wet to cool the air.

Eurasians Those of mixed European and Asian origin.

Crannies Eurasians.

A fat lot of good a certificate will be Farrell often shows indifference to consistency of style. A senior administrator in 1856 would never have used such a phrase, which is more appropriate to the colloquial speech of the mid 20th-century.

transitory Quickly passing away, not enduring.

Bacon Sir Francis Bacon (1561–1626). English philosopher and
Elizabethan statesman.

Milton John Milton (1608–74). Great English poet, author of *Lycidas*, *Comus*
and *Samson Agonistes*.

peremptorily Commandingly, abruptly.

alabaster Semi-transparent, white chalky rock.

granite principles Rock hard.

chignon Coil of hair.

filaments Threads.

gup Gossip.

Chapter 9

Fleury finds Louise in the Sunday School, where he becomes involved
in a dispute with the Padre, the importance of which is revealed later.
The incident of the crystallized fruit gifts to the native Christians is a
further example (as is the episode of far greater consequence, the
greased cartridges) of the ineptitude of the British in their dealings
with the Indians.

Fleury attempts to convey to Louise his own enthusiasm for a form
of human progress based on brotherly love. Here his high idealism is
placed alongside observations on his tendency to sweat freely when in
a state of excitement and on a filthy, diseased dog which he kicks when
it tries to pay him attention – an ironic clash of idealism and reality!

As the mutiny spreads Lucy arrives at the Residency, having been
won over by a letter from Louise. The cantonment burns while the
Collector takes dinner with his guests and muses on the benefits to
mankind of electro-plating. The burning houses remind him of Prince
Albert's model houses designed for working people, near the Crystal
Palace. The Collector and the Magistrate disagree strongly on the
significance of these gestures towards the improvement of the lot of the
poor, the Collector taking an optimistic and the Magistrate a cynical
view.

Having taken Hari and the Prime Minister virtually hostage when
they arrived to claim their certificates of loyalty, the Collector makes
his apologies to Hari. Circumstances have forced the Collector to
betray personal feelings of friendship. Hari is less than pleased.

explications Explanations.

Discountenanced Put to shame, disconcerted.

penitence Shame for having sinned.

heretical Unconventional (in religious sense).

Atonement Reconciliation of God and Man through Christ.

feringhees Hindu term for Europeans.

Excalibur King Arthur's sword. Arthur was proclaimed king, by virtue of being the only knight who could pull the sword free from the stone in which it was embedded.

claptraps Empty words.

lodestar Star which guides.

pariah dog Ownerless cur.

broached Stolen in transit, broken open.

Benvenuto Cellini (1500–71). Italian goldsmith, sculptor, and engraver whose bronze *Perseus with the head of Medusa* won him much fame.

punctiliousness Exactness, scrupulousness.

portentously With an air of importance.

sepulchral As if from a tomb.

impermeable to optimism Not able to be influenced by a more hopeful view.

occluded Blocked.

connive at To allow something to happen.

contagion Infectious disease.

Revision questions on Part 1

1 Write a short essay on what is revealed of social life and attitudes in British India in the gathering at the Dunstaples' house, the picnic at the Botanical Gardens and the ball in Calcutta.

2 What do we learn of Fleury's character in Chapters 2 and 3?

3 What seems to be the role of women in British India in the early sections of the book?

4 In what ways does Farrell make General Jackson a figure of fun (Chapter 4)? Why is he made to appear ridiculous?

5 How does Farrell attempt to make his description of the Maharajah's palace as vivid as possible? Do you think he succeeds?

6 What is the cause of the misunderstanding between Hari and Fleury? Why is it important?

Part 2

Chapter 10

The attack on the Residency begins. Before it develops, the Padre, increasingly frantic, goes about distributing tracts and exhorting everyone to abandon sin – not, perhaps, the best advice under the circumstances. Dawn breaks, and the first shells land on the Residency. We join Fleury and Harry at their post. Their position is hit almost immediately by a shell and several of their men are killed. Harry receives a painful – and embarrassing – blow but is hurt only temporarily.

Note the repeated comic elements even during the worst of the fighting: Fleury's fantasies, Major Hogan's death, Fleury's confusion of a grape for an eye.

ferreting out sin A ferret is a small polecat used for unearthing rabbits; here it means driving out sin.

hydra-headed Hydra was a many-headed water-snake. It was one of Hercules' twelve labours to kill it but as soon as he cut off one head, two grew in its place. Hence 'hydra-headed' a difficulty which increases as it is combated.

beatifically cunning Heaven-blessed cunning.

contiguity Nearness.

axiomatic Taken for granted, accepted.

fire and brimstone Punishment awaiting the damned in Hell.

disaffected Unfriendly.

pan Betel leaf.

commandeer To seize, to take possession of.

Plato and Socrates A disciple of Socrates, Plato attended the former's trial and immortalized Socrates' attitude and manner of death in his dialogues *Apology*, *Crito* and *Phaedo*.

lugubrious Mournful.

canister or grape Canisters were containers for shot; grape, a type of shot.

limber Fore part of a gun carriage.

drift Steel bolt.

Chapter 11

A brief chapter, in which the Collector reflects upon the animals, mainly dogs, in the compound. They include Chloë, the beautiful

Chapter 13

The Collector visits the ladies' quarters. Despite the overcrowding, intense heat and foul smell they are still determined to retain the social divisions and practices of their normal lives; their attitudes remain petty and ungenerous. The Collector feels superior among them and is annoyed when he finds himself disturbed by the proximity of half-clothed young women and soft muslin garments strewn about. He reflects on the sheltered, useless lives they lead. They merely wait in their quarters for their husbands to come: they have no resources of their own.

The Collector, the Magistrate and Fleury discuss the natives' rejection of the advanced civilization the British are trying to impose on them. The Magistrate says it doesn't affect him, and Fleury refutes the idea that it is superior anyway; his views are dismissed by the other two.

With the Collector we visit the hospital where conditions are gruesome. Dr Dunstaple, showing increasing signs of strain, continues his violent criticisms of Dr McNab. Dunstaple supports the old and tried methods in medicine, regarding as wicked and irresponsible the experiments carried out by Dr McNab. But it is Dr Dunstaple's methods that are primitive, misguided and dangerous; over a hundred years later Dr MacNab's 'experiments' can be seen to have led the way to modern medicine.

dal Well-cooked lentils mixed with Indian spices, which forms a purée.

rowelled Stabbed as if by a spur.

sobriety Soberness.

homily Lecture.

confinement The time for the baby's birth.

deference Respect.

vindicated Upheld.

ostracized Excluded.

at a small, but eloquent distance The gap, though small, clearly indicated Louise's disapproval of Lucy; she did not wish to be too closely associated with her.

Pleased with this scientific observation When insight and understanding fail him, the Collector falls back on what he thinks is scientific observation; only one of many instances in the book where a reliance upon rationalism in the guise of science actually obscures vision rather than illuminating it.

spaniel brought by Fleury as a gift for Louise, and pets belonging to other Europeans. There is also a group of pariahs – disgusting native creatures. These dogs develop a symbolic significance later in the book in that they mirror the distinctions between the British in their affluence and the Indians in their poverty.

khet Thicket, plantation.
somnolent Half-asleep.
parody A playful imitation.
ricocheted Rebounded.

Chapter 12

The chapter begins with Harry's instructions on maximizing the destructive power of the rifle. It continues with the Padre's attempts to prove the existence of God to Fleury by pointing out various wonders of Nature which, he argues, must have been designed. There must have *been* a designer, therefore a God. The Padre's timing is hardly opportune, but he is fearful that Fleury's beliefs may so offend God that they are all being punished for his heresy.

The sepoys make their first charge and are mown down in large numbers by the cannon fired by Harry and Fleury. These two then follow this up by attacking the sepoys in hand to hand fighting. Fleury is nearly killed by a huge sepoy but is saved by Harry. The attacking sepoys are thrown back.

Slough of Despond A marsh, or bog, which Pilgrim had to cross in John Bunyan's allegory *Pilgrim's Progress* (1678).
Sodom and Gomorrah Biblical cities of sin.
Paley William Paley (1743–1805). British clergyman and philosopher, remembered for his 'argument from design' to prove God's existence. This is, of course, just the argument used by the Padre.
frays its diurnal passage Makes its daily journey.
viviparous Producing live young in an advanced stage of development.
patent Absolute rights of designer over his own creation.
carnage Slaughter, killing.
ecclesiastical Relating to the Church.
heft Lift.
pinions Wings.
proboscis Trunk-like nose of some animals and insects.
equivocations Quibbles.

Miss Nightingale Florence Nightingale (1820–1910). Famous for revolutionizing the nursing profession during and after the Crimean War.

perhaps because his senses, usually kept under lock and key The Collector denies himself, as a rule, the bodily pleasures, particularly in relation to his sexual desires.

voluminous Full, lengthy.

narcosis A drugged state.

Bengal One of the principal areas of India ruled by the British East India Company.

anarchy Chaos, lawlessness.

Haileybury or Addiscombe English public schools.

Truth cannot be resisted Repeatedly throughout the book 'ideas' as here are immediately made to look foolish by events.

decadence Decay; absence of morality or vigour.

amputations The cutting off of limbs.

putrefaction Rotting, usually of flesh.

frenetic Frantic, mad.

metacarpal Between wrist and fingers.

haemorrhage Severe loss of blood.

sutures Stitching of wounds.

Sultan i.e. of Turkey; a reference to the Crimean war. The whole song is about this war.

integuments External covering.

flaccid Slack.

sanious fluid Seepage from wounds.

mortification Death (i.e. of a part of the body).

gangrene Rotting of flesh of a limb usually caused by obstructed circulation.

granulations First particles of new growth.

bilious remittent fever Unpleasant, but not deadly, stomach disorder.

iniquities Disgraceful aspects.

quackery Of a fraudulent doctor.

specific Remedy for a particular disease.

aperient Laxative.

parody Distorted version.

gruel Thin, watery broth.

cadaverous Like a dead body.

Chapter 14

There is a detailed description of the vile smells building up in and around the Residency. The Collector agrees with Lieutenant Cutter on a plan to undermine and blow up a section of the enemy lines. The Collector has been studying military mining from books, the availability of which he regards as yet another example of western superiority.

After musing on the benefits of statistics, the Collector visits Hari, whose spirits are now reviving as a result of the Magistrate lending him a book on phrenology. It is at once comic and sad that an Indian should be taken in by one of the false 'sciences' of Western progress.

The Collector helps the Padre to dig the graves, and is overwhelmed by the misery of human suffering. One of the few moments of genuine human contact in the novel is when he silently puts his arm round Miriam.

Dr McNab records the death of Mrs Scott and her still-born baby as meticulously as he records all things medical.

halyards Ropes.
olfactory background Background of smells, stenches.
hermetically Closed completely.
effervescent Frothing, bubbling.
cardinal Essential.
obliquely In a slanting direction.
Vauban Sébastien le Prestre de Vauban (1633–1707). Marshal of France and celebrated military engineer.
place assiégée, place prise A place besieged is a place taken.
sap A trench by which approach is made to the enemy position. Sap: undermine.
spiking Rendering useless (of guns).
bobbery A pack of dogs of mixed breeds.
sitars Long-necked Hindu plucked-string instruments.
caprice Change of humour.
ryots Indian peasants.
cranium Skull.
cerebellum Rear and lower part of brain.
Mr F. Rabelais and Mr J. Swift François Rabelais (1494?–1553?). French satirist. Jonathan Swift (1667–1745). Irish-born satirist of English parents; author of *Gulliver's Travels*.
his understanding ... from Hari Hari's explanations only serve to confuse the Collector.
Amativeness Tendency to love.
propensity Tendency.
mastoid Area behind the ears.

sang-froid Coolness.
ineffably Beyond description.
Caesarian section The process of childbirth in which a cut is made in the abdomen of the mother; the emperor Caesar is said to have been born in this way.
uterus Womb, in which baby grows before birth.

Chapter 15

Lieutenant Cutter fires his mine under the sepoy defences. In the ensuing confusion Harry, Fleury and others mount an attack on horseback. Fleury takes his new weapon, the Eradicator, with him but it proves a ludicrous failure. During the attack they spike a number of guns and blow up an ammunition store, but their leader Lieutenant Peterson, is killed despite heroic efforts by Fleury and Harry to save him. Note again the combination of action, tragedy and farce.

idiosyncrasies Strange characteristics; peculiar to one person.
anaemic Pale and bloodless, insignificant.
sceptical Having doubts.
crozier Pastoral staff or crook of a bishop or abbot.
tamping Material used to fill a hole for blasting.
extemporized Improvised.
vacillate Waver.
gutturals and sibilants Grunts and hisses.

Chapter 16

Fleury is praised and admired by the ladies for his brave deeds during the attack. From this point on he inclines to a 'manlier' attitude to life and begins to abandon his previous poetic pose.

Louise is increasingly concerned about her father's attacks on Dr McNab, who in turn appears to be showing some interest in Miriam. Lucy is busy captivating Harry; Fleury is now making a more favourable impression on Louise. Fleury is given a green jacket by the ladies at his birthday party.

litany A prayer.
solstice Climax, high point.
decorous Proper, decent.
unctuous Smoothly graceful.

infatuated Inspired with foolish passion.

semaphore A signalling device with movable arms.

on this, apply cosmetics ... betrayal of her sex Even though Louise might try to find excuses and reasons for it, she was forced to the unpleasant conclusion that Lucy's behaviour was a slur upon womanhood.

exonerating Circumstances which free from blame.

obnoxiously Objectionably (clearly not to Lucy).

Chapter 17

This chapter centres on the burial of three corpses by the Padre, the Collector and, later, Fleury, and once more Farrell finds humour in the grim situation. The Padre ponders the religious controversies of the day on the literal truth of the Bible and the extent to which Man, through the use of his mind and reason, is responsible for his own destiny or whether his fate is governed by God who rewards and punishes him according to his achievements and beliefs.

Under the pressures of the siege the Collector's own faith is badly shaken. He plans to reduce the size of the enclave in order to facilitate its defence.

Thirty-nine Articles Articles of religious belief agreed by bishops and clergy of the Church of England in 1562.

the Fall Christian doctrine relating to Man's original sin: the fall from Grace and expulsion from the Garden of Eden.

Rationalism A system of belief which attributes all phenomena to natural rather than miraculous causes.

From the farmyard ... rationalism and despair A metaphor meaning that under the pressure of the horrors of real life in the siege, the Collector was losing faith in all the beliefs and supposed truths taught him by the Christian religion.

disclaimer Denial.

wraith Ghost.

cunning as a serpent The serpent was the devil in the Garden of Eden, yet the Padre is attempting to act as the agent of God.

the method of philological and linguistic investigation An example of rationalism; methods of studying the Bible by means of scientific analysis of its language.

Coleridge Samuel Taylor Coleridge (1772–1834). Great English poet and philosopher. His most famous works were *Kubla Khan* and *The Ancient Mariner*.

apostasy Abandonment of one's religion.

positive assertions ... vague equivocations Confident statements as opposed to unclear statements of doubtful meaning.

arid Dry, unfruitful.

ratiocination Reasoning.

Machiavelli Niccolò Machiavelli (1469–1527). Florentine statesman and writer, noted for his lack of political morality. His most famous work was *Il Principe*.

another member of his staff of nocturnal counsellors In his imagination the Collector receives advice during the night from previous experts and writers whose works he has read.

disparate Separate and diverse.

impregnable That cannot be taken or defeated.

velocipede An early form of bicycle.

barbican A projecting watch tower.

firmament Heavens, sky.

shrapnel-pocked Bullet-scarred.

this once beautiful ... grieving mind The shattered state of his room exactly resembled the destruction of his own former contented state of mind.

Revision questions on Part 2

1 What is the effect of punctuating the description of the first attack (Chapter 10) with the Padre's comments on Sin?

2 Give as many examples as you can find of 'black comedy' in the description of the first attack (Chapters 10–12).

3 Examine closely the Collector's thoughts on animals, pets, the poor and wives in Chapter 11. What conclusions are we to draw from them and from the order in which they appear?

4 Examine carefully the description of Lieutenant Peterson's death (Chapter 15) and the attempt to rescue him. In what ways might it be called 'mock heroic'?

5 What does Fleury's birthday party reveal in terms of the characters of the young people present?

6 What is the author saying to us about religion when he shows us the Padre and Father O'Hara quarrelling over the burial of the corpses?

Part 3

Chapter 18

The monsoon rains threaten, but continue to hold off. There are two more deaths, those of Lieutenant Cutter and a little girl; the tragedies shake the camp. Dr Dunstaple seems to be completely deranged. The Collector is troubled by an eye infection. Hari is released.

monsoon The rainy season.
oration Speech.
Providence has denied ... of fame His death has prevented the country from rewarding this young man's bravery.
valedictory Farewell.
Cawnpore ... Delhi Scenes of sieges during the mutiny. See section on 'Background'.
Death was ... drinking-companion i.e. the doctor was so accustomed to the presence of death that it had become like an old friend to him.
deity God.
inanimate Without life.
succumbing Giving way to.
fetid Stinking.
Sircar The government, authorities.

Chapter 19

The Collector's condition worsens as the moment for retreat arrives. Sensing the garrison's weakness, the sepoys launch their anticipated attack. However, the explosion in the Cutcherry causes the papers to be hurled into the air and to descend in what appears to be a snow-storm. More explosions and cannon fire drive the sepoys back and the attack fails. The Collector collapses unconscious.

seared Scorched, burned.
train i.e. of gunpowder.
Even in his fever ... continued to itch The same image occurs in Chapter 17, p.223, where it is developed more fully.
Pain The Collector has now become so delirious and his pain so severe that in his confused mind it has detached itself from him and is now a separate being, his companion. An example of the figure of speech, personification.
impropriety Impoliteness.

The wave toppled Throughout this attack the charging sepoy forces are compared with the waves on the sea which threaten to engulf and obliterate the defenders.

Sikh A north Indian religious sect; a soldier belonging to this sect.

unadulterated Pure and simple.

ubiquity The quality of being everywhere; omnipresence.

Chapter 20

Miriam nurses the Collector, who is now in a delirious fever. The friendship between herself and Louise deepens, despite their contrasting personalities. Louise is worried lest Lucy should ensnare her brother into an unsuitable marriage.

The monsoon rains begin.

erysipelas Disease (usually of the face) causing inflammation and redness.

once in her life ... for the last time A metaphor comparing a tragic relationship with the experience of drowning.

vortex A whirlpool.

debilitating Weakening.

arrowroot A plant part of which was used for the treatment of poison.

Commissariat Army department which supplies provisions.

rigors Chills.

aperient Laxative.

alimentary canal Passage of the body which carries food.

antagonize To counteract the action of.

laudanum A sedative of opium, widely used in Victorian times.

solecism Something improper.

prudish Over-modest.

carnal conversation Sexual intercourse.

And everywhere he is in chains The complete quotation is 'Man is born free but is everywhere in chains.' (J. J. Rousseau). It is heavily ironic that when the Collector quotes an enlightened French philosopher, he should be regarded by the two ladies as merely delirious.

quadrille A dance performed in groups of four.

Eheu, fugaces (Lat) alas, time flies.

Chapter 21

The Collector slowly recovers. The rains bring some relief from sepoy attack, but they also bring terrible damp heat, mould and a foul stench.

morbid agent i.e. poison.

pyaemia Infection of the blood.

choleric aether A sedative.

ammonia in effervescence A reviving agent.

convinced that ... packed them off The use of the words 'brood' and 'parent' indicate the remoteness between the Collector and his children.

diabolical Devilish.

offal Refuse; waste meats, particularly the internal organs of a beast.

miasma Foul-smelling cloud.

camphor A powerfully perfumed oil.

palliate Reduce the worst effects of.

fatalism A despairing sense that nothing could be done.

proof Secure.

India itself ... be sustained Note the relationship of this idea to the theme of the book.

He saw his reflection ... Magistrate As the Collector loses his faith in his old beliefs this is reflected even in the colour of his hair.

Chapter 22

While conducting one of her teas for selected guests in the Banqueting Hall, Lucy is suddenly covered by swarms of flying black beetles. Horrified, she tears off her clothing in an effort to rid herself of them, fails, and falls in a faint. Fleury and Harry rip the covers off a bible in order to scrape her body clean. In the midst of the operation the Padre, Louise and Miriam arrive – and react as one might expect.

Again the author brings a note of farce to a frighteningly unpleasant situation.

hermetically sealed Airtight.

barter Exchange of goods not involving money.

whorls A turn in a spiral – in this case, of the ear.

pullulating Heaving, throbbing.

chemise Smock.

effervescent Bubbling.

carp A freshwater fish.

Chapter 23

Apparently concerning a baptism, this chapter is, in fact, an excursion through some of the Collector's innermost feelings and serves to show that he is inclined to let his mind wander. We learn something of his taste in women, what angers him, what rouses his sympathy, his reaction to doing his own washing, old age and death. Apparently attentive to the religious occasion, his mind is far away: another emphasis in the novel of the gap between appearance and reality.

zenith Highest point.

without discrimination ... thrown in An ironic reference to the equality of men in death, thereby poking fun at the artificial divisions so dear to men in life.

Madonna Picture of the Virgin Mary.

churched A church service performed to give thanks for a particular event, i.e. childbirth.

fissures Cracks (caused by despair).

dhobi Washerman.

'bolting' party Those who wanted to escape from the troubles before they began (deemed cowardly by the others).

workhouse Dreaded institution to which were committed the old and the poor, and those incapable of working.

prosecute these petty feuds Keep up these quarrels between different groups.

debauchery and sensuality Immoral sexual behaviour.

ejaculations Words forced out or exclaimed.

Saint Peter The saint said to stand guard at the gates of heaven.

Chapter 24

The Magistrate, taking tea with Lucy, experiences a powerful urge to carry out phrenological investigations of her skull. The rains threaten to wash away the ramparts, so the Collector orders that all moveable articles be used to reinforce them. No possession, however prized, is spared. The Collector accepts Harry's suggestion that the undergrowth should be mown down by chain shot.

vestige Trace.

the Padre ... and Fleury A splendid example of comic understatement.

Why did they ... to find any An example of the narrator's use of another 'voice' – here, Lucy's.

Cupid Roman god of love.

inion Lump at the back of the head.

Sahib Indian term of respect.

marquetry A type of inlaid decoration usually in wood, ivory etc.

haemophilia Disease of the blood causing uncontrolled bleeding, through failure of the blood to clot quickly.

vertebrae Small bones of the spine.

clemency Mercy.

tumbrils Carts used to carry victims to the guillotine during the French revolution.

samplers Pieces of embroidered cloth, usually in the form of a text.

humidors Moisturising containers.

college eights Rowing boats for racing.

you would … at this time One of the rare moments in the novel when Farrell communicates with the reader with any degree of intimacy.

sortie Raid.

Sappers and Miners Army personnel expert in military mining.

chauvinism Narrow, petty devotion to one's country (or other cause).

Please yourself … not yet noon That the Collector should so defy the conventions of normal bedtime was taken as a sure sign of his mental collapse.

Chapter 25

After evening service Dr Dunstaple launches the first of his public attacks on Dr McNab on the subject of cholera, the terrible disease which is sapping the strength of the besieged camp. Dr Dunstaple insists the infection is carried by foul air, Dr McNab rightly believes it to be water-borne, and begins to employ up-to-date methods based on records, statistics and research. The members of the enclave are deeply suspicious of his new-fangled ways. The quarrel is bitter and arouses strong feelings on all sides.

The Collector remains in bed – why, we do not know.

It was because an epidemic … of the enclave An image comparing the deadly disease with an advancing force of enemy troops.

supplication Plea.

adherents Supporters.

Nunc Dimittis Latin title for a canticle from Luke, 2,29.

travail Toil.

impugn Cast doubt upon.

pathology The study of diseases.

charlatan Fraud.

Dr McNab ... by drinking In fact, as we now know, Dr McNab held the correct view about the transmission of cholera.

morbific matter Infected matter, poison.

august Noble, distinguished.

premonitory Warning.

Newton or Faraday Sir Isaac Newton (1642–1727). Great English mathematician and scientist. Michael Faraday (1791–1867). Distinguished English natural philosopher, chemist and electrician.

Bengal Club Cup, Planters' Handicap Horse races.

When you inhale the poison The remainder of this section contains numerous technical terms of the day which are of little significance to us now. Individual notes on each of these are not necessary to an overall understanding of the argument.

leeches Blood-sucking creatures much used in early medicine for bleeding.

lugubrious Gloomy.

infusoria Minute organisms which breed rapidly on stagnant matter (here, people's minds unused to activity).

lassitude Weariness.

pulmonary Of the lungs.

Chapter 26

In the Collector's absence, the Magistrate decides on an auction as the best means of distributing the stocks of food which have built up as their owners have died. During the auction, it emerges that a number of the bidders have been standing proxy for Mr Rayne, who has hitherto been in charge of the stores: it is his intention to resell at a profit. The Collector returns and is shocked by Rayne's behaviour. He cancels the auction and orders the food to be shared equally among the besieged.

Following the auction, Dr Dunstaple returns to his medical feud with Dr McNab; the battle highlights the chasm between reason and prejudice, science and bigotry. The audience, however, would seem to be on the side of prejudice. As a final gesture, Dr Dunstaple drinks a quantity of clear fluid, pronounced deadly by Dr McNab, as proof of his infallibility.

expiate Make good.

radical Thorough-going, reforming.

1832 The date of the Reform Bill which, to the great disappointment of those who shared the Magistrate's views, gave the vote only to the middle classes.

Chartism Reform movement of 1837–48. The name is taken from the manifesto 'People's Charter'.

gavel Auctioneer's hammer.

abashed Downcast.

ceded Gave up.

aria Long accompanied song for one voice in an opera.

podium Raised platform from which to speak.

saline Salt.

privies Lavatories.

adjudicating Judging.

ingest Take in.

cerebral Of the brain.

visceral Relating to inward feelings; i.e. though Fleury saw the reason behind Dr McNab's arguments, he was inclined to believe Dr Dunstaple because of the physical discomforts he was currently suffering.

alpaca A type of wool which comes from the South American llama.

Chapter 27

Food and ammunition are now desperately short. The behaviour of those trapped in the Residency becomes increasingly primitive, reason loses its power. Even Chloë, the beautiful spaniel, is behaving like the pariah dogs. Note how the animals have reflected human reactions throughout the novel. Dr Dunstaple contracts cholera, and reveals that what he drank was harmless water. By so doing he exposes himself as a fraud while at the same time accusing Dr McNab of fraudulance. Despite her father's orders to the contrary, Louise pleads twice for Dr McNab's help, and Dr Dunstaple revives. Once conscious, he flies into a rage and rejects the treatment that is saving him. Shortly afterwards Dr Dunstaple dies – of a heart attack.

Despite all evidence to the contrary Dr McNab's methods are still frowned upon by the people in the camp.

obtuse Stupid.

mange Skin disease found in dogs.

like a trout in a restaurant tank Some restaurants keep live fish so that they are fresh and can be selected by the customer. The fish image is continued to the end of the paragraph.

Chloë The beautiful dog originally valued by Fleury for purely decorative reasons. When she reverts to her 'natural' state he has her shot. Farrell's use of animals throughout is finely ironic at the expense of the humans.

How strange it is ... poetic thoughts In this paragraph is a statement of one of the major themes underlying all Farrell's work. Fleury feels ashamed of his 'lapse into sensitivity', while this is clearly the novelist's own view of life.

composing drought A sedative drink.

imperceptibly So slowly it cannot be noticed.

Revision questions on Part 3

1 Why does the Collector imprison Hari and later release him?

2 'Even in his fever the Collector's amputated hopes and beliefs continued to itch.' What does this mean and what does it tell us of the development of the Collector's character?

3 What is the effect of the rains on the siege?

4 Note the stages in the development of the episode of the flying cockchafers and show how the comedy is achieved.

5 What conclusions is the reader to draw about human nature from the auction of provisions?

6 What is the significance of the death of Chloë?

Part 4

Chapter 28

The rains stop. The spectators return. As the garrison is increasingly tormented by disease and starvation, so its obsession with food grows. Louise's birthday is a sad affair, with her loose teeth making it almost impossible for her to eat Fleury's rock-hard cakes.

debilitated Weakened.

executors Those appointed to ensure that the terms of a will are carried out.

to lend substance ... arrangement To make this vague arrangement seem more likely to come about.

in the wake of Behind.

scurvy A disease caused by a lack of vitamin C, which is found in fresh fruit and vegetables.

Chapter 29

The sepoys prepare for their final, massive attack; their main ammunition store is just beyond the range of Harry's cannon. The Collector plans the garrison's defence, and arranges to blow up all survivors in the event of defeat. The Padre conducts a last service; again the Collector's mind wanders. Even he is reduced to eating a large, black beetle.

Islam The Muslim faith.

magazine Ammunition and gunpowder store.

gentlemen now ... not here A near-quotation from Shakespeare's *Henry V*, IV,3, when Henry encourages his troops before Agincourt: 'And gentlemen in England, now abed,/Shall think themselves accursed they were not here.'

He urged the garrison ... den of lions Three bible stories in which the weak conquer the strong.

brunt Main force.

Veneration Deep respect.

Credulity Excessive willingness to believe.

mercantile Business.

Chapter 30

The day of the final attack dawns. Fleury and the Collector arm themselves with pistols. The Collector gives the order to fire prematurely and the sepoys burst through; the defenders are forced to retreat into and through the Residency buildings. Throughout the withdrawal, each room is the scene of bloody battles. Fleury's pistol jams and he is so absorbed in releasing it that he misses the signals to retreat. There follows another splendid example of the fine line Farrell draws between horror and farce in his description of Fleury's ferocious – and comic – battle with a sepoy.

When all seems lost there is an enormous explosion. Harry has succeeded in destroying the sepoy ammunition store.

He remembered how ... a reprieve to Note the heavy irony in the use of the word 'innocently' in connection with blowing human beings to pieces.

hosiery shop One which sells socks, stockings etc.

ellipse Oval.

impetus Force.

muezzin The caller of Muslims to prayer – usually from a minaret.

salvo Several shots fired together.

optimum Greatest, best.

just as he was leaving ... so much about the sepoys The Collector is almost destroyed by the principal symbol of British patriotism and duty: the flag.

contingency Possibility.

in concert All together.

ravening Desperately hungry.

anthracite Non-bituminous variety of coal which glistens.

carnal Of bodies.

patchouli A perfumed oil from an East Indian plant.

Boney Nickname of Napoleon Bonaparte (1769–1821). Emperor of France.

elevation The angle at which a gun is fired according to the distance required.

Chapter 31

The Collector moves among the survivors in the Banqueting Hall. Their condition is appalling, yet each one of them, with the exception of the Padre and Miriam, has acquired a new set of values as a result of their experience; some have even undergone a change of personality.

A young British officer arrives unexpectedly to inform them that they are to be relieved. The siege is over. The officer turns out to be one of Louise's old admirers, but now his ardour is somewhat dampened: Louise, like everyone else in the garrison, smells abominably! The General at the head of the relieving force is equally taken aback by this ragged, filthy crowd of evil-smelling oddities – how on earth could the British allow themselves to get into such a state? He is consoled by the vision of himself prominently placed in the foreground of the inevitable commemorative painting of the siege of Krishnapur.

gothic Usually of architecture, this style was prevalent in churches etc. from the 12th–16th centuries and favoured pointed arches. The term can also be applied to furniture and literature (the gothic novels of the 18th and 19th centuries).

Jesuits An order of Catholic priests.

feudal retainers Servants attached to medieval households.

Saxon thanes Nobility of one of the races which conquered early England.

trenchers Large dishes.

Vanity Fair A novel by William Makepeace Thackeray (1811–63).

innocuous Harmless.

gutta-percha A substance like hard rubber.

ensigns Junior officers.

chains ... shackles The apparatus used on negro slaves.

embrace this conviction Hold this belief.

apotheosis Highest glorification.

taken its toll of the billiard room i.e. many of the ladies who had occupied the billiard room had died of cholera.

anaemic-looking As if she had too little blood.

stucco Type of rendering plastered onto the walls of buildings.

mandrels Cylindrical rods around which the paper is shaped.

Lucy's grease ... with pleasure See 'Indian Mutiny' in the section on 'Background'.

ballistic Relating to bullets, shells, cannon balls etc.

locks i.e. of hair.

effects Possessions of a dead person.

popish A derogatory term for Catholic.

Tractarian Anglican, of the Church of England.

Voltaire Jean François Marie Arouet de Voltaire (1694–1778). French sceptic, dramatist and historian. The irony here is that supposedly 'good' objects relating to art and religion have proved adequately destructive, whereas the head of a worldly cynic has refused to be so used.

Saint Sebastian A captain in the praetorian guard and a Christian. He was said to favour Christians and Diocletian ordered his execution. But the archers did not quite kill him and he was nursed back to life. When he upbraided Diocletian for his cruelty, the latter had him beaten to death with rods. He died in AD 288.

I'm referring to a leading article ... as wise as God himself The Padre is arguing that any departure from a belief in the total truth of the account of Man's creation and Fall as found in Genesis in the Bible is a sin and bound to bring disaster to men.

Beelzebub One of the fallen angels; a devil inhabiting Hell.

Baal ... Mammon The first is a false god, the second came to personify the evils of wealth and miserliness.

circumspectly Cautiously.

invested Besieged.

pandies Nicknames for sepoy mutineers (see section on 'Background').

Bahadur A title of respect, here attached to the name of the British East
  India Company.

two giant white faces i.e. the statues of Plato and Aristotle.

untouchables The lowest caste in India.

predicated Based.

emaciated Terribly thin, wasted.

sherry pawnee Sherry and water, or soda.

given the soft pedal Played down, treated without fuss.

Chapter 32

As the Collector crosses the Krishnapur plain for the last time he sees
the two men with the bullock carrying out their eternal task of drawing
water. We saw them first at the beginning of the book; and it is an
image the Collector will always carry with him.

  Life goes on for the survivors of the siege. Some return to England,
others remain in India. The Collector, back in London, is a silent
spectator of the general scene: he sees no point in exerting himself any
further. Fleury is now married to Louise, Harry to Lucy and Miriam
to Dr McNab. Years afterwards the Collector meets Fleury in London.
Theirs might have been an interesting talk but Fleury is obviously
impatient to be gone. Fleury, the man of high ideals – and given to
forcing them on his children – hurries off to meet his mistress.

Crossing for the last time ... on the ground Man and his affairs are
  dwarfed to insignificance by Nature.

hector To bully.

Culture is a sham ... its ugliness. There is no irony here. This belief is
  the underlying message of the novel.

ideas These have been shown throughout to be more destructive and
  deceiving than anything else. They get between people and reality.

Revision questions on Part 4

1 Which details most powerfully convey the depths to which the
besieged garrison has sunk? How is contrast used to heighten this
effect, particularly in Chapters 28 and 29?

2 By what means is the suspense built up towards the final attack?

3 The account of the battle (Fleury and the sepoy included) becomes more and more improbable. In what ways does it resemble popular cartoon films?

4 What evidence is there that some characters appearing in Chapter 31 have undergone change in the course of the novel and others none at all?

5 What dramatic effect does the author achieve in suddenly shifting the viewpoint from the besieged to two members of the relieving force, Lieutenant Stapleton and the General?

6 In what ways could it be said that Fleury and the Collector have changed places by the end of the novel?

General questions

1 The book begins with a description of a deserted cemetery. Why do you think Farrell introduces his book in this way?

2 Though he has seven children the Collector has not made a will. What does this tell us about him?

3 What does their attitude towards dogs tell us about the British?

4 'What could be easier to change than an idea?' This is the Collector's belief at the beginning of *The Siege of Krishnapur*. How is this idea related to the theme of the novel?

5 In what ways is Miriam different from all the other women?

6 'The foundations on which the new men will build their lives are Truth, Science, Respectability, Geology, Mechanical Invention, Ventilation and Rotation of crops!' How does the Collector come to change his views?

7 'He can't see things from their point of view because he has no heart!' So says the Collector of the Magistrate. To what extent is this true but why also is it full of irony?

8 What significance do the machines and statues belonging to the Collector have to him and to the theme of the novel?

9 The deaths of people are often turned into comic episodes. By giving some examples, show why and how Farrell does this.

10 Giving examples, show what use Farrell makes of descriptions of clothing.

11 Describe four views of 'progress' as held by different characters in the book.

12 Topics of conversation are often in stark contrast to events taking place at that very moment. Find three examples and discuss their importance.

13 '. . . nobody is superior to anyone else, he only may be better at doing a specific thing.' So thinks Fleury during the first attack. Show how this thought is developed throughout the novel.

14 '... the other and atrocious inflexibility of all human habits and beliefs'. The Collector believes this to be the root of all conflict and misery. What evidence is there to suggest that this is what Farrell intends us to believe also?

15 'Ah, Mr Hopkins, the abuse of man's power of reason is the curse of our day.' In what ways do you consider this to be true in the light of what happens in the book?

16 'India itself was now a different place; the fiction of happy natives being led forward along the road to civilization could no longer be sustained.' Discuss.

Pan study aids

Henry Fielding Joseph Andrews

F. Scott Fitzgerald The Great Gatsby

E. M. Forster Howards End A Passage to India
Where Angels Fear to Tread

William Golding Lord of the Flies The Spire

Oliver Goldsmith Two Plays of Goldsmith: She Stoops to Conquer;
The Good Natured Man

Graham Greene Brighton Rock The Power and the Glory
The Quiet American

Thom Gunn and Ted Hughes Selected Poems

Thomas Hardy Chosen Poems of Thomas Hardy
Far from the Madding Crowd Jude the Obscure
The Mayor of Casterbridge Return of the Native
Tess of the d'Urbervilles The Trumpet-Major

L. P. Hartley The Go-Between The Shrimp and the Anemone

Joseph Heller Catch-22

Ernest Hemingway For Whom the Bell Tolls
The Old Man and the Sea

Barry Hines A Kestrel for a Knave

Gerard Manley Hopkins Poetry and Prose of Gerard Manley Hopkins

Aldous Huxley Brave New World

Henry James Washington Square

Ben Jonson The Alchemist Volpone

James Joyce A Portrait of the Artist as a Young Man

John Keats Selected Poems and Letters of John Keats

Ken Kesey One Flew over the Cuckoo's Nest

Rudyard Kipling Kim

D. H. Lawrence The Rainbow Selected Tales Sons and Lovers

Harper Lee To Kill a Mockingbird

Laurie Lee As I Walked out One Midsummer Morning
Cider With Rosie

Thomas Mann Death in Venice & Tonio Kröger

Christopher Marlowe Doctor Faustus Edward the Second

W. Somerset Maugham Of Human Bondage

Arthur Miller The Crucible Death of a Salesman

John Milton A Choice of Milton's Verse Comus and Samson Agonistes
Paradise Lost I, II

Sean O'Casey Juno and the Paycock

George Orwell Animal Farm 1984

John Osborne Luther

Alexander Pope Selected Poetry

Siegfried Sassoon Memoirs of a Fox-Hunting Man

Peter Shaffer The Royal Hunt of the Sun

William Shakespeare Antony and Cleopatra As You Like It
Coriolanus Hamlet Henry IV (Part I) Henry IV (Part II)
Henry V Julius Caesar King Lear King Richard III
Love's Labour's Lost Macbeth Measure for Measure
The Merchant of Venice A Midsummer Night's Dream
Much Ado about Nothing Othello Richard II Romeo and Juliet
The Sonnets The Taming of the Shrew The Tempest Twelfth Night
The Winter's Tale

G. B. Shaw Androcles and the Lion Arms and the Man
Caesar and Cleopatra The Doctor's Dilemma Pygmalion Saint Joan

Richard Sheridan Plays of Sheridan: The Rivals; The Critic;
The School for Scandal

John Steinbeck The Grapes of Wrath Of Mice and Men & The Pearl

Tom Stoppard Rosencrantz and Guildenstern are Dead

J. M. Synge The Playboy of the Western World

Jonathan Swift Gulliver's Travels

Alfred Tennyson Selected Poetry

William Thackeray Vanity Fair

Flora Thompson Lark Rise to Candleford

Dylan Thomas Under Milk Wood

Anthony Trollope Barchester Towers

Mark Twain Huckleberry Finn

Keith Waterhouse Billy Liar

Evelyn Waugh Decline and Fall Scoop

H. G. Wells The History of Mr Polly

John Webster The White Devil

Oscar Wilde The Importance of Being Earnest

Virginia Woolf To the Lighthouse

William Wordsworth The Prelude (Books 1, 2)

John Wyndham The Chrysalids

W. B. Yeats Selected Poetry

Australian titles

George Johnston My Brother Jack

Thomas Keneally The Chant of Jimmie Blacksmith

Ray Lawler Summer of the Seventeenth Doll

Henry Lawson The Bush Undertaker & Selected Short Stories

Ronald McKie The Mango Tree

Kenneth Slessor Selected Poems

Ralph Stow The Merry-Go-Round in the Sea   To the Islands

Patrick White The Tree of Man

David Williamson The Removalists

The Bellmakers

She hoped Ginnie would go on talking for she suddenly felt as if she could not think quite rationally or perceive the world beyond Ben Robertson. He was so close he took her breath, obscured her whole horizon – with his index finger making a hook for his jacket, his black and white striped shirt, grey braces and black Sunday trousers. He was so near she could even catch the aroma of shaving-soap, and the clean, cottony, flat-iron smell of his shirt – it seemed a poignant intimacy to her, making her realise how all these masculine things had disappeared from her home.

Jean Chapman can trace her family back to the 1700s and its roots are to be found within two miles of where she now lives with her husband, deep in the Leicestershire countryside. Her short stories have been published in a wide variety of markets and she has also published a number of novels, including *The Bellmakers, Fortune's Woman, A World Apart* and *The Red Pavilion*. Jean talks widely about her work and creative writing. She is an East Midlands Arts lecturer and tutor in adult education.

GU00371914

The
Bellmakers

Jean Chapman

Woman's Weekly Fiction

A Woman's Weekly Paperback
THE BELLMAKERS

First published in Great Britain 1990
by Judy Paitkus (Publishers) Ltd
This edition published 1995
by Woman's Weekly
in association with Mandarin Paperbacks
an imprint of Reed Consumer Books Limited
Michelin House, 81 Fulham Road, London SW3 6RB
and Auckland, Melbourne, Singapore and Toronto

Copyright © 1990 by Jean Chapman
The author has asserted her moral rights

A CIP catalogue record for this title
is available from the British Library
ISBN 1 86056 005 9

Printed and bound by
HarperCollins Manufacturing, Glasgow

Chapter One

The compartment had been empty when Leah had boarded the train, but at each village station more early morning workmen filled the long seats facing each other, settling themselves while the churns of morning milk for the city were loaded. There was mail and boxes of spring cabbage, parcels, and once a young collie dog, to be lifted into the care of the guard. Good will seemed to abound to match the brilliant May morning, greetings were exchanged — men greeting their fellows — men laughing.

Leah supposed on market-days it would be different. Then the women would be travelling early, to sell and buy in the town, but on a Monday their tasks were in the home. She remembered her grandmother's sombre words of the night before, that it was a "man's job" Leah would be attempting. So it was, but what choice did she have? There they were, three women without a man between them – and a living to make. The quicker she became used to moving in a man's world, the easier she would feel.

Peering from the window at the station's flowerbeds, bright with red tulips and awash with the powder-blue of forget-me-nots, she was aware that several older men hesitated about entering the same compartment as a young woman, but a younger man nudged his companion to draw attention to her. They laughed as their hands fell together on the thick brass handle. She felt they looked rather disconcerted, as they stepped up on to the running-board, to find that there were already five other workmen seated at the far side of the compartment. These men had all greeted Leah courteously,

1

then talked quietly among themselves. The newcomers were of different intent, and one obviously considered himself irresistible.

He sat directly opposite Leah, tipped his cap to a rakish angle and stared. She stared back, resisting the immediate feminine impulse to check that her thick dark hair, so difficult to manage, was still neatly rolled around its ribbon in an unbroken coronet.

She saw his gaze take in her blue cotton dress with white cuffs and collar, go down to her black-buttoned walking boots, and the soft black cambric sacks she had placed tight against her legs.

'What'yer selling?' he asked.

Leah was aware that the quiet conversation between the other men stumbled and failed as they too listened for her answer. She felt her colour rise, and tried to smother her indignation, running a disparaging glace over the questioner's darned and patched hand-me-down clothes, and boots home-cobbled with all the delicacy of the hoofs of a shire horse. 'if I thought you were buying, I might tell you!' she answered tartly.

'There's some things I'd buy at any price,' he quipped back, to the amusement of his companion — and some of the other men.

'Aye, and there's some things such as you could never afford,' she retorted, angrily aware that he represented the upper – respectable – end of poverty, to which she knew her own family were fast slipping, that frightening down-hill path she glimpsed ever more often. She turned her burning face towards the window, grateful to realise that her destination was the next stop.

'Oh, Miss Hoitytoity! You'll not sell much like that.'

One of the older workers remonstrated with the younger man. She turned to stare sightlessly at the passing countryside and clenched her teeth tightly against any further repartee, because she knew he was right. She had things to sell, and couldn't afford either too much in the way of pride or to take offence. She also had to remember that she might be travelling on this same train a month from today – if all went well.

She rose as the train drew into Kibbly Junction, aware that every eye in the compartment was focused on her as she let down the window, waited until the train stopped and then alighted, turning back to pull her bundles out after her. The young man forestalled her and with a little bow handed them out to her. She felt contrite, thought she must make amends, thank him, but as she looked up into his face, he touched his cap to her in mock salute.

'Good day to you, pedlar-girl'

He hung out of the window, laughing at her, as the train took up the pressure of steam again and lurched forward. She wasn't going to let him get away with that, and conveniently forgetting she was nearly twenty, stuck out her tongue as far as it would go –then noticed several workmen peering with fixed curiosity from other compartments as the train drew away.

Her composure shattered once more, she hurried along the platform, unceremoniously thrusting her ticket into the porter's hand, then out through the ticket-office into the sun beyond. Here she paused, resolving there had to be a fresh start made to this day. She would forget everything that had happened up to this moment . . .

'I'm seen those two black sacks afore!'

She swung round to see the railway porter, nodding towards her bundles, and still holding her solitary ticket.

'They used to come 'ere regular, I reckon. Belonged to Fred Dexter, him as sold his woollen underwear and stockings on the monthly. Been coming round for twenty years and more.'

'My grandfather,' she answered the phlegmatic porter.

'I 'eard he had died . . .' he said with ponderous slowness, still seeming to address the bags rather than Leah.

'At Michaelmas,' she told him. 'I'm taking on his round. Which way is it to Soston?'

He lifted a long thin arm, indicating the road to the right, and remained quite still reminding Leah of a finger-post dressed out by some joker in the dark navy serge of the Midland Railways livery. 'Just follow your nose,' he said, still pointing, and adding with awesomely slow wonder, 'Fancy! A lass taking on a tally-man's job.'

3

She walked quickly away, anxious to be on her own, feeling her self-confidence hung in tatters around her like an old coat, with barely enough left to cover her decently. She kept up the pace for some distance, then the solitude, the clamorous birdsong and the beauty of the morning, made her slow down, laugh at herself, look around.

The hedges were still festooned with heavy drops of dew, but the sun was high enough to use them as prisms, jewelling them with every colour found in palest sunrise to deepest sunset, and changing shades with every step she took. She breathed deeply of the scents of the hedgerow: the May blossom was just coming into full flower, its sweet scent heavy in the warming sun; occasionally she caught the sharper, but lighter fragrance of a lime tree; underlying, came the ditch-rank smell of cow-parsley.

It tied up in her mind with the smells that emanated from the poorest cottages, where any effort at respectable standards of cleanliness had been long abandoned, and the earthy sourness of the unwashed and unhopeful met any caller long before the door-knocker was grasped.

She recollected the ornate knockers, shaped like inverted-dolphins, on the great main doors of the town workhouse. These doors were thrown wide for the Union's governors, local dignitaries. The doors at either end, marked "Men" and "Women" were more reluctantly approached, more swiftly closed, and should perhaps have been more properly marked "The Destitute" and "the Despairing".

She trod more resolutely, ringing her heels as best she might in the grass-grown mound between the cart-ruts. No matter how many miles she had to trudge, whatever prejudices, she had to overcome, she meant to see that neither her mother nor her grandmother came to that "worse than death" end. She squared her shoulders, realigned the two bags, taking care with the balancing of them this time, and patted the deep pocket in her dress, checking that her Grandfather's tally-book and the indelible pencil were still safe. She came to a cross-roads where the wooden signpost indicated Soston downhill to her left.

Something about the black-painted lettering struck a cord of recognition. Leah pulled out the tally-book, full of strange,

4

semi-literate notes in her Grandfather's hand – the few words drawn rather than written – only the figures bold and clear, with a "d's" or an "s" before each amount owing. She opened the well-thumbed pages and there was the name "Soston". The large "S", made slightly ornate and backsloping by the signwriter, had been meticulously copied by her Grandfather. She swallowed, felt her lips tremble with tenderness for the old man who had for so long taken on the role of both parent and grandparent. Leah's only recollection of the word "father" was linked with walks to the village cemetery, putting flowers beneath an inscribed slate headstone. She disciplined her sense of loss into a new resolve as she set off down the hill, towards the small village – where the Dexter's first customer was indicated in the book by a drawing of a cottage with low thatch and beams in two curiously irregular 'Y' shapes.

Soston was a string of cottages down to a village green and a pond – then the lane climbed up the opposite hill to more cottages, a farm or two and a Norman church. She had passed and scrutinised several cottages before she realised how quiet the village was for a Monday morning. She listened for sounds of washday activities, but could hear nothing; no sound of punches being splotched in tubs of wet clothes, or of huge wooden mangle-rollers thudding back together, to the peril of unwary fingers.

Then, at the foot of the hill rising to the church, she saw the cottage with the Y-shaped beams. Her heart gave a lurch of anticipation as she prepared for her first encounter with a customer, a good customer if the amount owed meant anything. She checked in the book before going further: s2. d11. That was clear enough.

Her mother's mild comment that the debts had been let go on too many months for folks either to admit owing or to want to pay came to mind as she went slowly passed the double-fronted cottage. Pedlars and tinkers round the back, she told herself, and walked up the mossy cobbles at the side, around to the backdoor. This stood open, and obviously the family washing had been recently done for the paving slabs around the pump were wet and the red quarries in the kitchen still shone where they had been scrubbed. 'Anyone at home?' she called, and stood listening.

Long lines of linen was already billowing in the garden, and she walked a way up the garden path. 'Anyone about?' she called again, going further to where rougher items of clothing, corduroy trousers and farm smocks, had been thrown over the back hedge to dry. There was clearly no one within earshot.

A sense of frustration coupled with a new determination to find this missing customer took her to the next cottage, where her intrusion was greeted by the furious barking of a dog from an outhouse, but no one came to investigate.

It was as if everyone had been called suddenly away, leaving everything behind them – doors standing open, dogs abandoned. Monday morning wasn't a time when a whole village went off gallivanting! She wondered if there had been some terrible accident somewhere, or a fire, and they'd all gone to watch? Something like that affected the whole community, they would all be involved in a tragedy. She wandered back to the green, sniffing the air – there seemed no more smoke than she would expect, lingering from cottage fires that had boiled kettles and made breakfasts, and been damped down to cook dinners later.

As she walked on, through the village, she stopped to listen — she could here something — it seemed to be coming from the church. All she could see of the building as she approached because of the unusually high wall around its churchyard was the tall square stone tower, but even from a distance she could see great beams seemed to have been braced through the top louvres on either side of the turreted tower. The noise resolved itself into many voices: a loud babble of conversation, rising and falling in pitches of interest and excitement. It became increasingly obvious that the entire population of Soston had gathered there for some momentous occasion. She found herself hurrying to the gateway.

The crowd was gathered around the west front of the church tower, looking up to where, on the side facing Leah, a construction like the top of a massive gallows protruded from the louvres of the tower.

6

'She won't be long now!'an old man declared. 'We'll soon see 'er'.

'Who are you waiting for?' Leah asked him.

He turned and regarded her with eyes like dark marbles, the pupils wide-ringed with the white of age, and seemed to view her appearance with great suspicion. 'Where'm you sprung from?' he asked.

'I've come to see Mr Fred Dexter's customers, he was my grandfather, come to collect some money that's owing and to sell more of our wares,' she told him. But before she could ask him anything further, he declared; 'Don't reckon you'm chosen a good day,' and turned his attention back to the tower.

'Why not?' she asked. 'What's happening?'

'T'aint the day for a strange young wumman to arrive, that's all.'

'Tek no notice,' a buxom young matron, balancing a baby in one arm and a toddler on her opposite hip, told her. 'Elijah by name and Elijah by nature, 'e is – full of old tales.' Leah thought her strong red arms and hands certainly looked as if they had been immersed in the weekly wash-water, but her clothes and those of her children looked as if they should have been included in the routine.

'T'aint no tale, neither!' the old man retaliated. 'But you'll see, soon enough, Bessie Yarrup, you'll see! And she'll wish she'd come nowhere near Soston the day the old Monk's Bell was brought out into God's light.'

'What's the Monk's Bell?' Leah asked.

The old man lifted a prophetic arm to the tower. 'It's been in that dark place for more than four 'undred year, keeping its curse to its'sen – but now . . .' He paused to grumble incoherently to himself, then went on, addressing Leah as if she had made some personal verbal attack on him, 'I'll tell you,' he said, 'I'll tell you! A young wumman – she suddenly appeared when that bell was cast at a monastery, as all God's bells used to be. And she warn't no better than she ought to be!' He paused to glare at both the young women, as if he included both of them in the same class. 'The bell-founder, he saw the wumman in that place – where she had no business to be – watching, right at the moment the bell was drawn from

7

off its core – and that monk, he declared the bell cursed and had it thrown outside the monastery grounds – and the wumman out of the parish.'

'And some men gathered it up, cursed or not, and put it into a church . . .'

He ignored Leah's comment and issued a last dire warning before moving away, 'Ah, you wait – wait till they all read the inscription on the Monk's Bell . . .'

'You doing the round, then?' Bessie asked, nodding at the ware-sacks. Leah saw an acquisitive look in the woman's eye, but before their conversation could go any further a sudden gasp, and a concerted upturning of everyone's eyes, diverted them.

Shading her eyes from the sun climbing at the far side of the tower, Leah could make out a young man in shirt sleeves, leaning far out, then edging along the top of the main beam to adjust the chains around a kind of double pulley system on the end. It seemed a precarious and foolhardy act, but the young man's movements were confident and athletic, and from his length measured along the beam he was tall and well-made. The older of several men standing on the ground at the base of the tower shouted up to him, but he waved aside the warning.

There were more shouts, orders, and two workmen at the bottom of the scaffolding took up the slack on one set of chains. 'Slowly, slowly – quarter of an inch at a time,' the young man shouted from the tower, and infinitely slowly there emerged from between the open louvres the outline of a great bell. The crowd gasped, every glance fixed as it was drawn slowly into view from the shadow of the church. All were somewhat awed by its size, its rim only just passing between the twin-arched louvre. The central oak beam creaked in protest as the bell was fully pulled out, where it hung, swaying a little, slightly sinister in its dusty, dark age as it hung above the crowd.

'The Monk's Bell – there y'are – very nearly a ton of it!'

Leah recognised the old man's voice again somewhere nearby. At the same moment her foot twisted under her as she stepped back to see better. Limping, she found what she had fallen over was the clapper of the bell, a piece of metal like a great thistle-head on a staff some four feet long.

Testing her ankle gingerly along the grass behind the crowd, she heard more about the village event.

'Tis good riddance to that old bell. It's allus been odd-struck. It's made every telling of a death, and every Pancake Day sound cracked.'

'They reckon as how they panelled the inside of the tower so the light shouldn't get up to that old bell.'

'Taking one down to put up six. Seems daft to me!'

'Good business for the bellmakers!'

The crowd were good humoured, and gave the two young men a bit of a cheer as they emerged from the church door, to help with the final lowering to the ground of the bell. Everyone was kept back until the bell finally rested on the grass, and she heard several already trying to read the inscription, with words like "curse" and "evil" being triumphantly read and repeated. Leah too dropped her sacks near the base of a thorny Judas tree and pressed forward. 'Why, tis just words scratched in the bell, not a proper inscription at all,' Bessie Yarrup declared as she established herself and her babes on the front rank.

'Had to be. The bell was cast before the monk saw that terrible wumman! It had to be scratched on.'

'That's right, Elijah, you tell'em!' there was a lot of laughter, above which Elijah shouted, 'you read 'un then! You read 'un.'

There was some muttering and sidling of heads to bring into focus the deeply etched letters which as far as Leah could see ran all around the bell's rim. She had just pushed her way in against her acquaintance's side when Bessie announced, 'Here's the start,' and begun with much labouring to read the old fashioned script. "Cursed I be and cursed I stay . . ." Then she couldn't read further from where she stood, and a man a little further round took up the quotation, repeating, ". . . and cursed I stay . . . N'er let me see the light of day." Elijah, with dire and ponderous tone, and much head nodding, took up the third section, "Cursed in bright May by eye of wumman. . .' And the tall young man from the tower finished the text, "Evil powers release them that ME again summon.'

9

'Reckon that's you and me done for then, Ben Robertson,' the younger of the two said cheerfully, and Leah found herself eagerly storing the knowledge of his name.

'Aye, and prophecy is being fulfilled, – 'tis May!' Elijah shouted excitedly.

'No one's denying that, old man.'

'And we have the eyes of a strange wumman on the old Monk's Bell again!'

This last did give rise to some consternation as Elijah's gaze picked out Leah. She looked over the shoulder-high bell first at the old man, then at Ben Robertson.

It was the first time most of the villagers had noticed there was another stranger in their midst – the men from the bellmakers had seemed excitement enough – but now there were whispered questions, and people around her stepped back. Leah's lips parted in consternation as she found herself the centre of superstitious scrutiny, suddenly isolated by their hostility. She remembered old stories of women burnt as witches, screaming their innocence, and of local "wise women" revered when they achieved a cure – dammed, cursed, and sometimes, to her own knowledge, driven from their homes if events took a turn for the worse.

It was as if the same thoughts were in many minds, and the crowd ebbed away from her a little more, beaching her on their distrust, good humour gone, silently surveying the stranger – all except Bessie Yarrup. She suddenly screamed out with laughter, startling the crowd and her babies. 'She's come curse you alright!' she shouted above the wails of her offspring, 'She's the old tallyman's granddaughter, come to collect your dues for your stockings and your combinations – them as some o'you thought you were getting away with!'

It took a moment for the woman's words to register, then there were one or two shame-faced glances at Leah, one or two laughed or humphed their astonishment or displeasure. The moment was over but the chill remained with Leah. She wanted away from the place, away from Elijah and the Monk's Bell. She raised her chin and her eyes met those of both men and women prejudiced against her honest intentions. She tossed her head a little higher and addressed them all, 'Yes, look out your purses and your money-stockings,

10

I've debts to collect, and goods to sell.' She met Ben Robertson's searching gaze and felt her colour mounting; she could have wished he might have seen her other than as a pedlar-girl.

Bessie Yarrup's raucous laughter at the crowd's expense, and Leah's announcement, seemed to turn passive, superstitious animosity into active prejudice. 'A girl like that – collecting!' Those who did not pass comment registered varying shades of displeasure on their faces.

Ben Robertson raised a quizzical, sympathetic eyebrow, as if he too knew what it was never to please. Then, as if to divert further unwelcome attention from her, he suddenly raised a sledgehammer above his head, crying out, 'Make way! Stand clear!' There were immediate cries of protect. Some were still pressing forward to read the inscription for themselves. She heard the old man, Elijah, querulously complain the bell shouldn't be broken up in a churchyard, a holy place.

'Easier to move in pieces,' Ben added uncompromisingly. 'It has to be melted down to go in the new ring of bells.'

'Yer – what's it matter where it's done?' Bessie actively supported.

'You've never bothered about that, have you, Bessie?' a voice called from the back of the crowd.

'I've never bothered about you, Fred Downes, that's f'sure!' Bessie retorted 'Got you salted years ago.'

There was much laughter as Bessie correctly identified the wit, but just as the good humour of the occasion seemed restored, there was an impatient shout from inside the tower.

'Ben! Nat! Get over here to these beams and chains. Let's get finished.'

'Come on, Ben, the old man won't stand for any messing about, 'the shorter of the two advised.

'Right!' Ben agreed. 'But we'll just make a first break in this old monk's curse.'

He stretched himself up, poised the hammer at the zenith of his height and strength, stood motionless for a few seconds as the last of the circle of villagers hastily pulled back out of range, then brought the hammer down with all his strength, aiming at the base of the bell where the circled inscription ran.

11

The blow fell and the bell rang out for a last time. It was a strange and awesome sound, reminding Leah of the rending, like pain, as a great tree falls – but this was a deeper note, forced down under the grass-muted rim. Like a new curse, she thought, expressed deep under the earth, vibrating under the churchyard. She had the strangest sensation – a premonition perhaps – and shuddered involuntarily, reminded of the old saying about someone walking over her grave.

Then a piece like a great bite fell away from the bell, the moment was past, and the morning's drama seemed played out. The villagers began to disperse and Leah looked to express her gratitude to Ben Robertson, but a further impatient bellow from the inside of the tower had Nat again urging his brother away.

Leah left the churchyard with Bessie, who stayed close, enquiring if she had any boys' stocking in her bags. She found herself expressing her gratitude for the woman's support, with three pairs of boys' stockings taken from her sacks for a mere half-penny deposit. Bessie had gone home clutching her wares as if they were trophies of war, leaving Leah with the uneasy feeling that the collection of that new debt might take a long time.

She returned to the house with the beams, where she was met by an unsmiling buxom woman who, after handing her two pennies, folded her arms across her sacking apron and told her they wouldn't be buying any more clothes now Mr Fred Dexter wouldn't be calling. Leah resisted the urge to make an apology because her grandfather had been inconsiderate enough to die. Instead, she assumed a stony-faced neutrality to counter the woman's aggressiveness, and replied that she would be along in a month's time "as usual" for a further instalment — and there would be more choice in her sacks if anyone cared to look.

Chapter Two

Leah left Soston having collected two and a half pence, and
parted with goods worth two shillings and three pence. The
only other house she had been able to identify from the tally-
book had been a house with a pump in the middle of the front
garden – and though the area round the pump was still wet,
and smoke drifted from the chimney, no one came to the
door. She wondered if her public announcement in the
churchyard had given this debtor time to go to earth.

The next entry of s1. d9. was after a line drawn under
"Soston" and before the next village of "Unthorpe". What
looked like a rotten row of teeth, with a knobbly stick poised
almost threateningly above, was her grandfather's identification of this customer. She laughed aloud when on an isolated
stretch of road she came to an old house, with a row of
stones set brokenly about the front door – the pattern
unmistakable.

This time she resolved the woman of the house would look
at her goods whether she wanted or not – and took time to
untie the necks of the cambric sacks and roll them down to
display the woollen garments before she knocked on the
door.

A child was crying inside, and something was either
dropped or thrown down. The door opened a crack and Leah
saw first a thin, bare-footed child in a little ragged shift. The
child's eyes were surrounded by clean circles where fresh
tears had bathed the dirty skin.

Leah looked up to see a woman, barely more than a girl
herself, with another baby in her arms. Her dark hair hung

13

lank around her shoulders, her hazel eyes were sunken in dark sockets, and on one side of her forehead was an angry bruise. Before Leah could speak the girl shook her head at her anxiously, attempting to shepherd the visitor back off the doorstep and pull the door closed behind them.

'Not today,' she whispered, ''e's drinking.'

Such was the urgency in the girl's voice that Leah stooped immediately to retrieve her bags, but she had barely bent down when the door was violently wrenched open, making the woman stumble, while the child who was leaning on her mother's legs fell down heavily. Leah half expected tears again, but instead the mite scuttled and scrabbled like a frightened rain-beetle to save itself from the threat of the man who now stood on the doorstep.

There was a timelessness about the hatred and the bitterness on this man's face, though she guessed he would be still in his twenties. Unwashed, unshaven, in filthy trousers and vest, he swung his arm in more swipe than gesture. 'Ger inside!' he growled. Keeping her eyelids lowered as if to conceal her feelings, the woman retreated into the stark stone-flagged interior with their children.

The man stood, swaying slightly, taking in the woollen garments, and looking Leah up and down. 'I do the buying in this 'ouse,' he said with a leer, 'you have to deal with me.'

'You always do the buying, do you?' She tried to sound casual as she pulled one of the sacks back from the step, so she could repack and still keep an eye on him.

'Called 'ere before?' he demanded, as if suddenly spotting a trap in this conversation. 'Well 'ave you?'

'No,' she replied, but straightening herself up she noticed the vest he was wearing had the bone buttons sewn on in her family's distinctive manner both crossing and taken around the four holes, so the pattern of the cotton resembled a tiny flag. The amount owing also exactly tallied with the cost of such a man's long-sleeved, button-necked vest.

'She don't owe you anything then, so you needn't come agen.' She saw the crafty look of triumph on his face.

'She couldn't if you do the buying,' she replied carefully, 'could she?'

14

'And if you've never been before . . .' he sneered, not bothering even to look at her face, his gaze fixed on her breasts so she felt dirtied, devoured – infuriated.

'No, but my grandfather sold you that vest you are wearing, and for which you owe one shilling and ninepence. I'd be glad to have something on account.' She feigned a businesslike manner, and produced the tally-book from her pocket.

For a moment, from the sudden fury on his face and the way he lunged forward, she thought he was going to strike her. Instead he swept the account book from her hand, and rifling through the pages, first looked surprised then began to laugh. His laughter becoming more and more obscene as he went from page to page, pointing at her grandfather's drawings.

'Oooh, you'll collect a lot from this! A tallyman who couldn't read and write! All these years and nobody guessed!'

He began tearing the pages from the book and throwing them about. Leah flew at him. 'You stop that!' It's not yours! Even the vest you're wearing's not yours!'

'Prove it! Prove it!' His laughter was maniacal as he teased the book in front of her face. Leah had a glimpse of the woman behind her husband as she jumped to try to retrieve her book. He pushed her away, his hand deliberately falling on one of her breasts. He was mocking her startled exclamation as the door opened wide behind him and his wife came out, holding something in both hands. Before Leah had time to understand what she was about, she brought down the heavy leg of a stool on the back of her husband's head. He fell as if poleaxed. The child emerged again and stood by her mother's side, with a look of some relief on her face.

The two women stood either side of the fallen man, Leah holding her breath, until a sound, half groan, half snore, gently erupted from his lips.

'What will you do?' Leah asked.

'Pour some more beer down his throat, and tell 'im he fell.' She held out her hand and Leah saw she held a penny.

'It's all right,' Leah began, but the woman's face hardened and she pushed the coin at her again. 'I had it put by for the tallyman,' she said, with a glimmer of pride in her achievement.

15

'Thank you. I'll put it down to you.' she scooped up the book and began to collect the scattered pages.

'You coming agen, regular, like the old man? Today month, I'll be walking along the road towards Unthorpe. That's what I allus used to do.'

Leah nodded, then for a moment they both stood regarding her unconscious husband. 'I've done it once before,' the woman commented. The small girl held up another page from the book. Leah took it gently. 'Thank you,' she said, and meeting the mother's eyes shared with her a mutual feeling of hopeless frustration about all their futures. What could she do to help? What could women do to help themselves? Without speaking again, the woman nodded, took the child's hand and went inside.

Leah walked on, angry that she had been the cause of such violence, resenting her own lack of knowledge. If she had been a boy, she would have known all about the customers – where to call and where not to – and there would have been no gap in the service. It would have been an automatic take-over of responsibility within the family.

She had hero-worshipped her grandfather, had dogged his every activity from the time she had taken her first step – and he had stitched her first soft pair of walking boots. She had begged, times out of mind, to be allowed to go with him on the train. They had all laughed at her precociousness.

Instead she had been taught how to pick up and splice stitches, seam stockings and under-garments – skills she found difficult to find patience for. She remembered in the early days of her apprenticeship throwing down the stock-inger's mending-hook and needle, declaring that if she'd got to stitch anything she'd rather be a milliner and make pretty hats for church and chapel, hats for weddings – with ribbons all the colour of the rainbow. She sighed, as she climbed the hill towards her next calls – to think she had ever been that innocently rebellious!

The sun was well past mid-day when she rested, to unwrap her cloth of bread and cheese on a pleasant grassy bank where a few late primroses still bloomed. She had a farthing short of two shillings in her money-bag, sore feet and bruised pride.

16

It had not come easy having to push to show her wares; having to stand stolidly on doorsteps; having to prove her identity, displaying her grandfather's figures in the tally-book – careful now to hide the fact that there were no names, only drawings, to identify the debtors.

Few who owed money were pleased to see her, that was for sure, though she felt sympathy for the women who were genuinely fussed by her arrival, and their inability to pay anything. 'Didn't expect you, see.'

The words had become very familiar, as had the glances, both open and covert, which seemed to contrast her appearance with her calling. She realised now why her grandfather had always worn his working clothes, not, as she had done, neatest Sunday dress and decent boots. She had made the mistake of looking better off than her customers, which neither invited their sympathy nor their pennies. Though if she had been a smart working-boy, she guessed, their reactions would have been very different – there might have been offers of drinks of new milk, or a slice from a pie. But the arrival of a girl was, as one woman put it, "Enough to flummoxed decent folk."

She had three more hours before she must complete the half circle of villages and end her day's travelling at another railway station on the same line. she stretched her legs and wriggled her cramped toes inside her boots, which were already showing the damaging effects of several hours' hard walking. If she took her train fare and her boots into consideration, she must so far be out of pocket.

Her greatest failure, she thought, was that apart from the stockings to Bessie Yarrup, she had only managed to place one garment, a pair of men's combinations. How to make people take garments they apparently did not want was a skill she had not yet acquired. The art of selling, of balancing supply and demand – she vaguely remembered hearing her grandfather and the other men talk of that in the stockingers' shop where many subjects, economics, politics, morality and religion, were aired in their turn. She had not been interested then. Her meal over, she rose and was struck by the sight of a young boy in a nearby field, being shown how to use a hoe to single out young turnip plants. The man watched him for a

17

few more minutes, then left him to work the huge field all by himself. He was clumsy and slow, and bent once to replace young plants he'd taken out by mistake. He saw her watching and she gave him a cheerful wave of encouragement. 'At least you had a little instruction' she breathed.

The boy in the field could not be more than nine years old. Her grandfather always said he began working at seven – helping to tend flocks of sheep, living out in the fields with his grandfather – and he had worked, with at least outward cheerfulness, until the day he died. Surely seventy years of hard work should have produced more than three women at the door of destitution? As the boy struggled in the field to come to terms with a man-sized hoe, so she tried to reconcile herself to the prospect of a life of lowly, unremitting work. There had to be a better way. All she needed was the idea. New ways of selling, perhaps? A way out of this spiral of work which, as far as she could see, was taking them downhill instead of up. She thought of the text, in red and black Gothic script, which hung above her mother's bed: "Labour and Do Not Seek for Any Reward". Who could believe such sanctimonious rubbish? she wondered. And how many large factory owners had such a sentiment framed above their beds?

For at least two miles she passed by the side of a high wall with herring-bone insets and elaborate coping, telling the boundary of the parkland to some great manor house. She also saw the many fences marked out for convenient jumping by the local hunt, the well-tended copses in great stretches of pasture. The lord of the manor would also be master of the hunt she guessed.

It was a surprise to come to the village in the middle of this affluent-looking countryside, and find it a poor place. The vicarage, church, and Elizabethan beamed house with the doctor's plate outside, looked well enough, but most of the cottages of Church Lacey needed much repair – sparse straw-thatch black with age, broken window glass so glued with paper as to admit little in the way of light. There was a general air of apathy in the many unscrubbed doorsteps and unswept yards, that even the sunny day could not lift. If the local squire owned this village, it seemed he was a selfish man, for it contrasted sharply with the boundaries of his personal interests, his land and the care taken in pursuit of his leisure activities.

She became aware of some activity at the far end of the village street, and as she drew nearer could see that a number of women, and one or two ancient men, were grouped around a cottage which seemed in danger of sliding backwards to final dereliction at any moment. Some were going inside then returning with odds and ends of household goods – pots, pans, a rush-bottomed chair – and pushing a few coppers into the hands of an old man who sat on an old millstone placed near the front door. Leah approached with some curiosity, but catching the word "Union" looked sharply at the rheumaticky hands and the two thick walking-sticks propped by the side of a frail old man who was obviously hardly able to walk – certainly not to work.

She faltered. The downcast eyes of the old man, the people obviously buying up his final few sticks of furniture and meagre cooking utensils, told that he had arrived at the end she so dreaded for her family. A cart approached from the far end of the village street, its funeral pace and the glances of the little crowd from it to the old man indicating that this was the vehicle which would take him away. "The last but one journey," she had often heard it called.

Another man, who must have been a contemporary, suddenly shuffled forward and took his friend's hands, 'Sorry you've come to such an end, Smiler. Pity your son was killed.' The old man looked up briefly, and their hard old hands clasped tight for a moment. He nodded, then let his head fall again. Leah felt tears prick her eyes, the old nickname so poignant, so inappropriate a reminder of youth and optimism.

This should not happen! Where was the milk of human kindness or God's mercy now? She wanted to shout out. Her anger must have been in her face for a woman next to her said, 'Ah! Nobody wants you when you can't work. Cowman for Squire Lacey for forty-two year – now he's out!' She paused, then gave an ironic laugh and jerked her thumb at the tumbledown cottage. 'Though what the new cowman and his family'll make of that when they arrive, I don't know!'

19

Squire Lacey . . . Leah had heard her grandfather talk of the family that had dominated the area since Norman times. Four villages commemorated their name – though little else did. The family had enclosed their land in the 1600s to breed huge flocks of sheep. Their serfs who had strip-farmed, paying their tithes in produce, were turned away – ridge and furrow showed where they had laboured, and the sites of deserted villages where they had lived.

The woman turned to regard Leah and her sacks with more interest. 'Who are you then?' When she explained, her inquisitor was suddenly inspired by an idea. 'Wait here,' she instructed, and quickly went from person to person and to the doors of several houses nearby, even stopping a passing doctor's trap. 'Conscience money,' she commented, adding, 'Come on, girl, spread your wares along the wall here.' A small crowd gathered to help choose a parting gift for the old man. Leah accepted a shilling for a long-sleeved vest.

The old man was helped painfully on to the back of the dray, and sat with his new woollen over his knees, a handkerchief full of possessions by his side, hands shaking uncontrollably as he clutched at his walking-sticks. Leah, overcome by concern, was shocked to hear a man behind her complain, 'I had to *carry* my old dad the eight miles to the workhouse – took us all day.'

As she turned sadly away, she was alerted to the fact that several people were still fingering her stock and sensed business. 'It's quality wool, guaranteed for wear. Just give me your name and address, and say how much you would like to put down as a first payment.

Interest seemed to pick up as she talked, so much so that she wondered if she wouldn't do better to arrange her stock in the middle of each village and invite customers. She collected another one shilling and sixpence in deposits, and left this village to make the final stage of her journey to the railway line, with at least her sacks much lighter.

'She's here, Nellie!'

Leah heard her grandmother's voice from behind the front parlour window as she wearily pushed her aching legs and sore feet the last few yards along the street, every cobble a torment. Before she had entered the arched brick entry running between the two cottages, she heard the kitchen door opened, and her mother and grandmother were there in the yard to welcome her home, full of questions and anxieties.

'You're tired out!' her mother exclaimed, hurrying her to the cane-bottomed rocking-chair by the table. 'Put your feet on the stool, I'll take your boots off.'

The tall figure of Miriam Dexter was already stooping to lift the great black kettle from the hob. Her face, bent to her task, was reserved, and private. Grief at losing her beloved Freddie had left her unbowed but a little detached from life, her greatest joy gone.

Leah wanted at first to protest at her mother's fussing, taking off her boots, but so profound was her exhaustion she just leaned back and inhaled the rich smell of one of their last precious pieces of home-cured ham gently frying on the far side of the fire, with cooked and refried potatoes to go with it. Tiny involuntary moans of pleasure escaped her lips as her mother began to massage her feet. She saw a faint smile like a fleeting memory cross her grandmother's face, and remembered how she had performed the same sympathetic service for Grandfather. Leah realised for the first time how much he must have appreciated the attention – and how much he had done to deserve it!

She took three sips of the reviving tea, then as her meal was served, and the older two women settled themselves on either side of the table, she related some of the events of her day. They listened intently, and Miriam murmured approval as she added, 'I'm going to make myself a diary so I know exactly where I should be going each Monday.'

'So you will go again?' her mother queried.

'The bags look a lot lighter,' Miriam commented, nodding at the two sacks abandoned just inside the up and over door-step.

'Yes' Leah felt cheered as she thought of the new customers she had found. 'I've not collected much on the old debts, but I've taken money on quite a few stockings and vests.' She reached down into her pocket and brought out the tally-book, pencil, and canvas money-bag. She tipped out the coins. Her

21

mother came to look, her grandmother to push them about, separating farthings, halfpennies, pennies, a couple of silver threepenny pieces and one sixpenny piece. Then Miriam counted it, 'Well,' she decided, 'it's five shillings, one penny three-farthings more than we had this morning.'

'God be thanked,' her mother said.

But Leah was aware of some want of enthusiasm as her grandmother lifted the limp ware-sacks to one end of the table and spread out what there was left. Two pairs of long woollen hose, three long-sleeved men's vests, two pairs of men's combinations.

'I know Grandpa collected much more, but . . .'

There was a knock at the door, then the latch was lifted and they heard the voice of Sam Elliott, a contemporary of her grandfather's and now their solitary employee, who took the adjoining cottage as part of his wages.

'He's come to see how you've got on,' Nellie told her daughter cheerfully, but Leah was watching her grandmother's face. Something was amiss, she suspected, and as Sam's glance went from the money on one end of the table, to the goods on the other, her suspicion was confirmed.

'What have I done wrong?' she asked quietly. Her mother looked as puzzled as she felt, but Sam and Miriam obviously knew.

'Looks to me as if you've not collected tithes,' Sam said, compressing the corners of his mouth into a grim downwards curve.

'Tithes?' she queried, but a suspicion of what he meant came coldly with the memory of the many goods put down in her tally-book after the old man's garden wall had become a kind of stall – and after she had consulted her customers as to how much they would like to put down as a first payment. Many had gone away grinning, seeming scarcely able to believe their good fortune.

'A tenth of the price, to be put down as first payment – folks as can't afford that usually can't afford to buy anything,' Sam said bluntly, sticking his thumbs into his waistcoat pocket and letting his fingers hang like tools from a rack.

'But no one told me,' she protested, feeling her colour rising, and panic threatening to overtake her, as she wondered if she hadn't made the family finances worse rather than better.

'No one had a lot of time to,' Sam answered.

Leah heard her mother protesting on her behalf, but it was true – she had certainly mulled over the idea of going on the tally-round, but had told no one until late the night before, and made sure the discussion had been confined to the females of the Dexter household. Sam and Clarrie Elliott next door had not been consulted, though they had been part of the Dexter Yard stockingers for as long as Leah could remember.

She tried not to but she resented Sam Elliott and the easy way he had always walked in and out of their home – she would have liked to have seen a little more propriety in his manner – and he in turn, until her grandfather's death, had exposed her wish for more deference as he greeted her arrival in the knitting-shop with an ironical, 'Hey-up! Here's gaffer's granddaughter.'

She regarded him now and let out a hearty sigh, full of her sense of failure. So much effort put into what was fast being revealed as a disaster. But for once the cynical look was missing from his eyes. 'You did your best,' he said. This was highest praise from Sam, and she must have looked startled, for he tempered it by adding, 'As well as you knew how to.'

Chapter Three

The round of work at the stockinger's shop came in seasonal rushes, usually picking up at Whitsuntide, after the post-Christmas slump. This year the expected upturn in business had not come.

Leah felt they were pinned down – like an adder she had seen caught, held by its head in a cleft stick, helpless. Their willingness, their freedom, to work was just as effectively curtailed by the town manufactories. At the slightest dropping off of demand, supplies of wool to the independent stockingers ceased. This, even though the town factory owners paid lower rates for the work produced by the small, self-employed "bag-hosiers".

'If you rely on a capitalist for your raw material, you're his man whether you like it or not. And if you're any sort of a small craftsman, that's worse still,' Sam philosophised as Leah watched him make up the last cone of wool on the loom.

'You're at the bottom of the pile, and everybody stands on your shoulders, exploits your wares.'

'That's not true if you sell directly to your customers on the tally-book,' she reminded him. He laughed loudly, and she hoped he wasn't going to refer to her failure to collect good deposits.

'Well, profit's always good when you don't pay for your wool.' He paused to look at her, adding, as he shook his head at her, 'You really don't know what I'm talking about, do you?'

She shook her head, mystified and apprehensive.

'Where do you think we get the wool from to knit up the garments for the round?'

'I thought we bought it from the factory . . .' she began. But seeing the look on his face, she asked fearfully, 'We don't steal it, do we?'

He laughed longer this time, then he paused to consider before answering, 'Well, yes, we do in a way – but only in the same way as any other stockinger trying to keep body and soul together. Come on, you're gaffer's granddaughter! Think what we do before we pack the stockings for the factory . . .'

Leah thought how the piles of stockings were spread out in serried ranks, and how either Sam or her grandfather would fill their mouths with water from a brown earthenware quart jug kept specially for the purpose. Cheeks full of water but lips kept tight, almost it seemed to bursting point. They blew out a fine spray of water over the work. The stockings were then smoothed, tied in neat bundles, and packed into great wicker skips.

She searched the old man's face for a clue, and he repeated the action of blowing out his cheeks. When she did not speak, he shook his head in obvious amusement at her naivety and explained; 'The wool's given out to us in pounds and ounces – we send the same weight back as finished stockings, plus a little water. In two skips we reckon to make thirty-two ounces of surplus wool for ourselves.'

Leah felt her mouth drop open in surprise. 'I thought it was just to make the stockings lie flat and look tidy. But that's . . .'

'Dishonest, were you thinking? It's no more dishonest than some of the over-wet wool we get handed out to us, if we're not careful. Why do you think your grandmother, and my Clarrie, allus keep sweet with the chap who picks up our wool from the factory and takes the finished work in? T'aint his personal charm!' They laughed together then as they thought of the broken black teeth and notoriously foul breath of their local carrier, and Sam added, 'No, the odd cup of tea, a few bits from the garden – if we can possibly manage it, a cockerel at Christmas – and he makes sure we don't get any bad wool. 'Wheels within wheels, m'gel.'

She silently digested this latest revelation as she watched the skill with which Sam used fingers, thumbs, arms, legs and feet, to call various sets of needles into action; to raise and lower the horizontal webs of threads; to send the shuttle flying across. It always amazed her that he could work and philosophise all at the same time, though it was said the work kept a stockinger's mind, as well as his body, nimble. 'There must be some answer, some other way,' she brooded.

'If you can find it, reckon we'll make you queen for the day,' Sam declared drily. 'This all happened to the hand weavers up North a hundred years or more ago. They were all reduced from craftsmen to factory hands generations back. Maybe I should think of working in town.'

'A factory owner wouldn't pay the right rate for all your skill.'

'He wouldn't need to!' Sam retorted impatiently. 'In a factory I'd just tend a machine that worked itself, powered by belts, driven by steam, making more in one day than I can on this old loom in a month.' He paused, then added, 'But at least I'd have someone to talk to again.'

She hadn't thought before how much he must miss her grandfather, but found herself defensively replying that he wouldn't be able to talk inside a factory anyway, because of the noise. He didn't answer, and though she had always resented his teasing, his easy outspokenness, she felt suddenly fearful for their future without him. 'Perhaps I could learn to work a loom?' she ventured.

'What'll we make? Fairy stockings!'

'I'll think of something,' she said stubbornly.

He swept the last section of a long-sleeved vest from the loom and pressed it into her hand, and for a moment she saw kindly concern in his face. 'I'm not going anywhere, there's too many young men looking for work. I'll do all I can, m'lass, but I'm thinking we're in for a lean time.'

It moved and concerned her that old Sam Elliot should drop his brusque manner. She murmured her thanks, but nothing could have come as greater confirmation of just how precarious their position was.

During the following days, the clattering of the foot pedals and the hiss of the tides of ebbing and flowing needles stopped in all the village workshops.

The stockingers began to look to their other food source, the land – and the allotments just outside the village, where one or two had laboured alone, suddenly became alive with people. The hillside was a favoured spot – despite its name Gallows Hill – and now whole families brought bread, cheese, bottles of cold tea and home-brewed beer with them, staying for long hours to cultivate the soil on this south-facing slope, where the heavy Leicestershire clay mingled with a more workable vein of sandy loam.

Work on the Dexter land had been taken up late, after the trauma of losing their man. At the far end of their plot Leah contemplated the sturdy green square of rapidly growing broad-beans, set the previous November by her grandfather. She marvelled, now that he had gone, at the mountain of work he had accomplished for one old man.

Then she found her mouth watering at the sight of the first green ferny fronds of carrots pushing through the ground. She seemed to feel hungry most of the time, but these, planted only a fortnight before, would take weeks before they were large enough to be thinned out, and they could have the threadlike carrots as a first delicious foretaste of the crop to come.

Miriam Dexter had thinly sliced the last Brussels-stalk into rings and boiled it in salted water some weeks ago. The last of the camped turnips and parsnips had been eaten just after Christmas. The only vegetables they had left now were some half dozen leeks – and the potatoes they had brought to set.

It would grieve her grandmother, but it seemed they would have to spend good money on vegetables this year. Leah had often wondered why money suddenly became "good" when no one wanted to spend it.

It was as Leah and her mother worked at the last section of digging, planning to set as many potatoes as they could before the sun set that day – that Nellie, stopping to straighten her aching back, gave a humph of disapproval before commenting, 'Here's Ginnie! Pity she's nothing better to do.'

Leah's face brightened as she looked up and saw her best friend, whose father, Walter Hobbday, was landlord of the Stockinger's Arms. 'She helps her father and her brothers – she works hard,' Leah said defensively, then struck her spade upright into the ground, as Ginnie beckoned urgently.

'Some nonsense,' Nellie said, resuming her digging.

As soon as she was near enough, Ginnie reached up to hook her arm around her taller friend's shoulders. Ginnie was some three inches smaller than Leah's tall five feet seven inches. 'As different as chalk from cheese,' as Nellie frequently reminded her daughter. Leah's dark hair and pale smooth complexion could sometimes make her seem stand-offish, even cold in reflective mood, like a stone-cut cameo – there was nothing of these traits in either Ginnie's appearance or nature. She was rosy-cheeked, hair a mass of natural waves, with more than a hint of red, bonny, warm-hearted, always one to throw her arm around her friend, or touch, or hold an arm, when talking.

'What you been up to then?' Ginnie asked, giving her a coy, questioning, look.

'Me!' Leah exclaimed, then laughed. 'I've cut up a whole stone of potatoes into eyed-pieces for planting.'

'Last Monday,' Ginnie said impatiently.

'Oh!' Leah exclaimed, wondering which part of that disastrous day Ginnie had heard about. She heard practically everything – her bedroom was immediately behind the painted signboard of the Stockinger's Arms and directly above the front door. Come closing time, she overhead many a juicy story or piece of gossip as she lay in bed – kept awake by customers leaving the four-ale bar who carried on their conversation just outside the porch.

'Well?' Ginnie was almost dancing with impatience as she propelled her friend to the far end of Gallows Hill, out of hearing of the toiling villagers. 'Who did you meet?'

'No one I want to see again before I need,' Leah vehemently declared.

'Oh, Leah! What about Nat and Ben Robertson?'

'The bellmakers?' She frowned. 'What about them?'

'They've only been here looking for you!'

Leah's mouth dropped open in surprise, then she shook her head in disbelief. 'Never!' she exclaimed.

'It's true! Last night, Thursday, it was practice night for our church bellringers. Well, these two lads came – to try out the bells, they said! Then they come in the Stockinger's Arms, asking if this was the village where the old tallyman used to come from, him whose granddaughter has took up the round.'

'Perhaps they want to buy something?'

'Perhaps cows might fly! Come on, tell's what happened. What did you say to them? Which one did you like the best?'

'Did you see them?' Now it was Leah's time to be curious.

Ginnie laughed provocatively. 'You tell first!'

'I never spoke to them,' she said quite honestly, and yet it seemed less than the truth. 'We looked at each other – that's all.'

'Oooh! It seems that was enough. But which one? Which one did you "look at?" Ginnie danced in front of her, like a young child begging favours from an adult.

'The tall one.'

'Oh, good!' Ginnie declared. 'I liked the look of the shorter one best.' She laughed up at her friend. 'I called to them out of my bedroom window when they left.'

'Ginnie!' Leah was frankly horrified at such brazen behaviour. 'What would people think?'

'Don't worry, I made sure there was no one else about. Anyway, they're coming Sunday afternoon. I said we'd meet them at Old Brig . . . I've already told my dad you've asked me round Sunday so you can look at my latest catalogues, so that's settled.'

Ginnie's catalogues had become a feature of the village. She loved to have a letter through the post, and had developed a mania for sending for every free catalogue or brochure she saw advertised in her father's copy of *Chamber's Journal*. They came addressed to V. Hobbday, Esquire, Care of The Landlord, Stockinger's Arm, Tur Lacey, Leicestershire. Ginnie had found from experience this never failed to bring a satisfactory reply, while a request from a Miss Hobbday was often ignored by the advertisers. After Ginnie had poured over them, they were borrowed and scanned printless, all down the hierarchies of the passing-on list.

Leah felt speechless with a mixture of embarrassment and excitement – and guilt, as over Ginnie's shoulder she saw her mother picking up the bag of potato pieces and the wooden dibber. 'I must go,' she said. Her mother was curiously inept when it came to dropping a section of potato into a hole before the sides caved in.

'See you Sunday then. I can drop the catalogues in before we go for our walk – to Old Brig.' Ginnie bobbed her head and fluttered her eyelashes meaningfully, then added triumphantly, 'I've been saving the lamp-black!' She swept her finger over her eyebrows, and Leah remembered the last time they had tried using the soot from the oil-lamps to darken their brows and lashes. A fine mess they had got into!

'You, Ginnie Hobbday, you'll have us both in trouble yet.'

'Chance'll be a fine thing,' she replied and, tossing her curls, ran back along Gallows Hill path, waving and calling to Mrs Dexter and others who waved back and watched her youthful, skipping passage along the sombrely named way leading to the old place of execution.

Even before the bells had begun calling out their message of early morning service the following Sunday morning, the two girls met outside the Church School gates, where both had graduated from pupils to assistants and undertook bible-story reading with the younger children.

Their eyes sparkled and they had some difficulty maintaining any appearance of decorum as they entered their joint classroom. Village boys created the odd diversion, but boys – young men – coming from another village some distance away, was quite another matter. It implied a seriousness, a sense of purpose, which awed Leah yet gave her a satisfying feeling of significance.

She had great trouble concentrating on her group of four year olds as she kept encountering Ginnie's broad grin, or watched as her friend cupped her hand to her ear and entreated the little children under her charge to, 'Listen to the sweet bells calling them to . . . church', but to Leah she mouthed, 'Old Brig'.

The skeletal figure of the Sunday School Superintendent suddenly appeared in their classroom. He looked over his pincenez and frowned disapproval at his two grinning assistants. 'Sunday,' he pronounced, 'is for sober reading of religious texts. I trust you are both setting good examples to your little flocks.'

'Oh, yes, Mr Warburton,' Ginnie said, demurely fluttering her eyelashes at him. A slow surge of colour and a sharp cough overtook him, and he retreated to the safer waters of the next room and his wife's class.

They were just attempting to regain control of themselves after the encounter when Mrs Warburton sailed majestically into the room. Ginnie always referred to her as the "S.S. Great Britain", and Leah always had difficulty looking straight at the rigid, whaleboned figure. It was easy to imagine that she too consisted of metal plates – though her progress at that moment suggested more battle-ship than peaceful steamer.

She regarded the two girls critically, and demanded, 'You are only *reading* to the children?'

Leah and Ginnie looked slightly puzzled.

'I mean, not talking – not attempting to *teach* that of which you have no knowledge.'

The two girls spoke together.

'What would that be?' Ginnie asked provocatively.

'Just reading, Mrs Warburton,' Leah replied darkly, a warning in her voice if the woman had sensitivity enough to hear it.

'Ye-es, Good. Because —' Mrs Warburton drew the words out as if extending a whip-lash to its fullest extent 'I understand,' she paused again as if to rid herself of an unpleasant taste in her mouth before she could continue, 'that you, Miss Dexter, travelled by train to sell, door to door!'

'Ye-es' Leah drew out her quiet reply in sarcastic imitation, 'just like a pedlar. Just as my grandfather did before me,' she went on with a lift of her head. 'In fact, all the years I've been coming to Sunday School, once every week my grandfather walked his round. He was a pedlar every Monday. Didn't you

31

know that, Mrs Warburton?' Her voice trembled with quiet anger now, and Ginnie was watching with some apprehension.

'Don't be pert, Miss,' she snapped. 'It is a man's employment, part of his trade – but not for a decent woman, a mere girl, to be walking the highways, and byways – alone.' She attempted to end the exchange, her eyes going from Leah to Ginnie whom she obviously found no more pleasing – but Leah had not finished.

'Perhaps you'd rather we starved in a quiet, decent, manner?'

'You've only been reading too, I trust, Miss Hobbday?' Mrs Warburton raised her voice and veered her glance further to starboard, attempting to eliminate Leah from her consideration.

'Don't worry, Mrs Warburton,' Leah went on just as determinedly, rising to her feet, 'we've not contaminated the children, even though I'm turned a pedlar-girl and Ginnie's a publican's daughter.'

'That remains to be something we shall have to guard against.' Mrs Warburton's face was stony, and her knuckles white as she clasped her hands beneath the ramparts of her bosom. 'Something the Sunday School Superintendent and I shall have to consider very seriously.'

'No!' Leah raised her voice now. She looked across at Ginnie, who rose in support of whatever her friend was going to do. 'No, you don't need to consider.' She paused as Mr Warburton came cautiously to the door of the room, his manner, his hand wringing, suggesting extreme agitation. 'In future you can teach your own little flocks without our help.'

'This is nothing that can't be put right very easily, I'm sure.' Mr Warburton bent solicitously towards the two girls. 'Some misunderstanding?' he suggested.

'Yes,' Leah confirmed, 'we thought you were Christians too.' She swept up her prayer book and bible and walked quickly and directly towards the door. The Sunday School Superintendent's wife, and the Sunday School Superintendent, who were in her path, stood hastily aside.

'Well! Did ever you hear the like? The scandal . . . the brazenness . . . You're a brazen hussy, Leah Dexter!' Mrs

Warburton's furious tones followed the two girls. 'You've not heard the last of this!'

'Now what do we do?' Ginnie asked, tripping over Leah's heels in her eagerness to be out of the school. Leah was too furious to answer, as she tried to reconcile facts with emotions. Why should the way one earned one's living, kept a crust in the pantry, be so important? Why had she herself resented being called a pedlar-girl? She had found it difficult to go from door to door, but hadn't that sanctimonious Mr Warburton gone from house to house collecting the meagre savings of the poor for a Friendly Society? Wasn't that how he had met Mrs Warburton? And wasn't she trade – the daughter of a butcher? Who was she to be so . . . Ginnie's voice wailing for her to slow down finally broke into Leah's racing thoughts.

'Where are we going? What are you going to do?'

'I'm going to church,' Leah decided, with a touch of bravado, 'and I'm sitting on the back row, and Mrs High-and-Mighty Warburton can sit at the front and look after the kids – see how she likes that!'

'Ooh-a!' Ginnie exclaimed biting her lip. 'We'll get told off.'

In spite of her heroics Leah's heart bumped furiously as she led the way into the church and sat in the back pew. She was almost at once nudged in the back, and the verger's voice near her ear demanded to know what they were doing and where were the children?

'We are no longer attached to the Sunday School. We are part of the general congregation,' she replied, without turning her head. There was silence for a moment, then the creaking of boots as the verger went to the vestry to report to the vicar. More silence, then as the final calling bell was rung down, the sound of many little pairs of boots on the stone flags as the Sunday School came into church. They heard Mrs Warburton snort as she passed behind them, and watched with some satisfaction the way her fruited and feathered hat hung dangerously loose on its hatpins as she ushered the youngest children into their places on the very front row.

The morning service proceeded with seemingly indifferent calm, but there were covert and speculative glances at the two displaced Sunday School helpers. Ginnie, who usually enjoyed singing, never uttered a sound, though Leah sung determinedly, if tunelessly, on.

As the service drew to an end, the notes of the recessional hymn and the vicar's final blessing had hardly died away in the choir vestry before the two of them were out of the door and away down the path. Their walk became a run and for a moment Ginnie giggled hysterically. Then they heard the door of the church opened fully and the first members of the congregation began to spill out, the swelling tide of their conversation, deep-toned and significant, beginning to flow — it seemed in pursuit of them. The two exchanged swift, panicky glances, their nerve temporarily gone. They had sinned against the establishment, and both were anxious to be home to tell their version of the event — before the families heard it from someone else.

'See you s'afternoon,' Ginnie said as they parted. 'Two o'clock . . .'

Leah nodded, but there was doubt on both their faces. It was possible the storm might break before then; the consequences of one impropriety might catch up with them before they had a chance to commit another.

Chapter Four

Ginnie arrived at half-past two, looking flustered and furtive. She carried a large brown paper parcel which she deposited in Leah's arms. 'Some catalogues and the new *Young Ladies' Journal*. Thought I'd better not carry it through the street on a *Sunday*.'

Leah took the parcel, trying to read on her friend's face how she had fared since Morning Song, but Ginnie's eyes revealed nothing as she asked, 'Can you come for a walk, Leah?'

'That alright, Mother?' Leah ventured.

Nellie hesitated, and looked at her mother-in-law for guidance. 'You can't lock her up for speaking her mind,' Miriam said, 'and the two of them are hardly likely to offend any more Holy Joes just by going for a walk!'

Her grandmother spoke with more spirit than she had since her beloved Freddie had died. Leah met her eyes across the table and lifted her head, proud she had aligned herself with her grandfather and his trade. She smiled, aware how much she owed her grandmother, a clever woman whom for as long as Leah could remember had regularly read to them all from her favourite Dickens, and who still regretted his death some eight years before, leaving that uncompleted story *Edwin Drood*.

'Remember it's still Sunday though,' Nellie added mildly, as Leah gave her the parcel for the privilege of first perusal.

More cautionary words followed the two girls out on to the village street, and as they passed the adjoining cottage, Leah whispered, 'Clarrie Elliott was in church!'

35

Neither spoke again until they were beyond the last cottage on the road leading down toward the River Sence. Nearly a mile away, it was no more than a large stream at this stage of its journey to join the mightier River Soar near the ancient city of Leicester.

The place they called 'Old Brig' was held in special affection, a trysting place for generations of young lovers, witnessed by the initials, old and new, carved in its thick oak hand-rail. New footbridges spanned the stream in many places – but those bridges with their metal handrails were merely for getting from one place to another.

'I wonder how old you have to be before you can really please yourself?' Leah mused. 'I mean, without half the village thinking it's their affair!' She stepped out angrily, deciding, 'Never – not if you're a girl!'

Ginnie grunted agreement, adding, 'I'm supposed to be in my bedroom.' Leah stopped and looked at her friend in concern. 'We'd better not go.' Ginnie's father had a reputation for two things: generosity with his poorer customers, and ruthlessness with anyone who disturbed his well-ordered house.

'Oh, blow that for a game of soldiers!'

'You might be missed, or we might be seen.' Leah amended her statement. 'We most likely *will* be seen!'

'Oh!' Ginnie screwed up her face in disgust. 'I don't care!'

'Not until we get back, you don't,' Leah decided dourly. Then the two of them began to laugh. They joined hands and ran, slowly at first, but then ever faster, as if to escape the strictures of close community life.

'Hold on!' Ginnie pleaded after a few minutes. 'you and your long legs! Anyway, we don't want them to see us running!'

The thought of two young men who should be waiting, who they might even be able to see from around the next bend, brought them both to a standstill.

'Perhaps they won't come.' Leah was not sure whether she felt it would be a tragedy or a relief.

'Oh, don't say that!' Ginnie at once took up the look of someone struck by sudden disaster, then glared at her friend for suggesting such a thing. 'They will. I know they will.'

The two of them composed themselves as they approached the bend in the road. Until they turned the corner they were hidden by the high hawthorn hedges, the blossom banked like snow, and by the first of the great willow tress which became more numerous as the land fell to the lush water meadows.

Having plucked their skirts straight, tucked stray wisps of hair into place and flicked the light film of dust from their boots on a sturdy clump of grass, they approached the first vantage point they would have of the river. Leah found courage in acquiring a slim stick, which she ran through the burgeoning verge grasses. Ginnie span a cowslip, until the head of long stalked flowerets twirled like a miniature yellow roundabout. 'I can't see anyone,' Leah hissed.

'No, neither can I,' Ginnie whispered back, both seeming casually engrossed, but in reality looking up under their brows and fiercely scanning the countryside ahead of them.

'It was a put on,' Leah decided, 'they were just pretending they would come.'

'Perhaps they're hiding!'

'They're scared of us, you mean.'

Ginnie stopped to giggle, and the two of them turned to look back the way they had come, as if this gave them a greater freedom to discuss the matter – though they were still a powerful shout away from the water.

'No, stupid! I mean, they may be somewhere looking us over,' Ginnie said, giving way to a delicious shiver of excitement. 'Men do that. I've heard them talking . . .'

'So, what do we do?' Leah questioned anxiously. Her friend was the authority on men.

'Oh!' Ginnie tossed her hair and assumed a dignified manner. 'We just pretend we don't care. Just walk and talk – naturally,' She advised, strutting forward, head held high and slightly sideways – the way Leah had seen her pose before the looking-glass above their parlour sideboard. 'Come on.'

Leah followed a little reluctantly. Ginnie said one thing, but did another. And fancy agreeing to come to meet a young man she have never actually spoken to, the arrangement made by Ginnie shouting to someone in the dark – could be anybody! She felt her spine become sensitive, prickle with apprehension. Her first meeting with the bellmakers had been traumatic enough . . .

She studied the countryside ahead, but the absence of anything other than a large number of very old willow trees, and a smaller number of brown cows ambling down to drink, then lingering ankle deep in the water, reassured her.

'I don't think anyone is there,' she commented as she noticed how swallows swooped undisturbed over the stream.

'You don't want them to come!' Ginnie remonstrated. 'You go home, I'll go by myself.'

'We do things together.'

'Shut up then, and come on.'

'This a private quarrel, or can anyone join in?'

A man's voice made them both jump. Coming across the field footpath, behind them and to their right, were the two young men Leah had last seen in Soston churchyard. They had taken off their jackets and had them slung on negligent fingers over their shoulders, their boots were brushed gold with buttercup pollen, and both sported elegant neckerchieves secured by gold pins.

Leah felt her face flame with confusion and embarrassment, then her throat tightened with unspent laughter at the nonplussed expression on her friend's face. But Ginnie recovered her voice first.

'We didn't see you coming over the fields.'

'We didn't think you had!' Nat grinned, and looking at Ginnie added, 'Our turn to surprise you this time.'

'We thought you'd be waiting for us at the bridge.' She achieved just the right amount of censure in her voice, to quell any further embarrassing questions.

'We came over the fields – took a short cut . . .' Nat began to explain.

'It would have been, if we hadn't taken the wrong path out of Black Pool Spinney,' Ben added, coming a few steps nearer to Leah.

She hoped Ginnie would go on talking for she suddenly felt as if she could not think quite rationally or perceive the world beyond Ben Robertson. He was so close he took her breath, obscured her whole horizon – with his index finger making a hook for his jacket, his black and white striped shirt, grey braces and black Sunday trousers. He was so near she could even catch the aroma of shaving-soap, and the clean, cottony, flat-iron smell of his shirt – it seemed a poignant intimacy to her, making her realise how all these masculine things had disappeared from her home. She had not thought, until that moment, how they must have been privily put away.

The other two were laughing together about Ginnie calling down from behind the public house sign, but she merely exchanged glances, and rather shy smiles, with Ben as the four of them began to walk on together.

She noticed that the hands that had wielded the sledge-hammer were well shaped with long fingers; his hair, that had been grey as the old bell from the dust and grime of the belfry was a glossy dark chestnut; the chin was angular, she had remembered that correctly. He cleared his throat a little as if preparing to speak, and she looked up at him. His eyes were blue, but dark and disconcerting, as if the long look questioned her existence, or searched her for the answer to some question that had so far not been asked. Perhaps her own scrutiny lasted a second or two too long, for whatever it was Ben had been preparing to say, it seemed he forgot – and he cleared his throat again, as if the irritation had been real.

Leah wondered if he could possibly be feeling as awkward as she did – while the other two seemed perfectly at ease, still chattering on, with Nat saying he thought there should be a warning on the front door of the Stockinger's Arms about female eavesdroppers.

'They say you hear no good of yourself, but I don't know . . .' Ginnie lifted her voice at the end of her statement as if all she had ever heard of herself had been very good.

'Did you finished breaking up that old bell?' Leah asked at last, her mind jumping from good to evil, though her tongue felt awkward and stiff, as if from years of disuse.

'It's all in pieces, ready to be melted down, along with its old inscription,' he replied, then asked with rather stilted formality, 'I hope you had a good day – sold a lot of things.'

'No, not really.' She found herself relating some of the less painful episodes of her day, and the other two stopped their gentle banter to listen too. Ben and Nat jointly related their version of the incident of the bell and the old man. 'Like an

Old Testament prophet he was, going on about hell fire and damnation!' Nat told Ginnie.

'He made me feel like the reincarnation of the woman of ill-repute he kept on about.' Leah was relieved to hear their roars of laughter at her reaction, but she saw Ben's understanding glance, knew he had shared the real trauma – that moment in the churchyard, when she had realised how easy it was to become a victim, just by arriving at a place at a wrong moment.

Nat too seemed to sense there was more hardship in her role than she was revealing, and he asked: 'Isn't there anyone else who could go out on these rounds?'

'You mean, a man?' Leah began defensively.

'No, there's not,' Ginnie interrupted, as if she felt the tone of the conversation might become too serious. 'It's all women in Leah's house, and all men in mine!'

'With one pretty exception,' Nat said, quickly taking up the change from conversation to boy-girl banter again.

They walked on, listening to Ginnie's tales of her family, laughing, flirting outrageously. Leah felt inhibited by her friend's gaiety; her careless easy gestures – an arm flung wide here, a step or two danced in front of the group there.

Ginnie might feel on safe and familiar ground – her days were full of men, young and old, related and unrelated – but Leah felt uneasy. She remembered Ginnie had years ago mischievously warned her that she shouldn't even look at men, when she had become "a proper young lady" – which had been the full extent of her mother's information, on what, she had believed at the time, to be the beginning of her own demise. Though Ginnie had immediately denied it was anything more than a joke, the remarks, and the memory of that first bleeding she had thought would never stop, sooner or later came to mind when she considered the mystery of men, and marriage, and "falling for" babies.

Ginnie had often, embarrassingly, pointed out the antics of animals in the fields – the rams, the bulls, the dogs that roamed the streets – and from the giggling she did about it, and the remarks she made, Leah knew was supposed to link this behaviour with "falling". She found it impossible to relate such activities to herself or any other human being. But

Ginnie said -. . and Ginnie had four elder brothers as loquacious as herself.

They had reached a place where a well-trodden path left the road and made its way over towards the stream. 'Shall we go over the fields?' Nat proposed.

Leah, relating the proposition to her thoughts, felt a moment of complete panic. 'Ginnie shouldn't be out,' she said quickly.

'Oh! Who cares?' Ginnie said defiantly, glaring at her friend.

'Neither should we, come to that – or not out here,' Nat answered.

'Where should you be?' Leah asked, full of curiosity. She wondered what rules applied to young men, who, as the village matriarchs expressed it, "Didn't take their troubles home with them."

'We're supposed to be going to Flaxhill, the deserted village, to see if the old tower that still stands has a bell in it,' Ben told them, adding dourly, 'If we're going out, it has to be with profit in mind. No such thing as time-off, not with our step-father about.'

'So we thought if we "got lost" this Sunday,' Nat said, leaning forward to give Leah a cheeky grin from the far end of the four, 'we could go and find the tower next Sunday . . .'

'In fact,' Ben added, his voice lighter, full of amusement, 'we lost our sense of direction in the spinney and found ourselves nearly at Flaxhill.'

The four laughed comfortably together, then Leah asked: 'Who would the bell belong to? If there was one there.'

The two young men were silent for a moment, then Nat answered, 'Left to the boss, I don't suppose we'd bother to find out.'

Leah opened her mouth to protest, then remembered the damping down of the stockings. She could hardly afford to cast the first stone.

'We could meet you at the spinney,' Ginnie proposed, her eyes shining with the prospect of such an adventure. 'I'll see my friend here doesn't get on her high horse and upset everyone – again!'

41

Despite Leah's appeals for her to be quiet, Ginnie related the morning's events – and the four of them approached the stile as they listened, as if not aware of their own actions.

Nat led the way with an easy athletic vault. Ginnie followed and managed to find herself standing on the top but one rung on the field side. Nat accepted the invitation and neatly encircled her waist with his hands to lift her down.

'Who's next?' he asked.

Leah indicated that Ben should go next, though she deemed it a mistake when all three then stood waiting for her to climb over. Self-consciously, she began what seemed like a serious attempt to scale a mountain, with all the world waiting for her to fall off. She put one leg over the top bar, and turning her foot inwards to find a purchase on the lower rung, slipped, and found herself blushing furiously again as Ben rushed forward to help. She recovered quickly, though she could not ignore his hand raised to steady her as she stepped from gate to ground.

'Thank you,' she breathed with prim correctness, though her palm burned from the momentary experience of his supporting hand. She thought how strong he seemed. His hand had not given even a fraction of an inch as it had supported her weight.

'So Ginnie should be at home?' Ben asked, as the two of them fell behind the others. 'Will she get into trouble?'

'She certainly will if her father finds out,' Leah confirmed, 'but Ginnie and her brothers are a happy lot and are always covering up for each other.'

'They're lucky then,' he said quietly, and his face fell into such solemn lines, she wondered how happy his own home was. They walked in silence, Leah thinking how different all their family circumstances were: Ginnie with no mother; Ben and Nat with a step-father; herself with neither father nor grandfather. She drew in a deep breath, noticing the distance shimmered with the first heat haze of the summer, and the long-stemmed grasses already head-heavy with seeds – the work of haymaking would begin early this year.

They had nearly reached the water, where it flowed here deep and smooth between the bankside willows, there shallow and broken over boulders and pebbles. For a moment they stood watching where the breeze pressed the slender foliage gently down to the water, tantalising the surface with images of silver shoals of leaves.

Leah caught an exchange of glances between the two brothers, and Ben laughed, exclaiming, 'I know what he's going to do.'

'What?' the two girls wanted to know.

'He's going to paddle!' Ben tried to sound scornful, but could not. 'He's just like a child when there's water about. He's got to be in it.'

Nat was laughing with his brother, but at the same time he began hopping about pulling off his boots and his socks. Then rolling up his trousers to just below the knee, revealing milk-white calves, he stepped into the stream, shivering and exclaiming at once with cold and ecstasy. 'Ooh! It's lovely. Wish you were here!'

Leah looked apprehensively at her friend, and the expression on her face told everything. 'You can't!' Leah breathed.

'Just watch me,' Ginnie replied, disappearing behind the trunk of a willow. She reappeared seconds later, and with a flash of bare feet beneath her skirts was standing on two flat boulders in the shallow water. 'It's cold!' she exclaimed delightedly, moving from stone to stone.

For a full minute the other two stood on the bank watching, the Ben turned to Leah and asked, 'Do you remember how your feet felt after that day on the roads?'

'Do I!' she repeated with emphasis. They looked at each other, and suddenly the moment was all holiday. Ben sat down to pull off his boots, and Leah sped to discard her own boots and stockings on top of Ginnie's. A minute later she was gasping with the cold and pleasure as she curled her toes tight around the first smooth boulder in the brook. 'It's freezing!'

'It's lovely,' Ginnie echoed. 'I haven't paddled for years. Not since I was a kid and my brothers brought me here.'

'I've not been in the water since my grandfather brought me fishing here. We were using a stick, a piece of thread and a bent pin, and I caught two fish on one worm. I was so excited I fell in. We were both in trouble when we got home!' Leah forgot all her inhibitions in relating the memory, holding her

43

skirt up so it drew tight about her legs at mid-calf. She stepped down off the boulder into the sandier stream bed and walked along, feeling the sand between her toes and sometimes the sticky slip of the mud-bed beneath that. For a moment or two it seemed she could almost hear the water moving silkily over her ankles, then it was obliterated by a heavier, splashier tread as Ben caught up with her.

'You were fond of your grandfather.'

She stood still to reflect on her answer, then moved one foot around, watching the fleeting pattern of circles she drew in the water. 'I often wished I had been a boy, just for his sake. We were so close, there was so much he would have liked to have taught me, and so very much I wanted to know — but being a girl . . .

'Like my grandfather . . . he's taught me all I know about bell-making.'

'Not your step-father?'

'No!' The denial was quick, all revealing. 'no, anything of any merit my step-father has in this world, he acquired by marrying my mother.'

'So it's your grandfather's business . . .'

There was another very long pause, so long Leah began to walk slowly forward, keeping her feet below the level of the water. She made little noise, not wanting to disturb this moment of quiet confidences.

'It was, but he assigned two-thirds to my mother and father when they married. Then, when my father died, his share went to my mother, and when she remarried . . .'

'That two-thirds went into your step-father's name,' Leah said quietly, wondering about the justice of the law that automatically assigned all a woman's property to her husband. Women were not supposed to be able to deal with business. She herself was not so far a shining example, but surely she could learn!

'And now he's got control, he holds the purse-strings very tight. We keep the peace for my mother's sake . . . though I'm not sure how much longer I'll be able to hold my tongue about some things.'

'He sounds a bit of a tyrant,' she said, but softening her tone to suit the shortness of their acquaintance.

44

'That's how it is.'

The quiet affirmation was disquieting, and she remembered the woman with the frightened children and the bruised face, and in a whisper hardly louder than the rippling water, she said, 'A home should be a sanctuary, not . . .'

'Not . . .' he took the word up from her, then seemed unable to go on, 'not . . . well, not what it is at our place.'

She stopped to plunge one foot down into a deeper colder pool in the stream's heart.

He stood close by her side as she explored the icy depths, and put one hand under her elbow as she stretched too far and was in danger of toppling over. 'I seem to be burdening you with my family worries very quickly,' he said, 'it must be paddling – no shoes and sock, no restraints!'

'Well, you've heard mine, and Ginnie's, so why not?' they exchanged gentle smiles and walked slowly on.

The stream meandered here, and following between the banks, the next bend took them out of sight of the other two. A sudden breeze ruffled the water ahead of them, disturbing the sun into a dappling of sparkling ripples. Instinctively they both stopped as the broken, golden water came hurrying towards them, and washed around their ankles like an offering of wealth. Leah lifted one foot out of the water through the golden light, and was almost surprised not to see the colour stick there, like buttercup pollen.

The afternoon seemed to hold a deep listening silence. Leah thought it an extraordinary day, more like high summer when the birds have finished rearing their young and have quieted their parental clamour, and the young calves and lambs have become used to long days in the freedom of the fields. She was full of a sense of wonder, and when she would have moved on, Ben squeezed her forearm, pointing a little way in front of them.

'Don't move,' he whispered. 'Look at the next bend, where the watercresses grow. There's a brown trout, a beauty.'

After a few seconds' peering she could make out the brown speckled back, so carefully camouflaged it looked like part of the pebbled stream bottom. 'Oh, yes!' she breathed, then her stomach rumbled and she felt a bit ashamed to realise that her

45

mouth was watering as she thought of its deep pink flesh on a plate surrounded by some of these same young watercresses.

With a sudden swirl of its tail, it rose, took a fly from the surface and was gone.

'Years ago my grandfather caught a great pike in this river, a twelve pounder . . .' She broke off, exclaiming as a flurry of minnows came shooting over their feet. For a second she wondered if a pike was chasing them, but then the splashing and laughter made them realise it was a different chase.

The next moment Nat came into sight around the bend, running and stumbling in the water with Ginnie in pursuit, holding a bunch of nettles in her handkerchief, and adding to their threat by dipping them into the water as she chased him.

The two of them joined the laughter and horse-play as Nat tried to dodge behind them. 'This girl plays rough,' he complained.

'Who picked the stingers?' Ginnie asked, advancing meaningfully.

Some movement behind a tree downstream caught Leah's eye, and she wondered what anyone would think, seeing them in this unladylike state – on a Sunday – paddling in the stream with two strange young men!

The next second she had to dodge quickly out of the way to avoid Ginnie's energetic swish at Nat. The lunge nearly brought real disaster, as Ginnie slipped and looked bound to go sprawling full length in the water, but Nat plunged forward and caught her up in his arms, carrying her to the bank. As the nettles fell from Ginnie's hand and floated downstream, Leah saw the dark form of a man step back behind one of the great pollarded willows.

'Someone's watching – behind the trees!' she exclaimed as they followed the others to the bank.

'Where?' Ben demanded, and as she indicated, the two men ran along the bank as fast as their bare feet would allow.

'Hope they get him,' Leah said angrily. 'Peeping Tom!'

'I hope it was a stranger,' Ginnie wished urgently.

'Fat chance!' Leah answered, watching as Ben and Nat reappeared.

'There's no one there now,' Nat reported, 'but we could see where someone stood in the long grass.'

'Hope he enjoyed what he saw,' Ginnie said, but her face had gone pale. There was little or nothing that went on in the village that was not sooner or later reported and mulled over in her father's four-ale bar, or more privately in his brewhouse.

'Perhaps we should go home,' she decided in a small solemn voice, as if already certain trouble would be waiting. But she added defiantly, 'We'll see you next week, like we said.'

Chapter Five

'Stay down, Ginnie, if you know what's good for you.'

She heard her brother's boots clatter up the stone steps which formed part of the brickwork supporting the huge brewing copper she was cleaning.

She opened her mouth to protest as the small wooden stepladder she had used to climb down into the copper was whisked away almost from under her hands. She did not relish the prospect of any lark that left her trapped inside the vessel. Then, hearing the unmistakable footsteps of her father approaching, she gripped bath-brick and cloth tighter and sank slowly and noiselessly lower.

'Where's your sister?'

'I saw her at breakfast.'

She raised appreciative eyebrows, Charley could always manage to tell the truth, and deceive, at the same time. Her father's rumble of response suggested he too knew his youngest son's abilities. He tried a different approach.

'Did you know she went out last Sunday afternoon, after I had told her to stay in her room?'

'Who told you she did?'

'Never mind who told me . . .'

'I expect it was the verger. Old Pask's not happy unless he's hopping from church to taproom, carrying tales.'

Ginnie held her breath – feeling a bit like a cannibal's meal, and the fire about to be lit under her. The silence outside stretched to an intolerable length. She recognised her father's devastating habit of never repeating a question. By merely waiting he usually unnerved his erring offspring into speech – or rather a gabble, to fill the guilty silence.

'Why don't you ask the others?' Charley suggested.

'Robert's busy in the stable, and the other two have gone to look at the grass – we may cut this afternoon.'

There was another ominous silence. Ginnie prayed for Charley to hold his tongue. If it was decided to cut the hay in their fields behind the pub, she might have until the evening to concoct an acceptable story. The verger was not given to long walks, he might only have seen her in the village. If, on the other hand, her father knew the whole story . . . She shuddered to think of the consequences.

She strained at the silence until it too seemed to ring like an accusation in her ears. One second she was tempted to stand up and wave her cloth, to release Charley from the necessity of circling around the truth, like a dog round a hedgehog – the next, she crouched lower, putting the cloth over one ear and bathbrick over the other.

The sudden raising of both hands made her lose her balance on the shiny copper surface. Her feet and back slipped slowly but inevitably, silently at first, then she took on a faster spin as she swirled into the cup-shaped bottom – grazing the bathbrick on the side. The brewing vessel seemed to magnify the sound, tittle-tattling her presence. Ginnie groaned.

The silence lasted a mere second or two longer as Walter Hobbday summed up the situation.

'Put the ladder back in,' he ordered. 'Then fetch the yokes and you start carrying the water – forty full buckets, mind. I'll pour in the barley.'

'But it's Bob's turn to fetch the water. I . . .' Charley protested.

'The next time I catch Bob out in a lie, he shall take your turn.' The tone brooked no further argument, and Ginnie tried to regain a little composure as she heard her brother climbing up the exterior stone-steps. The top of the small wooden stepladder appeared first, then his red hair and redder freckled face. He pulled down the corners of his mouth in a sympathetic grimace, waiting to give her a hand as she climbed the ladder and stepped out beside him.

'Get on then, lad, we'll have evening on us before half the work is done.'

Charley went to where several different sizes of yokes hung on the brewhouse wall, and choosing the middle pair departed in the direction of the village pump.

'I'm waiting, Ginnie,' Walter Hobbday added as she lingered, fidgeting the stepladder against the wall.

She gave up all pretence then, and turned to her father, protesting, 'It's not fair, Father. I can't do anything, or go anywhere, without somebody spying.' Lacking the courage to hang on his arm as she usually did when cajoling him, she tossed up her head in a hurt manner, bottom lip as petulant as she dared.

'No one could have "spied" on you, in your room' he began, 'and I tell you this much, Ginnie, I'm sick to my heart, of people coming into my house and telling me of your . . . your . . . goings-on. First the verger, then the Sunday School-superintendent . . . then his son!

'Levis! Levis Warburton!' the mystery of the secret watcher was solved. It was just the sort of action his contemporaries would expect of Levis. His ingratiating manner, inherited from his obsequious father, had made him an unpopular boy. Now as a rather solitary young man, apprenticed to pimples and his father's Friendly Society, he took pleasure in living vicariously by repeating scandalous tales.

Ginnie was too angry to care what she said now. 'Wait until I tell Leah! Levis . . .'

'Ah!' Her father's heavy and meaningful exclamation prevented her going on. 'We've come to one matter that can quickly be put right. You are not to associate with that Dexter girl any more. She's always had ideas beyond her station.'

Ginnie laughed, incredulous. 'Her station! You have to be joking, Father. They're poor as church mice these days.'

'Poor has nothing to do with it. That girl wasn't brought up to know her proper duties. I wouldn't want to be in the man's shoes who attempts to keep her in her place. He'll need a horse-whip, like as not. Now I hear she's traipsing around the countryside, touting for business . . . no wonder Mrs Warburton dismissed her from the Sunday School.

50

'No!' Ginnie protested. She would not endure this untruth. 'That's not true, none of it is true!' she exclaimed. 'We. . . resigned.'

'Listen to me, m'girl – half the trouble in this world is because people don't listen. This is what I am saying to you. A bad influence! You don't resign . . . you don't do anything. . . unless your olders and betters tell you to. But what you will do,' he paused to raise a stubby finger at her, 'is take yourself along to both the vicar and Mrs Warburton – apologise – and say you'll be back at Sunday School this coming Sunday.

'Father, I just can't,' she wailed at the thought of such humiliation. 'You don't understand! They look down on us – you and the public-house, and now because Leah went on her grandfather's old round . . .'

'Now we come to Sunday afternoon.'

'It's right what Leah told them. they're not Christians,' Ginnie went on, but her heart and stomach seemed to make a brave attempt at changing places as her father went on.

'It's more Christian than what I heard you were doing.'

This second silence was broken by Charley returning with the wooden yokes over his shoulders, his hands steadying the two brimming pails of water hanging from the chains and hooks.

'What were you about, half-undressed in some strange man's arms on Sunday afternoon?'

Even Charley looked impressed at the enormity of this sin, and water slopped over his boots as he lost concentration. He tried to linger, but as soon as he had climbed the stone steps and sent the water swirling down into the empty depths of the copper, he was motioned away, back in the direction of the village pump and nineteen more journeys across the village green.

Her father stood, hands on hips, waiting for an answer. Though the sandiness of his hair was faded and thinned, though he was little taller than his daughter and shorter than any of his sons, he had the air of one who expected to be answered and obeyed.

'It wasn't like that,' she began. 'I'd arranged to meet Leah to go for a walk on Sunday afternoon.'

51

'You'd been told to stay in your room!'

'And I didn't feel I could let her down – she was expecting me.' She glanced at him to see how he was taking the story so far, but though there was a terrible tension in his stance and he seemed to be listening intently, his eyes were downcast. 'And. . . and then we met these two young men who Leah knew. They're very respectable . . . and we paddled . . . That's all, Father! We just paddled. There's nothing wrong in paddling.'

'Carried in his arms,' he repeated, still looking down.

'I nearly fell in – he rescued me.'

'Rescued you!' he repeated, raising his eyes – and his voice, which was unusual. She backed away, chewing at her bottom lip. He lurched forward quickly, unexpectedly, and caught her by the shoulder. She was startled more by the look in his eyes than by his grasp, for she recognised both hurt and uncertainty such as she had never seen before – not when Charley had broken his shoulder falling off the trap-pony; not when a hogshead of best bitter had dropped from the brew-house thrall, splitting open his foot; not when serious fights erupted in the bar. He shook her with a slow controlled gentleness, and his voice was husky, almost inaudible. 'Don't you let me, or your dead mother, down. I'd never forgive you . . . not this side of the grave.'

He paused, searching her face, his question no more than a whisper. 'You know what I'm talking about, girl?'

She nodded urgently at him. 'I never would, Daddy, never!'

He stood still, looking at her, assessing, making judgement. Then he released her and stepped back, blinking, as if to shutter away the dark fears he had envisaged for his daughter.

'So these men had really come to see Leah Dexter,' he said. 'You stay away from that girl, you hear me!' When she did not immediately reply, he repeated, 'You hear me?'

'I hear you.' The words came reluctantly, but the uncertainty and concern she had seen in his eyes had touched her.

'And you go and see Mrs Warburton before the weekend.'

'Oh!' she exclaimed. This was quite another matter, but as she assessed her father's steady gaze, she knew she had reached the limits of his patience. She lowered her head to hide the thought that it would at least give her a reason to go out. . .

Leah worked the wooden rake, expertly drawing the lines of cut grass together, turning, and then respreading for the heat of the sun to do its work in making the hay.

The sun was as hot and the day as balmy as the previous Sunday had been, but comparing the two days was like comparing warm creamy beastlings from a newly calved cow with skimmed milk.

She remembered the delicious feel of her feet in the cool stream, and the breeze beneath the willow-trees. Now the frill at the back of her sun-bonnet stuck to her neck, and her arms burned with the heat of the sun. She paused, leaning on her rake, the air around her heavy with the already proving hay. She recalled the aroma of shaving-soap and newly pressed linen. She remembered how tall Ben Robertson had been beside her, how angular his jaw, the strength of his hand . . . His concern for her, his interest in her selling trip. She sighed for the pleasure of it all, and two days more would bring Sunday again.

She lifted her gaze in the direction of Black Pool Spinney, wondering what Ginnie had been up to and where she had been all week – while noting that a solitary rider had emerged from the spinney, both figure and horse looking broken and unreal in the shimmering heat haze. She watched a moment or two longer, then speculated that it might be the farmer coming to inspect her work.

Glancing up at the noon sun, then at the remaining three-quarters of the twenty-acre field she still had to turn, she began to work again. Thinking of the farmer, Ambrose Clarke – that drove away the day-dreams, and brought an anger that made her sweep her rake faster! She had been content until she had overhead him boast that he had "saved a full three-pence" by having a field turned by a lass. She, doing just as good a job as a man or a boy, had been persuaded that sixpence was the proper rate for the job!

It wasn't just the three-pence short she resented, it was the air of patronage the down-at-heel tenant-farmer had given himself when agreeing to let her do the work – though pride was just another straw in the wind when hunger threatened.

She had that morning caught her grandmother spooning extra bread and milk from her own breakfast dish into Leah's, and when she would have protested her mother hastily silenced her. 'It's her way of helping,' she whispered urgently, 'because you're working today.' Leah had self-consciously emptied her bowl.

The smooth rhythm of her work was upset at the thought, and she stabbed and swung erratically with her rake, making herself hotter, the toil harder. 'No,' she told herself, 'make a new start. Think about something else. Think of ways of using Sam's skill, of the loom and the tally-rounds. If I can think long enough . . .'

The swing of her rake became disciplined and controlled again as she went to her two tasks. "Queen for the Day" Sam had said, if she could think of a way of making the old shop profitable again.

So involved did she become in her thoughts that until the sudden half stumble of a horse nearby made her start, and a shadow fell over her, she had forgotten the figure she had glimpsed in the distance. She knew immediately by the size, of the well-muscled chestnut horse, and the gleam of its coat, that it was not her temporary employer who loomed over her.

'A village girl?' the man asked without preamble, easing himself out of his saddle with a forward thrust of his hips.

'From Tur Lacey, yes,' she answered, looking up from the fine leather riding boots in the stirrups, the well-cut breeches, to a pristine frilled white shirt, a riding coat across the horse's withers, and finally into the face of a man she judged to be in his late forties. His hair and moustache were of a gingery-red, his skin of that ruddy hue that often accompanies such colouring, and his eyes were a brown that held the same reddish hue. "Sly fox," she thought. "Sly old fox."

'Push your bonnet back, girl, let's see your face properly.'

She made no move, wondering at the authority he thought he had over her.

'Come on now!' Again he eased himself up out of his saddle with a movement that was curiously and disturbingly suggestive. His tone too altered. There was a token of banter, but impatience as well. 'You never know, your face could be your fortune – all else about you looks healthy.'

'Like a good filly, you mean?' She deliberately kept her face lowered as she answered.

He laughed aloud then. 'With a bit of spirit, that's right! That's how I like 'em.' Before she could answer or move, he lightly tapped his horse's flanks with his heels. The responsive beast shot forward, the rider leaned over a little as he passed – and the bonnet was pulled from her head, to hang on its strings down her back.

'Ah! Worth the effort.' The man laughed at her fury, but his expression changed as she took a fresh, aggressive grip on the wooden rake as he circled the horse around her.

'I'll bring this down on its rump if you come nearer.'

'You touch my mount at your peril!'

'And you touch me at yours!'

'The likes of you are mine for the asking,' he said without particular emphasis. 'You'll be one of Ambrose Clark's brood He's better at producing daughters than he is at farming, that's for sure.' He paused to consider her. He seemed able to see through her clothes, so she felt naked before him and had to fight an impulse to cover herself with her hands. There was a new persuasiveness in his voice as he went on, 'A fair maid like you never need work this hard for pennies. You are a maid, I would say.' He circled his mount around her once more.

'And your horse, I would say, is a gelding.' Her voice was low and shook with anger at his remark, and the audacity of her own.

He sat deeper into his saddle and studied her. 'The vicar and his village education ideas have a lot to answer for,' he judged, but before she could correct him either as to her parentage, or her grandmother's tuition, he added another inducement, 'You know, you could be the reason I don't turn your father and his broken-down collection of animals off my land, and your family out of your house.'

She was appalled at his calm assumption that he could order her, or any girl, to his will by such blackmail. Ginnie always said she had led a sheltered life – until now, until necessity had forced her out to earn what she could, how she could. . .

The confident smirk on his face made her want to strike out at him. Instead, she drummed the hay-rake on the ground, sounding it like the warning thump a rabbit makes before springing away from danger. She had little enough time for Ambrose Clarke, but now she had met his landlord, she could find more sympathy for anyone in his power. Another suspicion flashed into her mind. this field was the furthest south of Farmer Clarke's rented land. The rest stretched in the direction of Church Lacey where she had seen the stockman evicted – and there was certainly no compassion or compunction in his man.

'It seems, Squire Lacey, I know you better than you know me.'

He raised his eyebrows. 'Well, of course, and I suppose news travels fast where there's so little of importance happening in your lives. But I'll know who you are before the day's out, you may be sure of that.' He made it sound like a threat, and seemed to have lost all patience with her. He touched the horse's flanks, and made as if to ride at her again. She raised the rake shoulder high. His laugh was humourless as he violently pulled the reins, making the animal half rear before wheeling it away.

'The kill is always more enjoyable after a good chase,' he called. He rode away, deliberately guiding his gelding along the nearest line of neatly spread grass, disturbing and scattering the turning she had just done.

She stood watching him go, despising him as much for his pettiness as for his lustful arrogance. He reached the end of the field and urged his mount at the five-bar gate. Horse and rider took it impeccably. Squire Lacey turned to see if she still watched.

The display of balanced power made her feel somehow older and more sober as she retied her sunbonnet and took up her task again. The Clarke girls did not know how fortunate they were to have shapes like boiled puddings and complexions to match the pudding-cloths. She could imagine Ambrose Clarke first touching his forelock in acquiescence, then turning his back and closing his ears if Squire Lacey put the same ultimatum to him – and what other choice would he have, if he wasn't to render his whole family homeless?

Powerless, she decided. That was what it was to be poor. But she thanked God, and Heaven above, that she was in no way tied to, or in the power of, a man like Squire Lacey.

She had worked only another half row when a fresh voice hailed her. 'Ginnie?' she questioned the figure that came running towards her, looking rather overdressed for the fields on a weekday.

'I'm really supposed to be going to old Warburton's – to apologise!' The tone of the announcement she called to Leah was as dramatic as the story she had to tell. The two went to sit in the shade of the hedge, the better to discuss all the implications of Levis Warburton's gossiping. The story told, and her own anger satisfactorily mirrored in Leah's, Ginnie looked over the remainder of the field still to be turned. 'Come on,'she said, taking up a shorter rake Leah had also brought to the field, 'I can give you half an hour.'

'So we are not to see each other?' Leah said, still mulling over all she had been told.

Ginnie laughed. 'What do you think! And what about Sunday? Don't you worry. I may have to go and eat humble pie to old Ma Warbo, but Dad'll mellow after a bit – I think!'

'I hope so. I couldn't bear to lose you too.'

The next moment Ginnie's arms were around her neck. 'No one will keep us apart,' she declared.

It was well past dusk when Leah finished her work, shouldered the two rakes the three-quarters of a mile to the farmhouse, and received her sixpence from the hands of Ambrose Clarke. As she crossed the yard to walk the last mile home, she caught a glimpse of two of his daughters in the dairy, throwing buckets of water across the floor in a desultory fashion. She waved to them; they paused to look stolidly back at her. A bit like a couple of dun cows over a gate, she thought.

She trudged home alternatively plagued and angered by the thought that they would probably feel quite flattered if Square Lacey wanted his way with either of them – and any resulting child would be nurtured as insurance against future hostility from their landlord. It would not be the first boy or girl brought up among the village urchins whose different features and mannerisms were discussed at length in the close circles of the village matriarchs. The spurious offspring never themselves knew the reason their gazes were drawn with such curiosity to the occupants of the carriages they competed to open field-gates for – the farthings reward thrown as carelessly as their chance existence to the recipients.

Clarrie Elliott was in the Dexter kitchen when Leah arrived home. In contrast to her sombre thoughts, the women's chatter was all animation and excitement.

'What's happened?' she asked, brightening as she saw their smiling faces.

Clarrie hastened to tell of her sister's girl who was a dressmaker and seamstress in the home of Lord and Lady Nubury. Their third daughter was to marry Squire Lacey's son in the autumn, and there was much extra work to be put out to village women to ensure the full linen closets and chests of the Old Manor House at Tur Lacey where the couple would live.

'Clarrie has already put in a word for Miriam and Nellie Dexter to be included.' Her mother nodded, beaming at Leah and adding, 'And she said there will be at least six to eight weeks' work for us!'

So this was the news Squire Lacey thought all the countryside was rapt with. 'Why do names have to be given?' she asked.

'Everyone would have to be vouched for as being honest as well as good with their needles,' Clarrie explained, full of knowledgeable importance. 'Some of the stuffs, the cottons, silks and satins, would be pounds a yard.'

Nellie exclaimed at such a thing, and Miriam expressed an eagerness to work with such fine things. 'Make a change from the old worsted,' she said, adding, 'you know, our Nellie, we'll have to get our hands smooth – thank goodness it's summertime! We couldn't work fine fabrics with chaps and rough fingers.'

Leah hoped it wouldn't be the name "Dexter" that would stop them working – surely fate couldn't be that unkind!

Though she did not think of herself as superstitious, she wondered again about that old Monk's Bell and its curse. She, a strange woman, had seen its emergence into the daylight . . . Oh, no, she told herself, what nonsense! And hadn't she met Ben Robertson because the bell was being replaced – and weren't they all meeting at the edge of Black Pool Spinney come Sunday?

'Is your name to go down too?' Clarrie was asking. 'For the sewing . . .'

Chapter Six

'What did you say to Squire?' Ambrose Clarke' face was red with fury as he stood on the doorstep of the Dexters' cottage.

'Come on, what did you tell'un?' He gestured aggressively towards Leah and stepped uninvited into the kitchen, his burly, untidy figure blocking the morning sun, and his odour of the farmyard, the freshness of the morning.

Leah stepped forward to meet him. 'I told him – nothing.'

'What is this about, Mr Clarke?' Miriam put a chair before him. 'Sit down,' she added briefly.

He nearly obeyed the older women, but then waved the chair impatiently aside. 'I'll tell you what it's about – I had Squire at my house yester'even, wanting to look around the house, the farm – poking his nose in – asking to see my daughters . . .'

'Your daughters?' Miriam queries.

'Aye – then wanting to know who I had turning the hay near Tur Lacey.' He turned and glared at Leah. 'You!' he accused. 'Outcome is, he's coming back in a few weeks and wants this that and t'other doing about the place.' He broke off, shaking his fist and whole great forearm at Leah again. 'You put'un on my back! Women! More trouble than they're worth. Don't come asking me for work agen! There won't be none for you, nor any of you – either from me or the Squire. I've made sure he knows your names, where you live and what you do. Don't you fear, there'll be nothing for you!'

His glance swept around the three women, but he encountered an uncompromising alliance. Lost for further ways of abusing them, he turning, blaspheming, from the kitchen,

60

grasping the handle of the door and pulling it to with such violence the inner latch disappeared and they heard the splintering as the handle was wrenched from its moorings.

The iron fitting was thrown violently on to the cobbles outside. They heard Sam's voice raised, remonstrating, questioning the departing man, but in the kitchen no one heeded the spiteful vandalism. Nellie turned to her daughter. 'What have you done, Leah?' the tone rather than the words questioning the depth of trouble she had made for the family – the possible loss of earnings. It made Leah feel she had squandered the very food from their table. Her mother and grandmother had become so sure of the sewing work, of all those weeks, even months, of employment.

'What happened?' her grandmother asked more gently, and motioned Sam to come inside as he appeared, carrying the door handle.

She had no choice but to tell the full story, wondering as she did so at the nature of such a man, someone of wealth, who had gone from the home of Lord and Lady Nubury on the business of his only son's wedding to that of a lowly tenant farmer, just to find out the name of a girl who had defied him.

'I'm not sure what we'll do if we don't get this work,' Nellie began, sounding near to tears. 'I dare not think of it.'

'I'd rather think of that than of Leah being forcibly put upon by any man, be it lord, squire or . . .'

Sam made a noise of agreement in his throat. 'I know one of the huntsmen who was employed by t'old Squire. He said the Laceys were all ruthless. Hard-hearted with their dogs, horses, and their servants – using them and casting them aside without feeling.' His voice lower, he added, 'There was the girl from East Lacey, in the old Squire's time, who threw herself under a train . . .'

'Oh!' Nellie lifted her arms, appalled at the prospect that was being described, and hurried forward to envelop her daughter in a close, appeasing embrace. 'I'd rather starve!'

Miriam declared there had been other bad times they'd got through – this too would pass.

'But to bother to find out who I was!' Leah exclaimed.

'Aye, well, he knows something special when he sees it.' Sam commented in a more light-hearted manner, and laughed as she blushed, adding as he shook the door-latch in her direction, 'Come help me find some nails.'

Leah followed him to his cottage, knowing there was more to this invitation than the need of her help to find nails.

He sat down at the table where he had been straightening a wire noose. 'I didn't want to alarm your mother – but I do want to warn you, Leah. Squire Lacey is a bad man to cross, as many of his men have cause to know. They say he never forgives a slight, and will hunt a quarry, or an opponent, to the bitter end.'

'So you don't think we'll get any of the sewing?'

'Sewing! I'm not talking about sewing. I'm talking about you!' He leaned forward over the table to emphasise his point. 'I'm telling you to be watchful. Not to go off over the fields alone – not towards his land anyway. Not that you'll get any more work from Ambrose Clarke, that's for sure.' He wagged the wire snare at her. 'You be told now – be careful.'

'I will, don't worry. I can look after myself. I'll be on my guard.'

He regarded her as if trying to decide if he had said enough on the subject, then broke into husky laughter. 'I should've like to see Squire's face when he was shown the Clarke girls . . . not got quite the same class as Gaffer's granddaughter!'

For the first time she forgave the old man the nickname, and exchanged knowing looks, each acknowledging how much more affection and merit they were each finding in the other, in these days of growing adversity.

She picked up the last of a few pairs of men's stockings that Clarrie had painstakingly reknitted from faulty work and flattened them on the table. 'I wondered if it would be worth taking what goods we have into Leicester market? After all, I could get a lift on one of the farmcarts easily enough.'

Sam looked at her thoughtfully, as if gauging her reaction to what he was about to say. 'it might be an idea . . . and perhaps you could go to the factory and find out why some shops in the village have had wool this week, while we haven't. It's the first time I've known it happen.'

'Sam, you didn't tell me!' For the first time Leah felt a touch of real despair.

'Didn't know it was right until I asked around in the Stockinger's Arms last night.' He paused, trying out the wire he was making into a snare, pulling it tight around his wrist.

'I'll go to Leicester on Wednesday, but on Monday I'll do the next tally-round. It's not so far, I can start early and walk –so there'll be no fare to pay. I might collect some of what's owing. And I'll wear my gardening clogs,' she added, mindful of the thin fraying layer of leather on the soles of her best boots.

He nodded approvingly. 'And I've a few rabbit runs marked out for snares. We'll have a Sunday dinner between us, with a bit of luck.'

The sound of his wife, Clarrie, bustling up the entry made him add, 'We've 'undred and one shot today – a 'undred to one shot you get a bit of meat, boiled in a suet pudding.' Leah laughed, though she remembered grumbling many times in the past at the often produced suety meat pudding. Now she would have welcomed the chance for a good slice of the glutinous meal that could lie in your stomach for most of the day.

'Oh, Leah!' Clarrie exclaimed, as she bustled in. Though no taller than Sam, she seemed robust against his rib-bone thinness. 'I've some news for you. We've all to go to the Church Hall on Monday evening. Lady Nubury is coming personally to discuss with all the sewing women who is to do what. And you must take a sample of fine sewing. My sister's girl will be one of those with her, and she'll look out for us!'

The words implied that the young woman would see that her aunt, and the Dexters, were singled out for special work. When Leah's face showed her doubts, Clarrie hastened to reassure her that she had added Leah's name to the list sent forward for approval.

Sam diverted his wife from the sewing question by asking after his dinner. Leah left Clarrie remonstrating that she couldn't be in more places than one at once, or do more than one thing at once, however much she tried – while at the same time she bustled about to put his meal before him.

Her grandmother questioned whether the names would even reach such as Squire Lacey's household. 'After all, it's Lady Nubury's daughter. Perhaps we're bothering our heads about nothing.'

63

'Let's not think about it then,' Nellie said, restless with the worry of it all. And as she glanced anxiously at Leah, her daughter smiled reassuringly and said, 'Sam's hoping to get a rabbit for tomorrow.'

Nellie looked relieved. Here was a more homely matter she could deal with. She went to push the kettle over the hob, thrusting more kindling under it. In her faded pink floral dress, Leah though she looked like a rose that still hung upon its stem long after it should have fallen. Every ill wind brought it nearer to the moment that would send it tumbling. Perhaps this was what Sam saw too.

Her mother busied herself fetching milk from the pantry, and watching her anxiously, Leah thought of the long years of widowhood – from first blooming to well past middle-age. It seemed so unjust that both her mother and her grandmother should be bereaved, and that poverty now came hanging around their door. Leah felt close to angry tears but Nellie was already talking of thyme and parsley for the rabbit stock, brightening a little more as she speculated about a little suet to make dumplings. Only the china cups and saucers brought from the parlour, on a Saturday, revealed how much in need of extra comfort Nellie felt.

Sunday blew in with great banks of rain clouds looming low over the horizon, and Leah could smell the rain in the wind. After the weeks of hot weather it was a disappointment, but the rain still had not come when it was time to meet Ginnie, and Leah went casually from workshop to garden, down the entry and out into the street. She wondered what excuse Ginnie would find to be out. It was all becoming much more fraught and difficult – much more enticing and exciting!

She was hurrying on when she heard a call, and turned to see Ginnie running to catch her up. They linked arms but Ginnie seemed in a sombre mood. She told of the indignity of having to take her Sunday School class in the same room as Mrs Warburton. 'With the old battleship interrupting every few minutes. Then I had to sit next to her in church. I thought you might at least be there! I'd planned to sit with you at the back, no matter what. Then you didn't come!'

'We've been busy. Gran's got me the promise of a corner on a market stall in Leicester on Wednesday . . . we've been scraping things together.'

'Oh, you lucky thing! I wish I could come.'

'I wish you could.'

'Though if I get caught out today,' Ginnie added dourly, 'I'll probably never be allowed to see the light of day again. I've left Charley polishing the brass beer-taps and spittoons for me as it is. I've got to mend his best trousers before Father sees them, mind.'

'That's fair,' Leah said, realising that even her best friend had no idea how bad things were for the Dexters. They left the road near the point they had encountered Ben and Nat the week before, and struck off diagonally across a field of barley where a wide grass-edged footpath was maintained. The wind drove the clouds across the sky as if taking pleasure in its power. One moment the sun was full of heat, the next the brightness was gone and the clouds seemed to threaten a great downpour. To the two girls, the dramas of light and shade only added to their happy anticipation. From time to time they ran laughing before the shadows over the grain fields and the meadows.

'They're at the edge of the trees,' Leah said as they climbed the last field towards Black Pool Spinney.

The two young men raised themselves from their stance leaning on a stile, and came smiling to meet them.

'You've managed it then?' Nat asked.

'Of course,' Ginnie replied, 'no problem.'

Leah smiled up at Ben and he saw her amusement and raised his eyebrows. 'Not so simple, I expect.'

'No, certainly not so simple,' she repeated.

'So which way do we have to go?' Ginnie asked, hands on hips, confronting the diverging paths through the Spinney.

'Follow your nose,' Nat said, 'straight ahead.'

The open aspect of the trees at the edge of the spinney, with the sun shining through the leaves of hazelnut bushes and the larger oak and ash trees, made their way for a time idyllic and sunlit. Then a greater, darker mass of cloud plunged the party into gloom, sometimes so deep the couples stumbled upon each other and had to stop for a second or two as their eyes adjusted. Ginnie squealed her delight. She had determined that the afternoon would be an adventure.

The trees were much closer and the undergrowth thicker as they walked on. In places the ground had that peaty blackness that never dries.

Ben took Leah's hand, guiding her around the worst places, and as they came to a firmer path again, kept it and squeezed with firm gentleness. She felt breathless and bold as she tightened her fingers around his, just ever so slightly. The other two ran ahead, larking like children. Leah felt a lifetime older than her friend at that moment, and found herself tutting as she realised Ginnie had run ahead and concealed herself.

They came level with Nat, who was laughing and searching. 'You go that way,' he instructed his brother, 'and you that.' Leah felt her lips part in disappointment as Ben dropped her hand and made off in the direction Nat pointed.

'Ginnie!' she called, the tone half appealing, half annoyed, wanting to add, "For goodness' sake, grow up!" Instead, she listened. At first there was the disturbance of the two brothers going off in diverging directions, then the noises lessened and the wood seemed to listen.

One moment she had been surrounded by friends, her hand held by Ben Robertson, and now . . . She tutted again to herself, and walked in the direction Nat had pointed her. In the distance she heard movement again, but from quite a different direction. She opened her mouth to call Ginnie's name but some instinct made her stop, her heart beating faster. The sounds were not those made by someone hiding for larks. The slow crack of a twig seemed broken by a cautious, heavy footstep – a menacing sound. It came again, and she stepped silently aside under the cover of a thick hazel bush.

Someone was moving covertly along the path towards her . . . Then, it seemed at some great distance, she heard Ginnie's muffled but unmistakable giggle. The noises nearby stopped. Whoever it was paused, and listened too. Pressed back in the bush her view across the path was limited to where the branches thinned near the ground. Into sight came a man's highly polished leather boots, breeches, and the end of a gun-barrel. He was obviously listening intently for he moved very cautiously, one step at a time. It seemed that he must see her, or that she would give herself away long before he passed.

She bit her lip as she remembered Squire Lacey's polished riding boots – and Sam's remark that the Laceys had a reputation for always hunting a quarry down, never giving up . . . She wondered if a girl could defend herself in a situation like this?

She pressed a hand to her mouth as the man turned towards her, his toe-caps seeming to point out her hiding-place. then in the distance came Ginnie's laughter, the sound of Nat's voice and Ben's deeper tones answering. The man hesitated, then turned on his way again.

She stood quite still a moment or two longer, then she began to run in the opposite direction as fast as she could, back the way they had come, just wanting to be out of the spinney.

She wanted no more of Ginnie's games of hide and seek and forgot her self-appointed role as the strong member of the Dexter family, feeling as vulnerable as a small frightened child, one who needed protection herself – needed her grandfather. Suddenly it was all too much: Levis Warburton, Ambrose Clarke, Squire Lacey – not a fit person for Ginnie to associate with – no wool from the factory – no rabbit for dinner – Sam's snares stolen. . .

She ran unheeding now, feeling her skirts drag on twigs and branches, her hands scratched by briars as she protected her face. The tiny physical hurts suddenly brought a prickle of tears, which once begun she found she could not stop. She wiped her eyes dry with her fingers, then must use the palms of her hands to sweep the wetness from her cheeks.

She must go home – no one must see her like this. Now for the first time she truly wept for her grandfather – grieved unrestricted and unshamed by her grandmother's self-control. Leah had seen her do no more than bow her head, close her eyes against the pity of her granddaughter, and let her heart break with quiet stoicism. 'She should cry – really cry,' she found herself whispering as she ran, her way blurred by the copiousness of her tears.

Then she heard someone nearby, someone who came after her. Friend or foe? she wondered, running faster, until, finally she realised it was Ben calling her name, catching up with her. She stopped, caught her breath, trying with all her might to stem the tears, angry with herself. She pulled two huge dock leaves to cool her cheeks, throwing them down before he reached her.

'What is it?' he asked, his voice full of concern, and the next moment he had hold of her, holding first her forearms, then seeing her distress, close in his arms, soothing her. She realised his heart was soon beating as fast as her own.

'That was a silly game to play when we none of us know the place well,' he judged as he saw how she had been crying, how her cheeks burned.

She shook her head. 'It wasn't that – it was a man with a gun, and the sun going in . . . it was just . . .' She stopped and tried to laugh at herself. It was a shaky and unconvincing effort, but she knew the tears were finished and added with quiet certainty, 'It won't happen again.'

'A man with a gun?' he questioned. Then, as there was an explosion of laughter nearby, called out, 'Call it off, you two! The game's over.'

Ginnie came first, pretending petulance like a disciplined child, but was immediately curious and contrite when she saw Leah had been crying. Ben fended off her questions, ushering her and his brother on their way to Flaxhill. 'Let's get out of this spinney. It's as dark as night in here when the sun goes in.'

Nat and Ginnie walked ahead, and Ben shouldered aside branches, brambles, whole bushes it seemed to Leah, so he could walk by her side, and keep his arm around her. She began to feel very comforted, with her shoulder so snugly fitting under his arm, the warmth of his hand on her waist.

They emerged from the hill-top spinney, and stood looking down towards where the medieval village of Flaxhill had once been – all that remained were mounds of earth, graves of dwellings which had lined the main village street and circled a market cross. At the far side of the valley, the hill above the deserted village held the circular base of the windmill that had worked there. Below the ruin a pond still existed, behind great growths of reed, where it was said flax was laid to rot away the unwanted vegetation, and leave the fibres for making linen from which activity the original village had taken its name.

Only the Norman church remained in truly recognisable shape, looking from a distance untouched by time, its thick stone blocks impervious to man's history or nature's ravages.

'If it's coming on to rain, we'd find shelter in the church,' Nat said, looking over to where the next great bank of cloud was looming from the West.

They had barely time to assent before the first spots began to fall. 'Like cold half-crowns!' Ginnie decided. 'Come on!' For once she led the way, running downhill, but Nat caught her up in a few strides, and Ben and Leah overtook them both, Leah having to laugh at their exaggerated protests as she and Ben sprinted on – down the hill, along the grassed-over street, between the mounds, to the ruins of the church.

There was no door inside the broken porch, and Ben still held her hand as he led her inside, which was gloomier still, 'I want to know what upset you in the wood.' He paused, then added quietly, 'And I wondered if you would meet me somewhere . . .' The laughter and chatter of the other two reached them and he added, 'Without that scatty pair!'

'I . . .' she hesitated. The question was unexpected, her breathing erratic for reasons other than their run. 'I'd like to,' she agreed at last, just before the other two came clattering into the church.

'Oooh!' Ginnie shuddered with obvious enjoyment. 'It's dark and creepy. My brothers would love this.'

'Not for long, it isn't.' Ben took a candle from his jacket pocket, a match flared and he cupped his hand around the flame to steady it. 'Might as well have a look in the belfry while we've got it lit,' he added, and led the way across to the bottom of the tower.

The church was an eerie place by the light of one flickering candle. As Ben moved, the wavering flame sent the shadows of pillars, of the high stone-canopied pulpit, altar table and a great sepulchre with its solemn image of sleeping crusader processing ponderously across the interior, like worshippers intent on some strange religious ceremony.

Leah caught her breath as Ginnie's face was momentarily picked out by the pale light, making the rosy cheeks wan. She shivered, reminded of the moment Ben had brought his sledge-hammer down on the old Monk's Bell, feeling the same sense of premonition. She moved closer to Ben's side, and he took her hand, drawing her under the tower, pointing up to a wooden ceiling some fifteen feet above their heads. 'There was one bell at least,' he explained. 'See the small round hole? That was where they would have a bell-rope through to the ground floor to ring the communion bell. But we shall have to go up to the bell-chamber to find out if anything's still there.'

'I'll wait here with the girls, while you go,' Nat said.

'I thought we were all going,' Ginnie complained. 'It'll be more fun than just standing here.' She nodded to where the rain beat down like a solid, cold curtain, splashing for some yards inside the church. 'We're game, aren't we, Leah?'

'I've never been up a church tower,' she said, preferring to climb up with Ben than be left playing gooseberry with the other two.

'It's a lot of steps,' Nat warned, but allowed himself the pleasure of being persuaded and coaxed by Ginnie.

A small arched door led to an enclosed spiral staircase. The four had hardly begun the long climb up to the top before Leah realised this was going to be quite an experience. In the centre of the spiral, the steps tapered to nothing and were barely wide enough for a foot at the outside. There was no hand rail and it was dark, the heavy smell of stone all around them like a tomb.

'It'll be lighter higher up,' Ben reassured them, 'there'll be open louvres.' Leah held on to his jacket with one hand and pressed the other to the outer wall. Nat came next with Ginnie hanging on to him.

They quite soon came to a tiny stone-flagged landing and a door to their right. 'The ringing chamber,' Ben explained, trying it, but the oak door did not move.

'They don't want any Tom, Dick or Harry alarming the neighbourhood by ringing the bells,' Nat commented. 'Now the real climb begins,' Ben said, leading the way again.

70

They went on for some minutes in silence, each concentrating on keeping their equilibrium.

'How far is it? How many steps . . .?' Ginnie asked somewhat pathetically from the back of the line.

'Some of these towers can have hundreds,' Nat replied.

'I think it would have been more fun at the bottom.'

'I bet it's worse coming down,' Leah speculated.

'No turning back now,' Ben declared, 'onward and upward'

They reached the first of the slits, which let through a welcome if cobwebby breeze. Leah peered through as they passed. 'The sky's lighter,' she said.

'It's more than my legs are then,' Ginnie called. 'I've lost count how many steps!'

Leah began to feel disorientated as they circled and climbed, circled and climbed. The higher they went, the dustier, narrower, and more precarious the steps became. Even Ginnie had fallen silent long before they arrived at a door that barred their way. Ben made sure they were all carefully balanced below him before he tried to open it.

'Locked or jammed?' Nat queried, but as Ben put more weight on the door, it gave slowly, grating on dry hinges. Both girls cried out in surprise as from inside there came a great flutter and squawk of disturbed birds.

'By heavens!' Ben exclaimed triumphantly, leading the way in.'Look at those! They went in when the tower was built.'

Leah and Ginnie stepped cautiously into the bellchamber, where a stone thrall made a walkway around what seemed, from their elevation, a kind of pit, across which great oak beams had been built into the wall. Bolted to the beams by many radiating spokes of iron were four bells, varying in height from the size of a child to that of a small man. Alongside each was what looked like a cartwheel with a hollow rim. Remnants of old bell ropes still hung around two of the wheels, passing through the floor, down into the ringing chamber below.

'I think you're right. The argent and canons have to be seventeenth century.' The enthusiasm in Ben's voice fascinated Leah though the technical details meant nothing. She was more concerned with a solitary starling, deserted by its fellows, and unable in its panic to find the way out of the belfry.

Nat swung himself down under the bells and reported the clappers all there, though one or two "wouldn't stand ringing". The two men were obviously completely enthralled with their find, talking of weights, and the composition of the bell-metal. Leah and Ginnie stared round at the chamber with its larger carved arches open to the elements, and to what looked like tons of straw, twigs, feathers and bird droppings that had accumulated over the centuries. Every possible ledge inside the belfry showed signs of having been used for nesting or roosting.

'Do we tell the old man?' Nat asked, tapping the largest bell with his knuckle. It gave out a low hollow note.

'I think not,' Ben said briefly. 'It'll do nothing for any of us for him to know, and we've work enough.'

'Where do those go to?' Leah pointed to a flight of steps cut into one wall of the tower above their heads.

'Out on to the battlements,' Ben said. 'Want to see the view?'

He climbed this final flight alone first, clearing them of debris as he went, then used his shoulders to lever up the trapdoor above him. A ray of sun, brilliant and swirling with newly disturbed dust-motes, broke through into the gloomy belfry. It reminded Leah of an old picture that hung in the Sunday School, of a saint lying in a dark dungeon with a ray of sun, signifying hope, pouring down on him from a high barred window.

Ben climbed through on to the roof of the tower and stood waiting to help the other three up.

'It's so high! I didn't expect to feel so high,' Ginnie exclaimed, going to the battlements and peering over.

'Make sure it's safe before you lean on anything,' Nat warned.

'You can see so far – right up the valley – right to. . .' Leah pointed to a distant village as Ben came to stand next to her.

'Church Lacey,' he supplied.

'Oh!' she said solemnly, and walked around to the far side of the tower to view the other way.

'East Lacey,' Ben supplied before she asked.

'Lacey, Lacey! I can't get away from the name, even up here. They're a menace! I suppose it was the Laceys who turned the peasants away from Flaxhill, to enclose the land and farm sheep, and become richer and richer – greedier and greedier?'

'I suppose that's true. They've been the biggest landowners this side of the county for hundreds of years . . . but why a menace?'

She leaned against the tall castellations, the heat of the emergent sun seeming the greater after the cool interior of the tower.

'Is it anything to do with your running away just now – with the man carrying the gun?' This time his tone demanded an answer.

She leaned further out, watching the wind moving the tops of the full-foliaged trees, like green clouds, below them. The cows and horses in the fields, the distant farmhouses, looked like mere toys.

'Leah?' He came close, putting his arm around her waist, pulling her back from the battlement.

His hand felt warm through her clothes, and she wondered if it was possible that there was a man in her life again. 'I think they must be terrible people . . .' Quietly she began the story of her encounter with the latest squire of the Lacey family.

Nat and Ginnie came to their side of the tower and stood listening. Ginnie was surprised she had not been told when she had helped turn the hay. Then she made it a joint tale of woe by revealing her father's ban on her seeing Leah.

After a pause, she added with a giggle, 'He says any man who takes her on will need a horse-whip. So be warned, Ben!'

'I'll risk it,' he said with such alacrity Leah caught her breath, and as if the simple statement was the signal for some mutual show of intention, the two couples moved to adjoining battlements, looking out at the rolling Leicestershire countryside, with clouds and sun racing across it. They leaned, arms around each other, taking pleasure in the comfort and the dawning of deeper emotions.

Chapter Seven

Ben watched his step-father over the core of the new bell he and his grandfather were working on. His grandfather reprimanded him as he placed the shaped bricks carelessly on the heavy cast-iron base-plate.

'A good bell starts here,' he stated, realigning the bricks so they rested firmly in between the cinders and coke, used to help disperse the gases which would accumulate during the casting. Already by their side were piles of red sand, and burnt black sand from previous bellmaking, and Nat came into the casting shop pushing a barrow-load of fresh horse manure, all of which they would mix to a smooth loam to cover the inner bell-shaped mould of brick and coke.

They all three worked steadily enough, quietly enough – but all were watchful. These days Caleb Berridge was inclined to wander away from the scene of the work, and back to the house. Ben was becoming more and more disturbed by the way his mother either immediately found some excuse to come and linger in the foundry yard – or, when they returned to the kitchen for their mid-day meal, they found her pale, unwilling to meet their eyes or answer their enquiries with more than quick, anxious, unconvincing reassurances. Caleb seemed to find her manner a cause for sardonic amusement.

He wondered if the sweet hours he had spent with Leah the last two Sundays had made him more mindful of a woman's lot, more sensitive on his mother's behalf. It had certainly made him think of the time when he might wish to set up a home of his own – though long before that there had to be a confrontation with Caleb.

He noticed how his grandfather's hands trembled as he made the final adjustments to the bell-shaped structure, and the swing of the spade in Nat's hands paused as he mixed the loam. He knew without looking that his step-father had passed the open double doorway on his way to the house.

He rose slowly from his haunches, turning just in time to see his mother step from the kitchen threshold, only to be recalled by the harsh voice of Caleb from inside. She turned back. Swift anger made Ben's face burn as he watched her trail a hand behind her, tracing the line of the door jamb, then the surface of the open door, like a reluctant child recalled from play. He heard another barked order, and as she moved inside the door was slammed shut.

'Boy!' his grandfather warned sternly. 'You'll only make more trouble for her. For better or for worse he's her husband, as both he and she have often reminded me.'

Ben stood glaring at the house, knowing two things – that his grandfather was right, and that he could not tolerate it any longer. 'There must be some reckoning with the man,' he said with quiet purposefulness, glancing at his brother. 'We do the work. He pockets the profits, and makes our mother miserable.'

'He drinks all day, and takes her to bed in the mornings because he's incapable at night.' Nat was more specific.

Ben glanced at his grandfather, saw the agony for his daughter on his face as he asked in no more than a whisper, 'What more can we do? He only makes it worse for her if you interfere, and she'll vow she's quite all right.'

Ben knew his mother's strict sense of duty, reinforced by her religious fervour. She had made her vows to this second husband, and regarded them every bit as sacred as those she had made as a young bride to their father. 'We could manage without him,' Ben said. 'We're the skilled workmen – he's nothing.'

'She'll never leave him – not this side of the grave. And we can't make bells without the equipment and the furnace,' Josiah reminded him, sitting wearily back on his haunches.

'A furnace? It's only a fire, for Lord's sake!'

'Leave it, Ben.' Nat nodded sympathetically to the kneeling figure of their grandfather, who suddenly looked so frail and old. They both knew he blamed himself for losing control of the bell-foundry.

'How long can we leave it though?' he muttered, as if to himself. He felt suddenly impatient with his grandfather and his brother, each in their own way advocating that they should just carry on as they were. He felt he must get away from them for a few moments, be on his own to calm down, to think. If there was ever going to be anything done about their step-father, he would have to do it.

'Ben! Where are you going?'

'I'll fetch the sweepboard,' he called back, going off in the direction of the brick hovel where they stored the moulding tools.

'We're not nearly ready,' Josiah protested, for the sweep-board was used after all the loam was plastered on the core, its bell-shaped profile being swept around and around from a central shaft to form a regular shape and remove excess material.

Ben was already half way across the yard, and ignored the anxiety in his grandfather's voice. Though he did go first in the direction of the open hovel, he did not pause there but went on to stand under the shade of the nearest trees in the orchard. The Bramley cooking-apples were swelling a lighter green against their foliage, and Queen of Bath, the early eaters, were rosy skinned, nearly ready for picking. There was the slightest of breezes here. It cooled his cheek and he thought of that first Sunday afternoon meeting by the river; of Leah, Ginnie and Nat, paddling. That innocent time had been marred by a Peeping Tom, just as his home was marred by his step-father's presence.

He turned to look at the house again, at the fine deep yellow rambler-rose on the trellis arch around the doorway. His real father had erected that and planted the rose. "A cottage with roses around the door", as the old saying went – though he had heard another version that said, "Roses round the door, and thorns in the bed." That, he thought, was what his mother now had. The family home was the same, but the man who shared her bed was the thorn in all their sides.

He turned back to the house, and without further thought went into the kitchen. It was empty, but from the bedroom

76

above he could hear voices: his step-father's husky, half-coaxing, half threatening; his mother's low, placating.

He sat in his father's old elm carver chair near the kitchen table, gripping the smooth-worn arms as if to hold himself there, forcing himself to stay and listen to her submission, her humiliation. Once she cried out like an abused child, and he rose to his feet, bile in his throat. Only the thought of how much it would devastate his mother stopped him from rushing upstairs and dragging Caleb away from her. Then a further thought occurred to him, as hateful and perhaps more devious than Caleb Berridge himself. Being with detestable people made you become much the same, he thought.

At length he heard the stairs creak under the weight of a light footstep. He swallowed hard and waited for his mother to emerge from the enclosed staircase.

'Ben?' she queried, surprise making her come forward and search his face anxiously. 'How long have you been here? Is anything wrong?'

'It's what's wrong for you,' he began, his voice low and shaking as he saw in her eyes all she usually managed to conceal – the vulnerability, the stifling of her finer feelings.

'Why are you here in the kitchen? You have your work to do, and I have . . . mine.'

'Work? Mother! It shouldn't be regarded as work, should it? Not what you and he – not what husband and wife . . .'

'You have a lot to learn about life,' she said gently, putting her small heavily veined hand over his. 'I am . . .' She searched for a truthful word of reassurance for her elder son.

'You are abused and bullied,' he said, covering her thin hand with his, 'and I can't stand it any longer.'

'Ben, if I can stand it, so can you – what I cannot bear is trouble between my sons and my husband. My duty is to all of you.' She paused and pulled her hand from his, listening as she heard heavy movements in the bedroom above. She turned to go towards the dresser, reaching down the quart tankard Caleb used for his ale. 'Don't tear me apart, Ben,' she begged. Don't use me as the excuse.' She pressed her arm and hand tight to her side and chest as if in physical pain.

Ben stood up and faced his step-father wordlessly as he pushed his way through the stairs-door.

'What d'you want?' he growled. 'What you bin talking about?' His glance went from Mabel to her son. When neither answered he gave a dismissive laugh, waving his arm in the direction of the tankard. 'Come on. I've earned my ale, haven't I?' He laughed again and sat down at the table, while Mabel, with an appealing glance at Ben, went through into the back kitchen. Ben waited until he thought she was out of earshot, then turned and bent over Caleb.

''ere, what's this?' he demanded.

'This is a promise,' Ben hissed at him. 'I promise you that, like today, every time you come into the house during the daytime, I'll be here.' He indicated the chair, then went to the door of the stairs. 'Or perhaps even in the stairwell . . . listening to you. Listening to you earning your ale . . . if you can.' He paused to let the implications of what he had said bring a suffused purple colour to Caleb's face. 'Knowing your efforts are . . .'

'You'll get on with your bloody work!' Caleb shouted him down, and attempted to rise, but Ben stepped forward aggressively. The action seemed to unbalance the older man, making him fall back into his chair.

'I'll get on with my work when you're out there, supervising, telling us how to do the job – after all, you're the gaffer. You can tell us how much copper and tin to put in the furnace – you should really wield the old willow branch, stir the bell-metal in the cauldron as it runs from the furnace.' It was Ben's turn to laugh as Caleb moved uneasily in his seat. There was much about bell-making that was mystery and superstition to him, and Ben and Nat played on his ignorance whenever they could.

'Seems like we've got rebellion in the camp,' Caleb said, addressing Mabel who came back with a frothing tankard of ale. 'Young man here thinks he knows better than I do about bell-making.'

His mother looked pleadingly at Ben, but did not answer. 'I know all there is to know about bell-making. My grandfather has taught me everything.'

'So we could cut out a little dead wood then,' Caleb said, his face triumphant as he found a new way to discipline his workforce. 'No need to keep two men to do one man's job.

78

You can take over from the old man, and Nat can do Cuddy's work any time.' He gloated, sat smiling. 'What do you think, my dear? Saving money – isn't that a good business idea?'

'My grandfather's money!' Ben put in, gripping the back of a chair, wringing his fists, white-knuckled, around the rail to stop himself attacking the man. 'And my father's – and my mother's!'

'Now all in my control – all of you, from that no-good idiot Cuddy with his days off, you and Nat, your aged grandparent . . .' he paused to curl his lip in a sneer, '. . . and your dear mother.'

'Ben meant no disrespect,' Mabel began.

'Didn't I?' Ben interrupted, adding, 'And I would remind you that Cuddy has gone to his mother's funeral.'

'So you'd rather take Cuddy's part than mine?' Caleb said. 'Perhaps we should find out just where the loyalties lie in this family. Why I bother to keep us all together.' He paused, his glance going like an order to his wife.

She went hastily to stand behind her husband, and without looking at her son, placed a hand on each of his shoulders. 'I'm sure we're all wanting and working for the same things, to be all together . . .'

'That right, Ben? What your mother says? All working hard, doing as you're told.' He reached up and took one of Mabel's hands, in a manner which suggested it could become a cruel and punishing grip if Ben did not provide the right answer.

'We work hard,' Ben answered, 'and I can make as good a bell as any man – and I want a man's wage.'

He was almost as surprised as his step-father to hear this new demand so bluntly stated. This was not something he had planned for this particular confrontation – but it was time. Leah was desperately struggling in her efforts to keep her family – a girl almost running a business – while he received his keep and pocket-money.

'Huh! Full of whims and wants today!' Caleb said, throwing Mabel's hand fiercely from his to grasp his drink in both hands and take a deep draught. 'When you make me a good bell – from first to last, mind – then we'll talk about wages!'

His mother began putting bread, cheese, a cold piece of bacon on the table, signalling as she moved out of her husband's view for her son to go while the temper of the encounter remained cooled.

'Will you write that down?' Ben asked. 'Give me a written promise.'

The atmosphere in the kitchen was suddenly tense again, Caleb's tankard stationary halfway to his lips. Mabel gave a minute shake of her head at Ben who stood his ground determined now to extract something from his stepfather.

At last Caleb gave a "humph" of amusement and replaced the tankard in Mabel's hands, who stood at his elbow for that purpose. 'Why not?' he said. 'Why not? I'll have it all written out and signed for you by dinnertime.'

'There, Ben!' Mabel's voice had pleasure and life in it for the first time for many months. 'There!' she repeated, going again to stand against Caleb – who began to chuckle, quietly at first. By the time Ben closed the back door behind himself, the laughter was uproarious.

'What's he going to do?' he asked his grandfather, having related the encounter to Nat and Josiah.

'I suppose he could always interfere with the casting in some way.'

'I'd stand guard, night and day, until it was finished,' Ben vowed.

'And I'd help,' Nat said.

Caleb handed over the paper at the end of their evening meal. Ben unfolded it, and read it over to himself slowly – for long moments not trusting himself to raise his eyes. He was aware of the silence at the table, of Nat and his grandfather holding their breaths, waiting to hear the outcome of his demand, and as the silence lengthened he felt his grandfather's figure slump a little in his chair, as if he already knew that they had been outwitted again. Caleb thumped his empty tankard down on the table with a grunt of amusement.

Nat nodded impatiently, urging his brother to reveal what it said. He passed the single sheet of paper:

I, Caleb George Berridge, agree to pay Benjamin Robertson a top man's wages from the day he makes a good and true bell, of half a ton or more in weight. This bell to be tendered for by him, and moulded and cast by him in premises at least two miles from the bellfoundry known as 'Robertson's' in the County of Leicestershire, and without the use of any tools or equipment from said bellfoundry.

Dated this Thirtieth day of August One thousand eight hundred and seventy-eight.

The signature had been made with great flourishes, curls and embellishments.

'A pretty turn of legal phrasery, don't you think?' Caleb asked, and leaning forward he placed a forefinger on a blob of sealing-wax he had put at the end of the epistle, saying, 'And I deliver this as my act and deed. There!'

Red hot anger blurred Ben's vision, but he vowed with more deadly seriousness than ever his step-father had done, that no one should see it. 'Very pretty,' he said, rising, and though he could see no way he would ever fulfil the conditions, he took the paper from the table and placed it before his grandfather. 'Perhaps you will kindly witness the swearing by adding your signature?'

Caleb spluttered with laughter as this was done, and Ben folded the paper and put it carefully into his waistcoat pocket.

'When I make such a bell, I'll make sure it has a suitable inscription,' he told Caleb.

'When he makes one . . .' His step-father choked, spluttered, and beat the table with his fists in an outrageous display of amusement.

Not sure how he found the control, Ben left the house, closing the kitchen door quietly behind himself. Unaware of any conscious intention he walked to the foundry room and stood pondering over the bell-core made that day and now ready for drying and stoving at the heat of a moderate oven. He had heard his grandfather tell of the days when, three generations back, the Robertsons were itinerant bellmakers, going from district to district, setting up furnaces, finding all their materials and their business locally. And when no more bells remained to be cast in that area, then they moved on.

'If they could do it . . .' he said aloud. 'And if it's the only way to beat Caleb . . .'

Chapter Eight

Ben strode away from the house feeling like a wounded animal who never wants to return to the scene of its hurt. For a time he walked without conscious thought of his direction – just away as fast as he could. Caleb's laughter burnt into his mind, and the paper in his pocket felt like so much ash.

But if the law could give his step-father what was, by all natural justice, his and Nat's inheritance, then the law should be made to enforce a man's written promise. His hand went to his waistcoat pocket. He would make Caleb either stick to every word of his elaborate script – or else push the paper down the man's greedy throat.

He turned over in his mind the materials he would need to build a furnace; bricks, heavy clay, turf for insulation. Were there other possibilities? There were other bellfounders . . . one in the town, for instance. Though they would hardly be likely to let a competitor walk in and cast a bell . . . But he might be hired, at a skilled man's wage. But . . . 'Aye, but!' he exclaimed aloud.

He picked up a stout stick and lashed at the wayside nettles, laying them flat, and making the cow-parsley crackle like gunshot as he fractured its hollow stems. He reached the end of the lane, and followed the footpath into the fields. A familiar figure sitting on the far stile caught his eye, and his conscience.

'Cuddy,' he breathed, tutting at his own forgetfulness. He raised his arm high in greeting, palm spread as if asking Cuddy's forbearance. After a few seconds Cuddy's long arm went slowly into the air, but the fingers spread before the face, uneasy, defensive, and he turned, walking away towards Soston his home village.

Cuddy's mother had protected him like a tigress. He wondered who would now stand between Cuddy and village children who mocked his heavy-shouldered, long-armed stance, or those who took advantage of both his amiability and great strength, using him for long laborious tasks and rewarding him with a few words of praise and encouragement, and if he was lucky the price of a drink.

Cuddy too he realised was part of the "but", the reasons he could not just walk away – and then there was Leah. With her own problems – with the dark eyes that dealt his heart a blow at a glance – businesswoman yet child – coldly proud and austere one moment, but so warm and pulsating with life when his arm had encircled her waist on top of Flaxhill tower. He breathed faster. At that moment the old tower had seemed like the highest pinnacle in the world.

He felt he must have some definite plan before he could bring himself to return to the foundry. But now his thoughts were interrupted for he began to encounter many labourers and maids from the farms, the countryside suddenly busy with folk using paths and short-cuts between work-place and home.

'Hay finished then?' he asked.

'Near as may be.'

'Stacks only need the thacking.'

Their voices and laughter held the satisfaction of work well done, their arms were tanned deep brown from long days in the sun with scythe and rake, their faces tired but content. A fair day's work for a fair day's pay . . .

A horseman came upon him unexpectedly in the lane, the man cantering too fast for a blind corner and Ben deep in a new wave of bitterness. Ben swore, and the man returned the compliment. His irritation increased as he heard more horses approaching. He held himself ready for battle but around the corner came a bent old man in coarse working smock, leading three shire horses, two full-grown and a colt. The man gestured to a nearby gate and as if to make amends for his unwarranted aggression Ben ran to open it. He stood watching as the two older mares, released from their head-collars, shook out their manes, like women releasing long hair from pins, while the horseman refused to be hurried by the impatient colt.

'You take your hurry.' He held the colt's head-rope authoritatively while the mares ambled away, beginning to graze. 'Right – now's your time,' he told the young horse, slipping the rope off and shooing it, so it ran from them far into the field. It charged around, bucking, galloping, lifting its heels and back-kicking with a force that could have taken a man's head off. The old man drew the gate closed and stood leaning on it, chuckling. 'You wouldn't believe it, but I know how he feels.'

They laughed together companionably, but as the old man looked up at him, Ben felt his dissatisfaction was revealed in the lines of his face. The old horseman nodded as if remembering those feelings too, and added, 'You make the most of your young life – it's soon over. Now's your time too. You be off to your wenching, or to whatever you're about.' He lifted the head-collars and made as if to shoo Ben on his way.

'You know, I might just do that!' He felt his spirits lift at the thought of seeing Leah that very evening. 'it's a fine, night.'

'They'll not come much finer for you.' The words were quietly spoken, but in their wisdom seemed to pinpoint the long June evening, the young man's good looks and fine physique. And goodness, Ben thought, an eight mile walk was nothing.

Leah was pleased when Sam made his final departure from their kitchen for the evening, for she was weary of his anxious and detailed instructions about how to find the town factory the next day, and what to say when she got there. What had seemed like a simple expedition was becoming loaded down by everyone's "look fors" and "take cares". Most of all she had been completely mystified by her mother's reaction as her grandmother had told her the name of the stallholder she was to find.

'Oh, no! You had no right!' Nellie had shouted.

She could not remember her mild, even-tempered mother ever raising her voice like that before.

'He wrote to me – and needs must when the devil drives.'

One glance at their grim, tight-lipped faces told Leah she was not going to learn any more that evening, and for the first time since she could remember the two women went about their evening's activities entirely separate and in complete silence.

She wondered outside, wishing she might slip away and talk to Ginnie. She stopped to pluck and smell the dusky heart of a deep red rose. Its fragrance reached her still from its place tucked into the waistband of her skirt.

She sighed then frowned as above the noise of a cart passing on the street she heard a man whistling, sweet and clear – but it was what he was whistling that made her heart beat faster. First there came a scale of eight notes, each rising from the other, then the whistler caught out first the odd notes, then the even, winding them together like a peal of bells.

Catching her breath, she found herself drawn willy-nilly towards the entry. The clear whistle began: "Oranges and Lemons, say the bells of St Clemens. You owe me five farthings, said the bells of St Martins' . . . and Leah was running tip-toe between the two cottages. "When will you pay me? said the bells of Old Bailey." She was out in the street – the empty street. "When I get rich, said the Bells of Shoreditch," came from around the corner. "When will that be? said the bells of Stepney." Leah followed the Pied Piper around the corner. The whistle slowed to ponderousness: "I do not know, said the great Bell of Bow", as they confronted each other at the street corner – so close they both gasped with laughter, and Ben was hard put to it not to catch her up in his arms and twirl her around for sheer ecstasy.

Caution overcame him as a door banged nearby, a man shouted and a herd of cows came towards them, on their way back to pasture from the milking sheds. They must either stand aside while the lowing, lumbering beasts passed, or go ahead.

'Come on,' Ben urged, and took her hand. He saw her startled glance around to make sure no one had observed such a brazen act in the open street. He hurried her along because he could already see the cowman straining his neck to make out who it was ahead of his herd.

'We'll hide and let them go by,' he said, and once they were sufficiently ahead to be unobserved, drew her into the gateway of a cornfield. He unlatched the gate and they slipped through, walking quickly along the headland between hedge and crop. they reached a spot where the headland widened to leave room for the butt of an ancient oak.

'Shall we sit here?'

She nodded, pulling self-consciously at a few wheat-ears, yet regarding him anxiously as she sank to her knees beside him. 'Is anything wrong? I mean, why have you come tonight instead of Thursday as . . .' She had been about to say "as usual" but stopped, thinking he might feel it presumptuous of her to lay claim to his time.

He remembered the cavorting colt and the old man. 'I just needed to see you.'

A handful of bright chaffinches, a yellow hammer and a few belligerent sparrows rose and resettled further along the hedgerow as the cows approached. The two fell silent until they heard the soft-hoofed cows ambling past, smelt their milky-dung warmness, and held their breaths as the collie-dog came and sniffed at them under the hedge. The man grumbled at it for leaving its work.

When the birds had flown back to the nearby hedgerows, Leah knelt rubbing the wheat-ears between her palms, separating the grains from the stalk, then looked at him quizzically.

'I asked for a proper wage.' And he took the paper from his pocket and showed her.

She read it twice, slowly. 'You asked for a wage . . . and he gave you that!' She shook the paper and demanded, 'Is it possible?'

He was aware of the scent from the rose at her waist as her indignation made her lean forward, questioning him. 'Could you do it? Ben, could you?'

'At this moment – I could do anything,' he said.

She tilted her chin to him, wanting him to tell her about bell-founding, yet felt herself blushing, and lifting her hand dropped the wheat-grains from her fingers into his palm. He rubbed them thoughtfully, then blew away the chaff. Some of the seeds from the top of the ear were already golden brown, ripe, while others from the bottom were still green. Leah took one of the green seeds back and bit into its milky centre.

'Leah?'

She heard all the questions and all his hopes in the way he spoke her name. Her quiet, formal 'yes . . .' gave him permission to go on.

'Until I've means enough to support a wife . . .' he paused to take up the paper from the grass. 'At the moment this is all I can offer – well, of course, it's nothing. But I'll make it happen . . . I'll work . . .'

'Ben!' The realisation of what he was saying, what he was meaning, flooded her being. There was no room for thoughts or breath to make words.

He waited for her to say more, then began to see all the reasons why they should not marry. 'Perhaps you'd tire of waiting? You may not . . . I couldn't expect . . .'

'I'll ask if you can come to tea on Sunday,' she said quickly. If her family agreed, then they both knew it would be recognised that they were officially walking-out.

'Oh, Leah!' He drew her to him. 'We're promised then?'

'We're promised,' she whispered back. He leaned towards her and they kissed, lightly. Then he startled her by drawing her to him and kissing her with such a different strength and passion she was at first overwhelmed, wanting to be all his. Then a sense of panic swept over her. It was surely too soon for this? Like one on the point of drowning, she struggled to be free, to surface before it was too late. She scrambled to her feet, feeling hot and prudishly correct as she straightened her skirts.

'Perhaps we should go,' she said, suddenly wondering what Ginnie would have made of it all, then glad she had not thought of her friend before she had disentangled herself. 'No one knows where I am,' she added, 'they may be worried.'

'Yes,' he said huskily. 'I'll walk you back to the village. Sorry,' he said, and leaned forward to kiss her cheek. 'Sorry,' he repeated, touching the red rose at her waist.

She looked down, then pulled the rose free, teasing out the crushed petals, smelling the deep sweet perfume before reaching up and putting it into his buttonhole.

Such a wave of wistfulness for her innocence came over him as she looked into his eyes, smiling. He took her hand. 'I'll walk you home.'

But she insisted on walking part of his way as he had so far to go. Then even when they parted she wilfully ran to the top of a hill so she might see him further on his way.

She stood laughing and waving to him as he went on, and he occasionally stopped to wave and blow kisses to her, then more emphatically signalled for her to return home.

At length when his way took him on between high hedges, she stood on a stile to give a final wave.

'See you Thursday,' she whispered, then turned to run home. She raced down the hill through the bare hay-fields, arms outstretched as if with a little effort of will she might just fly home. Ben Robertson, who would make the great bell that would mean they could marry! When she reached home, she thought, she might just not tell of the trouble with his step-father. They would be impressed that his family owned a business, a bell-foundry . . . Time enough for the rest when they knew him . . . when he had been to tea . . .

The gates between the stripped fields had been left open, so she ran unhindered, her cares for the future pushed away by this golden present.

'A very pretty picture.'

The shock of a man's voice so close as she passed into the next field made her try to stop mid-stride, made her stagger and fall to her knees as a horse and rider came from behind the hedge. Recognition made her unable to move. There was no bonnet this time to hide her face, and she realised with dread and apprehension, no hay-rake to defend herself with.

'We meet again – in the hayfield – with you taking a tumble. Dearie me!'

Anger brought her rapidly to her feet and she made as if to move defiantly away, but Edgar Lacey barred her way.

'Not so quick, Leah Dexter of Dexter's Yard. I've not finished with you.'

'Knowing my name is not gong to help you!' she retorted, though recalling all Sam had told her. She could expect no sympathy from this man she had made to look a fool – and she had no hope of outrunning a horse.

He drew the animal close alongside her. 'You've been a foolish little thing, do you know that?' he said, looking down, smiling. She saw the spite in his eyes, and as his horse tossed its head nervously, foam splashing from around its bit, she was aware of more than just the usual horsy mixture of leather and farmyard; she smelt fear on the animal's coat. Poor beast, to have such a master. She scanned the fields all around, and the man laughed. 'There's on one within shouting distance. It's just you and me.' He raised his thick foxy eyebrows in pleasurable anticipation.

And a nervy horse, she thought, wondering if she could make it throw him. What satisfaction!

'I'm a generous man,' he was saying, 'prepared to let bygones rest in their beds. You need never soil your hands again, either in that old stockinger's shop of your grandfather's or in the fields !' His tone cajoled, almost seemed to court as he added, 'If you're a good girl to me.'

'Being a "good girl" hasn't much to do with it, has it?' she endeavoured to sound calm, as she tried to find space enough to frighten the horse. But the man had it so disciplined it obeyed the slightest squeeze on its quivering flanks, and he kept the beast close in upon her, trapping her against the hedge. Perhaps if she could trick him into dismounting . . . If only Ben were still within shouting distance . . . If only some labourer might be late on his way home . . . 'I heard you didn't take a liking to either of the Clarke girls?'

She saw immediately that his good humour did not stretch this far. His face altered to match the cold calculation in his eye, and he raised his riding-crop. She instinctively pushed further back into the hedge. 'No *man* talks to me like that, let alone a . . .'

She thought this might be the moment she was waiting for; a swipe with the stick in any direction seemed likely completely to derange the horse.

But he paused with the stick still above his head, then laughed, and brought it slowly down to his side again. 'You've quite a few things to learn about me – and I am going to enjoy teaching you them!'

He made a swift downward lunge, attempting to grab her arm. Instinctively she ducked away, and while he recovered, having to circle his horse, she ran back towards the gateway. She grabbed up her skirt and sped along the far hedgeside, in the direction of four new haystacks built close together in the corner of the field.

He was soon alongside her again, trotting his horse to keep pace. Then, looking to where they were heading, he laughed indulgently, and became inclined to coax a little again. 'You have your family to think of,' he told her, relaxing, sitting deep in his saddle, enjoying himself. 'I could do such a lot for them. There's your mother and your grandmother. What ordinary man could afford to marry you and keep *three* women?'

She was appalled by all he had discovered about her family, and tormented by the recollection that she had prudishly struggled from Ben's arms while now . . . She about turned suddenly, determined there should be no tumble in the hay for this casual predator. He must have been alert, waiting for her to do just this, for he threw himself off his horse, landing against her. A grip like an iron band encircled her arm. She fought with all her might to free herself, but found her arm wrenched up behind her back. The ease and ruthlessness with which he handled her made her painfully aware that he was well practised in the use of force.

His mistake lay in trying to hold on to her and his horse – which shied away, and as he clung to its bridle pulled him with it – though barring her way back the way she had come.

There was no choice but to make for the rectangular stacks. Dusk was beginning to come, and perhaps he might grow tired of too long a game of hide and seek.

There was just room for a person to run in between the stacks. She hoped he would think her stupid enough to stay there. She pushed through to the other side and then threw herself on to the ground, struggling and forcing herself under a small gap in the hedge, into the wheat-field on the other side. The one in which she and Ben had sat. She rolled over several times, then crept away carefully at a right-angle to conceal herself, lying motionless, biting her bottom lip to control her breathing.

She heard him arrive and gallop the horse all around the four stacks, like a general inspecting the city he was to lay seige to. Then she heard the horse making the circuit at a slower pace. A large natural cobble lay near her hand. She waited until he was at the far side and, lying flat, sent it high, to drop in the middle of the stacks.

She felt scornful as she heard his satisfied laugh, and then lay rigid as she heard the horse brought to the side and hitched to the hedge only yards from where she lay.

'Remember, you chose the hard way . . .' She felt her skin rise as she recognised the tone of a man who would enjoy seeing a quarry torn to pieces, enjoy the frenzy of a woman's resistance. Her own determination not to be a victim sharpened her senses, made her instincts keener. She listened until she knew he had gone in between the stacks, and when she judged the right moment, threw a second stone as far as she could, to the farthest side of the stacks.

She was through the hedge, even as she heard his self-satisfied, 'Ha!' She unlooped the hitched reins and threw her arms into the air, flapping her skirts at the horse like a demented creature. It reared, showed the whites of its eyes, skittered away from her and was off at a gallop.

Leah was down on the ground again, under the hedge and running along the edge of the wheat-field to reach the road back to the village. She looked back once, saw the horse take a hedge in fine style, but the only sounds she could hear were her own laboured breathing and heart-beats. Only when she reached the first cottages did she slow down and try to compose herself.

At her own street corner she paused, leaning on the brickwork at the spot where she and Ben had nearly walked into each other it seemed several lifetimes ago. Then as casually as she could manage, she walked past Sam's cottage. The lamp was lit and through the window she saw Clarrie, her mother and her grandmother sitting sewing. It seemed she had not been missed.

Then with sinking heart she realised they were working on the fine embroidery of the sheets allocated to them by Lady Nubury. Her mother moved the piece of linen on her lap and Leah could see the entwined letters, the "L" dominating the "N", as if the Laceys must brand and stamp their will on all things.

One thing was certain: if Edgar Lacey found out that the Dexter family were working on his future daughter-in-law's trousseau, that meagre and temporary source of income would swiftly be taken away.

Chapter Nine

The early morning start in the half light made Leah pull her shawl close about her, huddle and hold herself against the cold and the motion of the wagon on the rutted road. She had slept only fitfully, twice sitting bolt upright in her bed as the nightmare of capture came upon her.

She listened to the regular clop and scuff of the horse's hooves, to the stones crunched beneath its wheels, and knew today was to be decisive for the Dexters. The regular carrier said the factory had just heard her grandfather had died, and thought his stockinger's shop finished. Sam stated this was rubbish. They had known nine months ago, and who did they think had been returning the finished goods since last October! She meant to solve that mystery today.

She took more interest in her surroundings as the number of wagons on the road increased and they began to pass more and more houses. She scrambled to her knees on the back of the load of hay and looked towards their destination. slender spires of churches and of factory chimneys overlooked what seemed to Leah hundreds upon hundreds of houses. In some directions they straggled out into the countryside, but from the vantage of the hill they had just climbed, the town looked more as if it sprang directly out of the fields, like a great awesome feat of nature.

Though the hay-trusser driving the wagon had promised to direct her to the market, it seemed well nigh impossible she would ever really find her way into and out of that place. To the left she recognised the imposing complex of buildings that was the old but ever spreading town infirmary, and to her right the huge wall and turrets of the prison, built fifty years before. She was not sure which filled her with most dread: the infirmary, linked with village stories of those who entered "to be cut", never to return; or the prison with the memories of its treadmill, hard labour at best, hanging at worst.

The wagoner finally stopped his horses near a trough, and while he allowed his animals a drink, he directed Leah at a right-angle to his own way to the provender mart.

'Keep as straight as you can in that direction,' he advised, a downwards signal of his arm pointing her way up a cobbled side-street. 'You can't miss it.'

She thanked him, swung her ware sacks over her shoulders and took up her basket full of small bunches of fresh herbs and garden flowers. She had brought as much as might sell that she could lay her hands on and carry.

She walked quickly. The old dwellings leaning inwards over the cobbled street soon oppressed her, as they blotted out the morning sun. It was like walking in a tunnel, she thought, though she sensed she was being watched from many a cracked and dirty window. These were the remains of the old rookery dwellings, which provided roofs for many under their crazy crumbling timbers. In many places the old mortar had fallen from between the beams and been replaced with a hotch-potch of bricks, giving them a patched and cobbled-up appearance.

The few people she encountered all seemed poorly clad, thin, pale. "Starvelings" her grandmother would have called them, and many were badly pox-marked – survivors of the smallpox epidemics that had ravaged the town some years before.

Entries and passages emitted a rank odour, more appropriate to stables than houses, she thought, wishing she had a free hand to cowl her nose. She walked faster, wanting to leave these shambles behind, but the street came to an end and she must choose either to turn left or right. She took a first left, then a right in an effort to describe the straight line the wagoner had advised. A man leaning in a corner doorway startled her. He laughed harshly at her surprised gasp and spat into the street narrowly missing her skirts.

A bent crone lifted her head to look into Leah's eyes, as if assessing the prospects of a handout. The crone was no more than a girl herself, though the pale face was pinched and deep-lined with grime. Leah was startled both by the frank and hungry appraisal she and her burdens were given, and by the swiftness with which the gaze slipped away. Was it so obvious that she too was close to the line when her day's bread might depend on another's charity?

It was with a sense of relief that, after taking one more turn left, then right, she glimpsed a wider street.

Here was much more the town she expected. New brick buildings, three-storied, decorated with imposing Victorian stone arches, pillared porticoes, short flight of elegant steps to the front doors. Here was the evidence of trade and prosperity she sought, monied people who could buy, make deals, who could give or withhold opportunities of advancement.

She was just turning the corner when there was the sound of a moan, and someone falling just behind her. She turned to see what looked like no more than a heap of black clothing. She laid down her basket and sacks and knelt by the figure, taking an arm frail as a stick. 'Are you hurt?'

It was the girl who had appraised her earlier. After a few moments she summoned the energy to sit up and nod to her. 'You go on to your market,' she said, and looking at the gutter in which she had landed, added, 'This is my lot.'

Leah was appalled, but could not find the right words to tell her she must never accept poverty as her lot. She must fight it, she must strive! She took a handful of the bundled herbs from her basket and thrust them on to the girl's lap, saying huskily, 'You go to the market.'

The girl's face took on a look of such joy it might have been sovereigns not thyme, parsley and sage. 'God bless you,' she whispered.

Leah left her with a feeling of guilt, yet of obligation to be about her own business. She walked on into another aspect of the town as she emerged on one of the main thoroughfares. This road was busy with every kind of horse-drawn vehicle and the pavements crowded with factory and shopworkers hurrying to their places of work. In the distance a train whistle blew. This was the town businessmen and visitors saw when they arrived by the ever expanding railways, the new front-ispiece overlaying the old. Here were the workers, not the beggars. Those in service were scrubbing the elegant steps, sweeping the pavements, polishing the brass plates on the new buildings. "Josiah Needham, Gentleman" adjoined "Higgs Bros. Cotton Factors".

Further on white-aproned men pulled out shop blinds, boys ran errands with interesting-looking parcels. Boot-boys were beginning to find their first customers of the day. A huge wooden figure of a turbaned black man leaning on a cutlass was being carried to stand alongside a shop-window display-ing samples of flake and plug tobacco, with great blue Eastern storage jars at the back. A plate beside an adjoining flight of stairs invited suffers to find the benefit of "Painless Dentistry" and to have "Artifical Teeth by Atmospheric Pressure". Alternatively there was Bunter's Nervine, recommended to the public to stop up a troublesome hole in a severely aching tooth.

The next alleyway revealed the way through to the mar-ketplace. Here all was bustle, shouting, confusion.

'How much?' A hand took up a bundle of parsley, and Leah found herself addressed by a buxom woman, who tutted at her slowness. 'I'll take two of each for a penny.' The deal was done without Leah doing more than hold out her hand for the money.

'I'm looking for the button stall,' she said before the woman could escape.

Pointing to the far side of the market square, her customer hurried away with the impatient remark that she had dinner to cook for thirteen.

She's like the White Rabbit, Leah thought with a lift of her spirits. Before she had reached the far side of the market she had sold all the bunches of herbs, but seeing the poor quality of those on the stalls, half the size and twice the price, she understood why.

There seemed hundreds of stalls, made of thick planks set upon wooden trestles, crowding the wide cobbled square. The fresh vegetables and fruit, gave way to a section for meat, fish, pets – dogs, cats, monkeys, linnets in cages – then, at the far side, stalls with great bales of cottons, serges, oilcloths, and finally right at the opposite side was the button stall.

Its sign proclaimed "FREEMANS". Leah wasn't quite sure how she felt about the great letters proclaiming something for nothing, followed by the end of the stallholder's name. There were already several customers sorting through boxes containing every kind of button from covered metal for underwear, to great carved bone decorations for fashionable ladies. Other boxes held buckles, studs, papers of pins, small squares of material with one needle, cottons, threads. One old woman, snorting with laughter as she fumbled in her purse, exclaimed; 'Ar! Gerron wi'you, John White! Ge'us these buttons for a farthing and have less of y'lip.'

As the woman moved away, Leah caught her first glimpse of Mr John White. He was a tall robust man in his forties with a mop of hair, chestnut once but greying now, hearty, and someone she knew instinctively that women would feel comfortable with. He could pull their legs, and get a bit of cheek in return. She found herself smiling at him, and over the heads of other customers coming early to his stall, he called, 'Hello, m'flower. What can we do for you?'

'I'm looking for Mr Freeman, the stallholder,' she said. 'My grandmother . . .'

'Name of?' he questioned.

'Miriam Dexter,' she replied a little cautiously, for he had dropped the bantering tone now, and gestured to his wife to look after the customers.

'She said you might let me have a corner of your stall for . . .' She stopped for he was not listening to her, only looking, shaking his head for a time. Then he gave a grunt of laughter and nodded to her instead.

'You know why?'

It was her turn to shake her head.

'Well . . . if I'd have been a bit sharper when I was younger, I might have been your father. Instead of which, I got my nose pushed out by young Fred Dexter. Then, when he died, leaving you nothing but a tiddler, I wrote to your grandmother and said if ever there was anything I could do for you . . . Leah, they called you, didn't they? Your mother alright, is she?'

98

She nodded in answer to both questions.

'And Miriam Dexter remembered . . . after all this time..'
He gave her a deep searching glance. 'Times hard,' he stated.

'John?' His wife's voice called and queried as she held up a
large bundle of buttons, tape, pins and thread. 'Comes to a
shilling' she said.

'Oh, for a regular customer, I reckon a nimble ninepence is
better than a slow shilling any day!'

The customer went off with a laugh and a bargain. It was
the first lesson she learned from John White, alias Mr
FREEMAN.

The second was as he and his wife made space at the end of
their stall for her row of men's and boys' stockings and a few
pairs of mittens. 'Coals to Newcastle!' he commented.
'They'll have to be dirt cheap to sell in Leicester market.
Every other person works in a hosiery factory here.'

By mid-day Leah had cut the prices pinned to her goods by
half and sold nothing, finally leaving Mr and Mrs White in
charge of her goods while she found her way to the factory
which had supplied the Dexters with wool for as long as
anyone could remember.

The factories were fairly new, most built since Victoria had
come to the throne, and were not far from the market centre
of the town.

She found 'Glenfields, Spinners and Dyers' easily. Not too
sure which door to enter, she stood watching for a time. She
decided it was a little like the Workhouse. The top-hatted
went into the heavy plate-glass front doors, the workmen and
the carrier's carts entered a cobbled yard through high double
gates. She lingered around the gates, seeing skips of wool
being loaded, and approached the loading bay as a cart drew
away.

She looked up at an amiable-seeming man with long side-
whiskers and a great quiff of hair like a grey coxcomb. He
seemed well disposed to her and listened to her query seriously, nodding to acknowledge the truth of all she said.

'I was told your shop was finished,' he said simply, 'but you
wait here and I'll ask if they'll see you in the office.'

He returned quickly, solemn and regretful as he told her,
'They say there's no more business to be done with your

family – special instructions.' He pushed a hand into his bush of hair and scratched as if trying to puzzle this out. 'They say it's come from top brass. I don't understand it – as long as I've been here there's been wool for your place, and your work's been better than a good many other's.'

Leah was angry now. 'Perhaps they think I can't run the business . . .'

'Aye, its likely,' he agreed. 'Though perhaps it's the new owners. There seem to be changes coming – and not for the better for the likes of us, I can tell you.'

It was with a feeling of apprehension that she asked, 'Who are the new owners?'

'From your part of the world – landowners putting some of their money into industry. Got all them villages named after them . . .'

Surely no man so rich, his days so full of every good thing in life, would go to such lengths? It had to be coincidence. 'How long has he owned it?' she asked, and the man looked at her curiously.

'Some six months or more, though "he's" only just begun to take a personal interest, like.' His manner became a little more distant, as if her casual reference to the new owner put them on opposite sides. He lifted an empty skip and placed it tidily against the wall. 'Do you want to go and have a word in the office?'

She shook her head and took her leave of the man, aware that he stood looking critically after her. She seem to stumble from pavement to road, road to pavement, not watching where she was going, her mind full of disbelief and hopelessness. Last night she had found means and energy to escape, but this! She thought of the changed attitude of the man on the loading-bay. He knew nothing but seemed to condemn her, the woman. 'Damned if I have, and damned if I haven't,' she muttered, not sure what way she went, or what length of time it took her to find her way back to the button-stall.

John White greeted her with some concern, and when she leaned pale and silent on the end of the stall, he was immediately by her side. She closed her eyes against his solicitous enquiries, but then his wife's gentle voice was in her ear. 'Come on, my dear, we'll go and sit down.'

Mrs White led her away from the centre of the busy market, a little distance down a narrow alleyway and into a coffee house. Sitting her at a table she came back with two cups of strong, treacly-sweet liquid. 'Go on, m'dear. You've had some sort of shock, haven't you?'

Leah nodded, sipping the drink, one moment sure she could never tell a stranger her problems, and the next telling all in a low husky whisper. Jane White leaned over her, her face growing ever more grave.

'I'm glad you've told me rather than my John. He can be as generous with his fists as he can with everything else.'

Leah smiled briefly and shook her head. 'There's nothing he can do.'

'You don't know my John.' There was a hint of pride and of exasperation in her voice. 'I shall tell him tonight when we're home. I don't want him rushing round to the factory.'

When they returned to the stall, John White questioned them both with an imperative, 'Well?'

'She needs your help, John. There'll be no more wool from that factory, that's for sure.'

He accepted his wife's judgement without question, and got down to practical matters.

'You have your own knitting frame?' He waited for her nod and continued: 'Then you've no frame rent to pay and you're under no contract to anyone – your grandfather was a shrewd man. What you must do is buy your own wool, knit special goods that factories can't bother with – fancy goods as'll sell on this stall. It's no good bringing ordinary stockings to Leicester where everybody has a relative in the hosiery!'

'He's right,' his wife nodded affirmation. 'Every market's different – John knows.'

'Look!' he went on enthusiastically. 'I'll get you a good exchange.' He indicated her stockings still untouched on his stall. Before she could answer, he had scooped up the goods and strode off with them.

Leah looked doubtfully after him, and Mrs White added gently, 'You see what I mean? If John gets the bit between his teeth, there's no holding him. I don't know what he's thought of, but he'll get you a bargain.'

The stall was busy again for a few moments. Leah helped match some buttons for a young mother, then John returned, beaming, and carrying great hanks of grey and brown worsted. 'There!' he said. 'Make it up and sell it on your rounds. There's three or four times what you had for sale. And there!' Like a magician, he produced several smaller hanks of coloured wool – red, green, yellow – from his coat pocket.

She took them, forming a smile, wondering what on earth she could do with them – and dreading what Sam might say about exchanging made-up goods for great skeins of inferior-looking wool.

'You write to me, and let me know how things are with you all,' John instructed when it was time for her to find her lift home, calling after her as she threaded her way through the stalls, 'or I'll be over there myself to find out!'

Chapter Ten

The public bar of the Stockinger's Arms already had a half dozen early evening customers. Ginnie passed the door that led from kitchen to bar and heard the name of Dexter mentioned. She stopped and put her ear close and listened.

'He'd lost his best terrier down a rabbit-hole that morning and gone back to try and dig'm out. He saw it all.' The man spoke with an air of final authority.

'Squire, you say?' another voice enquired.

'Wonder if he caught 'er?'

There was some laughter and the first speaker added, 'If he did, time'll tell.'

'From what I hear, she's always down the fields with some chap or other. Feeling her feet since old Fred died, off on his rounds an'all! A girl!'

'Need a firm hand, young women.'

Ginnie raised her eyebrows at her father's statement, then tutted as she remembered the locked backdoor, a habit Walter Hobbday had long ago adopted to keep tabs on his lively sons and daughter. But she must know what had happened to Leah! She ran to snatch up a couple of magazines from the kitchen table, then walked rapidly through the bar and out of the front door, waggling the books at her father behind the counter in explanation.

'No lies, no pack drill,' she thought, walking sedately along the main street, only as she turned into Leah's entry giving a quick look round to see if anyone was about.

'So why didn't he show himself, whoever he was? That would have helped!' Leah asked indignantly as Ginnie told what she had overhead. 'I could have been . . .'

'So it's true!' Ginnie's eyes were wide, and Leah drew her further away from the kitchen door and into the tiny walled garden behind the cottage. Ginnie listened agog to the story of Ben's unexpected visit and the traumatic end to the evening. Leah went on to give details of the visit to Leicester, and of the Lacey family buying up several hosiery, spinning and dyeing businesses.

'He means to have you,' Ginnie breathed as if enthralled by one of her magazine dramas.

Leah was both disconcerted and alarmed by the whispered comment. But she had kept the most startling news until last, ending with 'So Ben's coming to tea a week on Sunday!'

'Ooooh!' Ginnie exclaimed, snatched back to reality. 'Fancy not telling me that first! You're spoken for, Leah Dexter. You've beaten me to it!' Then she beamed, and threw herself on Leah, hugging and kissing her. 'Now I've just got to catch Nat.'

Leah tried to calm her down, but Ginnie was irrepressible. 'We'll have a double wedding!' she cried. 'We will!'

'We'd better not book the church until Nat knows.'

Ginnie fell on her and they hugged each other again, until they were laughing and crying. Nellie came to the door of the cottage, knitting-needles busy in her hands, and shook her head at them both. But Miriam, looking over her shoulder, laughed with them. 'Now what are you planning, Ginnie Hobbday?' she called.

'Why is your mother hand-knitting?' Ginnie asked, changing the subject.

Leah confided the story of the hanks of wool which Sam was having problems with.

'Who's John White?'

It was Leah's turn now tactfully to steer the conversation off on another track. 'Come and see Sam. Perhaps you'll cheer him up.' And as Ginnie joggled her elbow as they crossed the yard, she whispered, 'I'll tell you later.'

Leah led the way to the workshop. Sam looked dwarfed as he sat on the bench bolted to the great knitting-frame. The last rays of the sun were caught by a water-filled glass ball over the window and reflected on to the work beneath his hands. He was in the process of disentangling a short piece of work from the needles. He gave a low disapproving grunt of greeting.

'Brought me something else useless?' he asked.

'Oh, go on, Sam! You don't mean that,' Ginnie replied with good humour. Leah caught the twinkle in his eye as he watched her spread her magazines out on his bench. She also noticed he had looped the three skeins of coloured wool on the end of an ancient knitting-frame that had stood in one corner of the shop gathering dust for as long as she could remember.

At last he managed to disengage the wool from the needles. He handed the piece to Leah. 'It'll all have to be hand knitted. I've tried everything: waxed it, soaped it, doubled it.'

'That's going to make a lot more work.' Leah tried to keep the note of complaint out of her voice, but the wearisomeness of handknitting . . .

'It is,' Sam confirmed uncompromisingly. A few months ago Leah would have tossed up her head and flounced out of his company. Now she knew it was more than part her fault, and she noticed how tired he looked. 'I think you've done enough for today, Sam.'

He shook his head at her. 'I've some hoeing to do, and some fruit to pick before bedtime.' She knew the long hours he was working was his way of fighting the terrible frustration he felt. She remembered his grim, cold anger when he heard of the ban imposed on their shop, and his involuntary, embarrassing outburst that the 'Bloody squire's no better than an old dog pissing everywhere, hankering after a new bitch!'

She also hoped, as Mrs White had done, that neither of the men would hear about her second encounter with the Squire. Yet with its being talked of in the public house . . .

'Oh, look!' Ginnie suddenly exclaimed. 'Here's an idea. There's a sketch of a man playing golf at Prestwich . . . and he's got socks with turned-over tops. What about that?'

'Golf?' Sam questioned as he finally slid from behind the frame to look doubtfully at the magazine article.

'A healthy game for royal gentlemen,' Ginnie read.

'Does anyone play golf around here?' Leah asked.

'No,' Sam said emphatically, but they left him poring over the magazine as Ginnie pulled her friend out of the shop, eager for more intimate conversation.

'Do you think Nat will come over on Sunday evening?' she quizzed, then bit her lip, planning. 'I could come to call to see if you were going to evening service. . . If you're promised, I don't see why my father should object any more to my coming to see you.'

'Oh! So I'm respectable again now?'

'I shouldn't go chasing around too many haystacks, unless you want to be bar-room gossip for the rest of your life.'

'They won't talk about the Squire though!'

'Well, everybody knows what he is,' Ginnie retorted.

There was a cold rabbit pie, the sliced meat set in its own clear juices; lettuce, young onions, and strawberries from the garden, and a sponge cake from the Stockinger's Arms. Ginnie had so far persuaded her father as to the true merit of her lifelong friend, and the standing of the foundry-owning Robertsons, as to be allowed to contribute to this official tea-party.

The three women, fussed, even got a little sharp with each other as each made final adjustments to the parlour table, until Nellie suddenly stopped in the doorway and exclaimed: 'It's never looked so well before.'

'With three of us at it every spare minute for the last week, that's not surprising,' Miriam said drily, but all three stood to admire the result.

The furniture shone from extra hours with the beeswax polish, the drawn-thread work table-cloth gleamed snow-white, the best tea-service, with its design of blue and gold ivy leaves, contrasted with the greens and reds, browns and creams, of the assembled feast.

'Hmm!' Miriam breathed deeply of the smell of strawberries and cake.

'You mustn't let him think we're hungry,' Leah said urgently.

Everything prepared, they all went to sit very solemnly in the kitchen and compose themselves. The deep tick and solemn swing of the brass pendulum of the kitchen clock soothed away the final minutes to four o'clock.

There was something both familiar and strange in the footfall that finally echoed in the entry. Leah looked sharply at her grandmother and saw the colour in her cheeks – she too had heard the same echo of another footstep in Ben's long stride.

'He should have come to the front door,' Nellie said primly.

'I told him to come to the back. We don't want all the village having a free look at him,' Leah said defensively as she opened the door wide, but the footsteps had stopped.

'Come calling, have you?'

'Oh!' All her old frustrations surfaced as she heard Sam intercept her guest.

'Do no harm for them to have a word,' Miriam said quietly.

'Don't see it'll do a lot of good either,' Leah breathed, hanging on every word from just inside the door jamb.

'Caleb Berridge!' Sam stated. 'Am I right in thinking he took over the foundry when your mother remarried?'

'Trust him to know things,' Leah hissed, and forgetting the display of dignity she had planned for the occasion, was out of the door and into the yard before Sam gave voice to anything else he knew.

'We're waiting for you.' It sounded disapproving.

'Perhaps I'll see you later.' Ben nodded agreeably at Sam.

'Gaffer's granddaughter permitting.' Sam stared at Leah, who tossed her head. Ben laughed uncertainly at the witticism he did not understand.

Leah thought he seemed much taller in their kitchen, as she introduced him and then led him through to the parlour and seated him in the carver chair at the head of the table.

'A cup of tea first, after your walk?' Miriam asked.

'Please.' He smiled at Leah's mother and grandmother, and seemed perfectly at ease, pleased with himself even, while she felt fussed. She swallowed hard, resolving to forget Sam's disruption to the gracious reception she had planned, and to make a fresh start.

'So when did you two meet?' her mother asked.

Leah felt he was far too eager to tell, too expansive with his explanations, in danger of any moment of letting her shrewd grandmother guess the conflict within his family. The progress of the tea seemed to her a series of impending pitfalls. At one moment the food was like sawdust in her mouth; at the next she hoped Sam's rabbit, Ginnie's cake and summer's plenty did not make him think she had exaggerated her family's troubles.

She lost track of the conversation, and when Ben suddenly laughed aloud she started and splashed tea on the best cloth. She just wished it all over as the others dabbed and dismissed the accident, and Nellie began to tell of other times her daughter had "got into pickles".

'Mother!' she protested. 'I'm dying of embarrassment here.' Her grandmother suggested if Ben had finished he should take him and show him the garden and the workshop while they washed up. Her mother gave her a beaming nod of approval.

'Let's go and see if Sam is still in the shop,' Ben suggested.

'Sam! I thought you'd come. . .' she began indignantly, but he caught her hand, gave it a squeeze. 'I've something to tell you.'

'And Sam too?' she queried indignantly.

'Yes – he knows my stepfather. I need to talk to another man – someone outside my family.'

'Curiouser and curiouser.' Leah led the way back into the shop, adding resignedly, 'We seem to spend all our time in here anyway.'

'Come to see the way I cast my metal, have you?' Sam joked as he lifted an old saucepan which still held a little liquid lead. 'I've been making some new blocks for these smaller needles,' he said, indicating a bench where the shiny metal was setting in small rectangular blocks with the shafts of the needles laid inside the mould.

'Ben's not interested in spoonfuls of metal you've heated up on Clarrie's hob. . .'

'Yes, I am,' he interrupted, 'and I wondered if Sam's got time to listen to a bit about casting a special bell, and whether I might persuade him to give me a hand when the time comes?'

'A special bell?' Leah queried. 'Not *the* bell? Can't be!' They had both thought and talked of that as being a far distant event.

'Something's happened, Leah,' he said with suppressed excitement in his voice, and she realised this news was the reason he had seemed so at ease over tea, so ready to enjoy himself. 'I have the chance to make the bell.' His hand went instinctively to his inside jacket pocket as if to check Caleb's signed promise was still there, then on an afterthought he drew out the paper and handed it to Sam to read.

Leah gasped in delight and amazement. 'But how?'

'It's through Cuddy.' He paused, laughing briefly as if he still hardly believed the stroke of luck. Sam was hooking his glasses back behind his ears as Ben explained, 'Cuddy is our workman. He's as good as they come, but . . . some ninepence to the shilling. He lives at Soston.'

Leah looked up sharply at the mention of that village, where she had seen the Monk's Bell and suffered public censure as the curse had been spelled out. Ben mistook her look and explained, 'He sets off to walk before first light every morning – but he always arrives at the foundry on time.'

Sam grunted as he finished reading. 'You don't expect him to honour this – not a Berridge? I knew the family well at one time. Rogues the lot of 'em!'

'I'll see he does,' Ben said with cold certainty, ' and it is through his efforts to cheat the parishioners who are buying the new bells for Soston that my chance has come. The Rector asked Cuddy how the work on the six bells was going. Cuddy repeated what he heard Caleb say: "Only making five. They've got to find out big bells is extra."

'His story was to be that the big bell, the tenor, was always quoted for separately. Unfortunately for Caleb, the Rector of Soston approached my grandfather to confirm the terms. The outcome is they are going to take the five smaller bells we've already begun, but they've refused to let Caleb have anything to do with the new tenor bell.

'This is where I saw my chance. Flaxhill comes under the same diocese and rectorship as Soston. I've approached the Rector and offered to cast the new tenor for him at cost, if he will let me work in the churchyard at Soston using the old bells from Flaxhill for the metal. Of course there has to be proper permission – a dispensation, I believe it's called – but it's a definite possibility. I'll never have a better.'

Sam unhooked his glasses and handed back the paper. 'I think you'll be breaking your back to no good end. He'll never stand by that.'

'He will.' Ben's face was hard. 'He has no skill in the trade. My grandfather and brother have promised they will do no more work for him *unless* he honours it.'

'A family Union.' Sam rubbed his chin, grinning and nodding. 'It could work. I'd like to see it work.'

'You'd help?' Ben asked eagerly.

'I don't know what I could do . . .'

'With practical advice. I'd have to cast the bell without the use of any of the foundry tools. I'd have no bell-case, no base-plate – nothing. I think I'll have to go back to the lost wax method. A core as we use now, then the bell built up in wax, an outer cover of clay and loam over that. Time to harden the mould then fires to melt the wax, letting it run away into pre-dug drains.

'Then you've got to have either a crucible or a furnace to melt your bell-metal,' Sam contributed and asked, 'How would you pour?'

'We dig a pit for the mould, so the liquid metal can be just channelled down.'

'Into the space left by the wax,' Leah said, jubilantly visualising the process.

'Ah! *Sounds* easy,' Sam said, suddenly pessimistic again, 'but there's a lot of work and a lot of skill . . .'

'I'm not afraid. The wax is the only material I've not used before . . .'

Leah was distracted by the sound of someone else coming into the yard. 'Ginnie.' She suddenly remembered their arrangement, and leaving the men talking went to meet her friend.

Ginnie looked curiously in at them, and lifted her eyebrows to question whether all had gone well. Leah nodded slowly and certainly in reply.

'I'm on my way to church really, but it's so nice just to be able to call in and see you again,' she said as Clarrie came to the back door of her cottage and waved to them both.

'Why don't you all come to Evensong?' Clarrie called as she came to join the group and be introduced to Ben.

'Nat is walking over to ring the bells before the service. He'd join us, I'm sure,' Ben added.

Ginnie's expression of simulated surprise at such a suggestion had Leah biting her lip to stop herself laughing aloud. 'I think that's a nice idea,' she added as Ben looked for her approval. He left a few minutes later to join the band of bell-ringers who would peal the bells for some three-quarters of an hour before the service.

'We must remember to leave room for the two boys,' Clarrie fussed as they took their places towards the rear of the central aisle. Leah, who was following Ginnie and tripping on her heels as her friend tried to catch a glimpse of Nat in the first floor ringing-chamber, thought that there was no danger of either of them forgetting that.

A loud and authoritative sniff drew attention to the arrival of Mr and Mrs Warburton and Levis, who made their way towards the front pews, just behind those belonging to the local gentry. Ginnie nudged Leah and they turned and sniffed at each other. Nothing and no one was going to dampen their high spirits that evening. Leah just hoped *everyone* would see Ben and Nat come and sit with them when the bells had been rung down.

She sat still now, for the organist had begun to play a gentle reflective composition as the pews began to fill. The ring of bells began tumbling faster down their scales and the tenor took up the final tolling to speak the last minutes before it was time for the service to begin. Ginnie wriggled for a moment like an excited child, and Leah, for no reason she could think of, found herself wishing it had been somewhere other than Soston where this new tenor bell was to be made.

In the choir vestry the voice of the Vicar could be heard, saying a prayer before the opening processional hymn. The deep tenor paused, sounded three more times, then was silent.

There was a little scuffle of feet behind them, and Ben and Nat came quietly down from the curtained ringing-chamber to join them in the pew. Ginnie hastily gave Leah a push to indicate she should stay at the end of the pew while she moved up against Clarrie – so leaving room for the two men between them.

As he sat beside her, Ben contrived to cover her hand with his as it lay between them on the seat. It seemed a very audacious act, a terrible deprivation when they must stand as the choir processed to the front of the church.

Chapter Eleven

Leah watched her mother's head drawing even nearer and nearer to the sock she was knitting. Her own eyes felt itchy and irritated with long hours of close work. Local people said you always knew a stockinger by the dark circles and red rims to their eyes.

'Are you going to finish that tonight?'

'Oh, yes,' Nellie replied calmly, while Leah felt the back of her head might well blow off with the frustration and boredom of handknitting. She thought there seemed a world of difference between what John White was achieving on his stall and the "bargain" wool he had acquired for her.

'Did you know John well?' she asked.

The tick of the clock filled the sudden silence, until Nellie gave a brief laugh. 'I did . . .' And for a rare moment she let the knitting rest in her lap. 'Your father came along just in time to save me.'

'Mother! do you mean that?'

Nellie chuckled. 'I do. He was the most dashing young man. He very nearly bowled me off my feet! But John is . . . well, he's too much of everything. Too impulsive, too generous, too hot-headed – while your father now, he had a gentleness about him. He was too good for this world.'

'Oh, don't,' Leah protested quietly, hot tears stinging her eyes, and went to kneel on the pegged hearthrug, arms around her mother's knees. 'And you've been alone so long.' The words tumbled out in the unguarded moment. 'I'm sorry, that doesn't help.'

Nellie put her had over Leah's cheek and said gently, 'There are moments when, as you half turn your face away . . . and you have his eyes . . .'

'I didn't know.'

'It's a joy,' she explained, 'not a sorrow.'

They were silent for a time, Nellie smoothing her daughter's hair were it lay gilded by the lamp light.

'Why were you so cross when Grandma wrote to John White?'

'Because looking at you and remembering your father is a kind memory. It brings me a gentle smile or a gentle tear, but John White . . . he's . . . so disquieting.'

'Like being in a gale, leaves you a bit breathless.' she wondered if her mother, even at her age, was not a little afraid of a reunion, of being disquieted all over again?

'A whirlwind more like!' Nellie laughed. 'Though I'm pleased to hear he's prospering. I always felt he could as easily run himself on to rocks as into harbour.' She was quiet then, but Leah could sense she had something else she wanted to say, and after a moment she went on. 'I'm glad your grandmother's still with Clarrie, and that we've talked about your father, because . . . I want you to have something. Sam has told me all about this bell that has to be made, and that Ben has not been able to obtain any money from the Church to buy the wax and other things he needs. But first you must make me a promise.'

'A promise?'

'A serious, solemn promise.'

Leah frowned, wanting to know more.

'You must not say one word, just take what I give you upstairs and put it in your drawer until you can sell it. You promise?'

She felt the weight and pressing seriousness of her mother's request as she heard her grandmother coming home.

'She knows,' Nellie said quietly, still waiting for the promise.

Miriam came into the kitchen, and stopped at the sight of her daughter-in-law and granddaughter, caught in the drama of awaited commitment.

'I promise,' Leah said doubtfully.

At her words Nellie took her daughter's hand and dropped something into her palm, closing the young fingers over it and pushing her away.

Leah opened her hand. 'Oh, no!' she protested, seeing her mother's broad wedding-ring lying there, yet still glancing to check it was not in place on her hand. 'Oh, no! this I couldn't . . . I couldn't!'

'Leah!' Her grandmother's voice was sharp, harsher than she had ever heard it. 'You made a promise. Take it!' Then, as Leah might have protested again, she saw her mother turn away so they could no longer see her face, and Miriam repeated in a low and weary voice, 'Just take it!'

She went quickly upstairs, closed her bedroom door and knelt by the bed, the ring clasped in her hands, weeping silently. Such a precious thing – the thought that had gone into the giving, the discussion there must have been with her grandmother, the tremulous moment of drawing the ring from the finger, the promise extracted, too painful to talk of the sacrifice. She buried her head deeper in the quilt for the given symbol of her mother and father's wedding-day, all the hopes they must have had – lasting so short a time. Then, bleakly, opening her hand and wiping her eyes to look again, she saw it as a symbol of how little they had – how very little separated them from destitution.

It was never referred to again inside the house but she found many an extra opportunity to give her mother and grandmother a hug. She made light of the tally-rounds with so little to show for the labour, and a game of hand-knitting the remainder of John White's inferior wool, comparing lengths and competing to finish socks, rather than making a burden of every push of her needles.

Ben returned interest fourfold in effort, in wood chopped, in water carried, in labouring on their allotment, in any and every chore he could find time to help with. As the summer months passed he spent more and more time at Tur Lacey. There were sketches of bell moulds and bells pinned up in the workshop, and minor experiments with wax models on the benches; a pair of his work-trousers hung on the peg behind the kitchen door where her grandfather's had been.

He and Sam had laboured long hours together, copying and reproducing bell-stickles and other tools Ben variously borrowed from the foundry, until Sam declared it was going to be a shame to just make one bell with all the preparation that was going into it. But still there was no word giving the go-ahead from the Church authorities.

'The mills of God grind slowly,' Sam quoted.

'Are they moving at all? Is this all for nothing?' He felt a sudden terrible impatience, and looking up as Leah came into the workshop, fresh, slim and smiling, his desire for her threatened to overwhelm all sense of propriety.

'It's time I took you home . . .' she began cheerfully but was startled by his dark brooding look. She frowned gently at him, questioning, and reached for his hand. She saw Sam raise his head to comment, and added, 'Ginnie's coming, so I won't be on my own coming back.'

It had become a regular event for the two brothers to walk to and from Tur Lacey together, the four meeting at Old Brigg when it was time to return. She sometimes envied Ginnie the extra time she had alone with Nat. Their secret friendship gave them the excitement of long stolen hours alone, while she and Ben were welcome to meet but expected to spend much of their time in her home and in the workshop, making plans for the future. While Walter Hobbday believed his daughter was safely being supervised by a friend now seriously attached and settled in her relationship with a man, she was having larks and good times enough. Ginnie's only frustration was that marriage did not seem to be on Nat's mind.

'I know how you feel,' Leah ventured as she and Ben walked away from the village.

'No,' he said simply, 'you don't. I don't believe any woman knows how a man feels.'

'Tell me, then,' she asked. 'I want to understand.'

'Oh!' The exclamation was almost one of pain. He stopped walking and shook his head. She went to him and put her arms under his jacket, moulding herself close to him, feeling the erratic pumping of his heart. He stood as if steeling himself against her. 'No, you don't understand,' he said. 'Let me go.'

116

She released him, feeling suddenly angry. 'Perhaps it's you who doesn't understand.' She swallowed hard, then blurted out what she felt. 'I don't want to start that . . .; She made another beginning. 'I don't want to start having babies yet, with any number from one to twenty coming once started! And not married or anything!'

'Oh, Leah.' He tried to catch her hand as they walked on, but she avoided him. 'I wouldn't want that for us, you know that.'

She was silent, a little angry still, thinking of Bessie Yarrup. Her ever increasing brood of hungry boys meant she still had not found a halfpenny more to pay on the stockings Leah had let her have on that very first tally-round. 'No, but *you* don't really know what it's like, baby after baby, dragging you down further into debt and destitution.'

He wondered how much she knew about such things, but it hardly seemed a wise moment to ask. They had reached the bridge, and though the other two were not yet in sight, their time together was short. 'It's this dammed bell! If I could only hear about that!' he exclaimed, leaning on the bridge and kicking at the grasses growing at its base.

Leah felt a chill start from the base of her spine, the gooseflesh prickling icily over her back, shoulders, arms. She made an effort to turn a shudder into no more than a shiver. The more she heard about the "dammed bell", the more apprehensive she became. 'Will you put an inscription on it?' she asked. 'Something good – though it's not really having a good beginning . . .'

'What do you mean?'

'The chance coming through dishonesty, planned in secret . . . tools sneaked out of your step-father's foundry, traced and . . .'

'Returned,' Ben interrupted firmly. 'As far as I am concerned it is rightly my grandfather's foundry – and will be mine and Nat's if there's any justice under the heavens.'

'*In* heaven perhaps.' Her tone suggested doubt of any on earth, and for a moment they both lapsed into silence as they heard the other two coming, laughing and chasing across the field to the bridge.

117

'It's just a means to an end,' he said, 'to my wage as a master-man, and to our being together. I don't know that I'm much concerned with the niceties.'

'Oh! Cheerful as a little snow in harvest,' Ginnie declared, peering at their faces as she and Nat joined them on the bridge.

'Lovers' tiff?' Nat exclaimed, smoothing his tousled hair back. 'Surely not!'

'It will all come right when you're wed,' Ginnie promised, looking provocatively at Nat.

'It's just the bell . . . *again*,' Leah explained.

''Tis cursed, you know,' Ginnie said dourly, stooping over, making a childlike impression of a witch. 'C. . .u. . .r. . .sed before 'tis cast.'

'Don't, Ginnie,' censured Leah, unamused. 'You don't know how I feel.'

'Then there ain't no sense in how you feel,' Ginnie declared, tossing her curls and linking her arm in Nat's. 'I should say you ought to thank the day you went to Soston – and to Flaxhill.'

Leah was silent, and none of them quite managed to regain his or her spirits before they parted. Nat reminded his brother that Caleb was taking their grandfather to inspect and tender for a new bell in Lincolnshire, so they would probably be able to come over for the whole day.

'We'll see how things go then,' Leah rather vaguely replied.

'What'd you got to say that for?' Ginnie remonstrated as they walked back together. 'Now I don't know what to do Saturday.'

'Bring that other picture you found of the men playing golf,' she suggested.

'Right!' Immediately content, Ginnie linked and squeezed her friend's arm.

Any plans any of them had made for Saturday were completely disrupted by the letter that arrived by that morning's mail. Posted the day before from town, the message was from John White, to say he proposed to hire a wagon and come to

Tur Lacey for the day to see them all. "The family could do with a day's holiday in the country," he wrote.

The idea threw Nellie into a complete panic, and Leah suspected her of trying to find some way of not being there as she reminded them there was likely to be gleaning to be had in the fields that day.

'If he knows wheat-ears as well as he does wool, he'll be no use at that,' Sam declared.

'No, I didn't mean . . .' Nellie began.

'One thing I know for sure, he could be here any minute,' Miriam declared. 'How many children has he got?'

No one knew, and as they all stood at the back door debating, there was the sound of a wagon in the street and of many voices, many lively children. Leah recognised John White's hearty 'Wooah!' She saw her mother's hand fly to her cheeks. 'He's here,' she breathed, and retreated into the kitchen.

The next moment boys first, then girls, came in a kind of wave up the entry into the backyard, hurrahing and calling back to those following. To the Dexters and the Elliotts, unused to young children for so many years, it seemed like the arrival of a Sunday School outing. Sam discreetly closed the workshop door behind himself and stood guard. Leah stood in the middle of the yard and the children collected around her as if she was to be the pivot of their day's outing. There were two boys of about eleven and twelve with curly chestnut hair, two curly-haired dark boys of about six and eight and three girls, all with straight auburn hair, who looked as if they were slotted between the other four, in order to keep a sense of proportion about curls.

'Hello! Hello!' John White came striding after his children, resplendent in green homespun with a red neckerchief. He was as her mother said just too much, too colourful, too big. '*You* didn't write to me!' He aimed a pretend punch in the direction of her shoulder, then took her hand and pumped it up and down, as his children dispersed over the yard and small vegetable garden, some going over the top of the wall into the flower garden.

119

'So now then! Where's my first love?' Then he saw Miriam and went to shake her energetically by the hand. 'I'm pleased you remembered me.'

'You're not one easily forgotten,' she replied with a laugh, but added more seriously, 'I still have the letter you wrote to us when my son died. There's not many in your position would have bothered.'

She introduced him to Clarrie and Sam, who seemed about to bring him to task on the matter of the wool when more footsteps sounded in the entry.

'Here's my Jane,' he announced as Mrs White appeared with yet another son, almost as tall as his mother, his chestnut hair as red as his father's must have been at that age. Leah found herself warming to Mrs White all over again, and as her mother came slowly from the back door, she thought what a contrast the two women were. Jane, medium height, neat, slim as a broomstale, dark wavy hair, quietly spoken; her mother looking a country woman in sacking apron, but her homely features coloured and were much enhanced by her embarrassment.

'Ah, Nellie!' John grabbed her by the shoulders. His eyes fairly seemed to devour her as he demanded, 'How have you been?'

'Fine, John, fine!' she replied, looking first shyly at him then with some embarrassment at his wife, as still he held her. There was something in both their faces that stirred recognition in Leah's heart. They really had been in love, there was no doubt about that.

'Shall I bring the baskets in, Father?' the boy who had come with his mother interposed.

'Yes, Johnnie.' John White kept one arm around Nellie's shoulders and drew her forward to his wife.

'You've been a lucky man,' Nellie said, leaning forward to kiss Jane's cheek, then gesturing to indicate the seven younger children, variously exploring the garden paths, eating the loganberries and playing leapfrog over an old trestle.

John picked out the various children. 'Matthew, Mark, Luke and big Johnnie here. Janie, Gertie, Maudie and Victoria.' He drew Leah forward to meet his eldest son.

'Nearly thirteen,' Johnnie said quietly as if in explanation as he offered his hand not his cheek to her. He went off then to fetch the baskets from the wagon, and returned in short time with helpers: Ben and Nat pottering two huge cloth-covered baskets each, and Ginnie with two smaller ones.

'Heavens above!' Sam declared as the children were attracted by the newcomers and the baskets. 'It'll soon be as noisy and crowded as bedlam.'

Leah laughed aloud as everyone crowded round, making introductions, hands crossing here and there in greeting, and felt a little thrill of pride, seeing how well her Ben compared even with larger-than-life John White. Across the crowd she disconcerted her young man, her smile clearly showing her pleasure in him. He smiled back, the tension of their last parting forgotten as they repledged their love across the nodding heads.

Then the conversation was stilled as the church bell suddenly sounded out, the adults hushing the children as they listed to see what it portended. Once the first three strokes had passed they relaxed, for it was not the death bell, patterned one for a man, two for a woman and three for a child, to be followed, after a pause, with as many strokes as the departed had years. This Saturday morning bell rang busily for some several minutes.

Once they saw the seriousness leave the grownups' faces, the children were loud in their demands as to what it meant ..

'It's the gleaning-bell,' Nellie explained. 'It means that a farmer has finished harvesting his fields and the people are free to go and pick up the stray heads of corn that have dropped from the sheaves.

'What for should they?'

'If they collect enough they take it to the local miller and he'll grind it down into flour for them, keeping a little for himself for the trouble.'

'Can we go? We'll get sacks full.' Little Janie stretched and crouched to describe the biggest circle she could manage.

'Sooner the better,' Sam said, nodding to where two of the boys were picking the half-grown cooking-apples. 'There's more room in the fields. City kids and country gardens don't mix.'

'We've brought food enough . . .' Mrs White began.

'For everyone. Come on, day in the fields! We'll all go gleaning - have a picnic.' John, his arms now around Ginnie's shoulders, took up his wife's lead. 'Load the baskets again! Everyone back on the wagon. Come on, you ladies, you shall ride. And, Leah, you young folk can walk ahead and show us the way.'

Sam took the suggestion that he might join them with raised eyebrows, and as the women collected sacks and sun bonnets waved a warning finger in their direction. 'You remember you don't go in any fields where there's still even a single stook – and if there's stooks lined up by the gate, that'll be the time you're allowed into that particular field.

'*We* know, Sam Elliott,' Clarrie told him. 'We've lived here all our lives too.'

'Aye, well, you'll maybe find there's more rules than them you're breaking . . .'

Clarrie tutted as he turned back into the shop, giving no further explanation. 'He's tired, that's his trouble. Messing about with that old knitting-frame, trying to make it do things it was never intended for,' she mumbled in explanation, as the four older women collected sacks and sunbonnets and climbed on to the wagon. At the last minute Sam came back with a wicker basket full of his best early eating apples, handing them in to the children.

Nat and Ben shouldered one each of the smaller boys, and as the party drew away began a jogging "horse" race with the mare in the wagon.

'Beat mine with a stick,' Luke ordered as Nat lagged behind.

'You dare!'

'I dare, don't you fret.' Ginnie darted to the hedgerow to select a twig, and Nat galloped off at a great pace, so it looked as if four-year-old Luke might well lose his seat and toss off his own head it shook about so. Ginnie gave up and walked on the other side of Ben until they reached the south-facing fields just beyond the allotment gardens. These were always the first to be carried, the first opened to the villagers for gleaning.

Four cornfields led off one another from the road. In the first, four women were already bent double retrieving the fallen ears of corn. There were stooks still across the gateway leading to the next field. Eleven, Leah counted. In the furthest field, the harvesters were still swaying and bending rhythmically as they worked in a diagonal line, cutting into the standing corn. Behind the mowers worked the binders, mostly women, pulling and twisting strands of corn from the swathes to bind them into sheaves, then carrying one under each arm to prop them together in stooks of six.

The gleaners turned as one to stare at the sudden crowd at the gate, then began to work even harder. No longer pausing to snap heads from the straws, but pushing them whole into their bags to be sorted later.

'Well, it's free for all,' Nellie said defensively as she and Miriam set to without delay, though choosing a line across the field furthest from the other village women.

Leaving John and his wife to deal with their party and belongings, the others too collected sacks and began retrieving the lost corn heads. Luke quickly joined his new hero Nat, shouting to the others, 'Bet we fill our sack first!' At the challenge the other children quickly chose who they would work with. Johnnie shyly putting his first handful of corn into Leah's bag, with Janie taking up the role of her second helper.

'Hey! What's this then – the Dexters hiring labour? This 'ere's supposed to be rights for villagers, not for half the county.'

'You must have jumped the bell anyway.' Ginnie gestured towards the woman's bulging sack.

'And you'll be making up for lost time,' the woman shouted. 'Fourteen, I count. Fourteen!'

'Eight are only children,' Leah retorted, 'come for an outing in the country.'

'But picking up! Picking up!' The woman was quite beside herself, and as Ben tried to intervene, she rounded on him. 'And who are you? Not of this parish. Clear off, the lot of you!'

Mrs White came hurrying from where John was tethering the horse to graze on the roadside. Jane rapidly took in the situation.

'Look,' she said, 'the sheaves are being taken away from the next field gateway. If you go on into that field, I'll keep my children in this field.'

The woman was torn between pursuing her quarrel, and fear of loosing the best pickings in the next field. Seeing the other women running forward, she gave them one last scowl and hurried away.

They gave a sigh of relief to see her go, but Miriam, who had not seemed to take much notice of the exchange, followed quickly into the newly opened field, and Nellie, giving Leah a nod to stay with the Whites, followed.

Ginnie soon had to leave to go home to prepare the mid-day meal, but promised to be back as soon as she could. By noon the sun was hot, the air and their hands full of the dry sweet smell of the straw. In the furthest field the last loads of corn were being carted away, the harvesters were moving as a band on to the next farmer's land, and there were some two dozen villagers gleaning industriously.

The children had long since tired of the useful task and run themselves to a state of heated exhaustion by the time John brought the great baskets of food and stone bottles of home-made lemonade and beer to the shade of a great oak in the middle of the first field. Once the food was broken out no one needed calling, the party was soon assembled. Great round flat loaves cut through and filled with thick slices of beef and cheese were broken into pieces for the children, but handed whole to the grown-ups. There was a mutton pie wrapped in many cloths to keep it cool, with jam and curd pastry turn-overs to follow.

Leah thought food had never tasted so good, and company was never so happy. She saw her grandmother's eyes begin to close as the meal ended, though once the food was de-spatched the children were eager for action again. When Nat suggested that he take them all to the brook for a paddle, he almost disappeared under a surge of children all anxious to be off that very second. 'Come on, Ben, I can't handle this lot on my own.'

'I'll wait for Ginnie,' Leah said in answer to Ben's glance.

'Five minutes' peace,' Jane said gratefully as they watched them go, and Miriam finally lapsed into sleep.

John who had lain back, head cradled in his hands, suddenly exclaimed, 'Oh, my! Look at this.' More by sheer determination than strength, the woman who had accosted them when they first arrived was slowly dragging three enormous sacks towards the roadway.

'She'll have the bottoms out if she drags them all the way home,' Nellie said drily. 'She lives as far the other side of the village as you can and still *be* in this parish.'

'She'll never carry them,' John decided, then looked to where several other of the early gleaners were beginning to carry their loads home. 'I might as well make up a wagon-load,' he commented as he roused himself and approached the woman with the three enormous sacks. They watched as for a second she seemed to fend him off, then looked round to the others hurrying to take advantage of a ride home. Disbelieving, she relinquished her burdens, walked a step or two more, then turned and gave them all an uncertain wave. Cheerfully, her gesture was returned. Leah felt the return of a tremendous affection for John White. He always meant well, and now no bad memory would marr this day.

Nellie, Jane and Leah watched him go, smiled as they heard him bantering with the women and their answering laughter.

'That's John White,' Nellie said, laughing herself.

'You remember him very well?'

'He was nineteen when I first met him, but he's not changed one little bit – not a bit! It was quite a shock.'

Jane sighed. 'He's like an aggravating child you cannot help loving.' Her voice softened as she added, 'But I would go to the ends of the earth for my John.'

Nellie smiled at her possessiveness, and added gently, 'As I would have done for my Fred – but *John* running a successful stall, now that was a surprise!'

'I do all the buying and the pricing. John is the showman in the markets. He loves it, and the women love him.'

'So really you are organising the business?' Leah put in, wanting to hear more.

'You mustn't let him hear you say that! He thinks the work is done behind the stall, not behind the scenes.'

'But . . .' Leah protested.

'I know, my dear, but there has to be a man up front.'

'But you're running the business side! It should be John and Jane Freeman on your board.'

'Even other women don't like to see another putting herself forward. We know how much we do, but have to content ourselves with that, with being in the background.'

'Not this woman,' Leah declared, 'and that's not how grandfather treated *us*.'

'Ah! Your grandfather was a law to himself.' Nellie declared.

'There are a few men . . .' Jane began, but seemed too lethargic to pursue the argument further. The two older women laughed indulgently. Then Nellie pointed towards the roadway. 'Here's Ginnie back!'

Leah felt a deep sense of rebellion, but she saw a rare smile of contentment on her mother's face as she leaned on the bole of the great oak – and she turned to watch Ginnie coming across the field. No wonder boys flocked around her. She looked all warmth and cheer and life with her chestnut curls burnished by the sun. The day was too good and too golden to spoil – but Leah remembered her friend secured the receipt of her catalogues and magazines by using initials, by the pretence of being a man.

'Where is everybody?' Ginnie called, and soon the two of them were on their way to join the others.

'Come on!' Don't waste a second!' Ginnie cried, catching her hand and running, but before they reached the brook they met Nat carrying back a large pile of clothes.

'We tried to get their clothes off before they went in but . . .' He indicated the saturated state of everything he was carrying. 'I wondered if their mother has anything else they could put on?'

'Not for that lot, I shouldn't think!' Ginnie relieved Nat of some of his burden. 'I'll go back with you, and we'll spread them all out in the sun.'

Leah was hardly out of sight of the other two when she heard them calling her. She turned to see them hurrying back towards her with a third person. A man, she thought, but a strange figure, stooped, with unnaturally long arms, the outline black against the sun. She went hesitantly to meet them, saw Nat's face alight with excitement.

'This is Cuddy,' he introduced the stranger, 'who works for us. He's come with a letter for Ben from the Rector of Soston.'

Her heart began to pound rapidly as she nodded to the odd-looking figure, neither man nor boy. He shook an envelope at her. 'For Mr Ben,' he said, his voice odd and muffled as if his tongue was too thick, out of proportion and difficult to control. She remembered he had recently lost his mother.

'Hello, Cuddy. How are you?'

'All right . . . thank . . . you,' he answered, blushing and swaying about like an embarrassed child.

'This may be what we are waiting for,' she told him. 'Come on, I'll take you to Mr Ben.'

They all returned to the stream together, and Ben came immediately to meet them, taking the proffered letter.

'Take Cuddy for a paddle,' he instructed his brother. 'We'll come in a moment.

He stood holding the letter until he and Leah were alone, then giving her a last look, like a man going to his fate, he broke the seal on the back of the envelope, and stood reading the contents.

'Ben?' she queried at last, as he stood as if turned to stone. 'Ben?'

At last he let out a roar of triumph and throwing the letter up into the air, caught her in his arms and twirled her round and round. From the stream came an answering shout, a pause, and then burst upon louder burst of cheering as Nat responded and John White's children followed his lead.

'There never was such a day,' Nellie declared as the heat of the late afternoon found them all reassembled under the tree for a final cut of cake and drink of water from the stone bottles, long since emptied of their original contents, but which John had carried to fill upstream of the paddlers. Cuddy, who had been taken in hand by young Janie, and had splashed around with the best of them, was persuaded to take a huge piece of cake with him as he determined it was time for him to go home.

Then the children were busy again, engrossed in finding a few extra cornheads with long straws as Miriam showed them how to plait a corn-dolly, for soon they all wanted their own dolly to take home. They flitted about like white butterflies in their underclothes, boys with just pants, one with only a shirt, bigger girls with petticoats, smaller ones with knickers — their outer clothing like a gipsy's washday on the hedge, and they like gipsy children with their red faces and arms and their hair wild from much wetting and wind-drying.

At last the time came for the horse to be reharnessed, its waterbucket and feedbag rehung on hooks under the back of the cart, the baskets and bottles, the seven sacks of gleanings and a hustle of tired children put aboard. John drove and the others brought up the rear.

Leah walked with Ben at the end of the party, his arm around her shoulders. She could tell his mind was already racing forward to the making of the bell as for a time he stared straight ahead. The he came back to her with a swift intake of breath, his eyes shining. He gave her a swift fierce hug, as if he hardly knew how to contain his excitement.

For a time the only sound was that of the horse's hooves, the crunch of the wheels, and the scuff of tired feet. Then John began to sing *Home, Sweet Home* in deep soft tones: 'Mid pleasures and Palaces though we may roam, Be it ever so humble there's no place like home!' At the end of each verse they all joined in the chorus: 'Home! Home, sweet sweet Home! There's no place like Home!' To the last dying slow repeat 'There's no place like Home!

Then he took up a more lilting air. 'Believe me if all those endearing your charms, Which I gaze on so fondly today, Were to change by tomorrow, and fleet in my arms, Like fairy gifts facing away, Thou woulds't still be ador'd as this moment thou art, Let thou loveliness fade as it will; And round each dear ruin each wish of my heart Would entwine itself verdently still.'

The words he sang solo, but they gave him a gentle sweet humming accompaniment. Leah wondered if he sang for her mother, and the sentimental song brought tears to her eyes. She saw Ginnie tilt her head on to Nat's shoulder.

Chapter Twelve

'These bellringers . . .' Charley Hobbday began as he and his brother David manhandled full barrels from the brewhouse to the shallow cellar behind the bar of the Stockinger's Arms.

'Bell *makers*,' Ginnie corrected, standing by with wooden wedges to secure the barrels once in position.

There was a pause as David supported a huge hogshead against his legs, turning it against his great thighs. The blue veins stood out in his forehead as he levered the barrel up inch by inch between his arched body and the brick thrall. Ginnie held her breath, fearful that even David's back would one day break under such a strain.

'Which one of 'em have you set your cap at?' David asked as he joggled the barrel until its base was tight to the wall. She was used to being teased, often enjoyed being the centre of her brothers' attentions – but was unsure where this particular conversation was leading.

'Come on' she demanded. 'Don't go all around the houses What've you got to say?'

'Well, it's as I was saying to Levis Warburton . . .' David began, having to duck as she threw a wedge. 'You can't tell! First she's over the fields meeting one of them, and then the other!'

'Spell it out!' she demanded, lifting another wooden scotch above her head.

'Tell her, for goodness' sake,' Charley pleaded. 'With her aim, nobody's safe!'

'There's confusion in the county, the neighbourhood's nonplussed, there's . . .'

'You'll be concussed, David Hobbday!' She aimed at her eldest brother, grinning in spite of herself at the old rhyming game. This had begun when they learned nursery rhymes one from the other.

'. . .bother in the bar, and tit-tattle in the taproom,' he went on, ducking as she awkwardly balanced her missile behind her head and made a determined effort to throw straight towards him.

Charley drew in his breath sharply as it hit the wall opposite his brother. 'That was close!'

'"Leah Dexter's so busy peddling her stockings around she doesn't see what's going on."'

David's imitation of Levis Warburton's whingeing tones was unmistakable, and she felt all the playfulness drain away as she demanded, 'Did he say that? DID HE?'

'He did until David leaned his weight against him when he went out the back.' Charley's voice was serious now. 'Made him explain what he meant.'

'And?'

'He said he'd twice seen you meet Ben Robertson on your own,' David explained.

'Leah is my best friend. I'd *never* do anything to hurt her. You should know that, both of you.' Distress set her voice wavering, making Charley add gently, 'We thought you should know what was being said.'

'I've met Ben alone just once. And then Nat was supposed to have been there. He'd stayed to finish some work for his step-father so Ben could slip away early.'

'So it's Nathaniel we have to watch out for?' David tried to restore her good humour.

'Shouldn't think you need worry.' She tossed her head, angry now and near to tears. 'There's obviously plenty of people watching out on my behalf.'

'You'll never stop folk gossiping. If it's not in here, it'll be round the village pump.'

'Always ready to pull a person down,' Ginnie protested, then another thought struck her. 'Father didn't hear, did he?' David took up a piece of brown paper and stood meticulously folding it into a neat strip then binding it gasket-tight around the stem of a tap. His silence answered her question.

'Levis is more to be pitied than blamed,' he reflected. 'It's the only time anyone takes any notice of him, when he's telltaling.' He moved to a barrel that had been thralled and pegged some days before, allowing the beer to settle.

'Oh, no! He's a real mischief maker,' Ginnie protested, 'a Peeping Tom, a . . .' She had to relieve her feelings somehow and kicked vigorously at a wooden tub used for beer fouled by hops or sediment. She found fresh inspiration. 'A bucket of bilge, the dregs, dottle and dross . . .'

David and Charley were now roaring with laughter at her tirade, and she went on kicking and chanting . . . 'bilge-pits and spoil banks . . .' Until a voice from the direction of the kitchen demanded, 'Is there any work going on!'

In automatic reaction David grabbed a mallet, and positioning the tap over the bung-hole, raised his hand to give a single mighty swipe, which should have driven the tap home with no spillage.

At the moment his arm began to swing down he caught sight of young Wally imitating their father's hands-on-hips stance as well as his voice. The distraction caused a misstroke. A great shower of best ale spurted over all of them as the tap slewed crookedly in the bung. Cursing, it took David three more strokes to hold the tap into the foaming mass of beer and drive it tight into place. They were all well bespattered and David soaked. 'You numbskull,' he began, but Ginnie's sharp eyes saw a familiar figure pass the latticed front window.

'Here *is* father!' she warned, and a wild mopping up began. Ginnie saw her opportunity. While they were all busy she slipped away. She heard her brothers' voices raised in conflicting explanations as she reached the village street.

She found Leah carefully and thoughtfully gathering huge dark green cooking apples, placing them upright in a basket of straw.

'You know I'd never do anything to hurt you, Leah. Never!' she vowed, and seeing the distant look on her friend's face, added, 'You believe me, don't you? I'd rather die.'

Leah looked up at the last word. 'I went to Soston last night,' she began. 'It was . . .horrible.'

'Horrible?' Ginnie questioned, but again sought confirmation that Levis's gossip was not believed.

Leah waved it aside, then drew Ginnie's arm through her own and walked her to the privacy of the empty workshop.

'Tell me.' Ginnie felt puzzled for all around in the Dexter shop was evidence of plans to help bring Leah's wedding-day nearer. Drawings of bells, lists, calculations, calendars, lined the walls. The beams, pulley-wheels and ropes ready to lower the old bells from Flaxhill Tower stood in one corner. She wished there were such plans and goings-on for her and Nat. 'Tell me,' she repeated.

It felt to Leah curiously like a loss of pride to admit fears which everyone else saw as groundless. It reminded her of how she had felt when labelled "pedlar-girl" by the young man on the train. 'I sometimes think,' she began, 'that holy places are no different to any other – they're just what people make them. And that old Monk's Bell and that awful old man have made Soston evil, for me anyway. I feel no good will come to me or . . .' she paused to look directly at her friend, 'anyone I love from that place.'

'So what happened? Ginnie demanded with assumed bravado. 'What was so 'orrible?'

'I was later than I meant to be setting out, so when I arrived it was nearly dark.'

'You shouldn't have gone on your own. I would have come.'

'Ben had borrowed a hack and promised to give me a ride home. It was supposed to be an enjoyable outing,' Leah explained with a touch of irony in her voice. 'The horse was tethered against the lychgate when I got there. But it was a different world inside those high walls. So dark and silent, with that great tower looming. I walked slowly round to the back, and first of all his jacket scared me to death. He had hung it on a thorn of an old Judas tree – and for a moment I thought it was a person hanging there.'

Ginnie tutted. 'Fancy going to a graveyard on your own, at night!'

'Then as I reached the back of the church I could see a glow from two lanterns on the ground. Ben was still measuring up where he has permission to dig out the bell-pit. He didn't hear me. He took up a spade and began to slice down into the grass.' She paused, remembering the energy he put into those first strokes. She had been amazed at his strength as great pieces of turf were thrown aside, and saw again how as he moved his shadow shot backwards and forwards over the ground, up the angle of the wall, like a giant. She shuddered then, crossing her arms over her chest, gripping her forearms, chilled by the unexpectedness of what had happened next. She went on, 'Then suddenly he stopped, sort of choking and retching, staggering over to lean on the wall. I ran to him – then I smelt it too. Huh!' She shook her head in disgust.

'Smelt?' Ginnie questioned in amazement, not expecting a smell to be the cause of the drama.

Leah swallowed hard. 'It was just as if he had dug straight into bad meat – rank – like bad suet, like that filthy village slaughterhouse in high summer. We had to move away before we could talk.'

'What was it?' Ginnie asked aghast at the possibilities, 'What did you do?'

For the first time Leah looked at her with a spark of humour in her eyes. 'We had a great argument! I said he must be digging into an unmarked mass grave from the time of the Black Death. He said Soston churchyard was still open for burials so it couldn't be that.'

'The Rector must know about these things,' Ginnie reasoned, 'and if Ben has permission to dig there . . .'

'Yes . . . but you don't know what it smelt like! I begged him not to carry on. To make the bell somewhere else, at least outside the churchyard. He said that would put him back months. He must get it all done before the hard frosts begin. He said the smell was probably something a fox had buried.' Leah paused then added, 'It was something dead, that was for sure.'

'Soston was a deserted village from sixteen forty.' Ginnie began dredging up scraps of information, local history not written but passed on in casual conversations over the generations. 'Time of enclosure that was, then the cottages began to spring up again at the beginning of this century.'

'So you're saying he was right?'

133

'There would not have been a great many funerals in Soston . . .' Ginnie added, with an air of superior logic.

'Oh! So we should be grateful to Squire Lacey and his ancestors? They enclosed their lands early for sheep, drove the people away and kept the churchyard empty. Good! Perhaps Ben should inscribe his new bell to them. To the Laceys, who kept sheep not men.'

'Leah' she appealed. 'I'm on your side. Remember me, your childhood friend?'

'I know!' Leah replied vehemently, then laughed briefly at her own intensity.

Ginnie looped an arm around Leah's waist and coaxed her to go on.

'Ben said he might wait years for another chance as good as this – which I know is true. He decided he would only stop digging the pit if he actually found . . . anything, any human remains – or if I had changed my mind about wanting to marry him. Otherwise . . .'

'So he went on.'

'He had to tie his kerchief around his nose and mouth – but he carried on. I couldn't bear it. It got worse the deeper he went. I kept wondering what he was going to throw up on his spade – and it became so cold, just watching. I didn't say anything but he saw me shivering, and stopped work to bring me home. He was not best pleased, said he'll never get on if he listens to my whims and fancies.'

'Sounds like a real married quarrel, does that.' Ginnie turned her mouth down in a comic curve.

'I know!' she agreed ruefully. 'it really was.'

'And all that ride home together wasted!' Ginnie shook her head sadly, ready to agonise over that.

'Well, not quite.' Leah smiled, remembering their closeness as she rode before him on the horse, the warmth of his body to her back, the strength of his arms around her, as he held the reins very short. 'We made up before we got home.'

'Ah! Then it was all worth it,' Ginnie declared, adding wistfully, 'I wish Nat would be more like Ben, more serious, less flighty. You can talk to Ben.'

Leah laughed aloud at the thought of Ginnie preferring someone she could talk to. 'Perhaps if *you* were more serious and less inclined to larks . . .'

'Me!' Ginnie exclaimed. 'I couldn't be more serious. Why I'm almost straight-laced.'

'Oh, Ginnie.' Leah fell on her friend's neck, holding her tight. 'Never, never change, will you?'

'Nor you! I'd never do anything to hurt you, you may be sure of that. I'd sooner cut out my own heart,' Ginnie vowed.

'We'll always be friends, no one will ever come between us.' Leah hugged her close.

'And no more going to Soston on your own,' Ginnie admonished. 'Remember, me and Nat still need excuses to be out together, not like you old bespoke couples.'

They both soon realised there was little likelihood of any of them being alone in Soston churchyard again. News spread of the undertaking, which became the source of much local interest.

Neither of them arrived there but to find some interested spectator offering advice. Elijah, who had linked Leah's name with the old curse, was a daily visitor. Leah felt she and he regarded each other with deep suspicion, but familiarity at least brought a kind of delicate if contemptuous truce. His one positive contribution was that he offered an explanation of the smell. He said it was because the land drained that way from the oldest part of the burial ground. The stench was certainly much less now the ground had been open and dry for a time, and there had been no gruesome finds. The only one who still regarded the place as positively biased against them was Leah.

Ginnie was at once pleased and peeved by the situation. Certainly her father's anxieties about her friendship with the Robertsons had lessened. She felt she had her brothers to thank for reassuring their ever concerned parent. But now she could meet Nat more openly, there was little or no time for the two of them to be alone together.

The two brothers and Cuddy devoted every spare minute to the work though their conversation dwelt more and more on when Caleb Berridge would hear the news.

'It was an act of God that he was away with my grandfather when we delivered these.' Nat nodded at the five new bells standing in graded shiny line at the rear of Soston church.

Ginnie went to stand between the two largest bells, lifting her hands to rest them on the shoulders of the bells, posing for Nat's admiration. 'Why don't you just tell him?' she asked. 'Bring the matter out into the open. He has to know.'

'You don't understand,' Nat replied solemnly. 'he has only just found out Ben is courting Leah. That has caused enough trouble. He's a violent man, he takes it out on our mother.'

'Can't you stop him?' she demanded, 'Surely you don't stand by and . . .'

'In the bedroom,' Nat interrupted quietly.

She was still wondering if he meant what she was thinking of as he added: 'My mother says no one must interfere between husband and wife.' He paused, his voice very low as he added; 'And I know she would as soon bear any humiliation as break her sacred word.'

He came to her and took her hand, spreading her fingers then interlacing his between hers, moving them gently up and down, and finally trailing his fingers down over her palm. For one breathless moment she thought he was going to tell her he cared, that he loved her, but grasping her hand gently he said, 'He punishes us through our mother.'

'That's really cruel.' Her voice was a little husky with emotion and disappointment.

'It'll be worse when he hears about all this.' He tapped one of the bells with his foot, making it ring true as crystal. 'Not only about the new bell, but the Rector won't have him back on the site and has commissioned us to hang all the bells when the tenor is completed.'

'So you'll be paid for that. It should help bring the happy day nearer,' she said, her idea of a double wedding very nearly tripping off the end of her tongue.

'What we need is money now,' Nat said with a rueful click of his tongue. 'We're still a long way short of having everything we need to make this bell.'

136

'Like what?' she asked.

'Bricks and fuel for a start,' he answered.

They had walked to the church door and could see that Ben and Cuddy were entertaining quite a small crowd of villagers. 'Why don't you let all these locals know what you need?' she suggested. 'Ask the Rector if you can put up the plans and drawings in the church porch. There's masses of stuff in the Dexter's workshop.'

'We shouldn't have to answer so many questions. It might be a good idea,' he said, laughing as he watched his brother have to angle his spade to avoid old Elijah. 'Come on, my bright beauty, let's see what big brother thinks.' He took her arm and smiled down into her eyes, so she felt she might melt away she loved him so.

Within the next few days a display was completed on the church notice-board. This included a new finely penned drawing by Sam showing how a hearth-furnace was to be constructed alongside the pit. The Rector added a letter to say the work was being done as a gesture of goodwill by Mr Benjamin Robertson on behalf of his grandfather, Josiah Robertson, the founder of their local bellmaking firm.

To Ginnie and Leah's amusement it did not stop the self-opinionated from giving Ben and Nat more unworkable pieces of advice, but some of these were followed up by offers of real value. The local blacksmith volunteered the loan of his old bellows, plus thin iron rods to act as grillage in the furnace; a local farmer offered a load of dry ash logs; the local thatcher "a roof" of dry blackened straw. The wood was delivered by horse and wagon the very same day. The rushes they must collect from Church Lacey.

Ben had reached the point of wanting to begin moulding the inner core of his bell, when the thatcher sent word that he was about to begin stripping the roof of the old cowman's cottage and had orders from the Squire to tidy up as he went along.

'The Squire!' Leah exclaimed. 'The cowman's cottage!'

'You look as if you'd seen that ghost at last,' Ben said.

'I told you, I told you all, about the old man being evicted. *This* will be his cottage! I don't want to be indebted to Squire

Lacey for anything.' Leah stood shaking her head very emphatically.

'You must just stay out of the way,' Ginnie said quickly, seeing a long-suffering look pass over Ben's face. 'I bet my brothers would help, and you could write to John White. He said he would come any time.'

'The thatch'll only be burnt, and rushes make a great amount of heat in a furnace,' Nat reasoned. 'It's no skin off Squire's nose.'

'It might somehow be skin of ours, though,' Leah added.

Ben turned away, unwilling to enter into another fruitless discussion about Leah's intuitions, and jumping down into the pit began to mix the loam he would need for the bell core.

As she and Ginnie walked home to Tur Lacey that night, Leah suddenly stopped, turned aside from their way and leaned on a gate, head in hands. 'Do you think I'm ill? Sick in the head?' she asked.

Ginnie opened her mouth to say a blunt, "Yes", but instead parried question with comment. 'I should think it's Ben who must feel heartsick. When everyone is working for you, all you can do is see bad luck or disaster in everything that happens.'

'I can't throw the feeling off,' she said with an air of desperation. 'Every time Soston or the bell is mentioned, my heart lurches and I just feel full of fear. Now this cottage and the Squire come into it.'

'Oh, Leah, you don't need to go anywhere near Church Lacey. You needn't even see the bell again, if you don't want to.'

'Will you go?' Leah interrupted sharply.

'I shall go to see Nat,' she confirmed.

'You didn't want me to go there on my own,' Leah reminded her.

When they separated at Leah's home Ginnie could not forget Leah's manner or her words. 'Full of fear,' she whispered to herself. Then she remembered how Nat had caressed her hand in those few brief moments alone at the back of the church. 'What a right game of soldiers!' she breathed lovingly into her pillow.

Chapter Thirteen

The door of the kitchen rebounded from the wall. Caleb Berridge stood hands on hips, face dark with fury as he faced his two step-sons. He spluttered, his anger too intense, too freshly roused for expression.

Ben regarded him cooly; it was almost a relief that the moment had at last come. 'So you've heard?'

'Heard!' he bellowed, walking around the table, elbowing the two of them out of the way as he went. 'Heard!' Making a bloody laughing stock of me.' He mimicked a smarmy, sarcastic voice as he went on, '"Hear you're giving old Josiah's grandsons a chance at last."'

Ben gathered he had not been able to conceal his surprise.

'So how long has it been going on? How long?'

'It'll be finished well before Christmas.' Ben continued lacing his boots, but Nat who had been putting on his jacket took it off again and hung it on the back of a chair.

'Will it? Will it!' He threw himself around the kitchen again. As he repassed the back door, Mabel came in carrying the shopping. She was pale and agitated. As Ben took the baskets, she whispered in a low shaky voice, 'You should have told him.'

'Oh, get upstairs, woman! It's all you're fit for.' Caleb snatched at her forearm and half flung her towards the staircase. Ben interposed himself between them, his hands by his sides, but his body hard against Caleb's waistcoat, moving in matched menacing dance, as his step-father tried to dodge away.

'Go on, go upstairs, Mother.' Nat supported her to the staircase, reassuring her but adding, 'This had to come. Better you're out of the way.'

'Yes, go on!' Caleb shouted. 'I can deal with you any time, any time at all. When your boys are busy making bells at Soston, I can deal with you.' He stood smirking at them, then laughed aloud. 'And when I've dealt with her, I can start on the old man.'

'You'd better sit down,' Ben told him. Nat, as if rehearsed, positioned a chair behind him, Ben spread a hand on Caleb's chest and pressed him on to it. 'Dealings in future will be made by consent, not as now . . .' Ben paused to restrain Caleb on the chair, '. . . by force. If you don't keep your promise to pay me a master-man's wage when I've completed this bell, none of us,' he paused to gesture to Nat, then towards the foundry yard, 'or my grandfather will work for you at all.'

'No work, no keep!' Caleb snarled back, thumping his hand on the table.

'No Robertsons, no business.'

'I'll manage without you, the lot of you,' he blustered.

'For a time,' Ben agreed calmly, 'but soon *you* won't be eating so well. And who'll keep you out of the poorhouse in your old age?

'Oh, I can handle you lot!' Caleb twisted in his chair to see that Nat had established himself at the foot of the stairs. 'You can't stay there forever.'

'You'll be surprised how long I can stay,' Nat answered quietly.

'Your problem is, the business and her,' he paused to toss a crude gesture upwards with his thumb, 'are legally mine to do with just as I please.'

'And yours is that if you don't keep your written – legal – promise,' he spaced the words with intent, 'we shall begin to play by your rules – two eyes for an eye,' Ben promised.

'I'll turn you out!'

'Try,' Ben said briefly, and going to the corner of the kitchen handed Nat a hefty stick. 'I shall stay,' he told his brother.

Nat nodded understanding. 'So shall I,' he said, tapping the stick on the stairs.

Ben left the foundry and finding his grandfather told him that Caleb had at last found out, and that he was going to stay overnight at Soston to make sure his step-father could do no mischief. 'Nat is staying here with you and mother.' He looked anxiously at his grandfather. 'You'll be all right? We've told him – as we planned.'

'It had to come,' Josiah said wearily.

Ben found himself repeating the same words to Leah and Ginnie when he arrived at Soston, and the three of them stood looking solemnly into the bell pit.

'Will Nat come later?' Ginnie asked.

'If Caleb drinks himself into his usual stupor after supper, he'll come then.'

'You're planning to stay late,' Leah commented.

'I shall stay all night,' Ben answered, nodding down at the completed mould of core, wax bell and casing. 'I feel I've put part of myself in that. I must make sure if he does turn up, there's no opportunity for him to do any mischief.'

'Surely he wouldn't!' Ginnie exclaimed.

'You don't know any step-father.'

'No, we don't know any of your family not really – only what you've told us,' Leah confirmed, suddenly struck by the realisation.

'Except Nat,' Ginnie put in with a beatific smile.

'Except Nat,' Leah repeated gently as Ginnie leaned against her. The warmth of her friend's close affection made her ask Ben, 'Where will you sleep?'

'Nowhere, I'll be working. We're ready for the wax to be melted out. I shall spend the night keeping the fires going.' Leah sensed the anxiety in his voice, as he contemplated the result so far of his long, patient, painstaking work. This she knew was the part he was most anxious about. This for him was the unknown part of the procedure, forced on him by the terms of Caleb's agreement – no tools, no bell casing, or lifting gear to be used from the foundry.

'If Nat doesn't come, will you work all alone?' she asked, her imagination furnishing the cold and fog that would certainly form part of that long late October night.

'The one person I *would* be pleased to have here for a time is Sam. We've done so many tests together on this wax.'

'I'll go and fetch him,' Ginnie volunteered. 'And I'll see if I can have our trap to bring him back. The boys've all gone to a football match in town, and father never gets out on a Saturday.'

'It would save Sam,' Leah readily agreed. She knew how concerned Clarrie was becoming about her husband coughing away in the workshop, spending hours reknitting other people's rejected old shoddy wool or renovating that ancient knitting-frame. 'Should I come back with you?'

'You stay with your chap. And, anyway, here's your other friend coming.' She grinned mischievously as she waved goodbye and old Elijah came around the corner of the church.

Leah tutted her annoyance. 'Can I do anything?' she asked. 'I can't bear to just stand around with him here asking daft questions and making dafter remarks about *women*.'

Ben laughed and seemed about to make some flippant remark but she glared at him and shook her head as the old man approached. Ben raised his eyebrows in pretended innocence. 'I was only going to say that anyone who comes this afternoon can collect firewood. I shall need to keep a steady fire going in the pit most of the night, and I want to save the good logs for the furnace.'

Leah made the first tentative trip to a small spinney behind the church alone, but was quickly joined by enthusiastic church workers and a few reluctant children, who did this chore too often for it to hold any attraction. Soon she had a regular platoon of helpers, some ranging further into the fields for sticks, discarded and rotted fencing, fallen branches. Anything that had been overlooked before was now collected, and piled around the edge of the pit until it looked like a flimsy stockade.

For the very first time Leah felt some excitement about the project. It was also the first time she had been able to do anything positive to help. 'A fresh start,' she thought, and hummed the light lilting air of *Believe Me If All Those Endearing Young Charms* which John White had sung on the way back from the gleaning. Others overheard her and took

142

up the words, then as befitted a workforce of ardent church supporters the song was replaced by lively hymns. *Forward Into Battle See His Banners Go* was followed by *Onward Christian Soldiers*. Leah sang and worked, and wondered if she could have been such a fool about this place. Surely there was nothing and no one here to fear.

It was almost four o'clock when Ginnie arrived back with Sam in the Stockinger's Arms trap. It was the first time he had seen the site, and it amused the girls to see him hold out his arms like a child for Ben to help him down into the pit. Sam wasted no more than a disgusted glance at them as he tapped the mould. 'You're sure it's dry? It won't crack?'

Ben shook his head emphatically. 'provided we begin losing the wax from the bottom first, as we planned, there'll be no problem on that score.'

Sam studied the channel dug from under the bell to a hollow reservoir for the wax to collect in.

'Nat's not come then?' Ginnie asked with a wistful shake of her head.

'Well, it's hardly suppertime yet, is it?' Leah whispered back so as not to disturb the serious assessment going on below them, then for no good reason except that her spirits had lifted so, was overtaken by a fit of the giggles.

'Young wummen!' Elijah exclaimed, waving his walking-stick around above his head. 'Only one thing wuss, and that's old wummen!'

Ginnie drew her away from the edge of the pit and the irritable old man, asking, 'How long will you stay?'

'Mother'll expect me back before dark.'

'I'll have to wait for Sam now – but father knows so . . .' she shrugged '. . . the longer I stay, the more chance I have of seeing Nat.

They joined the little throng of people who had been helping. The two men in the pit seemed about to light the low ring of sticks they had prepared around the mould.

'One more thing . . .' Sam stopped Ben as he was about to strike a lucifer into a bundle of dry grass. There was a slight groan of disappointment from the bystanders, as Ben was instructed to fetch an old iron sheet ready to drop over the channel near the mould. 'Once the wax begins to run we don't want it to catch fire near the bell, Sam reasoned imperturbably. 'We should keep the heat as even as possible all around.'

'That makes sense,' one man remarked, and patted Ben on the back as he vaulted out of the pit to fetch the iron sheet that had once formed part of a baker's oven.

He returned quickly, smiling as the crowd parted to let him through, and as he passed Leah, he paused and kissed her on the cheek. There was an immediate uproar of cheering and shouts of, 'Go it, boy' 'Bet he feels he could lift church tower!' 'Whose a lucky lass then!' Leah turned as she recognised Bessie Yarrup's voice, who beamed at Leah, adding, 'But you know what he's after,' and nodded down at the new baby she carried in one arm, while supporting another youngster astride her opposite hip.

'Some folk breed faster than rabbits,' Ginnie whispered behind her hand as she saw Leah blush furiously, but the crowd were good humoured now and closed around Leah and Ben, some passing down the metal sheet. Sam directed it should be leaned against the side of the pit until needed, and Ben rasped the match against the serrated metal side of its box and held the flames to the grass, which crackled into swift darting flame. This in turn he put to a pile of small dry twigs Leah had specially chosen. Another cheer went up as these caught and lively flames began to take larger pieces of kindling.

The light from the growing fire suddenly made the evening seem darker. Ginnie watched the flow on Leah's face as she strained eagerly forward, lit by the flames. After all the misgivings she had harboured about the place, Ginnie smiled to see her so happy, and felt it was her own turn to feel alone in a crowd, so wanting Nat to come.

'How long will it take for the wax to begin to melt?' Leah wanted to know.

'We've calculated about half an hour,' Ben answered, 'but that may be just a few first drips. It won't be really running out along the channel for hours perhaps.'

'It's beginning to get dark,' Ginnie reminded her.

Leah looked up at the sky, but decided, 'I must just see it drip!'

It was twenty minutes later when Ben lying flat on the ground reported the first spot of wax falling from the carefully aligned slots in the iron plate the mould stood on. Leah insisted on seeing for herself, and with a warning to hold her skirts well back from the flames, Ben lifted her down. She was surprised how hot it was in the pit even several feet back from the fire. He pointed where she might stoop to look between flames and mould. 'Yes! Yes!' she shouted up to Ginnie. 'It's dripping! It's melting!'

'I thought I'd get Cuddy to walk home with you,' Ben said as he took her waist to help her back up to ground level.

'I'll be quicker on my own,' she told him, 'and there'll be plenty of people on the roads. The Saturday carrier's cart from town will be due, with lots of people meeting it. I'm sure!' she emphasised as he looked doubtful, then added in a low voice, 'And I know from Clarrie's niece that the Squire and all his family are in London.'

They parted, with Leah promising to walk over early the next morning with provisions. 'Cuddy's feeding me,' he told her with a grin, 'it's all arranged – but come anyway.'

'It seems to me everything's arranged!' Ginnie exclaimed as she walked from the churchyard with Leah, a little disgruntled now at the thought of waiting hours for Sam. 'These men don't tell us half – and you can bet your last brass farthing Nat won't come now.'

'Oh, he might,' Leah answered, 'and we must let these men think they're in charge,' she added, thinking of Mrs White and the market stall. She gave Ginnie a quick hug and a kiss, with a promise to see her after evening church service the next day. 'Come down to my house,' she said. Ginnie agreed, urging her away on her walk home.

Leah took the longer roadway home, and looking out across the fields could see the mist from the water meadows rolling quickly across the countryside. She shivered, knowing from experience that even a simple well-known piece of shrub could look strange and menacing as dusk and mist took over. Even as this thought made her hurry on more earnestly, she started. The bulky form of a man suddenly emerged from a bank of mist, the vapours seeming to stream from him, rather than around him, making him an eerie sight. It was no one she knew, she was sure of that, and as he caught sight of her, he turned quickly away, leaving the path, climbing the grassy slope around to the far side of the church.

She thought of Cuddy and old Elijah and wondered just how many strange people did live in and around this place. She promised herself that once this bell was made and hung, she would never go to Soston again – well, she quickly compromised, only to collect the tally-money.

Ginnie looked after Leah with a tinge of worry. It was going to be really dark before she reached Tur Lacey. She also reasoned that if Nat was going to come at all, it would be soon – and that he would come their usual short cut over the fields. She made her way around to the far side of the church, where the ground was raised and she could see the glow of the fire from the far side of the church wall, as well as the other way over towards the water meadows and the path Nat was sure to use.

Her heart suddenly gave a great leap as through the mist which swirled, now thick now thin, she saw someone coming. 'It has to be him,' she told herself, and ran to meet him, calling his name.

'Nat! Nat! You're so late. I thought you'd never come.' She hesitated then, unsure as the figure seemed to stumble and disappear where the vapours had thickened to fog. In a second desire overcame her doubts, and she hurried forward again called his name. She was almost on the man when she realised her mistake.

He stopped, no more than a couple of yards away, peering closely and asking, 'Who were you expecting me to be? Nat somebody?'

'Robertson,' she answered, feeling foolish. 'I was so sure.'

'I know of him, if that's any help to a pretty young girl.'

To her surprise he turned back the way he had come, after a few paces looking back at her, repeating, 'I know of him.'

'He's coming, do you mean?' she asked, following, intrigued by the man's tone of voice. 'Have you passed him?'

The man chuckled deep in his throat. 'I have indeed. Come and see.' He walked purposefully back the way he had come.

'Nothing's wrong with him, is there? Nothing's happened to him?'

'No, no. He's just longing to see you.' The man was over the brow of the hill now, out of sight, but his voice drifted back to her. 'It's a surprise. Nat likes surprises, you must know that.'

She did know that. She smiled as she thought how like a child he was with his paddling and his games. 'Nat?' she queried as she too walked over the slope, out of sight of the tower and the light from the fire. 'Nat? What are you doing? You . . .' Then a cry half escaped her as she was grabbed from behind. One rough hand clamped over her mouth, while the man pinioned her against himself, an arm across her chest, his other hand gripping her upper-arm.

His voice was victorious, purposeful, spine-chilling as he breathed in her ear, 'I'm not going to hurt you.' Even as he spoke his fingers tightened excruciatingly on her arm. He turned her round to face him, and she caught a glimpse of lighter clothing and knew he had his trousers unbuttoned. 'Oh, No!' her mind screamed. She struggled furiously as he lowered his hand from her shoulder to her buttocks and pressed her to him, and she could feel his penis grow erect between them.

She remembered tricks her brothers had taught her, let her knees go so all her weight fell suddenly on to his arm. For a few seconds she was free. She opened her mouth to scream, but in a moment he had a handful of her hair and his other hand was over her mouth again. She bit at it. He swore under his breath, twisted her hair tight to her scalp. She ignored the pain and managed to twist and kick backwards at his shins. He grunted with pain, and if he had been determined before, there was now a calculated cruel intent. The hand that had held her hair now crashed down into her stomach and held her in a breath-denying clamp.

She remembered what David had said about disabling a man, and fought to turn and bring her knee up hard between his legs. It was the last thing she could think of. But she heard him laugh, and his fury at her biting and kicking seemed to have given him added strength. He turned her easily so her shoulders were again to his chest. But before she could kick

147

back at him this time, he brought one knee up hard under her bottom. She first sat then was pushed prostrate on the grass. She felt a moment of despair. There was more than an awesome determination about the man now; it felt more like a personal revenge he was taking. An eye for an eye. She fought with all the might she could muster, one hand clawing at his face, pulling at his hair, her mind still refusing to accept what was happening, what was going to happen.

The man's weight took her breath, and with one hand still clamped over her mouth and from time to time over her nose as well, she felt her strength lessening. In a confusion of pain and panic she felt her skirt dragged up, felt one of the man's legs between hers. She steeled all her will, all her strength, to throw him off, her mind loud with pleas for God and Nat to come to help her.

He touched her bare thigh, and she heard his breath catch and rasp in his throat. She thought she might choke on the bile that rose into her mouth. Then wished she could die as he forced his fingers up between her legs, finding her, forcing her open, her body hurting, her mind screaming. Then he came at her. She wondered if it would kill her, or why she did not faint, why was it all so real, as he pushed, and pushed faster.

Then it was over. For him it was over. He lay there panting, his weight full on her so her breath was in her throat only. Then she heard her own voice, no more than a whisper, and that sounding barely human,: 'Nat, Nat.' The man reclamped his hand over her mouth, while he lay recovering his breath.

'I just want to die,' her lips moved under his fingers, 'just die.' She lay limp under him, and uncaring as unable to breathe she felt herself drifting into unconsciousness. He had ruined her life. Nat would not want her now – nor her father – no one would want her now.

'Here! You all right?' He was suddenly panicked by her stillness, but as he released her mouth and raised himself up, she turned her head away from him. He cursed her then and getting to his feet spurned her with his boot, as if pushing a piece of rubbish aside into a gutter. 'Nat Robertson,' he said as if Nat too had been vanquished by the act, and went away, laughing.

Chapter Fourteen

'Ben! Ben!'

He turned on the field footpath, frowning at the urgent voice behind him, then forgot his unwillingness to be delayed as he saw who it was. 'Ginnie?' he questioned, walking back to where she stood half concealed by an overhang of wild red rosehips.

'I've been waiting for you,' she said. 'I . . . wanted to talk to you.'

The brilliance of the rose-hips heightened the pallor of the girl's cheeks. In little more than a week, she had lost her vivacious sparkle. He felt she had aged ten years, become like a woman ravaged by cares.

'We've all been so worried about you,' he said as heartily as he could, hiding his shock. 'Are you sure – are you better?'

She could never be better, never forget, never be as she was before. She had prayed and fasted – and spoken not a word of her ordeal. It had been Charley, trying faithfully to nurse her, who had finally urged her from her bed with his acute anxiety and the words, 'The Lord helps those who help themselves.'

'Ginnie, what is it?' Ben took her hands in his. They had no warmth. 'How long have you been waiting?'

'I don't know,' she replied truthfully.

'Come and sit down,' he said, feeling she looked too wan to keep warm walking. He led her to the long dead bole of a tree, and seating her there took off his jacket and put it around her shoulders. Then he took her hands between his own, trying to chaff some warmth into them.

'Please don't be kind to me,' she whispered, knowing she could well bring disgrace and unhappiness on him and Leah as well as Nat; on everyone she cared about, it seemed. 'I don't deserve it. I'm . . .'

He waited quietly, gently restraining her hands between his, her words and demeanour giving some substance to the worries Leah had expressed day after day. Leah had visited the Stockinger's Arms several times, but each time either Ginnie's father or one of her brothers had returned from upstairs with the message that Ginnie did not feel well enough to see anyone. Charley had added the cryptic message, 'She says she must have time,' and had looked as puzzled as Leah had felt.

'Did you see the doctor?' Ben asked as the silence went on.

'It's not an illness,' Ginnie answered, drawing in a ragged breath as she realised she had heard the doctor pronounce those same words about have babies. She wondered about the mortal sin of taking one's own life.

Ben had presumed that, like Sam, she had taken some bad chill from the night vapours and long cold hours she had spent at Soston. Now he was not sure, but still he felt responsible. Glancing at this changed girl by his side, he thought that if it was not illness, then it must be some terrible news, or disaster, that had come to the Hobbday family.

'What is it, Ginnie, what's happened? Nat's desperately worried about you and wants to see you.'

'Nat.' she breathed his name with low wistful tenderness. He seemed to belong to a golden carefree youth, while she felt old and soiled. How could she tell less than the truth? Nat wanted to see her, and how could she ever even raise her eyes to him again? A man might look the world in the eye, even gain a reputation from his fellows for being 'a bit of a lad' – but that man, that great heavy man, had been no boy by many years.

He waited for her to continue, but she merely shook her head, letting it slowly fall lower and lower, seeming to shrink into herself.

'I thought I could talk to you . . .' she began, but even in the beginning of it, her courage failed.

150

'Yes, of course you can.' The bleakness of her look appalled him. 'Is it something at home?' he asked. 'Your brothers or your father?'

'No!'

The reply was sharp enough to carry conviction but with an edge of meaning he did not understand.

'No,' she began again with more control, for there was one man she needed to eliminate from her mind before she knew how to deal in part with such life as she had left. 'I need to know,' she said, 'the night you lit the fires to melt the wax – did Nat, or anyone, go out?'

He rose to his feet, unable to sit passively and tell that story. 'Nat certainly did not,' he began, 'though my stepfather did. Nat said he took no supper-beer, stayed stone-cold sober and *said* he would take a short walk outside, and be back any minute. Nat stayed where he was, as we'd arranged, making sure he didn't take any kind of revenge on our mother.'

Ben paused to control his voice before going on. There had been recriminations between the two brothers growing from their mutual disappointments. 'Of course he did not go back "any minute", and though I never saw him anywhere around, he had obviously been to Soston. The next morning I found the far side of the furnace had been tampered with. The turf and soil dug out low down with a piece of slate and the inner bridgework of bricks displaced – it was ruined. I'm having to dismantle and rebuild it. The trouble was we were all too busy watching the fires'. He turned back to her, about to ask if she had seen anything.

'Yes,' she agreed, but before he could question her the image of the fires in the pit mingled with the story of the Monk's Bell and its curse, and without thought words came tumbling out. 'Leah was right, you know. All she said about that bell and Soston – that no good would come to anyone she loved. "Full of fear", that's what she said. That was what it was, full of fear. We should have listened.'

'Ginnie, I'm going to take you home. I'm sure you shouldn't be out.' He knew he must be decisive. She had obviously taken some kind of fever in the head, and was incapable of making rational decisions.

'No, I shouldn't be seen,' she agreed, for that was just how she felt; her worthlessness should not be about in the world.

Her answer astounded him, made him fear as much for her sanity as for her health. 'Leah wants to see you very much. Come back with me now.'

'Yes,' she agreed again, with that same wild distracted look in her eyes that made him unsure if she understood what he intended. He put an arm around her waist and lifted her to her feet, torn between feeling that she might either faint or run away. He wanted to talk to her, to reassure her, but so strange had been her responses, he thought it wiser to keep a solicitous silence until he had her safely back under the Dexters' roof. Perhaps a house where there were three women might be more conducive to confidences than the all male household of the Stockinger's Arms.

There was laughter coming from the Dexter kitchen when they arrived, and they heard Leah's voice proclaiming with disbelief, 'You called me Gaffer, Sam!'

'Slip of the tongue, slip of the tongue,' he was replying as Ben opened the door and gently propelled Ginnie inside.

'Ginnie!' Leah cried. 'Are you better? It's Sam's first day up too. Why wouldn't you let me come to see you?' The questions trailed away. Leah's heart leapt in alarm at the stricken look on Ginnie's face. How changed she was! She went to her, took her into her arms, held her tight to the exclusion of the need for words. Vaguely Leah was aware of Ben having a whispered conference with her grandmother, then of him and Sam leaving the house.

She pulled the rocking-chair nearer the hearth and gently seated Ginnie there, kneeling on the rug beside her. Miriam pushed the kettle over the fire, stirring the embers to life and announcing in businesslike tones, 'Tea first.'

By the time the tea was made, Leah was thoroughly alarmed about Ginnie who, having turned her face into Ben's coat, began to cry. Then after a moment or two she leaned forward out of the jacket and demanded, 'Take this from me!'

Leah complied, folding it carefully and laying it aside on the far end of the kitchen table. Ginnie continued to cry, softly at first, then interspersed with brief laughs and fiercer cries as if of pain.

'You'll make yourself ill, girl,' Miriam reprimanded gently. 'What's happened to you? Something's happened!' Ginnie only shook her head, covering her face with her hands.

'Where have you been since Leah left you at Soston?'

Ginnie again shook her head – the smell of Ben's jacket as it had warmed before the fire had finally explained why the image and the story of the old bell had so plagued her. The smell of the man's clothes who had attacked her had held the same half sandy, half fiery, smell of a foundry.

'That tells us nothing,' Miriam persisted, repeating the question.

Without removing her hands from her face Ginnie decided now was the time for real deceit, and for escape from the loving concern of Leah and her family, before the yearning she felt for confession overcame her, and destroyed them all. 'I've never left my room until today,' she finally answered Miriam's question.

'So it was something that happened between Leah leaving and you driving Sam home, or between dropping Sam off and you going to your room?'

Again Ginnie shook her head vigorously, and Leah half wanted to stop Miriam's head-on approach. But she respected her grandmother's logic, knew that whatever had happened must be brought out into the open. Miriam's next quiet words mirrored her thoughts, though they alarmed her none the less.

'Things fester if they're not cleansed.'

Leah opened her lips to ask what she thought might have happened; instead she found herself going through the time-table of events. 'I left you on the road, and you went back to the church to wait for Sam.'

Ginnie was still, cagey now, the probing reaching too near the nub of the matter. Leah's mother pushed a steaming cup of tea before her, with Nellie insisting she take it, lifting her hand and directing it to the tea-cup handle.

Miriam went to the pantry for more milk and Leah followed her, demanding in an urgent whisper: 'What do you think's happened?' Miriam looked at her, lips tightly pursed, then answered enigmatically, 'I've seen the same look about a girl before . . .'

'And?' Leah demanded. 'And, Grandma!'

'That girl had been taken away by a man and her life ruined.'

Leah almost laughed in relief. 'There wasn't time, Gran, honestly. I left her on the roadway, she went back to the church and waited for Sam. And she drove the trap back to the Stockinger's Arms. No one in the village would dare touch Ginnie. they'd know what Walter Hobbday would do to them if they did!'

Miriam regarded her granddaughter, acknowledging that the last part of her reasoning was certainly true, but nothing else made as much sense to the older woman as this explanation. She did not tell Leah that the girl she had known had taken her own life rather than face the shame of carrying a child out of wedlock. Instead she asked: 'Did Sam say how Ginnie was as they drove home?'

'His words were, "She were shivering w'cold, same as I was." It must be just a really bad chill, don't you think?'

'It's gone to her brain then,' Miriam said shortly, tipping milk from the can into the jug. 'you'd best persuade her to stay here where we can look after her and advise her. I could sleep in with Nellie, she could have my bed.'

Leah brightened at the thought of being able to keep a close eye on Ginnie and went to tell her mother of the idea. Nellie was bending over Ginnie, persuading her to sip the tea. She nodded enthusiastically. 'Good idea. I'll go and see Mr Hobbday, bring her some night things.'

'No!' Ginnie protested, 'No, I couldn't do that. I need to be on my own. In my own bed.' She pushed the tea aside and stood up. 'I'm much better. Just leave me be.' She side-stepped around them all, dodging as if they might any second lay hands on and restrain her.

'Ginnie,' Leah protested, 'please. Please stay.'

Ginnie was out of the door, and for a second pulling on the handle as if to prevent anyone following. Then she saw Ben standing at the workshop door, and though he made no move, she waved a dismissive arm at him, shouting, 'No, leave me alone, all of you.' She backed away as Leah and Miriam came from the cottage. 'I've . . . I must have nothing to do with you

154

– any of you. It's all finished. Don't come. Don't follow me – ever.'

'Go after her,' Miriam said, as Ginnie ran from the yard.

I'll go,' Ben said, and Leah followed. By the time they reached the public house Ginnie was nowhere to be seen, but her father stood on his front doorstep.

'What have you been doing to my girl?' he demanded.

There was endless discussion, continual heart-searching about Ginnie, with Miriam the only one who kept her thoughts to herself.

No one else in the village followed her example. Ginnie's disappearance from the daily village scene was the cause of much consternation. The inquisitive enquired directly and were stone-walled by Walter Hobbday's dour: 'What's that to you?'

On the Thursday Leah went again to the public house to invite Ginnie to go with them all to Church Lacey on Saturday, but she went prepared with a note just in case.

Dear Ginnie,

On Saturday John White is coming again with the wagon, and his eldest boy, to help Nat and Ben fetch the old thatch promised from the cowman's cottage at Church Lacey. Wrap up warm and come with us. Though you grumbled because you thought Nat not serious, if you could see him fretting about you now you would know he is *very* serious.

Cuddy is to be left guarding the bell mould at Soston as he has been every night since the furnace was damaged. He sleeps there, wrapped in blankets and hay, and the children wake him each morning on their way to school. Some throw hips and haws at him, the kinder bring him a piece of their breakfast.

You remember showing Sam the picture of the man in the golf socks? He says he's going to make that ancient old frame knit patterned sock tops! Can you believe the man?

Ben and Nat say bring as many of your brothers as you can to give a hand! But *please* make sure you come, Ginnie.

Your very best friend always,
Leah

She folded the note, hoping she would not need it, but feeling she had done her best to make it cheerful and interest Ginnie in trying to be her old self again.

Walter Hobbday met her at the door, and after scrutinising her for several seconds, held out his hand for the note she carried.

'Won't you ask if Ginnie will see me?'

'Don't you think you and your bellmakers have done enough harm?'

'Please let me see her.'

'She wants to see no one,' he stated, 'and least of all you.'

'That's not true,' she retaliated sharply, 'I know that's not true.'

He pursed his lips and nodded ponderously. 'Oh, yes, and if I'd 'ave stuck to my guns, when I stopped her seeing you before, we should not have this trouble now, should we?'

'You can't blame me! Anyone can take a cold.' She stood defiantly throwing answers to arguments he no longer made, merely standing there as immutable as Victoria on the throne of England.

She turned away, frustrated, condemned by his stony silence. As she walked the length of the village street, passing the small crowd fetching evening water, the conversation stopped as she approached. She felt those who had known her all her life regarded her curiously as if she was a stranger.

'Did she see you?' one asked.

'Ah, well, you know what my missus says.'

Leah recognised Sarah Bright, maid-of-all-work in the Warburtons' house. 'No, tell us, Sarah,' she said quietly.

'She says those that associate with the devil . . .' she paused eyeing Leah a little cautiously 'will surely reap their just reward. And,' she continued with more certainty, 'that time will tell!'

156

There was a murmur of assent to this last statement. Leah had been angry when her grandmother had uttered this glib phrase. She was certainly not going to let anyone else get away with it. But before she could give vent to her fury, the loud and authoritative tones of Sarah's mistress rang across the street.

'Sarah! Stop gossiping and bring the water.'

Sarah's red hands gripped the brimming bucket.

'No, let me,' Leah said, taking it from the smaller girl, carrying it across to the pavement and confronting Mrs Warburton, who raised a warning finger at her. 'I don't want any more truck or trouble with you, my girl. I should think you've done enough.'

'And you think "time will tell" for Ginnie, do you? Well, this is what I think of you!'

Mrs Warburton saw the intention, but could not escape. Leah swung the bucket backwards, and with all the skill acquired from throwing buckets of water to swill down the cobbled yard, caught the bottom of the bucket with her free hand and drenched the woman from head to foot, wasting not a drop. She rejoiced in the drooping hat feathers, the furious face that registered outrage near to tears. The crowd at the pump were at once astounded but unable to control their mirth. Calmly, she handed the empty bucket back to Sarah and walked home.

Clarrie arrived with the news shortly afterwards. Her mother was mortified. Her grandmother, pressed into comment, said she doubted the wisdom of taking sides, and making bad enemies worse, on a matter that would undoubtedly be proved one way or the other very shortly.

'You're saying the same thing again!' Leah accused. 'And I know Ginnie would have confided in me. We would have stuck together . . .'

'So what is the matter with her?' Miriam demanded bluntly.

'I don't know,' Leah began belligerently, then faltered, her voice breaking a little as she added, 'I keep thinking of that toddler who was scalded when the kettle fell from the spit. How she was changed from a bright little thing to a twisted idiot child.'

'Oh, Leah, even if what I fear may be true, Ginnie is not going to be like that.'

'No, it could be worse, couldn't it?' Leah drummed her fists on the kitchen table. 'An idiot child would at least be taken care of, while a girl might well be sent away, turned out by family and parish. No wonder they hang themselves.'

Chapter Fifteen

'Leah,' Ben prompted gently, 'I don't think she'll come.'

'No,' she answered, but still watching from beside the wagon as Nat walked up and down the road before the Stockinger's Arms, whistling *Come Into the Garden, Maud* with rather desperate, high-fetching flourishes.

She turned to shake her head, and he reached a hand down to her. She delayed for yet another moment, his fingers encompassing her hand, then he gave an extra squeeze and urged her to climb aboard. John White moved along to give her room between them. He looked very sober, as he had been ever since Leah had interrupted an early morning conference between him and her grandmother. It had sounded as if he had been pressing Miriam hard, but by the brooding look on his face now, she supposed her grandmother had finally passed on *her* views as to the cause of Ginnie's indisposition.

Nat, finally admitting defeat, flung himself on the back of the wagon alongside young Johnnie White, announcing, 'I'm going in that bar tonight. I'll not be put off by Walter Hobbday or anyone else. I'll *make* him let me see Ginnie.'

'Daughters are a big responsibility, worse for a man on his own,' John said as he slapped the reins on the cob's back.

'Why?' Leah demanded.

'Well, I mean' John laughed briefly, then added in deference to Nat, 'Now I'm not talking about Ginnie, only generally, but it is as they say — the women do take the trouble home with them!'

'And the men can just walk away.'

'Depends who the man is,' Ben said. 'If he's the Squire, or Lord Whoever, then yes, he has the money to buy off trouble.'

'Or if he's unknown to the girl,' John added darkly, a tremor of anger touching his voice, 'or the girl won't say . . .'

'If it's by force, you mean? Then I don't understand why the girl should be disgraced, made to suffer,' Leah stated, becoming carried away by the whole principle of such matters. 'If someone punches you on the chin without cause, you don't blame your chin.'

Ben caught the hand that waved so expressively about, making her aware she had overstepped the bounds of permitted conversation, and of the ominous silence behind them. She glanced back at Nat's slumped shoulders, hands clasped between his knees, and was sorry if she had caused him more hurt. 'I'm not talking about Ginnie.' The point had already been made, and she finished lamely, resenting the feeling of being put in the wrong. Why shouldn't she discuss such things?

John urged the cob into a brisk trot, and changed the subject as swiftly, asking whether they had to pull the thatch from the roof, or whether it would be down.

'If it is the cottage I saw, the whole lot will fall down if you all get on it,' Leah commented, resolving to make a fresh start, and whatever happened for the rest of the day to leave the vexed question of the exploitation of women alone. Her resolution was given immediate trial as John suddenly wondered how his wife was managing the stall without him.

'Perfectly well, I should imagine,' she heard herself say.

'It is a Saturday, you know, the market will be busy,' he answered, sounding surprised at her swift reaction.

'Mum will be all right,' Johnnie supplied confidently from the back of the wagon, 'Reckon she could do it all on her own if she had to.' Leah suppressed a smile at the look of complete astonishment on his father's face.

As they passed the long ornate wall around the extensive grounds of the manor house, she wondered if the Squire and his retinue were still in London. When they reached Church

Lacey, Ben's reaction to the village was much the same as hers had been on her first visit.

'Looks as if all the cottages could do with rethatching,' he said, and when she pointed out the tied cottage at the end of the street, added, 'We're too late. It's already fallen down!'

This was certainly the impression from a distance. The roof was partly off and several workmen were taking down sections of the front walls. Leah was curious; surely the Squire was not actually having repairs done. 'It *must* have fallen down,' she decided.

John drew up the horse in front of the cottage. 'It's being built up again though.' He indicated new roof timbers lying alongside the huge pile of discarded black thatch.

'That saves us a deal of trouble. I can back the wagon down there.'

Ben was about to jump down when one of the workmen came hurrying forward, waving them away. 'Hold on,' he said. 'What do you want?' When Ben told him his errand he nodded, checking. 'Name of Robertson? You're only just in time. I've orders to burn it if it's not cleared today. Thatcher was told to tidy up as he went,' he said, adding enigmatically, 'Squire has an interest in this particular cottage.'

'It belongs to him, doesn't it?' John asked.

The builder laughed, nodding along the street, as he returned to his work. 'Most of them do.'

Comically Ben shrugged his mystification to Leah, who grimaced back, though she felt nervous and apprehensive about anything that had to do with Squire Lacey. She also found the general poverty of the village and the memory of the old man taken from this very cottage oppressive. She remembered how she had thought she sensed business when she had displayed her wares on this same wall, where Ben now stood directing John as he backed the wagon. She had guaranteed the quality and the wool, and revealed to the world her inexperience. 'Just say how much you would like to put down as a first payment.'

She reminded herself she had come on this outing for her own ends: hoping first it might tempt Ginnie to come, but secondly having brought her tally-book, determined to retrieve some of her reputation as a businesswoman with Sam, as well as hopefully a copper or two from each customer. Her pretext for calling other than on her normal monthly day was to be that she was taking special orders for gloves and socks with patterned cuffs. She had several hand-knitted sample patterns in her pockets. She also had the reassurance of Ben's presence and the luxury of a lift home.

As she and Johnnie stood watching the final positioning of the wagon, a woman emerged from the cottage. It looked a little incongruous as with the roof agape to the elements she closed the door behind herself. She seemed to set her sights on the men with the wagon, but paused to exchanged banter with the workmen, urging them to 'Get on with it. Want more than the stars to sleep under tonight.' Her laugh was shrill, attention-seeking, as they answered her back, and she asked, 'Is that an offer?'

She went over to the men at the wagon, stood arms akimbo, laughing up at them. Leah moved nearer, noting she must be in her thirties, near the point of over-blossoming with riotous corn-coloured hair and a full bosom. She met Leah's gaze, and as they took each other's measure Leah saw that though she was fulsome in word, bodice all revealing and rosy of complexion, her eyes were sheer sharp calculation. She in turn took in Leah's youthful figure and smooth dark hair, and asked with a jerk of her head at Ben and Nat, 'You belong to one of them?'

'I *belong* to no one,' she answered, wishing women would not do themselves disfavours with such like remarks.

'You work for the Squire then?' This question was sharper 'You a maid or a governess or something?'

'She's with me,' Ben said.

The woman looked up at him and simpered. 'Don't know why she's ashamed of that then.'

'I'm not,' Leah answered. 'And who are you? Do *you* work for the Squire?' One of the workmen sniggered.

'This is my house,' the woman said, raising her eyebrows. 'The Squire is having it repaired for me.'

'So your husband is cowman to Squire?'

'That's right, Desmond Wilson's my old man, sent off to fetch some new cows from Bedfordshire.' The woman stared hard at her. 'What you got to say about that?'

162

'He must be good at his job,' Leah said, determined not to be browbeaten by this aggressive woman, and nodded towards the work on the cottage. 'The last cowman lived here forty years, then was sent to the Union for his pains.'

'Perhaps he didn't know how to please his employer,' she said, curling her lip. Leah felt her colour rise as she remembered the Squire's words to her when he had snatched the bonnet back from her face: "You need never work this hard for pennies."

'Some would rather starve,' she said very quietly.

'Let them then,' the woman retorted, laughing at the stupidity of the idea, 'the more fool them! Me, I take very bit of comfort I can get.' She gave John a come-hither look, which he ignored as if he had never exchanged a word of banter with a woman in his life, and with a cry of 'Mind your back', busied himself drawing the horse up a further few inches. The movement forced Mrs Wilson to step smartly away from the wagon. She retaliated with a short blasphemous string of words, adding, 'You best be out the way before the Squire comes, that's all.' And giving them all a last disdainful look, went back inside.

'Come on,' Nat said between clenched teeth. 'Bugger the straw, let'em keep it.'

Leah shared the sentiment. The woman had brought back to life all her fears of one day falling in the way of Edgar Lacey again.

'I need this straw for the furnace,' Ben said. 'Leah needs time to visit her customers.'

The nearest builder overheard and came over to advise quietly, 'You're here now, with your wagon. Load it and be away – don't miss the chance.' He jerked a thumb towards the cottage. 'She's more than willing, make no mistake.'

'One can see she's a lady,' John said, his cool irony easing the tension. He climbed into the back of the wagon and began throwing out the ropes they had brought to secure their final load. 'Come on, lads! Four of us – it won't take long.'

Nat shrugged and they all began work, leaving Leah little alternative but to be about her business as tallyman.

It had been a bad beginning to their day, and though she had the feeling that nothing would improve while they were in

163

Church Lacey, she resolved for a fresh, quick start. She marched straight across the road to the first address she had in her book – and found a friendly face.

'Why, you're the girl who came on the tally-round. Thought it must be about your time again.' The sturdy bustling woman who had organised the present for the old man beckoned her inside. She went immediately to a spillholder on her kitchen mantlepiece and tipped out a silver threepenny piece, instructing, 'Cross me off your list, mind! Jessie Haddon, owing another five pence for stockings after you've taken that away.'

'That's right, thank you.' Leah was cheered by this early success.

'He's dead, you know,' she continued as Leah marked off the payment. 'Only lasted a fortnight. Kept him inside, see, shut up, and he straining his nose for a breath of fresh air. Lived outside near all his life, hadn't he?' Without pausing for answer she pulled out a chair against the kitchen table. 'Cup of tea, and you've time for a sit down.'

'This is my first call, I'm best not . . .'

'Come back when you've finished, then.'

Leah felt to have refused would have been discourteous and nodded her acceptance, impressed as she looked round at the pretty pieces of pottery on the mantelpiece, the frilled cushions on the wooden settle by the fire, and everything from fender to saucepans glowing with a deep gleam. 'You have made your cottage nice.'

'More than can be said for outside, hey?' She laughed. 'Squire won't spend a farthing unless he's seeing a hundred-fold return.'

'I've come with my young man and some friends for the thatch off the old cowman's cottage.'

'Ah! That's a case in point. Reckon that woman won't be so pleased with herself when she finally finishes *paying* for all she's having done.' There was an ominous note in her voice as she added, 'He'll have the life from her body before he's satisfied.'

Leah's alarm must have shown in her face, for Jessie Haddon was instantly repentant. 'Ah, I shouldn't talk so! It's long past. There's no need for such as you to worry about him.

You be away about your business. I'll mash tea for you and the men.' She laughed, patted Leah's arm as she led the way out. 'They'll be black as the Old Man's hat – and lousy – when they've loaded that old thatch.'

That first call was the easiest found and the most enjoyable. Some of the cottages were tucked away in meagre little yards, the insides no more attractive than the outsides. But if Leah had expected resentment she did not find it, and most paid something, even if only a farthing. She had forgotten the patterned cuffs in Jessie Haddon's kitchen, and as she went round did not attempt to show them in the poorest of homes. Where she did pull them out, they were examined with keen interest, admiration even. 'Them's right toff's goods!' But they were handed back without any thought that the "like of us" would ever buy socks or gloves with such decoration.

Leah felt she had proved that even if Sam made his old frame knit coloured patterns, they would never sell in communities like this. The odd everyday items bought from such as herself were the luxuries here; there were no extra pennies to pay for frivolities like patterns. She finished her round in a tiny yard at the far end of the village, the old man there paying her a halfpenny and thanking her for calling. He had reminded her of her grandfather, made her wish she could afford to give her goods away.

She walked back, imagining the game of golf becoming popular and the Dexters making fancy topped half-hose for all the men, the money rolling in, her grandmother and mother counting . . . She was recalled to reality by the sound of a chest-tearing cough from close under the eaves of a nearby cottage, and thought of Sam labouring over that terrible old knitting-frame, stubbornly refusing to have the stove lit, saying, 'Time enough for burning fuel when the frosts come.'

From some distance away she could see the towering load of the wagon. A figure which looked as if dipped in the blacking pot jumped to grab a rope thrown from the other side. As she drew nearer she bit her lip to quell the laughter. It was John. 'You look like a blackamoor,' she called, laughing and running to stand by him as he hauled energetically on the rope, but he frowned and nodded his head in the direction of

165

the back of the wagon. A pair of quality horses were tethered to a post at the rear of the cottage. Leah recognised the glossy but temperamental creature that belonged to Edgar Lacey, and felt a moment of complete panic.

'We've got visitors just arrived,' her murmured. 'You keep out of the way. We'll be about ten more minutes.'

'The woman opposite has promised to make us all tea,' she whispered, 'I'll wait for you there.'

Leah began to walk away, but not quickly enough for Edgar Lacey came from the far side of the wagon and they met face to face. He was unable to hide his mingled surprise and fury, and Leah was unable to stop her automatic gesture of recoil. He laughed scornfully, tossing a remark to the man in his footsteps, a burly man of about the same age as the Squire himself but dressed in rust-coloured tweeds and black gaiters like an estate manager or agent. 'This is not it, I'm afraid, Barton. If it were, I'm keep it all to myself.' Barton laughed uncertainly, then with coarse understanding when he saw Leah, but before he could speak Ben strode out after them, ordering, 'Watch your tongues when there's a lady present.' Leah could see that under the black dust his face was pale with pent-up anger.

'Do you know who you're talking to?' Edgar Lacey demanded, turning aggressively back.

'I know!' Ben's tone was uncompromising and he put himself in front of Leah. John White closed up on the men from the other side, adding, 'And I've heard!'

'Stand away, the pair of you,' Squire Lacey ordered. 'Don't think the filth you're hiding under protects you. I'll know who you are.'

'Get back! Stand back from your betters!' Barton, his eyes fairly bulging with aggression, stabbed his riding-stick at Ben's chest.

'No man's my better,' Ben began catching the stick, twisting it from the man's grasp, 'less he earns my respect.'

'I'll have you in the dock for robbery with violence.' The Squire's tone was ruffled but confident. 'My word will convict any man.'

'There'll be a few witnesses to call,' Ben said, 'not all on your side. And no doubt the repairs to this cottage, out of all the others in the village, can be made to figure in the evidence.'

Leah felt a little thrill of victory as Edgar Lacey's red face fairly blazed with colour. For a second he was lost for words; when they came there was no mistaking the threat. 'There are other ways.'

'Aye,' John White agreed, 'and every man bleeds when cut.'

Ben put the riding-crop across his forearm and offered it back to the agent as if offering a choice of a duelling pair. Barton snatched it. At that moment the cottage door opened, and Mrs Wilson came from her roofless home as if to greet her landlord. He ignored her, leading the way to the horses.

'He's lost his appetite,' Nat commented from the top of the load of straw.

They watched the pair mount, dig their heels hard into their horses' flanks and ride away.

Leah took a great gasp of air as if she had not breathed for a long time. She had been terrified that either Ben or John might strike out. She leaned back on the wall to steady her shaking legs as she thought what might have happened. Then to her amazement she heard the men laughing at the Squire's retreat, and the next moment the cowman's wife was upon them, with such a stream of practised abuse the men pretended shocked amazement, then laughed all the more.

'You're all fools,' Leah breathed, unable to reconcile this merriment with what she knew of Edgar Lacey. The quiet certainty of her condemnation stopped their laughter. 'And you,' she raised her voice to the woman, 'he'll have the life from your body before he's finished with you.' She heard herself repeating Jessie Haddon's warning, then as Nat slid down from the top of the load to her side, she thought of Ginnie. How could men find any cause for amusement in such things? Then she wondered why she too was linking "such things" and Ginnie.

She turned and ran from Ben's extended, appeasing hand, to where there was another woman who seemed to know from experience to what extremes men such as Edgar Lacey would go.

Chapter Sixteen

There was a buzz of talk, a sudden roar of laughter from the men standing near the shove-ha'penny boards and the rattle of dominos in the bar of the Stockinger's Arms, as Ben and Nat walked in. They raised a hand to Sam, sitting in on a game of "fives and threes" at one of the domino tables. Ben bought three pints of best ale and took Sam one. In answer to his thanks he said, 'Your wife says we can stay the night in your spare room.' Sam laughed and took a hearty drink, 'Thanks for the rent,' then played a six-three domino, which with the double-six at the other end earned him and his partner eight points and won their game.

Ben and Nat moved to the counter where Sam joined them, eyeing them with just suspicion. 'What are you two here for?' he asked.

'I want to see Ginnie,' Nat said uncompromisingly. 'I'm not leaving until I have.'

'Hmmm.' Sam nodded to where Walter was busy replenishing tankards from a large jug. 'I'll tell you for nothing, this is not the time to ask. Walter Hobbday won't stand for any interference in the running of his house or his family – well-intentioned or not.'

'He won't let anyone over his doorstep at any other time,' Ben said, 'Leah's tried. We just want to know if there's any way we can help Ginnie.'

'Don't you think we've tried everything we can think of?' a low voice asked. They turned to find David by their side, his fingers threaded into half a dozen empty tankards. 'And she's gone away now.'

'Gone away!' Nat's voice rose in disbelief and disappointment. 'When? Where?'

'What's it to you?' Walter Hobbday demanded, attracted by the serious group at one end of his counter.

'We're all friends,' Ben put in, 'we're concerned.'

'I'm not talking to you,' Walter said.

At a nearby table a heavily built man, with a lingering smell of suet about him, raised his voice as if in support. 'Course they be concerned! Didn't you hear what his girl did?'

'Come on, George Heuitt, play your hand and stop gossiping,' his partner urged, nodding his head meaningfully to where Levis Warburton sat drinking with a friend near the door.

'I tell you, my old wummon was at the pump when it happened.'

'Ah, wummon's talk! You listen to too many wummon in that shop of yours.'

'I'm telling you . . .' George Heuitt pounded the air with a great slab of hand, then pointed a finger at Ben, added, 'Here, you'll know! Didn't that Leah Dexter throw a bucket of water over the Sunday School Superintendent's wife?'

The question secured a larger circle of listeners around the gaming tables, near the door and along the bar. Ben looked pointedly at Walter Hobbday and answered, 'She was defending her friend, Ginnie, from what she thought was malicious gossip.'

'Right! She douched Fanny Warburton! That's what I said.'

The bar erupted into laughter. Even Levis's drinking partner had trouble keeping a solemn face.

'Why have you sent Ginnie away?' Nat asked with quiet persistence.

George Heuitt muttered something, and those at his table obliged him with a laugh. Nat rounded on him. 'If you've more to say, we'd best all hear it.'

'I said,' Heuitt reiterated in loud precise tones, 'you should know!'

'What should we know?' Ben asked taking his boot from the brass footrail and standing upright.

'Well, one or other of you should.'

'Know what?' Ben repeated, as Nat squared up by his side, while Sam laid cautionary hands on their arms.

'Why she's been sent away – for her health. That's the term, isn't it? For their health.' Heuitt laughed in such a sarcastic, deprecating way there was a murmur of dissent around the bar. Someone called that his 'tongue would be better cooked and pressed', while one or two looked nervously in the direction of the landlord. His customers had a healthy respect for Walter Hobbday, and Ginnie was a village favourite. Walter himself looked momentarily stunned by what had been openly implied.

'You seem to know a lot,' Ben moved forward towards the table, 'perhaps more than's good for you.

'He only repeats what he hears in his butcher's shop,' the man still slowly shuffling the dominoes said derisively. 'He's a bigger gossip than his customers.'

'Here, don't you try to put me down! I know what I hear and I know what I see. I see plenty. Him!' He pointed at Nat. 'And him!' He indicated Ben. 'I've seen them both taking a turn with her in the fields.'

Anger rose from many throats, and Heuitt added hastily, 'Walking, I mean. Walking, with Walter's daughter. Of course you know who I blame? That same girl we was just talking about, that Dexter girl, brought up to have ideas.'

'Old Fred Dexter never would buy his meat from you, would he?' his partner commented, and began to stack the dominos back in their box as he saw Walter coming purposefully from behind his counter.

'You see, my mother was right though.' Levis Warburton's piping voice rose querulously and indiscreetly above the general muttered presentiments of trouble. 'No one can marry her now. Just the suspicion that she might have . . . well, it's enough, isn't it? And *we* blame her friendship with Leah Dexter – she thinks she's free to go about just like a man.'

Customers drained their tankards at some speed. Sam, forgetting his appeasing role, shouted back, 'Aye, and she'd make a better man than six of you!'

By the time Nat had launched himself towards Levis, Walter had the village butcher by the scruff of his neck, and every man was on his feet. Several hastily removed their precious spectacles as they made for the door. Levis too tried to escape but Nat grabbed his jacket labels and shook him like a limp cloth. 'You sanctimonious Peeping-Tom! Who are you to judge?'

'Here just a minute.' Levis's companion tried to intervene, was pushed back into his seat, then came back at Nat with renewed vigour. Those men who had thought of leaving were now prevented from doing so by the mêlée near the door.

Ben, seeing that Nat was more than holding his own, positioned himself between Sam and the struggle that was developing between Walter and the purple-faced Heuitt, who was endeavouring to keep all his weight down on his seat and stay there, shouting his claim as a "regular customer" to better treatment. Several other regular customers tried to assist the landlord by clearing the way of tables chairs and irate customers to aid the now plaintive butcher's ejection.

'No, no,' Heuitt objected, flailing his clenched fists in the direction of the Robertsons. 'There's your trouble-makers. Throw them out!'

'They're next,' Walter hissed as he finally dragged the butcher from his seat, and nodding to his son ordered, 'Fetch the others! Let's have them out.'

David disappeared into the back quarters, but as Heuitt again began shouting that it was "Them oddlings the Dexters who cause all the trouble in this village", Ben became Hobbday's temporary assistant in ejecting the village butcher. Walter looked a bit surprised as he found himself and Ben outside his front door and Heuitt pushed with such force he span and tottered to the far side of the village street before regaining his equilibrium. He retreated beyond the pool of light from the porch lanterns, still shouting his rights as a regular customer and a free Englishman.

Ben stayed the landlord from re-entering his pub with an urgent hand on his arm. 'Neither me nor my brother has done any harm to your daughter, Mr Hobbday, and never would.'

Walter glared at him, pushing had hand roughly away. 'I've only your word for that. You and your friends are banned from my house.'

171

'That'll include me then,' Sam declared as he was escorted out, with Charley keeping him at arm's length from Levis Warburton.

'That's as you care to make it,' the landlord growled back.

'Ah! You've always been head-down bull at a gate, Walter Hobbday. You want to try looking around a bit, finding out who are your real friends, or you'll lose your family as well as your customers.'

Nat was now propelled out through the pub door, fighting and struggling and only partly restrained by David and Robert Hobbday.

'Look at your great sons!' Sam advanced on Walter, wagging a reproving finger. 'Everyone of 'em afraid to say boo to you. They daren't have opinions of their own. You're a bully, Walter Hobbday.'

For a second the landlord looked as nonplussed as when the affair had begun, then he advanced on Sam. Perhaps he was only lifting a finger in return, but Ben and Nat both sprang forward, ready to protect the sparsely built old man they had both come to respect. David and Robert Hobbday immediately squared up behind their father.

Levis Warburton came back within the light of the porch lanterns and obviously felt secure behind the publican and his three sons as he shouted, 'What Mr Heuitt said was right! I've seen that tall one – that Ben Robertson – walking Ginnie in the fields . . .'

Ben launched himself through the middle of the opposition to grab Levis. 'Perhaps if I hold *you* under the pump, it'll stop your evil gossip,' he said between clenched teeth. He grabbed Levis and began to drag him back through the mêlée in the direction of the village pump. The level of shouting and fighting escalated quickly, with someone giving a new focus to the affair by calling for "the strangers" to be run out. This singled out Ben and Nat as the enemy, and Ben found it more and more difficult to keep his grip on Levis, but he was fiercely determined to give this trouble-maker a swift cold lesson.

The crowd seemed to grow rather than diminish as the noise of the fight stirred the silent village. A close crowd of onlookers came from nearby cottages and raised questions, mingled with the shouts of anger and cries of outraged pain – until in the distance a police whistle sounded. 'Bobby Woodstock!' a voice warned, and the shouting gave way to the sound of many boots scuffling to sidestep the fray and disperse into the darkness.

'This is no place for you.' It was as Sam spoke that Ben first became aware of Leah. As he turned she shouted, 'What are you all doing? Where's Ginnie? What about her?' as if to remind him of the reason for his outing. She caught his arm and tried to pull him away from Levis, but he shook his head. 'Go home! Take Sam,' he said as the warning whistle shrilled closer.

'So you've seen Ginnie, have you?' Leah demanded, her anger tinged with sarcasm. She indicated the final scuffles taking place before the public-house. 'This has helped!'

'Go with Sam,' was all he would say as he dragged the still protesting Levis towards the village pump.

'Leave him alone,' Leah demanded, 'he's only half your size.'

'His tongue's longer,' Ben said, pressing Levis's head down under the spout with one hand and using the handle vigorously with the other. The pump, ever primed by almost continual use, gushed water over the squealing Sunday School Superintendent's son. When the water was in full flood Ben released him and he lay spluttering in the trough worn by hundreds of years of buckets.

'He won't be the only one getting it in the neck for this little lot,' Sam commented as Leah strode angrily away.

'Go after her, Sam, while I find Nat.'

Leah would have strode straight home and to her room, but Sam came hurrying and calling after her, and when he caught her up led the way into the workshop, where he lit the lamp and ruefully examined his torn jacket pocket.

'Come on, gaffer,' he said, 'thread a needle and mend it before my Clarrie sees it.'

'Gaffer!' she exclaimed. 'Don't address me as a man. I consider it an insult after what I've seen tonight. I suppose you've left the other two still fighting? That must really have helped Ginnie. Her father must be pleased!'

'Shall I call you Gaffer's granddaughter still? And shall I tell you that the trouble in the Stockinger's Arms was sparked off by what *you* had done?'

She protested and questioned, but he let her stew a little as he took off his jacket. 'If women want to be partners, they should be partners all the time, not flutter around like outraged choirgirls when events take a turn they don't like. I shouldn't suppose Ben was too pleased to hear you discussed across the public bar, but he took your part, 'stead of siding with the opposition as you've just tried to do.'

'But . . .'

'Life won't let you pick the best bits out of a pudding and leave the rest,' he admonished. 'if you don't like the way men act, stay at home out of their world.'

'Since when has it been just for men?' she began, but her defiance held a hint of defensiveness. She expected him to regale her with the usual: God who created the world for men; with Eve as an unfortunate afterthought for Adam's amusement. When he didn't she glanced across to see him holding his right side as if in pain. She watched him with close concern. He looked up, immediately released his side, grinned, and held out his coat. She gave a sigh of feigned exasperation, and planned to talk to Clarrie about his health. As she prepared to mend the torn pocket, Sam told her that Ginnie was gone way.

The final bricking up of the furnace was near completion. The channel which would drain the molten bellmetal was bolted into place, the fuel was to hand, the furnace fully charged including the pieces of the broken Flaxhill bells. Their metal had been carefully assayed and Ben had spent the previous evening checking and rechecking his calculations of the amounts of copper and tin to make the perfect alloy. His aim was for a final mixture of seventy-seven per cent copper, the balance of tin – too much tin he knew would make the bell too hard and liable to crack, too much copper would produce an alloy that was too soft and produce a poor toned bell. He mortared in the last bricks. Once more he ran through the operation in his mind, then with a final tap of the trowel handle he acknowledged to himself that so far he had done all in his power to ensure success. His skill and knowledge neared the final test. He felt the challenge warm his stomach and the exhilaration colour his face. This was the time . . . He looked up eagerly – to see Nat scowling down at him, standing shoulders stooped, knuckles white as he gripped a spade.

'What is it?' he asked, alarmed for his brother. 'Are you all right?'

Nat turned away, continuing to tidy away the surplus sand from near the furnace. Then suddenly he straightened and turned back on his brother. 'You didn't touch Ginnie . . .?' It hovered between statement and question.

Ben slowly speared the trowel into the heart of the remaining pile of mortar. 'Do you need to ask?' His answer held the same tense neutrality.

There was a long pause. 'It'd help clear my mind. This way and that, I've gone . . .' Nat began, then sliced the spade down into the ground with all his force, leaned back on the slope of the furnace side, slid down to his haunches. 'I love her, I really love her.' He covered his face with his hands. 'We played around like children, I know. But now . . .'

'You know how you really feel,' Ben finished for him.

'If anyone's . . .' He looked up at his brother, and Ben saw tears on his cheeks. 'I'll kill him, whoever it is. It would be worth going to the gallows for.'

'That wouldn't help Ginnie much,' Ben said as gently as he could, 'and we don't know what her trouble is.'

'Everyone else seems to know.' His voice was thick with tears and anger. 'The butcher, the baker . . .' his voice spun off into wildness, then came down heavily '. . . that Levis!'

'Him! What he repeats is not worth the snuff end of a candle. And Leah is sure Ginnie would have confided in her.'

'Unless it's someone close to Leah. Someone whose coat she couldn't bear around her shoulders. . .'

For a moment Ben was not sure this was an accusation.

'Someone she waited for secretly in the fields, someone she needed to talk to.' Nat stared straight at the earth between his feet, but his crouch now held the tension of a spring.

Ben frowned, unable to believe he heard right. He gave a disbelieving laugh. 'What, me? I told you about the jacket.'

'Who else?' Nat glared up at him now. 'Who else is there!' He sprang towards Ben from crouch to attack like an animal.

Like past life flashing before his eyes, Ben realised just how withdrawn his brother had been since their evening at the Stockinger's Arms. Had he really believed the scandal and gossip? 'No, wait,' he protested, trying to fend off the hands that reached for his throat. 'You don't really think . . .' But the blind anger that had built with brooding, once unleashed, could not be restrained by words.

He tried to defend himself without hurting his brother, tried to understand, to put himself in the other's place.

'I'll kill you!' Nat clawed blindly at his neck, and all Ben could think of was how he himself had once flailed his fury at his mother as he demanded his dead father back. Then Nat fetched him a stinging blow to the side of the head, and he caught the arms and shook them as best he could, as if this younger brother were that same bereaved, misunderstanding child.

'Listen to me, I've nothing to do with Ginnie's illness, whatever it is!'

'You were seen with her!' Nat snatched his arms violently downwards, and attacked once more.

'I've been seen with *you* every day since you were born.' In spite of himself, Ben felt his own anger rising. All the years of their step-father's domination they had cleaved together. Other brothers might have had the security of a happy home to quarrel in, but needing each other they had drawn ever closer. 'Don't you know me any better than that?'

'I know Ginnie too!' Tears and anger mixed torment with wild aggression. 'Why should she hate your jacket near her?'

'Perhaps she thought it was yours!' He pushed Nat away so he stumbled and sprawled back again over the thick-piled turf insulating the furnace.

'I wouldn't hurt Ginnie! Never think such a thing.' He hurled himself forward in a fresh attack.

'Or of me!' The blows Nat rained on him now made Ben forget it was a brother who attacked, and restraining his strength no more he punched him in the ribs, then flattening the palm of his hand under Nat's chin, pushed him backwards, pinioning him down to the ground with his superior weight, repeating, 'or of me!' Nat struggled for a moment, but realised he could not free himself. Beside himself with frustration and fury, he snatched breath for a different attack.

'Is this how you took her,' he asked, 'by force?'

Ben looked at him as if seeing this younger brother for the first time, disbelief creasing his forehead, forcing open his mouth as if in pain. He released his hold and struggled to his feet, stepped rapidly backwards, utterly repulsed.

He turned away, hearing more bitter accusations and blasphemies as Nat struggled to his feet. He stood rigid with anger and hurt, fists clenched. He heard Nat snatch up the spade, but he would not turn. He felt bleakly that he had lost a brother, and if he came on the attack again, Ben felt no will to resist. The hurt was already too great.

'I can't kill you!' Nat shouted, his voice thick with tears as he found himself incapable of the act. The heavy spade came down, splitting the earth within inches of Ben's feet. 'But I hate you! I hate you!'

Ben listened to him moving away, slowly at first, then running. He remembered again his own fury when he had lost his father, but could not remember the last time he had fought tears.

Chapter Seventeen

'A guinea!' Leah exclaimed. 'I can't believe it.'

'I know,' Clarrie's eyes were wide with excitement, 'and you requested specially.'

'Why?' Sam accompanied the word with a thump on his kitchen table.

'Why not?' Clarrie tutted and turned on him, pulling up the blanket around his shoulders, almost covering his ears.

'That's no answer,' he persisted, freeing himself. 'And stop your molly-coddling, woman.'

'You stop opening your mouth and letting the cold air in, making you cough. And why shouldn't Leah be asked? Lady Nubury wants twelve pretty young women to hold flower garlands along the church path after the wedding. It's tradition, and this is not a hit or miss affair. The gentry do things proper.'

'Is this your sis's girl's doing? he persisted.

'No!' Clarrie denied vehemently, adding importantly, 'the list of girls came straight from Lady Nubury.'

'Did it?' Sam said ominously. 'Then Leah shouldn't go.'

'A guinea, Sam!' Leah exclaimed. 'For standing around holding a few flowers.'

'Think on the Squire, m'girl.'

For a moment her fingers nervously traced the outline of her lips. 'But there'll be crowds of people. The whole village'll be there to see . . . and surely the Squire wouldn't have any say in things like this?'

'You never know!' If you listen to me, you'll stay far enough away. Money doesn't cure all ills.'

'I know a lot of ills it does!' Clarrie said decisively.

'I wonder if Ginnie was asked . . . she would have loved it.'
Leah felt as if a light had gone out of her life, and still there
was no news of where her friend was, or how she was. She
wondered if she dared go again to the Stockinger's Arms to
ask if Ginnie would be well enough to go to the society
wedding. 'The Hobbdays are like a silent order of monks
these days,' she said as if thinking aloud.

'A guinea'll help just before Christmas, that's for sure,'
Clarrie said, and turning to Sam again ordered, 'And you can
eat a bowl of warm bread and milk with a little grated nutmeg
on top.'

Leah thought how frail Sam looked and how Clarrie bullied
him – with all the force of an embattled turtle-dove. She
compared their little pretences of argument with the bitterness that had developed between Ben and his brother, and in
so short a time. All her emotions and instincts spoke for Ben,
but she could see what the evidence said to Nat. The quarrel
she and Ben had had when she tried to show him his brother's
point of view was still too fresh to be completely forgotten.

As she crossed the yard, her mother came hurrying from
the back door of their cottage. 'We're to have an outing – this
Saturday afternoon!' she exclaimed as she waved a note. 'It's
from the Rector of Soston. They're having a gathering to see
Ben cast their tenor bell. There'll be refreshments *and* a pony
and trap to take us and bring us home!'

'Tomorrow? Why didn't Ben tell us?' Leah wondered,
though she knew their quarrel and her statement she would
never go to Soston again were reason enough.

Nellie passed the note to Miriam who put on her spectacles.
'The Rector says this is a "parochial event", not seen in a
churchyard in these parts for over a century, which will later
be followed by a formal blessing of the bells when they are all
hung – before Christmas, he hopes.' She looked over the top
of her small circular glasses. 'It's probably been arranged at
short notice. It'll be the Rector's way of saying thank you to
Ben, who as far as he is concerned is just making up for his
step-father's sharp practices.'

Leah had never met the Rector, and had no wish to. She
had it on the tip of her tongue to say anyone who went had

best take book and candle to go with the bell, for the place needed exorcism. Then she saw the excitement colouring her mother's cheeks and, turning, found her grandmother's gaze on her. 'We don't have many outings, and we should go,' Miriam said quietly.

The noise of the furnace was like that of a thousand tiny roaring devils bricked up in their beehive-shaped mound. The turf steamed with the heat beneath it, and Cuddy was at that moment throwing more soil and turf on top, while at the far side the light of the flames through the open stoke-hole door gilded Ben as he threw more wood inside, afterwards closing the door with his spade. Under the smell of hot steamy soil Leah caught the lingering foulness she had first smelt when the bell-pit had been dug, and a shiver of apprehension slithered icily down her back as she looked around at the burial mounds.

The grey sky threatened drizzle and even the crowd seemed ominous. She recognised many faces from that first occasion – the old man, Elijah, there as always, like the prophet of doom himself; Bessie Yarrup who cuckooed and waved; the woman who had steadfastly refused to buy from a girl at her door. She even recognised the woman from the house outside the village, who had laid out her husband with the stool – and the man he was there, carrying one of the children. These last did not acknowledge her, or she them.

The Rector's groom had been told to escort the Dexters into the rear of the church, and here, around the new bells waiting for the tenor to make up the ring, the ladies of the village had prepared tea, sandwiches, cakes – plain, seed, plus many examples of their Queen's favourite jam sponge sandwich.

'Ah!' The Reverend James Porter came forward, peering absent-mindedly at them, then as if cued by the presence of his groom who had fetched them from Tur Lacey, he added, 'Mr Ben Robertson's ladies. Thank you for coming. Isn't this all splendid?' He waved vaguely at the loaded trestle-tables. They introduced themselves to this kind-looking man who gave the impression of wandering vaguely through life, full of good intentions. Leah caught the glance of the lady at the tea-urn, who had just drawn off an excellent-looking brew, and to give some fresh impetus to the proceedings she volunteered to fetch Ben and Cuddy to take a cup before they actually tapped the furnace. The Rector agreed with great heartiness and informed them all that the fire had consumed first all the old rushes and now most of the wood. He made it sound like a greedy parishioner he was at a loss to know how to deal with.

Leah made her way through the crowd in the porch and round to where Ben stood, looking stern and anxious, while Cuddy, like a devoted dog, was watchful of every change of expression on his master's face.

'This is really not the time for drinking tea!' he exclaimed as Leah delivered her message. 'Why there has to be all these folk around – I'd rather've had just Cuddy here.'

'Nat's not come' She knew the remark was unnecessary from his expression. 'Just step briefly inside. I think that's all they want.'

Ben took Cuddy's arm gently. 'Come on, old chap, a cup of tea first.' Cuddy gave that odd, off-key laugh that at least here in his native village raised no eyebrows. As they entered the porch the Rector led a round of applause, and climbed up on his vestry steps, while his devotees shushed the less discerning.

'I, my vergers, the ladies of our Mother Church, felt we could not let this historic moment pass without some commemorative event – though we were rather late in that decision.' He paused for understanding laughter before going on with great sincerity, 'But diligence has conquered dalliance, as I'm sure you will agree looking at our table. I want you to join with me in thanking Mr Benjamin Robertson for his splendid efforts on our behalf, assisted by our own Cuddy.' There was more applause, and a few discreet shouts of approval, before the Rector invited all present to partake of the refreshments, and then to join them all to see the furnace tapped and the metal of Flaxhill bells run into the making of their new tenor bell.

Ben certainly took a drink of tea, but not much more before he was back outside with Cuddy. Leah followed. 'I need several men to keep the crowd well back.' he told her. 'This is

181

all experiment. I don't want anyone burnt should there be any sudden surge or splash.'

Leah could hardly believe that in spite of their quarrel Nat would not be there to help. His absence at this crucial time made the break between the two brothers seem permanent. She arranged with the Rector for several authoritative parishioners to keep control of the people, while at the same time giving everyone a good view. Leah, her mother and grandmother were given front row position to the right of the bell-pit.

'Now keep back,' Ben ordered. 'Whatever happens, keep well back. If you're splashed with metal, you're scarred for life,' he added as he drew on long leather gauntlets. Several mothers took firmer hold of their children.

He had manufactured a long angled crow-bar, with which he gently prised away the bricks he had mortared in over an inner small iron vent. The crowd was quiet now. He paused to check everyone was standing clear, his eyes holding Leah's for a few brief seconds, then he steadied the crow-bar to tap the furnace. The small plate was lifted away, and for a second there seemed to be an inner door of burnished gold. Then the bright metal ran free into the channel secured just beneath the opening.

There was intense concentration now as Cuddy came forward and put a thick stick into Ben's hand. This Ben seemed gently to beat the stream of metal with as it ran steadily along towards the bell-mould. The willow-stick burst into flames above the line of the metal, but these never became more than a frill of fire on the surface of the liquid. This practice Ben had told Leah dated back to medieval times and released salicylic acid from the willow which helped the metals fuse successfully.

The air above the flow of metal shimmered and the atmosphere was full of mouth-drying gases from the copper and tin, smoke from the wood.

Leah saw Ben was completely absorbed in the task. The only one he was aware of now was Cuddy whom he motioned anxiously on to the plank and trestles set up in the pit. This, she guessed, should have been Nat's role, as Cuddy glanced at Ben for guidance as he stood agitating a thin metal rod at the top of the mould to ensure the molten metal flowed evenly all around the bell. Ben nodded emphatically. 'All the time, Cuddy. Keep going, slowly and gently, all the time.'

Seeing the two of them so intent, both beating and stirring, the glow from the metal casting a strange upward light which in turn seemed contained by the lowering grey sky, Leah felt the old unreasoned apprehension creeping over her. She quietly slipped behind her mother, and then turned and walked back to the church where she sat first in the porch, then hearing someone inside, thought there might still be a lady serving tea.

A man stood near the line of bells.

'Nat?' she queried, and as he turned she was shocked by two things: his haggard look and the fact that he carried a thick staff. 'What is it?' She wondered if this was a new stage in their quarrel, if he had come to attack Ben again.

'It's the willow-stick,' he answered literally. 'The one Ben had prepared to use today.'

She frowned. 'But he's used . . .'

'I was too late to stop him. Caleb tricked Cuddy into bringing the wrong one, the old one we've used at the foundry. It invalidates the paper my step-father signed – or he says it does, which I suppose amounts to the same thing.'

She wondered if she could believe what she was hearing. She wondered at this brother who came late, implying what? Then she recalled the words of the paper Ben had preserved so meticulously: ". . . a good and true bell . . . without the use of any tools or equipment from Robertson's foundry." She shook her head at him in disbelief. She had been appalled by their fighting, but this was harder to accept. 'You mean Ben is out there doing all this work, for nothing? No prospects for us, your grandfather . . .' Leah broke off, incredulous and suddenly very angry. 'And you! If you'd been here, it wouldn't have happened. You'd have noticed!' She wondered if he saw this as a kind of revenge for what he thought Ben had done, was capable of. 'Why have you come now? To gloat?'

He laid the whitish staff down on a pew and walked towards the door. 'I came to stop him if I could. Though why I should bother . . .'

From outside came a ripple of applause and people began to talk again. 'You've no cause to quarrel with your brother.'

'I need proof of that,' he said without looking back, and as people began to come in again to finish the left-over refreshments, he made his way through them and away.

When she went back outside, Ben had taken over Cuddy's place, giving a final agitation to the last trickle of metal filtering into the mould. He looked up at her, relief on his face. The hard lines of tension were gone. Now an overwhelming weariness seemed to make his face longer and thinner, but he smiled at her. At the far side of the pit Cuddy grinned hugely, the discarded willow-stick in the grass behind him.

'Is Ben coming home with us?' Her mother's voice made her jump.

'No, he's staying with Cuddy until the bell is finished.'

'What is it?' Nellie asked as she caught her daughter's arm and led her away. 'You've gone pale. What's happened?'

Leah let herself be led out of the churchyard, almost to the spot where she had parted from Ginnie. She had left her friend, and Ginnie had never seemed herself again. She found herself telling her mother everything. 'I feel I can't tell him bluntly, then leave. It will destroy everything he's done. He's so tired – I feel I should stay with him, break it gently.'

'Yes,' Nellie's voice was quiet, 'it would come better after he's rested – and fed, come to that.'

They turned to look back, saw the Rector's horse and trap drawing up against the lychgate, her grandmother waving to them, and Cuddy going across to his cottage. They were both silent, but Leah felt they had the same thought as her mother indicated the young man. 'Come on. Ben will need you.' She led the way quickly across to the front door Cuddy had just closed. 'Stand by his side while he is there to need you.' Leah hurried in her mother's wake, surprised at her sudden decisiveness – and deeply moved. All the bitter experience of her mother's long solitary years had been in those few words: "while he is there to need you".

Cuddy came back to open his door and looked disconcerted by his visitors. As they tried to convey their meaning, the door of the neighbouring cottage was swept open and an old, small, but determined-looking woman asked: 'What is it, Cuddy?'

He moved uneasily from foot to foot.

'Do you know them?' The neighbour came and stood slightly in front of Cuddy, like an old Bantam hen defending a last chicken. 'Are they friends?'

To Leah's relief Cuddy nodded enthusiastically, and the woman's manner changed. 'You see, Cuddy here is *my* friend. He does much for me in the way of chopping and carrying, and I try to stop him being taken advantage of. He's too willing to work for nothing.'

'My daughter needs a place to stay overnight.' The story was precisely told, and even as the Rector's trap drew up alongside them the offer of a bed in Sadie Thompson's house accepted.

Leah was waving goodbye almost before she knew the matter decided. She thought even Sam could not accuse any of them of "fluttering about like outraged choirgirls" on this occasion.

It had all been quickly and quietly arranged – between women – not half the village engaged in fisticuffs.

'It isn't good news you have to break so gently,' Sadie Thompson guessed as Leah said she must go back to the church. 'Remember, they often blame the messenger.'

The advice was probably well meant, but it did not help Leah's decision as to how and when to tell Ben, or her composure as she met the villagers coming away from the celebration.

It was done. Ben inhaled deeply, and thought the last lingering metallic gases smelt sweeter to him than all the perfumes of Arabia. But he was tired – tired as the proverbial dog who had hunted all day. It was as if every ounce of energy had been drained from him by the tension of uncertainty: wondering if the furnace would stand up to the heat; whether the metal would flow properly, the mould hold; how he would manage without Nat. Now the experimental part of the work was over. He knew his own skill and ability to extract the bell from the mould, clean and tune it. His ear was true and his hand steady. There was many days more work, but all the rest he was confident about.

He had lingered over the last dregs from the furnace, and now as he looked around could see only a group talking at the lychgate. Everyone else had gone. He was surprised Leah had not come to take her leave as yet, and supposed they were still inside the church talking. He ran his hands through his hair, pulled his shirt straight, eased his shoulders back and went to find her. In spite of his bitter quarrel with Nat, he felt the uplift of achievement and wanted to share it. He looked with more confidence to the future, and the thought of setting up house together, set his heart racing. He met the ladies carrying away their tea-urn, who greeted him with smiles, nods, and from one of them a provocative, 'She's waiting in church.' They all laughed. He watched as they negotiated the lychgate, while on top of a great churchyard yew a mistle-thrush threw its heart at the sky. Ben searched to find the bird on the topmost thread of green, lifting its head, beak wide, working away to earn its winter name of "storm-cock".

When he looked down the ladies had disappeared behind the high stone wall, and he hurried into the church. Inside, all seemed dark until his eyes readjusted, then he saw Leah at the far side. She put something down on the pew seat and come towards him. He opened his arms and held her close.

'We're nearly there,' he said, his enthusiasm perhaps making him hold her too tight, for she struggled away, pushed her arms up between their chests. 'What is it?' he asked. 'Have you heard something about Ginnie?'

'No.' she dropped her head gently on to his chest, so he could not see her face. She had not intended to tell him this soon, but it could not be hidden. 'No, but Nat's been here.'

'Nat?' he queried. He felt her nod, and was suddenly aware of the chill in the church after the heat of the furnace. The granite of wall and pillar, the slate memorials, the grey marble of monument and effigy, the stone flags beneath his feet, entombed his hopes as she stood in his arms and told him of the willow-stick.

She wondered if he knew he had released her as he strode to the pew. He grasped the staff at either end, lifted his head and opened his mouth in a great silent cry, an image of agony sculptured on her mind forever.

He felt his mind like a mad eye try to blink away shock. Was this true? Why did he listen for the song-bird? He turned back on her, hoping for a reprieve. 'It's not true, is it?' Then, without waiting for an answer, ran his hands along the unscorched rod and added, 'it is. It's all been for nothing. Nothing! there's no lengths that man will not stoop to.' There was a long silence before he added: 'Caleb Berridge.'

He pronounced the name like a judge about to give sentence. It startled her for the tone held not defeat but intent, and she was suddenly afraid for him, and for what he might do. She understood Jane White's fear for her man. 'It's not all for nothing,' she tried to reassure him. 'You know you can do it, you accomplished the bell.' She knew he did not hear.

He was aware she came to his side, felt her grip his shirt sleeve, and half closed his eyes so she should catch no glimpse of the wild intensions running amok in his mind. He imagined belabouring Caleb, staining that pristine staff or casting him into a bell – what a note would that give out! He wanted to lay waste to someone else's world, as Caleb had lain waste to his hopes.

Sam had warned him, "He'll wriggle out, you'll see." He had been made a fool of. And Nat! He felt doubly wronged by his brother, misjudged and bitterly ill-served. His gaze fell on the row of bells, at the beams laid ready to receive the tenor. It meant nothing to him now.

As he moved towards the bells she felt he might almost attack the inanimate things. 'Come outside, Ben. Let's walk – and talk.'

'Why haven't you gone home? he asked.

He seemed to listen as she explained, and when she plucked his sleeve followed her along the path through the lychgate. It seemed suddenly important to get him away from that churchyard.

'In any case,' he said, 'even if I starve, I shall never work for him again.'

Chapter Eighteen

'I told him eating humble pie was better than not eating at all,' Leah related defiantly.

'Is it?' Sam asked mildly as he sat before his kitchen fire working on yet another adaptation for the small knitting frame.

'I think it must be.' Her answer was studied, weighing all she had seen of poverty, and known of lean times, since her grandfather had died.

'What about pride and self-respect?'

She did not answer as she pondered the fact that if her grandfather had not been such a hardworking provider, they might all have been destitute before now. The payments from the tally-rounds and the carefully worked garden and allotment land had kept them going so far, but the contacts he had built up, all his years of hard work, were slipping through their fingers like dry sand.

'What about the men who are prepared to die for their principles or for their country? Should a country eat humble pie?'

'Oh, I know men are prepared to fight!' She returned to the discussion with wholehearted sarcasm. 'Men are obviously prepared to fight about anything. You don't need to beat a drum or offer a shilling to set them off.'

Sam chuckled at her passion, while his fingers trembled in the fight to align a neat row of metal loops he was fastening through slim lengths of wood. His hands fell to his lap, resting. 'What do you think he should do? Go back to a house where he's been bested by someone he hates, and distrusted by someone he loves?'

'I hadn't thought about it like that.'

'Ah, there's a lot you should think about before you rush into action.' When she was about to protest, he went on, 'You've upset all the Warburtons, you've threatened the Squire with a hayrake and panicked his horse . . .'

'But that was different!' she protested.

'Yes, your pride was attacked in one case, and your honour threatened in another – a bit like Ben, wouldn't you say?'

She opened her mouth to answer back, then laughed and slipped to the rag-rug before the fire, leaning her head gently against the old man's knee. 'You're much too wise for me.' She felt his hand touch her hair, felt the tremor still there after several minutes' rest.

They were quiet for some time, both reluctant to break the moments of closeness. The fire slipped and crackled in the grate and she watched the flames circle and engulf a fallen log. 'What are we going to do?' she asked.

Although they had been talking of Ben, he knew she meant their livelihood. 'Well, thanks to old Fred, our roofs are secure – it's just the eating that's tricky.' He laughed gently at the fraught look she gave him. 'Come on, now, the women have some sewing money to come. When they've finished, I'm going to teach Clarrie how to do this.' He wagged the piece of wood towards the knitting frame, and the coloured spools of wool. 'As for the rest, your grandmother knows how to work the big frame in the shop, your mother toes and presses beautifully – and you have a nice copperplate hand for the office work.'

'But you always do the knitting . . .' Leah began. 'Sam?'

He leaned forward to drop another log on the fire, avoiding her eyes. 'I can't do it all,' he answered, and silenced her utterly for a moment as he squeezed her forearm almost fiercely and added, 'You'll manage.'

'What are you telling me?' she persisted, dreading a revelation about his health.

'That this idea for selling high-class fancy-topped golfing stockings through the post has to be made to work.' He held her gaze without blinking.

'Well, it won't be for want of trying on your part, will it?' Her voice wavered and she rose quickly, but before she fled she added, 'Or mine.'

She ran to the old workshop, shutting herself in. She shivered. 'He doesn't think he'll get better,' she told herself, trying to fight off tears. 'And now I love the old devil, almost as much as I loved my grandfather. Him and his Gaffer's granddaughter!'

She looked around at the silent frame, the cone-winding spindle and handle, the unlit lamps and candles behind the glass domes of water, and recalled the workshop when it was buzzing with work and voices. Her grandfather full of passion as he debated things like the new trade unions, or whether child labour under eight years would ever really be eradicated, law or no law; Sam, as she remembered, always managing to add a very pertinent point, which usually created laughter. Always work but always talk; always the stockingers' sense of humour lightening the long demanding work of the frames. Sam had that capacity for leg-pulling and self-denigration for sure, but she shook her head over herself.

The capacity to laugh at her own misfortunes always gave way to fear, for she had another memory of this workshop. She had been little more than three years old when a man had been found dying in the street, and carried into the warmth. She remembered his huge gaunt frame lying on the bench there, the skin stretched tight into the deep cheek sockets. She had been forgotten in the corner until the man's eyes had stayed staring open and his hand had clattered like thrown bones to the floor. She had whimpered then, and her grandfather had gestured hurriedly to her mother who had swept her up and run with her across the cobbled yard, back to the cottage kitchen. She remembered the words of explanation: 'No food.'

Hugging herself she walked around the room, looking at some of the plans, calculations and sketches for "their bell" which still decorated the walls. The bell they had thought would bring them together, hasten their wedding-day.

She remembered Ben's cold rage, his fear of returning home for what he might do to his step-father, and perhaps the greater fear that his mother would try to place herself physically as well as emotionally between husband and son. Sam had made her see how Ben was pinned down by circumstances – that old forked stick again.

She felt she had helped him come to terms with that first overwhelming anger. They had taken a very long walk that night. She had been silent, sensing his need for time and space, merely trying to keep pace with him, sometimes having to run a few steps to keep up. Her eyes adjusting as the night had deepened, they had gone on until she recognised Flaxhill Tower as a blacker bulk against the blackness. He had stopped then, suddenly, and she had to come back a few paces to be by his side. He let out a great sigh, then opened his arms. She had flown into them, and he had rocked her, though his was the greater need.

'We'll find a way,' she promised. 'It may take longer . . .'

They had begun their long walk back, and he had talked over his intentions. 'All the joy has gone,' he said, ' but I shall finish the bell. I owe the Rector that. Then there will be the hanging of all six. I shall be paid for that. I'll have to hire some help . . .'

He had asked her to stay for a few days, needing her to talk to. She knew this was when fears had overcome loyalty. She wanted to save the extra pennies she would have to offer for the lodging.

Early the next morning she had left him at Soston. She sighed as she reached up gently to smooth out a sketch of bell section. Her gaze fell on a small pile of catalogues and magazines lying on a bench. She had left Ginnie at Soston . . . She shuddered involuntarily. This place chilled her to the bone, was like yet another graveyard, full of dead hopes. She left the shop quickly.

Over the last weeks she had deliberately walked past the Stockinger's Arms every day. Each time she hoped one of Ginnie's brothers might see her and bring news, or best of all that the old Ginnie would come running out to link arms with her – full of news, wanting to tell every little last detail of all that had happened – and that the explanation for her absence would be straightforward, simple, innocent. She walked along the main street, desperately needing something good to happen.

As she approached the public-house she was alerted by the sound of a bolt being drawn. Was her need to be answered? The front door opened and Walter Hobbday came towards her. 'I've been waiting for you,' he called.

Her heart sank. His tone told her that it was not good news, and he looked ten years older than when she had last seen him. 'I've *seen* you every day, and I don't want to see you no more.' For a moment she thought he was going to take hold of her. His fists clenched and unclenched, and his voice shook as he went on, 'I'll tell you what you want to know! I've heard from my sister. The signs are my Ginnie is expecting a child. But she'll not speak, and her aunt says if she goes on the way she's doing she'll not live either.'

'Let met go to her, Mr Hobbday, please! She'll tell me what's happened, who it was, I know she will. Please!'

'Oh! I think we both know the name's Robertson – it's just which one that's the problem. But when I find out, I won't ask the law to deal with him.'

'You're wrong, Mr Hobbday,' she pleaded, her emotions held in check by her will to help Ginnie, to go to her. 'I know . . .'

'NO! You don't know!' He turned sudden, spiteful fury on her as he added, 'And you be careful, my girl, or you'll be marrying the father of my Ginnie's child.'

'Oh, no! How could you?' The insult felt like a mortal wound, but she heard the agony in the choking "*my* Ginnie" and tried again. 'Let me go to her, she'll tell me the truth. For all you know, you could be serving the man in your public bar.'

'She wasn't seen in the fields, or in the brook, with anyone who frequents my bar,' she said heavily. 'I hear the Robertsons've quarrelled, and yours left home. It seems to be where the finger points. Just a word from my girl, that's all I'm waiting for . . . so you can tell them both I'm keeping my gun loaded ready for that word. Truth'll out.'

'I can't wait for the day!' There was no reasoning with the man. Leah turned and walked quickly away. She did not stop until she was in her own kitchen, had closed the door behind herself with a slam and stood rigid before the table, her knuckles rapping the scrubbed wood.

'What on earth's the matter?' her grandmother asked.

'Walter Hobbday! He'd sooner let her die than let me go to her,' she said at last.

'Ginnie?'

'You were right about her,' Leah said quietly, the pent-up tears of the whole morning suddenly overwhelming her.

'Oh, I'm sorry about that,' Miriam said, coming to put her arms around her granddaughter. 'Poor Ginnie! Has she said . . .'

Leah shook her head against the older woman's shoulder. 'She's with an aunt. Do you know where that would be?'

'The Hobbdays originated from Staffordshire, somewhere near the Potteries, that's all I know.'

'We have to do something. This can't go on. Ginnie silent – and maybe dying. Ben and Nat enemies, and Ben left home.' The tearful list faltered into appeal. 'There must be something we can find out, something like clues, if we only think hard enough.'

Miriam tried to draw her to a chair, but Leah shook her head. 'Gran, you remember how we read that Wilkie Collins novel together? We read a little, talked it over, looked for clues.'

Miriam took her granddaughter's hands and shook them. 'This is life,' she began, but Leah had found new resolution in her speculations.

'You remember we were all in the kitchen when Ben found Ginnie and brought her here?' She paused. 'Though I always feel the answer is back at Soston . . . I always come back to that place.

'Begin there then,' Miriam said resignedly, 'if you must. The night Ginnie drove Sam over, and waited to bring him home – why did she go in the first place?'

'To keep me company, and hoping Nat might come.'

'But he didn't?'

'No.'

'Tell me where and how you left Ginnie. Did you see anyone?'

'We walked together from the churchyard to where there's a stile to the field footpath, but I kept on the road. I saw a man a bit later. He was on the field footpath.' She remembered the bulky figure made eerie by the evening mists. She had taken him for a man in his fifties and added now, 'But he was old.'

'Did Ginnie go straight back to the churchyard?' Miriam asked.

'Ben saw her once when he was pushing kindling into the fire. Sam said later she sat huddled in the church porch, waiting. She said she was cold when she drove him home.'

'And none of us saw her again until she came here with Ben,' Miriam went on. 'When she sat by the fire with Ben's coat around her.'

They were both silent as they remembered how violently Ginnie had suddenly demanded the coat be taken from her – how she had briefly laughed, then whimpered like a whipped child as Ben had taken the coat from her shoulders and put it aside on the table.

They both started as the door latch rattled and Nellie came in, beaming. 'Ben's here,' she announced, 'Sam spotted him through the window. He's just having a quick word, he'll be here in a moment.' She paused, looking from face to face. 'What's happened?'

Before they could answer Ben came in, his coat hooked on one finger over his shoulder. 'Clarrie's certainly keeping Sam warm – it's like an oven in that kitchen.' He dropped his coat on the end of the table.

Miriam hurried forward, swept it up and hung it on the back of the door. 'Sorry . . .' he murmured, surprised at the speed with which she acted.

'Ginnie is expecting a child,' Leah said.

He stood a moment, looking from one to another. Miriam frowned, sat at the table looking down at her entwined fingers. Nellie smiled in his direction, but her eyes did not meet his. Almost as if dreading what he might see, he looked from his coat hanging on the door to Leah. She looked directly back at him, suddenly understanding her grandmother's reluctance to go over all that had happened. She had felt her granddaughter might not like the conclusion they came to.

'What can we do?' she asked, and felt strangely as if she had grown up in that moment.

He held out one hand, took up his coat with the other, and they left the kitchen together. No sooner were they in the entry between the two houses then he drew her to him and kissed her. 'Forgive me,' he whispered, 'just for a moment I wondered if you thought I . . .'

She did not answer because she too had wondered, before his eyes had met hers so directly. Feeling his arms around her now, she felt she had come home after a long time away. 'We must never let anything come between us,' she whispered, standing tall against him, pressing her cheek to his.

'I do love you, Leah,' his voice was husky, 'but . . .'

'But?' The word frightened her and she pushed away to scan his face.

'I'm going away for a time.' He laughed at the expression on her face. 'Don't look like that. It's to earn money – good money. You should be pleased about that.'

She knew he meant no sarcasm by his remark. She knew she deserved the hurt it cause her.

'You were right anyway. All that work wasn't for nothing. The owner of the City Bell Foundry had heard and came to look at what I'd done. He has a lot of work in the city at the moment, but doesn't want to lose a contract to make a bell on site in Derbyshire. He needs an extra master-man just for a short time. He's paying me fifteen guineas.'

Leah gasped at the sum.

'He offered pounds. I asked for guineas,' Ben said.

There was also the guinea she would earn at the Nubury wedding, she thought, then despised herself for the calculation.

'Are you pleased?' he asked. 'You're very quiet.'

'We need money to be together, but to earn it you have to go away.'

'I'm hoping if I make a good job of this he may offer me something more permanent at his foundry. It's just my mother and grandfather I worry about.'

'And Nat . . .?'

'Nat.' He repeated the name as if it were a conundrum. 'I had to come to terms with all this after you left. With me gone, Caleb will need my grandfather for his skill, and Nat is almost as useful. My mother will always take her husband's side because of the vows she has made her scourge, her prison. While he lives she will stay with him, whatever. It was not easy, I had to make a choice . . .'

'And I'll never leave you to do that on your own again,' Leah vowed.

'Thank God for that,' he said feelingly, holding her tight to him again. She clung to him in the narrow entry, remembering how as a child it had seemed a special, safe place, hemmed in by all she knew – and now all she loved, even old Sam.

There was the sound of footsteps on the cobble yard and they drew apart, and would have walked on into the street, but Clarrie's voice brought them to a half. 'Sam wants you, Leah,' she called. 'I'll have to go,' she whispered, and Ben gave her a consoling squeeze.

'What is it?' she called back as they walked circumspectly out of the entry. Clarrie shook her head in comic disapproval. 'Something we've *got* to see.' She bustled ahead of them.

With no more than a wave of acknowledgement that they had answered his summons, Sam, his cheeks red with an unnatural flush of excitement, waved them all to come around him. With something of a flourish he took up the piece of wood he had been working on, checking that the spools of coloured wool were straight on their spindles. He used the loops to pull into action the needles he wanted to knit in one colour, then sent a shuttle flying across the frame carrying green wool. Closing their latches with the flat side of the strip, he then worked a shuttle with red wool.

There was no sound but the hiss of the needles and the clatter of the wooden shuttles as he worked. Before their eyes he manufactured a diamond-patterned sock-top. He ran the piece off the needles and handed it to Leah. 'Practice will make it quicker,' he said with modest pride.

'Then we put the stitches on the other frame and knit the body of the sock,' Leah said, 'so if we all do different stages it shouldn't take us any longer to produce than plain stockings. It'll just be buying in the wool.' She mentally committed her guinea from the Nubury wedding to that – and this time she would go with John Smith to buy it! She wondered if the Prestwich Golf Club had club colours?

'Is it only young Leah who sees the possibilities? The Dexters' first step on the road to industrialisation!'

'I'm just wondering which "step" I shall be taking,' Clarrie said cautiously, but Leah threw her arms around Sam's neck. 'We'll do it. We'll get there!'

'That's no way for a Gaffer to behave,' Sam said, disengaging himself, but not before he had returned her hug.

'Well then,' she ordered as another idea occurred to her, 'could you make me another top just like this one straight away? I'm going to send the first pair to Ginnie, with a letter. If I ask Charley Hobbday I'm sure he'll try to get them to her. She must be allowed to know we're all thinking about her.'

'It seems fair,' Sam replied, 'it was her idea in the first place.'

Ben laid his arms across Leah's shoulders. In the close friendly circle the others smiled, and pretended not to notice the intimacy.

Chapter Nineteen

No one in the village had seen a photographer outside a town studio before. There was much interest as he set up his tripod in the middle of the path outside the church.

'Hired by the Squire! He's going to take a likeness as they come out of the church door.' The verger accompanied his information to Leah with a sharp elbow in her ribs.

She drew in her breath with a tut of annoyance. Old Pask thought the younger generation of the village did not readily understand his remarks unless they were well driven home. 'You might be on the photograph, standing here,' he added, then directing a sharp forefinger in the direction of her ribs he pronounced, 'and lucky to be chosen, I should think.'

Leah drew back an inch and avoided the second prod. There was a minor diversion as the photographer's black top hat was accidentally sent skimming off the gravestone where he had carefully balanced it. It was hurriedly replaced while the man was still under the black cloth aligning his camera. It seemed to heighten the sense of nervous camaraderie among the villagers. A brief opportunity to laugh at the expense of the Laceys whom few in that curious crowd had cause to regard with anything but resentment.

Leah had taken her place with the eleven other flower girls only minutes before. She had not seen the bride and guests as they went into church for she had sped to the post office on a more urgent errand.

In response to a letter of enquiry from "Dexter Golf Stockings" she had just mailed their first samples to Prestwich

Golf Club. She still felt a thrill of excitement as she thought of it. The samples had been excellent.

'Come along, flower girls.' Mrs Warburton's authoritarian tones cut into her thoughts. 'Prepare to take up your garlands. Now!' Leah thought the woman would make a fine sergeant major; she had the voice and the build. The double line of girls stooped to pick up the ropes of flowers. In December Leah would have expected these to be mostly evergreens, chrysanthemums and Michaelmas daisies, but they were made up of sprays of tiny exotic-looking lilies, orange blossom, white and cream rose buds. The "glasshouse blooms" were as much a marvel to the men of the villages as were the fashions to the women.

Mrs Warburton leaned to eavesdrop at the church door, then strode down the path, inspecting her troops. She did not lower her dignity by looking at Leah, just gave a loud, disapproving sniff. Leah concentrated on the guinea. Certainly if Mrs Frances Warburton, wife of the Sunday School Superintendent, defied and drenched, had any say in matters she would not be in this line, and definitely not nearest the porch.

From inside came the sound of the final hymn and all heads craned forward, waiting for the doors to be opened. In spite of the fact that the villagers from all around had no time for any of the Laceys, Lord and Lady Nubury had a better reputation – kind, if vague as to the needs of ordinary folk, was the general judgement. Today in the thin December sunshine there was excitement for Flavia Nubury – perhaps even sympathy for a girl marrying into a family with such a long and black reputation.

Inside, the triumphal march announced the end of the ceremony and the doors were flung wide. People who had been talking and laughing quietly together suddenly took on louder more expansive tones, but every eye was on the porch. From the steeple the bells began a peal of full and joyous splendour, made more splendid for Leah because Ben was one of the band of ringers. He had returned from Derbyshire specially. John White had come too and was standing outside the churchyard with her mother, grandmother and Clarrie.

Leah could see into the church now; saw the congregation turning to watch as the bridal procession progressed down the aisle. Then, as the party turned the corner to walk out into the sunshine, she could see the bride. Flavia Nubury, now Mrs Lacey, come into view on the arm of her husband. Flavia was dressed in white velvet with real flowers of orange blossom pinned beneath an inset of rare white lace on the bodice. From her shoulders flowed a train of white silk, which as she came nearer Leah could see was embroidered in silver thread with fine sprays of the same orange blossom. Her breathtakingly beautiful finery, her straight proud carriage made her a dazzling bride.

Then Leah's glance went to the bridegroom and she felt as if an icy hand had been laid on her heart. Though he was taller than his father, he had that same red colouring. Even as she recognised the foxiness, she glimpsed it echoed behind the bridegroom as Squire Lacey followed his son. She heard his laugh, and though she knew he was powerless to harm her here, yet she dreaded he might pause and pass some patronising word. No longer did she study the dresses; the bridesmaids passed her in a blurr of pale pink velvet. It was not until the general congregation began to file out that she dared to look round.

The Squire of course was nowhere in sight. What a fool she was! The crowd quickly dispersed to the green at the far side of the church, all eager to see more of the fashions of the gentry, and to watch them pose for this outdoor photographer.

Her fellow flower-girls were full of chatter about the bridal party, while Leah just felt pleased it was all over. 'What do we do with the flowers now?'

'Just lay them carefuly down on the grass,' a man's voice instructed. A stranger appeared at Leah's elbow from inside the porch. He turned, smiled down at her and asked, 'Would you collect the garlands and take them to the carriage waiting over there?' He pointed in the opposite direction to where the crowds were viewing the guests. 'They're going to be used to decorate the Hall for the wedding breakfast.' Then, indicating a liveried servant talking to the other girls, he added, 'But collect your guinea first.'

To her surprise she found that instead of the pound note and one shilling which she had expected, she was given an old golden guinea last minted at the beginning of the century. 'A keepsake,' the servant said. Some hopes, she thought as she collected the first batch of flowers for the carriage.

Her mind was full of how much wool she might buy; she would ask John when they all got home. She wondered how quickly they would have a reply from the Golf Club – whether now was the time to advertise in a magazine? She wondered why the carriage (which was more like an old black closed coach than anything else) was parked the wrong way for returning to the Hall. As she approached, it moved off a little. She had opened her mouth to call out when it stopped again and a man got down from the front, ordering someone else to hold the horses steady. Then, seeing her coming, he raised a hand and opened the carriage door.

'Just lay them along the seat, will you?' he instructed, 'He'll help you.' And he gestured to another man already in the vehicle.

She put one foot on the step, and lifted the heavy garlands towards the hands of the man inside. It was at the moment she had her arms at fullest stretch that she sensed danger. It was too late. She was pushed violently from behind, sent sprawling on to the floor of the carriage, crushing the flowers. 'Here, mind what you're doing!' The words were automatic, as if her mind had not caught up with her predicament. But as she tried to raise herself, looked for assistance, she glimpsed the man's face full of shifty evil intention. A hand on the back of her head forced her face down into the pale fragrance of blooms. She shouted for help, rose petals against her lips, in her mouth. She remembered the sweet smell of hay when she had escaped from Edgar Lacey . . . Sudden panic gave her strength. She managed to gain her knees and began to shout again. The man tried to cover her mouth. She shook her head violently from side to side, shouting still. She felt the carriage tip and heard the other man urge the horses on. Her heart thumped violently. This time she had been caught.

Then the carriage rocked again, and there were more shouts. She heard the horse's hooves sliding and skittering, the wheels beneath her rolling forward. More shouting, and they lurched to a halt again.

The man's hold on her was suddenly relaxed and she fought amid torn roses, lilies and orange blossom to raise herself up, turning to see Ben in the doorway, grappling with her assailant. Part of her mind registered that the bells were still ringing.

'Get away!' he ordered as he fought with her assailant. 'Out, Leah! Get away!' he repeated. She half crawled from the carriage, avoiding the feet and fists of the two men. Outside she saw John White on the cab, fighting to gain a foothold as well as attempting to secure the reins. The driver was lashing at him with the whip. She glanced frantically up and down the street to see if there was anyone who could help. Two men stood near the church. One was the man who had instructed her to bring the flowers to the carriage. The other? She glimpsed morning dress, but he was careful to keep behind the first man.

A sudden cry made her turn back to see the whip lash catch John's face a stinging blow, making him lose his grip on the reins. The driver's foot came up and caught him full in the chest. He sprawled backwards, landing heavily on the footpath.

Immediately the horses were urged forward, whipped and shouted into action. Ben appeared momentarily in the doorway, then launched himself back inside. They both shouted to him to jump. He reappeared, struggling to bring the other man out with him. Leah saw the driver's hand come up and the whip lashed viciously backwards. Ben had the man as far as the doorway. He hung there perilously with one hand as he tried to prise the man out of the vehicle. Again the lash curled backwards.

'Let go, Ben! Please, let him go!' she shouted, but now standing on the bottom steps of the vehicle, Ben nearly had the man out.

'Jump!' John shouted, scrambling to his feet to go after the vehicle. 'Don't let them take you!'

The man so near to being ejected bellowed his alarm to the driver, and the next minute the carriage slewed violently to the right. Ben partly lost his grip on the man, grabbed backwards at the door-frame but could not reach as it moved away from him. He seemed posied for a moment at an impossible angle, like a music hall acrobat, then, assisted by a kick from the now secure passenger, he fell rolling and sprawling to the road.

Leah reached him first. As he struggled to rise and she saw his injuries were no worse than grazes she began to tremble. She knelt by him because she could not stand, but for him the matter was not over.

'Who told you to bring the flowers to that carriage?' he demanded. She turned to look back towards the church. 'He's gone,' she said, 'he was watching with – another man. He was against the church porch when we were paid our guineas.'

'I saw him,' John said grimly. 'I'll know him again.' He was away back to the church, running. Ben was up and urging her to her feet. 'Come on! I'm not leaving you alone for a second, and I don't want John tackling anyone on his own.'

Leah remembered what Jane had said about her husband's hotheadedness and forced some use into her legs. Ben put his arm about her and they ran to scan the crowd on the far side of the church. They saw John prowling around behind the official wedding party. They also saw him attract the attention of Squire Lacey, who spoke to him briefly then moved quickly away and beckoned two liveried footmen. The servants' heads went up to look in John's direction as their master instructed them. The Squire immediately turned away, chatting with his fellow guests as if nothing untoward was happening.

John had apparently finished his sortie among the nobility and made his way slowly through the villagers to where she and Ben stood scanning the rest of the crowd. There was no sign of the man who had instructed her about the flowers, but from where she stood Leah could see some of the village woman and children pulling apart the remaining rope of flowers and carrying away great armsful..

'It's all right, Miss,' one child informed her, 'Squire said we could have them.'

'The Squire?' Ben questioned. 'When did he tell you?'

'A minute since,' the boy replied. 'Honest!'

'Was he with anyone?'

'He were talking to a tall man in black, but he went off on a horse. He were about in a gallop when he left t'street!'

Sam's face was grim, but he nodded his complete belief, when the whole story was related and cuts and grazes were being bathed in the Elliotts' kitchen.

'So you were right,' John said.

'Right – what about?' Leah asked.

'Sam guessed there was something more behind this special request for you to be one of the flower-girls and wrote to me asking me to come,' John explained.

'And Ben thought the same as I did,' Sam added. 'He came without being asked, and arranged for everyone to think he was busy pulling bell ropes.'

'It was as well there were two of us,' John reflected.

'So you weren't in the belfry?' Leah remembered her moment of astonishment when Ben had suddenly appeared in the carriage while the bells were ringing.

'I was on the tower steps, watching from one of the window-slits.'

'You really thought someone was going to try to . . . take me away . . . abduct me?' The proper word for the act sent a chill down her spine.

'Not *someone*,' Sam said sternly, making himself cough, 'it's Edgar Lacey we're talking about. I told you he never lets a quarry go. I warned you. Now perhaps you'll listen.'

The experience had frightened her more than she liked to admit, but even so she felt rebellious. How could she live if she was to be afraid to walk out anywhere? 'I can still hardly believe it happened. It seems like a dream. He's got a wife and – and a woman in Church Lacey. Why should he want me?'

The kitchen was quiet for a moment, then Ben said grimly, 'He'd better *not* want you. I'll find some kind of work nearby. He won't get another chance, I'll see to that.'

'I told him not to expect to hid behind his money. If anything happens to Leah, I promised I'd find him and . . .' John broke off, seeing the appalled look on Nellie's face, and waved a hand as if to dismiss the seriousness of what he had promised Edgar Lacey. 'Anyway, he knows he has me to deal with.'

'John, don't make light of it.' Everyone's eyes were suddenly focussed on Nellie; her voice was quiet yet full of concern. 'It's dangerous to make an enemy of such a man.'

He laughed. 'I'm not tied to him for my living. What can he do?'

Nellie shook her head. 'I don't know, but I'm fearful.'

'No, no, Nellie, my old love,' he declared, jumping up and giving her a tremendous kiss on her cheek, 'never be fearful – not with all us men to protect you.'

'John White,' she declared, blushing, 'what would your Jane say!'

'She's probably saying it's time I started walking back. If I don't find a lift, it'll take me a couple of hours.'

Clarrie insisted he at least have tea and bread and jam before he set off. Then Leah and Ben walked with him through the village, past the church and on to the Leicester road.

All traces of the wedding were gone. Every last piece of rose-petal confetti, every last flower, had been scavenged by jubilant village children. Leah wished her memories of the day could be as easily dispersed.

Leah and Ben watched John go along the darkening road towards the town. 'It will be quite dark before he's gone far,' she said.

'I don't think that will worry John much.' He put his arm around her waist. They turned back, but before they reached the lights of the village street he drew her into a field gateway. 'It's been quite a day.'

She shivered, thinking of it all, and he unbuttoned his jacket, opening it for her to come into the warmth. A sense both of pleasure and of shyness came over her as she put her arms around his waistcoat, pushing her hands under it to feel his back through his shirt. He wrapped the jacket closely round her. 'You're so warm,' she breathed, looking up over his shoulder 'There'll be a moon in a minute. And . . .' She broke off with an exclamation. 'Why, there's snow coming! Look, Ben!'

Above them a myriad tiny twinkling flakes were drifting slowly, softly, down.

They stood fascinated, waiting for the snow to reach them. 'It's like looking into a different world.' she breathed, the moonlight on the flakes reminding her of the silver embroidery on Flavia Nubury's transparent silk veil. She lifted her face high, watched the first flakes touch Ben's hair, then felt the touch of cold and the thrill of wetness on her cheeks, and laughed up at him. 'It's on your eyelashes.'

'And on yours,' he whispered, bending his face to hers to kiss her. 'And on your cheeks and on your lips. I love you, Leah.'

'And I love you,' she said, taking a snowflake from his cheek with the tip of her tongue.

'Leah.' His voice was husky with emotion.

'It's stopped now – as quickly as it began.'

The snow cloud had passed and the rising moon showed ruthlessly each skeleton of tree, each bare field.

'What a strange day,' she murmured, 'all heights and depths. Nothing ordinary . . . nothing.'

'Nothing,' he repeated, closing his eyes as he clasped her to him, her innocence his pain.

Chapter Twenty

The weekend became a broken up bitty sort of time, with no one very settled to their chores. Every time they crossed each other's path, they could not help referring to Saturday's dramatic events, 'And another thing . . .' parting with trailing resolution, 'Well, we'll have to . . .'

Sam told them they were like a pack of old toothless dogs with a bone, getting nowhere. 'We have to finish our work. Ben has to go back to Derbyshire. And *we* all know we have to be more vigilant.'

Ben was still ill at ease on Monday morning as he breakfasted early with Leah and her family before leaving for the station. There was nothing very much left to say, and they all started violently as a sudden loud summons began on the front door. For a moment they looked at each other in astonishment. No one as far as Leah could remember had ever *knocked* on the front door. Front-door visitors were always expected and the door opened before they reached it.

As she ran from kitchen to parlour to answer, she wondered if it was about Ginnie. Had Charley brought an answer to the letter she had pushed inside one of the stockings? She peered through the window, saw a bicycle propped under it, and craning further towards the glass saw a youth in uniform. She ran the few steps back to the kitchen. 'It's a telegram boy,' she announced.

There was a concerted rise from the table. 'Are you sure?' Miriam asked. 'The nearest telegraph office is five miles away. You'd better open the door!'

Leah hurried back, followed by her grandmother and Ben. Hastily she drew aside the plush curtain and opened the street door.

The boy touched his cap. 'Telegram for Mrs Nellie Dexter,' he said, 'and could she sign, please?' He looked from one to the other, holding out the telegram in one hand and his pad and pencil in the other.

Miriam went to call Nellie, who came slowly, her face ashen.

'For me?' she asked. The boy touched his hat in acknowledgement and held out his pad. Nellie's hand shook as she signed in a round childish hand, and took the small brown envelope. She handed it to Ben. 'You open it.' He hesitated as if seeking approval from the other two, then eased open the flap, the envelope and message small in his hands. He read the contents silently and Leah saw his lips part in shock. 'What is it?' she asked.

'I think we'd better all go and sit down.' Without allowing any protest he shepherded them back to the kitchen, and waited until they were all seated. 'It's from Jane White's eldest son, Johnnie.'

'Johnnie?' Leah questioned, seeing in her mind the tall boy who uncomplainingly fetched and carried on the day of their picnic. Leah was aware of her mother hugging herself fearfully as Ben went on, 'His father has been found dead.'

'Dead!' She was not sure whether it was herself or others who repeated the word aloud. Shock lay like a crushing physical weight on them all. Ben placed the telegram on the table and smoothed it out with hands that trembled.

'Father found dead on road 2 am today.'

'Two o'clock this morning' Miriam queried.

'What would he have been doing out at that time?' Ben wondered. 'Where would he be going?'

'Home,' Nellie said quietly, 'he'd be going home – from here.'

'Oh, no, surely not?' Leah felt her heart marble cold. A link between John's death and what had happened after the wedding was more than she could contemplate. 'He went home on Saturday night, two days ago, mother.'

208

'Excuse me – only you left the door open.' All heads turned to see the telegram boy standing hesitantly between parlour and kitchen. 'I wondered if there was any reply?'

It was Ben who rose and motioned the telegram boy to sit down in his place and eat a slice of toast and dripping, and drink a cup of tea, while they composed an answer.

'I shall go to her,' Nellie decided.

'We'll come with you.' Leah looked across at Ben who nodded. 'We've fifteen minutes to catch the carrier.'

'All those children,' Miriam murmured.

In the end they sent the telegram boy away empty handed, deciding they would be in town almost as soon as an answer.

They found the back door of the Orchard Street house open to the bleak December morning and Jane White sitting at her kitchen table rapidly sewing buttons – odd buttons – on to small pieces of card. Huddled in the far corner were her children. The older ones had tear-stained faces, the younger looked bewildered and frightened, while Johnnie the eldest boy stood rigid and expressionless. Then, seeing who the visitors were, he came forward eagerly. His mother sewed a small brown button next to a large red one.

'Thank you for coming,' he said. 'I didn't know what to do.'

'Make some tea for us all, son,' Ben said as Nellie, holding out her arms to the younger children, was immediately overwhelmed by their need for a cuddle and reassurance.

Leah was appalled by Jane's obvious state of shock. She moved to the table, sat by her, tried to catch a hand as it reached for a button. Jane shook her off quite roughly.

Tea was made, the children given slices of bread and jam, and hot tea. 'Come on, Johnnie, we'll take this brood to see where they make bells. I bet none of you even know where it is?' Ben looked questioningly at Leah and Nellie who nodded their approbation of his idea. The children's coats were put on, and though some of the older ones attempted to speak to their mother first they went gladly.

Still the sewing went on; still they seemed unable to reach Jane in any way. She would neither look up, take a sip of tea nor speak to them.

'I know what she has lost, that's for sure,' Nellie said quietly. Then, as if not to distress herself and make matters worse, she began to tidy the room. She took the crockery to the back kitchen, and Leah heard her pouring water to wash up.

Leah sat next to Jane again, watched as first a blue button was sewn on to a new piece of card. Then, as Jane's hand reached haphazardly for the next, Leah pushed a matching button to her. Automatically, and seemingly without Jane's noticing, it was picked up and sewn on. Leah sorted four more of the same buttons from the mixed pile and put them in a neat square. This time the hand reached, hesitated, then went on. Leah began to sort the buttons and place the matching sets ready. Then another idea came to her. She reached over to a card Jane had already sewn with buttons in a medley of colours and sizes. She placed this alongside the matching sets.

Jane's hands slowed, then stopped. She looked up suddenly and voiced great long drawn out cries of anguish. 'Ooh! Ooh! Ooh!' repeated again and again. But her eyes saw how things really stood; saw Leah, and Nellie coming from her back kitchen; saw her loss. 'Oh, John, John! What can I do? How can I go on without him?'

She threw her head down on her arms pushing aside cards and buttons, sobbing. Tears coursed unheeded down all their checks, while Jane's sobbing increased until it seemed likely to crack her heart in two.

After a few minutes Leah became alarmed, and through her own stream of tears tried to quieten Jane. Her mother stayed her. 'No, let her be. This is the best thing.'

It went on so Leah felt she could hardly bear to listen. She put her own head on her arms, in despair as to what they would all do – then suddenly realised it was quiet, the sobbing had stopped. She sat up to see Jane resting on her arms across the table, eyes closed as if in sleep. 'Make some more tea,' her mother mouthed. She went about the task quietly, and when she brought it back to the table Nellie had Jane in her arms, the two of them crying still, but quietly.

'Take a drink,' Nellie said, 'then you must tell us what happened. If you say it out loud, it may help you understand too.'

210

Leah held her breath as she offered the cup, held it within Jane's reach, willing her to take it. At long last a hand came out, attempting to take the tea, but it shook so, Leah clasped the woman's hand and held all steady. Jane took one sip, no more than moistening her lips.

'Saturday morning John came to us at Tur Lecey,' Nellie prompted very quietly.

'I never saw him again.' Jane shook her head pitifully. 'Until they took me to the town mortuary.'

'No!' Leah had to fight to keep herself seated and behave with some degree of calm in the face of Jane's loss. 'But who found him, and where?'

'A drover found him – well, his dog did. He was in . . . a ditch . . . at the edge of town.' She paused, then added with a curious air of detached disbelief, 'He was nearly home.'

'But what had happened?'

'They said he had been knocked down – that was true. He had certainly been run over, by a heavy wagon.'

Leah closed her eyes as if to block out thoughts of the metal-rimmed wheels of the great wagons that plied their trade to and from town.

'How did you find out? Who came to tell you?'

Jane stared into space, her eyes bruised to a flat blankness, and for a moment both visitors thought she was going to lapse back into her trancelike state. Nellie questioned again, sharply: 'Who came for you, Jane? How did they know who John was, where he lived?'

'He had Sam's letter in his pocket, asking him to go over for the wedding.'

Leah felt as if she and her mother had exchanged deep meaningful glances, though neither looked at the other.

'What happened?' Jane asked. 'Why *did* that old man write to my John?'

Leah was surprised when her mother began in a simple, straightforward way to tell their part of the story. But she quickly realised it was right. There is a time to tell the whole truth, which if neglected never comes in quite the same way again. Leah took over when she reached the point where the wedding procession left the church. When she had finished,

211

Jane began nodding gently. They watched her silently for a long time.

'So there we have the truth of it,' she said at last. 'I always knew he would never die in his bed. He would *always* take up other people's causes – everybody's knight in shining armour, that's John – that *was* John. Now, he's no use to anyone – to me, to his children, nobody – though he's John Freeman alright!'

Leah felt the bitterness like a personal reproof. She shrank inwardly at the anger in Jane's voice, but it was better than the sobbing or her silence. The greatest shock for Leah to absorb was Jane's immediate acceptance that what had happened after the wedding *was* the cause of John's death. "So there we have the truth of it." So the conclusion was they were talking of a deliberate killing, of murder?

'No man is above the law, not Squire Lacey nor anyone else,' she said. 'He must be made to pay.'

Neither of the older women showed signs of having heard, and Nellie moved so as to screen Jane from Leah's sight, urging her to drink a little. 'Rest while you can, before the children come back,' she urged. Jane conceded by lying back in an old armchair. Leah was sent for a blanket, and it seemed in spite of herself Jane began to doze fitfully.

'She's worn out,' Nellie breathed, then drawing her daughter to the back kitchen began, 'There's a joint of meat she must have cooked . . .'

'Shouldn't I go and tell somebody?' Leah interrupted. 'Tell them everything?'

Nellie shook her head vigorously. 'You wait! I'm going to put some potatoes in the fire. The children can have those and some cold meat when they come back.'

'Waiting's not going to solve anything,' Leah began, and wished Ben would hurry back. When Jane woke the two older women seemed to her to be playing some game of make-believe, as if the meal was the most important thing in the world, playing at being busy, talking of the children.

They seemed to be away a long time. It was well into the afternoon before they heard the children returning. Ben brought up the rear of the group of boys and girls who regarded their mother first cautiously then with relief as she rose to help them off with their coats.

'We saw a bell being hammered out of its case. Bash! Bash!'

'And we went to the park with Johnnie.'

'We saw the prison.'

'It had a great wall as high as a church steeple.'

'And we 'ad jellied eels and licquorice root.'

'Oh, lovely!' Leah exclaimed with a shudder, but acknowledged what a relief it was to have children about, children whose mouths must be filled and whose very young lives would help fill the gap in the home.

'And we went to see the market manager. The stall's safe' Johnnie added. 'he says as far as he's concerned, I'm John Freeman now.'

'Women are not allowed to be registered stall-holders on the town market,' Ben explained. 'I learned that from Mr Champion, the bell-founder. In fact, I learned a lot from him.'

The words held the promise of much more, but it was obviously not information he intended giving out in front of all the children. It was not until they had all eaten and the younger ones been taken into the charge of a neighbour, just returned from her daily stint of step-scrubbing in the city, that the women were told all Ben had achieved in some three hours.

'First I went to the bell foundry. I saw the owner, Mr Lionel Champion. He arranged for the children to be shown round while I confided in him. I felt obliged to, not having gone back to Derbyshire for work today. That was quickly solved. He sent for his foundry foreman and he's going to Derbyshire for the next week to finish my job while I'm to take over his position here for the week.' Ben paused, his head lowered, and took a deep breath as if steeling himself for the grimmer part of the story. 'Jane?' he queried. 'Have they told you what happened?' He waited for her nod of assent before going on, 'I told all this to Mr Champion too. As soon as I mentioned Squire Edgar Lacey, he was vitally interested and most concerned. Lacey is recognised as one of the city's most exploitative industrialists, a man who buys his friends and uses them to his own ends.'

'While Johnnie took the children to the park, Mr Champion took me to the mortuary.' Ben paused and lowered his eyes. Only his determination to find out how John White had died had given him courage to request the visit, and now he did not wish any of the women, or John's son, to see a reflection of the experience in his face. For a start the building had been grim – a stark, windowless place, lit by a series of high barred arches near the roof. there were marble slabs, a stout locked door. He had thought it well placed with the town cemetery over the road, beyond that the cattle market and slaughter house.

'Champion is an alderman of the town,' he continued, 'and found the mortuary attendant's' position for him after he had been injured in a factory accident. He allowed us in.' The worst thing had been not recognising John. The shape beneath the sheet had not been in his living image: the face so pale, hair so lank, recognisable only with an effort.

'I doubt he knew anything about it,' he said, his voice betraying him by its gruffness as he pursued the matter to its bitter conclusion. 'He had received a terrible blow to the back of the head.' When he had asked if this had been noticed, the mortuary assistant said the doctor who had performed the post mortem had sent all the facts to the Coroner, who would decide whether or not there was to be an inquest – as he did with all sudden deaths. No one spoke, but Ben looked up to find Leah gazing intently at him as if urging him on to speak the logical conclusion.

'So I think we should go to the police and tell them what happened after the wedding,' he added. 'it would seem to me to be relevant evidence.'

'In a court, you mean? Oh, no,' Jane said, 'it'll do no good. I've seen such cases before. I don't want the agony of it. It won't bring my John back.'

'It will not, but isn't it what John would have wanted?'

'The truth brought out in the open?' Leah declared vehemently. 'Justice is blind, the law is the same for everyone.'

Nellie laughed disparagingly. 'You've a lot to learn!'

'So wasn't my father run over?' Johnnie questioned.

They had overlooked his ignorance of all the facts, and there was a moment's silence before Ben said quietly, 'We

214

believe he was attacked because he defied a very powerful man.'

'I think he died because he saved me,' Leah said.

'So he's a hero really? But what happened?'

The story was told again for his eldest son. 'So I think we should strive to prove what we suspect,' Ben urged, 'make sure there is an inquest.'

'Everyone should know, Mother,' Johnnie declared. 'He did stand up for lots of people . . .'

'Fighting to the end,' Jane said wearily. 'Yes, yes . . . the bitter end.'

'So I think Leah and I should go to the police right away. Mr Champion was of the same opinion. He's a man after John's heart, Jane. His life is spent fighting greed and malpractice within the town council. He calls Edgar Lacey the arch-enemy of the working man.

'Champion by name and champion by nature.' Jane's attempt at levity was more heartrending than any further protest. Young John went quickly to her side, putting his arm around her shoulders. 'That's right, Mother.'

'I expressed the same sentiment at the foundry,' Ben added wryly. 'It had obviously been voiced a few times before.'

'I really liked him,' Johnnie commented quietly, 'he was a kind man.'

'Now this is all very well, but we mustn't forget the carrier's cart leaves as five-thirty,' Nellie reminded Leah.

'Oh! I thought you would stay,' Jane said. For a second she looked so vulnerable, Leah wondered how she would ever manage if they left her alone so soon.

'They will be wondering at home . . .' Nellie said.

'If we write a note, we could catch the carrier's cart with it before we go on to the police station,' Leah suggested. 'But we'll have to hurry.'

'I'll show you the quickest way,' Ben said as the note was quickly composed.

Leah remembered some of the narrow streets from the first time she had visited John's stall. She recalled his bit of cheek with the women customers, remembered his saying: "A nimble ninepence is better than a slow shilling." For a moment tears blurred her vision and she stumbled. Ben immediately caught her arm. 'All right?' he asked. She nodded dumbly, suddenly overwhelmed by the enormity of what had happened, the price a man and his family had paid to save her.

They reached the old magazine gateway where all the country carriers gathered before returning to their various villages. Monday was not a particularly busy day, and Leah only just managed to stop the Tur Lacey man as he drew away a few minutes early.

'He'll take it to my grandmother as soon as he arrives,' she reported, adding, 'Now for the police station.'

'Just a moment,' Ben said, and drew her under a low stone arch. 'All this has made me realise we mustn't waste our lives, Leah, waiting and planning. Let's just marry. Let's make things happen for us.'

'Where would we live?' she asked, leaning against him, utterly weary, feeling she never wanted to let him go again but still asking, 'And how?'

'They say two can live as cheaply as one,' he said suddenly. 'And I could look out for you better.'

She looked up at him questioning. Was any of this more than wishful thinking? He bent and kissed her, a kiss that grew into a demand. She remembered she had left him when he had needed her before, and stood tiptoe to return his kiss, to reassure him that this time, whatever happened, they would go through it together.

The approaching ring of footsteps underneath the archway made them draw apart.

At the police station they approached the uniformed desk sergeant and said they wished to give evidence with regard to a sudden death. This introduction certainly gained his full attention, and he called to a constable to take his place while he ushered both of them to an inner office.

He listened to Ben's story, but shushed Leah when she tried to add details. 'But it's me he wants!' she exclaimed in exasperation.

'Is it indeed?' the Sergeant stated. 'And you both believe this is what this closed carriage was for?' He leaned back in his chair, a stout man whose neck bulged uncomfortably over his high uniform collar. 'Has this Edgar Lacey done you any real harm?' he asked. Then added sharply, 'Or has he ever *refused* you anything?'

'He stopped supplies of wool to our stockinger's shop,' Leah answered immediately.

'Ah, well.' The Sergeant sounded as if he now had the explanation of the story within his grasp.

'No, you don't understand. He did that because I . . . I . . . wouldn't do what he wanted. He said I need never work again.'

'The man has a reputation,' Ben began.

'You be careful what you say, unless you have witnesses who will stand up in court. Have you witnesses?' When there was no answer, he added, 'There's such a thing a defamation of character, you know.'

'But I can't believe John White's death was an accident,' Ben persisted.

'Look,' the Sergeant decided, 'you can sign statements, and I'll send them and a report to the Coroner's Office. You can say what you suspect about John White's death. I knew him, of course, from the market. Never did think he'd die in his bed.'

They were told that they would hear from the Coroner's Office direct as to the outcome.

'It sounded a stupid story,' Leah commented as they walked back to Orchard Street. 'It sounded as if we'd made it up out of spite.'

'I suppose it was a pity you mentioned the wool.'

'I know . . . now.

Notification that an inquest was to be held came the next day. Ben's opinion of the law rose a little.

Leah had imagined all courts to be packed with people, so it was a surprise when, two days later, they found themselves in a room where the court atmosphere seemed to have been scaled down in size. There was certainly a high chair behind a good heavy table, and a chair behind a rail which she assumed was the witness-box, and facing this on a long pew seven jurors. The seven men looked rather ill at ease, perhaps

217

wondering just what gory deails they were going to hear in court.

The coroner himself looked as ease but no less out of place, for his features met in the marketplace would have been taken for those of the quintessential outdoor man. Leah found herself judging him to be a gentleman who was regularly out with his hunt, a sportsman, probably with land on the side. She glanced sideways at Jane, sitting between Leah and her mother. Nellie had Jane's hand firmly grasped in her own.

A police officer gave evidence as to the finding and identification of John White's body. A doctor was called who gave details of what he considered to be the cause of death. 'The man had obviously been knocked down, then subsequently run over by a heavy wagon, suffering a heavy blow to the back of the head, and crushing to the lower chest.'

Jane screwed a handkerchief into a rag, her eyes never lifting from her lap. Leah felt Ben already half off his seat as one or two more medical details followed and the Coroner thanked the medical practitioner. She laid her hand on his sleeve and nodded towards the papers the Coroner was now consulting. She was sure they looked like the statements they had made at the police station.

'Is there any other evidence relevant to this man's death?' he asked.

Her heart bumped alarmingly as Ben got to his feet. 'I've made a statement . . .' he began.

The Coroner looked over his gold-framed spectacles. 'Benjamin Robertson' Ye-es' He picked up the papers again, considering. 'What did you wish to say?'

'Could I ask the doctor some questions?'

The police inspector made a few disapproving noises, but the Coroner reminded him that a properly interested person might be allowed to examine any witness. 'It is only the police who must not cross-question. This you must do through your counsel. Our task is to find out how, when and where John White came by his death. Dr Austen, would you mind . . .?'

Leah wondered if she imagined the touch of condescension and amusement in his voice as the Coroner dealt with Ben's request.

Ben waited until the doctor was again seated in the witness box, then asked, 'The blow to the back of the head – was it a heavy one?'

'Hmm, yes.' The doctor sat with crossed legs as if in his own consulting rooms, Leah thought.

'Did it seem to you the kind of blow a man would receive when being knocked down by a horse and heavy wagon?'

'A horse can cause more kinds of injuries than most people imagine. If the man slipped, the hoof of a shire horse could have split his skull open.'

'Was this injury made by a hoof?'

'Ah, well now . . .' The doctor uncrossed his legs and rested his hands on his knees, as if thinking hard. 'This injury *could* have been made by a hoof or a shaft. All I am sure about is that it alone did not cause death, and that it happened before the wheels passed over the body.'

'Do you think John White was struck over the head and thrown under the wheels of a passing wagon?'

'Hmm . . . the head wound was first, as I said.'

'But was it caused by the wagon?' There was a growing impatience in Ben's voice as the word game continued.

'But what else could it have been?' The doctor looked over at the jurymen. 'He certainly had not been robbed. His money was falling out of his pockets when I examined him.'

The Coroner interposed: 'So it is your opinion that all the injuries were sustained at the same time, and that the cause was the victim's being run down by a heavy wagon?'

'Hmm, yes, certainly.'

Leah watched the jurymen who had noticeably relaxed back in their seats when money falling from pockets had been mentioned. They had, it seemed to her, already made their decision.

'But our statements!' Ben exclaimed, gesturing in Leah's direction. 'What of that evidence?'

'Do you wish to take the oath and give evidence?' the Coroner asked.

'Yes,' Ben said without hesitation.

The story told in court seemed thin, and as the counsel for the police cross-questioned Ben, came to sound like a matter of personal spite directed against a wool factor who had refused work to the Dexter stockinger's shop.

Leah's heart wept for Ben as he tried to tell of Edgar Lacey's local reputation but was silenced by the Coroner, the healthy glow on his face beginning to be supplanted by an angry-looking flush.

'I would remind you, young man, that it is a misdemeanour in common law to obstruct the coroner and the jury in their duty to ascertain only how, when and where this person came by his death. I would advise you to hold your tongue before you find yourself answering charges before another court.'

Leah leapt to her feet. 'So one man dies and you threaten another with prosecution for trying to protect a woman from . . .'

'A fate worse than death! A male voice from the public seats in court provided.

'Yes – that's what I would call it, to be carried off by such a man,' Leah retaliated above a certain amount of laughter.

'Now, now,' the Coroner immediately interrupted, 'I will not have my court reduced to a place of public entertainment. Neither will I have it used as a platform for wild accusations. Sit down, both of you.' When neither moved he added, 'If you do not sit down immediately I shall have you forcibly removed from this court and consider charges to be brought against you both.'

'Please, leave it,' Jane pleaded, as several police constables readied themselves to obey the order. Leah suddenly wondered what would happen if Ben resisted. She could imagine the fight – hadn't she seen him in action? 'I think we're doing no good,' she said quietly, then turned and went back to her seat. Ben turned to look at the three women, and reluctantly followed.

There were a few more exchanges between police, their counsel and the Coroner before he summed up for the jury. He told them that the duty of a Coroner's Court was to ascertain solely who the person was, and how, when and where he came by his death. 'I would urge you to consider only those facts that relate to the cause of death. We have heard medical evidence, we have heard speculation and a little female hysteria. We have heard that John White certianly was not robbed.'

Leah had the feeling that the evidence hardly counted any more with the jury who had been subtly swayed against recording any verdict of murder. They did not even leave the jury box before the foreman stood up to announce a verdict of "Accidental Death" to the obvious approval of the Coroner who packed up his papers and dismissed the court.

A tall, imposing constable came over and introduced himself to Jane. 'I am the Coroner's Officer. If you would wait a moment, Madam, I have some of the deceased's effects I would like you to sign for.'

By the time he returned the four of them were alone in the court room. He went to the Coroner's table and produced a form for signature.

His huge hands then produced: 'One handkerchief and three buttons.' He placed a red and white spotted kerchief and three brown buttons before Jane. 'One letter.' The letter from Sam was placed next in line. Then, with a final conjurer's flourish, he ended: 'And one penny, one florin, and . . . five guineas.' The coins were placed on top of the letter.

None of them had expected a further shock that day. Jane's hands shook as they hovered above John's possessions. Her fingers circumvented the gold coins and closed over the three buttons. 'John never had a guinea in his pocket in his life,' she said.

There was some controversy over her refusal to pick up the guineas. 'Many wives do not know *everything* about their husbands.' The Coroner's Officer sounded almost belligerent.

'I know who it belongs to, I'll return it,' Ben said, sweeping up the gold coins.

Chapter Twenty One

'I'm not going to let my girl spend the rest of her life worrying about that lecher! And I don't want to feel afraid every time I move away from her side.'

Lionel Champion tucked in his chin and regarded Ben over his half spectacles, like a doctor making a diagnosis. 'Ben, I can help you only if you stay inside the law. I've kept you on as a labourer until there's a chance to use you again as a master bellmaker, but I can't . . .'

'No, no, you've done more than any of us had a right to hope. It's helped Jane White having me lodge with her, and with Christmas so near Leah comes every week and sells a few fancy socks and gloves on the stall, so that helps too.' He paused, twirling his work-cap between his hands.

'Tell me just one thing and no more: how did you know Edgar Lacey had returned from Paris?'

'I went into his factory office and asked.'

'Simple but effective.' Lionel Champion laughed then rose from his desk and put a hand on Ben's shoulder. 'And you're needing a day off in the middle of the week . . . I'll ask no further. Just remember, I don't want to lose you now. I know a true bellman when I see one!'

Ben returned to the furnace room where a cast had just been finished. Before the furnace cooled, his work was to remove all the residue of metal and clinker, a task Cuddy would have been set to at home. He doned an extra leather apron, added sacking to his legs and arms. Like preparing to meet the devil on his own ground, he thought, but his mind was on Edgar Lacey. He would be pleased to sweat to that end.

He started work with the long-handled scraper, keeping behind the protection of the wall as much as he could and still reach into the glowing interior of the furnace. Living under cover, concealing identities . . . he had planned for that too. The market men who were eager to help must be protected. He was determined that the only victim of his scheme would be Lacey.

A pile of glowing debris soon collected near his feet, where it quickly lost its redness, cooling to black and grey. He acknowledged the devil within himself as he hoped to see Edgar Lacey lie just as broken, rejected and useless.

It had been at John White's funeral that the possibility of organising real retaliation against the Squire had first occurred to him. The central church of St George's in the Market, by ancient custom the place of worship of all the traders, had been full. There had been a heartwarming resonance to *Abide With Me* and *Now the Day is Over* as voices more used to shouting their wares from their stalls joined in mutual grief for the loss of one of their own. The Vicar of St George's summed up their feelings. 'This man, generous and caring, big in heart, untimely ripped from life.'

As they had waited to file from the church Miriam had echoed Ben's thoughts when she said that most of the men seemed built like "sides of houses." Nellie commented she had never seen so many children at a funeral, but the women managed them with brisk efficiency, reminding Ben of the way a nod of assent had a market purchase wrapped before there was time for second thoughts.

After the committal in the churchyard, Ben had encouraged a silent Leah to go ahead with the other women to the church hall where the market people had provided the funeral repast. Some of the men had lingered, obviously anxious to talk to young John and Ben. These strapping chaps, used to hauling down and putting up their stalls and humping their stock backwards and forwards, were more than anxious to know the full story.

Ben, having pondered what one man alone might do, had seen in their clenched fists an anger he could use, and asked if he might meet some of them the following night. He was invited to the market tavern, to an upstairs room used for Lodge meetings, where they would not be disturbed or overheard.

'What happened to the five guineas?' There had been some recrimination as one beefy trader greeted the end of Ben's story with that question. Ben put his hand in his pocket and placed a single coin on the table. 'The other four I've given to young John against any family emergency. This one . . .' He paused to look round at the other five men, wondering if he was wise to go on and tell what he planned.

'Spit it out! We want to help grind this man into the dust too.'

'This one I plan to return.' While he had brooded alone over what he might do, his ideas had seemed wild and unworkable. But by the time he had met with the market men a second time, the scheme was planned in detail. Ben made one visit to Church Lacey, and all was arranged for the time Edgar Lacey returned from his post wedding trip.

Now the day was come. If justice loaded its scales with the money of the rich, he and the market men were now prepared to put a weighty thumb on the opposite pan.

They left the town early the next morning in a wagon belonging to Joe, a fruiterer, his name on the tailboard concealed by a large sack. Ben directed them through the cold and deserted December countryside, where hoar frost thickened every twig and the light was no more than grey. From the road they turned on to the grassed over bridle road to Flaxhill. Here the wagon was taken between the walls of a roofless shed. The horse was watered at the nearby stream then tethered in the church porch, with a net of hay to keep it quiet.

The men then set off at intervals in pairs to walk to Church Lacey. Two were to station themselves in the field behind the cowman's cottage where there was a convenient barn, two would approach the village cautiously from either end, and two – including Ben – were to make their way via the back door into Jessie Haddon's cottage. She had listened solemnly when Ben had come to ask about the Squire's visits to the renovated cottage opposite then said with great certainty that he would resume his Wednesday visits to his cowman's wife as soon as he returned home. 'Set your clock by him,' she had told Ben. 'Come eleven o'clock Wednesdays he'll be here.' She had paused before adding, 'And you can wait for him here in my cottage. Twenty years ago my sister hung herself because of that man . . . she was fifteen.'

Well before time, they were all in place. If Jessie Haddon felt anything other than glee at their impending attack on the most influential man in the neighbourhood, she certainly did not show it. 'I've everything I promised ready.' She nodded to a large can near the fire. 'Warm enough to spread easy,' she told them, 'and there's two old brushes, and that's the other.' She dropped a ticking full of feathers on to the table.

'Listen!' she said a few minutes later, forefinger raised. Ben and Joe leaned near her closed front door to hear the sounds of the church clock mingle with those of her kitchen timepiece as both struck eleven, followed by the noise of a horse coming at a brisk trot along the street.

'Give him about ten minutes,' Jessie said. She went to stand at the side of her window. 'There,' she reported, 'the curtains have been drawn.'

'He don't waste no time,' Joe commented, almost with a tinge of admiration to his voice.

'He didn't with John White!' Ben said.

Jessie made a token pass of the tar can over the fire. 'This is for my sister, Deborah.' Then she indicated a pile of hoods she had made from a flour sack. 'There's your head covers.'

'No one must see us go from here,' Ben said, handing Joe half the hoods and taking three himself. 'We go out of the back door, over the fields a way before we head to the road again. You make your way to the barn, put on the hoods, and wait for my *second* call.'

Joe nodded over the road. 'See you inside.'

Jessie saw them to her kitchen door. Ben caught her arm and kissed her briefly on the cheek as he thanked her. 'If there's any trouble afterwards, you'll let me know at once?'

She nodded, then asked: 'And you'll give me a call just now if you're successful?'

'We will be,' he said with a confident grin that made her pat his arm in motherly anxiety.

'Good luck,' Joe breathed as they both pulled on their hoods and separated as they reached the road. Ben gave the first call, the twice repeated extended crow of a cock, then went across to stand near the spot where John had helped load the old straw. He haad time to notice that the new thatch still had a golden glow to it even in the dull December morning – then the other two men were with him.

'Anyone about?' he asked.

'Narry a soul,' one whispered. The oother shook his head. He handed them their hoods, then nodded towards the front door. With utmost stealth they scaled the low garden wall, crossed the grass and regrouped under a new latticed porch. He grasped both their forearms, questioning if they were ready. The answering nods were eageer. Ben stepped just outside the porch, lifted his head and gave the second call.

Almost immediately there was the sound of someone opening the rear door. He did not need to give any further instruction. His men were already through the front door.

For a moment he felt a touch of comic hysteria as his hood slipped sidewards and he could not see. He pulled the slits back level with his eyes and followed Joe up the stairs. In seconds they were in the bedroom, viewing the Squire's bare hairy backside as he drove home into the moaning woman. All six men were in the room as the strokes finished. Ben felt ashamed as momentarily he felt sexually stirred himself, then he noticed how the man's hands were clawed into her shoulders like cruel talons.

Their mutual pleasure had deafened them to the presence of the hooded men. It was the stockman's wife who saw them first over the Squire's bare shoulder. She let out a cry of terror which made Edgar Lacey raise himself with a half articulated: 'What?' He saw the six huge hooded men, two either side, two at the bottom of the old limed oak half-tester, and looked as if he thought he had woken in hell with devils round his bed.

'What's this?' the Squire demanded. 'What's this?' It was difficult, Ben thought, to assert your authority naked as the day you were born. He moved forward Mrs Wilson rolled defensively on to her stomach; Lacey scrambled up on to his haunches on top of the pillows.

'What do you want? How much. . .?' he began, but Ben held up a reproving finger, taking the guinea from his pocket exhibiting both sides to the Squire, then placing it ceremonisouly on top of the man's riding breeches. Then he nodded. The group, drilled to a man, closed in on the bed.

Mrs Wilson whinnied with fear, but Joe caught her arm and urged her to get up from the bed, passing her and a bundle of clothes into the care of the man next to him who signed a warning finger over his shrouded lips. Mrs Wilson clasped her clothes with one hand and clamped the other over her own mouth as she was led downstairs.

Edgar Lacey was standing on the pillows now, casting speculative glances at both the door and the window. Ben shook his head at him. 'I'll pay! I'll pay!' the man cried. 'Anything.'

Ben found it difficult to keep the pact of silence they had sworn to and with a motion of his hands urged the action on.

Ryan the market butcher produced a filthy rag from his pocket. As the others grabbed a limb each and dragged Lacey back down on to the bed, Ryan thrust the rag into the man's mouth and bound it there with an old scarf. Ropes brought for the purpose tied him spread-eagled and helpless to the bedposts.

They took turns then with the paint brushes and the tar. They daubed his private parts, and as he tried to twist away, his buttocks then his torso. Ben remembered John, remembered Jane White's widowhood, Leah's ordeals, and took satisfaction in the terror in the man's eyes. Then he started as someone broke their vow of silence. Joe, tipping the last of the tar from the can into Lacey's crutch, growled, 'If we have to come again, it'll be hot. The third time, it'll be boiling.'

The feathers seemed almost an unnecessary embellishment, but not wishing to carry the full sack away again Ben shook them out on to the tar. Immediately what had been naked and an almost fearful desecration became comical. The hen feathers were a prudent mixture of brown Rhode Island, White Leghorn and black Bantam, and made the man look as if dressed for the part of an outlandish pantomime bird.

Ben sensed laughter under the other hoods and picking up can, brushes and sack, urged them away. He gave a loud and victorious crow for Jessie and Deborah as they left the cottage, but they were halfway across the fields towards Flaxhill before he let them pause properly for breath.

'I wonder how she liked her feathered friend?'

'What a terrible thing to do to a man!' Ryan exploded with laughter.

'He'll know what it's like to be plucked!'

'Though we've hardly hurt him at all,' Ryan said regretfully. 'We didn't really give him a hiding.'

'I think he'll be sore enough.'

'He won't be feeling very fruity for a time,' Joe said. 'I'll never be able to see tar and feathers again without seeing . . . and y'know what, lads? I reckon as how these high and mighty folk look just the same as anyone else without their trousers.' He shook his head as if in astonishment at what they had done and seen – and they all laughed until they hurt.

Chapter Twenty Two

While our days last may we walk in your ways.
Before our night comes help us all wrongs to mend.

* * *

God bless the rich and care for the poor.

* * *

A merry Chirstmas then to you, my dearest friend,
And a happy New Year to follow after.

The words of the printed Christmas card were over-pious,
and yet seemed to link with the note she had written to
Ginnie. She added, "All my love, and a great wish to come
and care for you, Leah."

She took up the note, staring at it without seeing the actual
words, rather reviewing in her mind the possible effects on
Ginnie should it reach her, and should she read it. It was
hardly a festive message to say that Nat and Ben were now
enemies, each blaming the other for her troubles, and that
Ben had left home. She focussed instead on the end of her
note. "I know we *all* love you, Ginnie, and need you to make
us whole – to make *our* matters mend."

She was still undecided whether to include the note when
she heard Ben's voice calling from the staircase. It would have
to do. She folded the note, sealed it in the envelope with the
card. They intended to catch Charley Hobbday as he fetched
water for the brewhouse from the village pump. Poor
Charley, caught in this routine chore, had little chance of
escape. When she had waylaid him the last time he had told

her that he and David were trying to persuade their father to let them go and visit Ginnie before Christmas.

'I'm coming,' she answered as Ben called again, but the next moment there was a tap on her door and he was inside.

The sight of him standing in her bedroom, his back to the door, made her heart pound. He seemed so much bigger in that confined space and for a moment she was overwhelmed by the idea that he had come to take her from the narrowness of her childhood bed straight to the marital chamber. She stood up quickly. 'I've written the Christmas card for Ginnie.'

'Good.' He came nearer, took her in his arms.

'Where's Mother and . . .'

'Both having instruction on the looms from Sam. We're quite safe.'

Safe was not what she felt. The bed that had seemed so narrow when he first came through the door, now loomed so large she found it difficult to look anywhere and not have it within view.

'Leah . . . what we were saying under that archway in town. Could we set a date to marry? Something definite to aim for? Christmas seems a good time to broach the subject with your family – while I'm here for them to scrutinise.'

'You know there's no need for that,' she laughed. 'They all approve. Can't wait to get you in the family!'

'And you?'

'Me?' She felt herself blush. 'I love you more than anyone else in the whole wide world.'

'But?'

'There's many buts, aren't there? Sam is far from well, and there are three other women in the two cottages – I couldn't leave them to fend for themselves. They need me.'

'I wouldn't want you to. They'd become part of my responsibility too.' He broke off as she shook her head resignedly. 'What is it?'

'The Squire told me ages ago that you would never be able to support all the women of my family.'

'The Squire!' Ben gave a hoot of derisive laughter. 'You don't have to worry about him any more.'

By the time the story was told the two of them were sitting on the edge of the bed together. 'That's what you were telling

Sam!' She suddenly recollected coming upon the two of them laughing in the workshop. They had refused to tell her what it was about. 'I hope there's been no come back on Jessie Haddon?' she said anxiously.

'She came to Orchard Street last week when she made her annual Christmas visit to town. She said the Squire rode away, somewhat awkwardly, two hours later. The cowman's wife has apparently come into some money and she and her husband are moving further south to a new position.'

Leah laughed with relief and astonishment, feeling as if a great weight of tyranny had slipped from her. No more looking over her shoulder every time she heard a horse. What had seemed impossible had been accomplished – at least the man had not escaped unpunished. She lay back on the bed, throwing her arms up over her head, and looked at him with new respect. 'Ben Robertson, I thought tarring and feathering belonged to the Middle Ages.'

'So do men like the Squire,' he said, and leaning over her trapped her arms with one of his, then kissed her gently on the forehead, cheeks, then her lips. 'Leah, I love you,' he breathed intensely, leaning down to rest his head gently against her breasts. 'Don't keep me waiting too long.'

How easy it would be to just give myself, to love him . . . Her mind threw up a picture of Ginnie laughing and chattering on about men. How easy to get oneself into trouble . . . like Ginnie.

'We'll see what the family say come Christmas,' she said huskily. Then was so completely overwhelmed by the look of joy that came to his face, she felt sure that with very little extra persuasion she would have succumbed entirely. But now it seemed he was content. His next kiss was hearty, almost comradely – and perversely not at all what she desired. 'Come on,' he said, 'let's go and find Charley Hobbday.'

It had not been with any great hope that Leah had given the card into Charley's hands, but on the last market day before Christmas she noticed his eldest brother, David, lingering near the village square. She wondered if he might have any news for her, but was surprised when as soon as he saw her coming he strode purposefully to meet her.

'I have a message from Ginnie,' he said without preamble.

'Oh!' Leah stopped in her tracks. 'How is she?'

David shrugged at this question. 'I didn't know her – at first,' he said quietly, turning and beginning to retrace his steps.

Leah hurried and caught his arm. 'Is there anything we can do? Could I go to see her? Just tell me where she is, I'll get there.'

'I'm not sure . . .' he answered, and she felt stricken by the sorrow in his eyes. 'Her message is that neither Nat nor Ben Robertson is responsible for . . . her condition. She broke her silence after she had read your note. It was obviously a terrible shock to her that such a thing had ever been suspected. But –' he paused and shook his head, as if in complete mystification, '– there's something that stops her saying more. It seems like torture to her even to think about it. That's why I'm not sure about anyone else going to see her. I fear for her . . . for her peace of mind, her sanity even.'

They both stood watching as the carrier's cart drew into the village square. 'I don't know how much it helps, but I thought you should know as soon as possible.'

'It may bring two brothers together in time for Christmas!' she told him. 'when I get to town, I shall go straight to Ben's workplace.' Though she immediately thought of it when talking to David, she mentioned neither to Ben nor anyone else that she also intended to go to the Robertsons' foundry to tell Nat.

The very next morning, on the pretext of putting in an extra tally-round before Christmas, she set off for the Robertsons'. There was no way she was going to let this festive season pass without both brothers knowing what Ginnie had said.

She made her usual early morning start, adding to the tally-sack a pair of the new gloves which, if the opportunity arose, she would give to Ben's mother as a Christmas present.

It was with a hollow feeling in the pit of her stomach that some two hours later, she approached the old Georgian house set to one side of a square of outbuildings. Towards the back was an orchard, while beyond that was garden ground fringed by a small spinney, as Ben has described to her.

She stood for a moment, shivering in the wind that had a touch of ice in it. She wondered if she was making a mistake, for she had encountered no one she could enquire of. Then the breeze brought the smell that was so familiar from Ben's clothes: a sandy yet metallic mixture. This, she reminded herself, was likely to be one of the few things that was familiar for so far she had not met his mother, step-father or grand-father. Her courage was in grave danger of failing and it would have been easy to have turned on her heel and gone about her tally-round.

Ben's reception of the news the day before had been rather non-committal. He had said he never believed Nat had taken advantage of Ginnie anyway, and he *knew* he was not respon-sible. But she expected a more positive reaction from Nat. She understood that Ben would not go to the Robertsons' foundry, but there was nothing to stop Nat coming to her home to see Ben over Christmas . . .

She concentrated on thoughts of Christmas with the two brothers friends again, and not her own misgivings, as she walked up the lane to the house. As she drew nearer she was aware of a man's voice shouting. there was a familiarity about that voice. She remembered it had been at Soston she had first heard those deep irritated tones as Caleb Berridge had be-rated his step-sons. Though she had never seen the man, she was well prepared to dislike him as soon as she set eyes on him.

She hoped she might see Mrs Berridge first, but just as she was passing the first of the foundry outbuildings Cuddy came hurrying around the corner, pushing a wheelbarrow heavy with black sand. He looked completely nonplussed to see her, and his obvious concern dried up both her greeting and her question. She felt the same look of panic must have been reflected in both their faces. She should not have been there and he knew it, but even so he gestured back the way he had come, as if urging her on to whatever purpose she had.

Her throat felt so dry she had diffiuclty in swallowing, and Cuddy had trundled his barrow away about his work before she regained her voice. For goodness' sake, what could they do to her! this was for Ben – and Nat if he did but know it – and somehow it was for Ginnie too, a first step towards the truth.

As she turned the corner she came to the doorway of the furnace-room and realised that a bell had just been cast, for slung on girders and chains above a bell mould was a huge cauldron from which the last of the golden metal was trickling. The air in the building was full of gases and steam but she recognised Nat standing to one side, holding that ill-fated willow branch, while a tall old man stood on planks above the mould, stirring a metal rod in its neck. The ore from the cauldron slowed and stopped, and as it was swung back to its upright position a man's bulky figure emerged through the steam, the wisps of moisture seeming to cling around his form – as they had done the night Leah had seen this same figure emerge from the evening mists of Soston!

She stood staring, her mind shaken, rattled, like a malcontent child's kaleidoscope. The pieces fell into a new pattern. One so novel, so unexpected, she could not at first make it out, could not believe it. The form, the voice . . . And yet! this sudden revelation made sense of the whole. She started forward, seeing all the truth – all the reason for Ginnie's silence. Her sudden movement distracted the men. She heard Nat's surprised ejaculation of her name, but she had eyes only for Caleb Berridge.

'You're the man!' she accused. 'You! Nat's step-father. No wonder Ginnie would not talk! No wonder she could not tell! You revolting beast!'

Nat was at her side now, and she smelt the ore on his clothes as he instinctively restrained her from rushing at his step-father. 'No wonder Ginnie threw off the jacket that smelt like *your* clothes.'

For a moment the man had come forward aggressively. Now he stood back, uncertain.

'I came to bring you a message, Nat.' she said, though her gaze was over his shoulder, pinioning the older man with her accusation. 'No I bring you an answer too. The message was from Ginnie Hobbday, my friend, whose life was ruined by some man after I left her outside Soston churchyard. The message was that neither you nor your brother are responsible for her unborn child. The answer. . .' Nat moved so he too could see Caleb's face as Leah pointed. The man made as if to side-step them both and make for the door. 'The answer is that it was your step-father who forced my friend.' Tears threatened to drown her voice but she did not care. She could cry and be angry.

'What's this?' The man on the planks used the metal rod to steady himself.

'Stand still, Grandfather. I'll help you down in a minute.'

'Go away, girl,' Caleb began to bluster, but Leah cut his words off with a withering cry of exasperation.

'Oh, no, I saw you that night! I didn't know who you were then . . .' She paused, shaking her head as if her very palate was soured. 'But you're that . . . creature. Look at him! See his guilt!'

'My God,' Nat breathed, and for a second there was awe in his voice, the awe that recognises extremes – and before him stood a perfect example of consummate evil in a man. His fingers tightened on the willow branch, and at that moment Leah felt it would have been just if revenge had been wrought with it. 'I'm going to kill you,' Nat stated.

'Nat!' his grandfather appealed. 'Don't do anything you'll regret!'

Caleb grabbed a metal stickle and flailing it around made for the door – just as Cuddy re-appeared with the empty wheelbarrow. As Nat raced to detain him, Caleb sidestepped the wheelbarrow, raised the stickle and struck down the man who inpeded his escape.

Cuddy half fell, half stayed himself in the doorway, then swayed back into Nat's arms. Leah was by Nat's side as he half dropped, half lowered, Cuddy to the ground, as if his will divided him between chasing the guilty and tending the innocent.

Then they both exclaimed as they saw the long jagged wound down the side of Cuddy's face, while he rocked like a child and attempted to cover the injury with his hands. Even as they tried to assess how serious the cut was, Nat muttered, 'It's true. That was why . . .' He broke off with a groan.

Leah gripped his arm as he lifted and cradled Cuddy. 'It all makes sense,' she breathed. For a moment their glances met. She saw at one and the same time the vulnerable eyes of the summer youth who loved paddling, and the opaque winter-ice of vengeance. 'Go before me to the house,' he ordered. 'Once I have Cuddy inside . . .'

Before they reached the house, the door was opened. 'Where's your *husband?*' Nat's lips twisted in scorn as he carried their injured workman into the kitchen. The older woman shook her head at him then exclaimed over Cuddy's wound, asking, 'He's done this?'

'And much more,' Nat growled, trying to coax Cuddy to let his wound be looked at.

'There's lint and iodine.' She directed Leah to a long cupboard by the kitchen range.

'Will you manage?'

His mother nodded, then added a questioning: 'Nat?'

'I'm going to find my step-father. Leah will tell you the full story.' He left the kitchen. Through a window Leah saw him meet his grandfather, and both went around the house.

Eventually, by dint of giving Cuddy a piece of a cold apple pie and the promise of a mug of milk afterwards, they were able to clean and staunch the wound.

'I think he should be taken home,' Mrs Berridge said tentatively, 'but we'll have to see what Mr Berridge says first.'

'I shouldn't think Mr Berridge will ever . . .' Leah began aggressively, but seeing the incomprehension and alarm on this meek-looking woman's face, she disciplined her tongue. She instructed Cuddy to sit quietly while she and Mrs Berridge had a talk. She began by introducing herself.

'My Ben's girl.' Mrs Berridge whispered the words, but her face was alight with pleasure as she leaned forward and took Leah's hands, and again in no more than a whisper added, 'Love him well, he's a good man – and Nat says how he loves you truly. My blessing to you, my dear.'

The sincere if furtive nature of her approval made the story harder to tell, but it was time for the truth. Leah described Ginnie first. How the four of them had been friends together all summer, how Nat and Ginnie had found they loved each other. The woman sat very still until Leah came to what had just taken place in the foundry. At that Mrs Berridge closed her eyes, and only the tightening of her clasped hands indicated she had heard at all. Then the door of the kitchen opened and Nat and his grandfather returned.

'We can't find him,' Nat began, then glanced at Cuddy. 'Is he all right?' he asked as his mother said something.

'Caleb's upstairs,' Mrs Berridge repeated. She sat as before but now her eyes were open, her voice more resolute as she again repeated, 'Caleb's upstairs.'

'Mother?' Nat knelt swiftly before her, as if needing some further sanction before he could act. She nodded vehemently and he leapt to the staircase.

'Mabel?' Josiah said as if questioning the wisdom of his daughter's revelation.

She shook her head at the frail old man. 'Father, this is too much.'

Leah realised she was witnessing something like a sea-change; blind loyalty had finally been eroded away by this tide of events. The meek wife was stepping out of the shadow of her husband and passing judgement for another woman. Leah went to her side and put her arm around the woman's tense shoulders as they listened to Nat going from room to room, and waited for the clamour of discovery. She understood now why Mrs Berridge had spoken in whispers, but was not sorry there had been time for Nat to bring himself a little more under control and to discard the willow branch. She worried instead whether Mr Berridge might not have found some weapon, and now be lying in wait for his stepson. Her glance went to Cuddy who lay curled up on the settle by the fire, cradling his face and rocking himself gently. But in a short time Nat called down: 'He's gone! Come and see!'

Leah followed Mrs Berridge and her father up the stairs and through the bedrooms, with Nat pointing to an open back window above a lean-to roof. 'That's the way he went,' he said, adding as he led the way to the main bedroom, 'And he's not gone empty handed.'

'No,' Mrs Berridge examined her jewel box, 'but there was nothing of great value there.' Then she pointed to where a brick stood slightly proud in a white-washed alcove near the window. Going to it she pulled it free and felt behind. 'But he's taken all the money there was in the house.'

'All the foundry money?' Josiah queried.

'It was all kept there.'

'He can't have gone far,' Nat said with renewed resolution. 'I'll get the horse . . .'

They followed him downstairs, but he was back from the stable immediately. 'It's gone,' he told them, 'and the orchard gate open. He must have led it away over the grass.'

'You'll not catch him on foot now,' his mother began practically, then implored, 'Let him go, Nat.'

'I hope he never comes back. I hope I never see him again in the whole of my lifetime,' Josiah said, his hands and body trembling as he sat down next to Cuddy. He patted the young man reassuringly on the knee. 'You can stay here. We'll look after you.'

'If he ever comes back, I shall leave,' Mabel said.

'I wanted you to do that many years ago,' her father wearily endorsed. 'Endurance is one thing, but when it is to no good end . . .'

'It was to keep you and my sons together.' She paused then recollected, 'Ben doesn't know any of this.' Nat rose suddenly and went outside.

'Go to him, girl,' Josiah said. 'He shouldn't be alone for a time.'

Following, Leah heard Nat before she found him. She went to him quickly, put an arm around his shoulders as he heaved and retched. 'Oh, Nat, don't! Don't' she pleaded. 'it's over now. The truth is out.'

'The truth!' He wiped his mouth on his sleeve. Leah slipped her arm around his waist and led him to an old bench she could see in a solitary outbuilding. 'It seems to me it would be better kept buried. How will Walter Hobbday feel when he learns the truth? Will it help him?' she watched the bitterness twist Nat's lips.

'I think it's better than rumour and gossip,' she ventured.

'My God, when I think of Caleb – think of it being his child . . .' He swallowed hard, as if bile again rose to his throat.

'But it is still Ginnie. Ginnie forced to be a mother to the child whether she wills it or not – unless she frets herself to death, which is what her brothers fear she may do. Not speaking, hardly eating . . .' She paused to look at Nat who

238

sat with his head despairingly in his hands, and added with heavy emphasis, 'And it in no way her fault.'

He did not answer, only dug his fingers further into his hair as if he would tear it from its roots.

She felt only impatience with him now as he repeated his intention of finding and killing his step-father.

'That won't help Ginnie,' she said bluntly, thinking he must know what would and waiting for him to say it – but he did not. She had heard before of women abandoned by "faithful" suitors and husbands because they had been raped; men who "loved" until some other man ravished.

The silence continued for a long time. Only the wind keened and whined, finding the chinks in their shelter. Nat still clasped his head in his hands, Leah still waited for him to make some generous suggestion towards the blameless Ginnie, but in the end she could sustain hope no longer. 'I thought you would want to go to see Ginnie, let her know that you still cared.' She gave him the benefit of a few more seconds, but he gave no sign. It was a bitter moment as she added, – 'I understand now why she has kept silent. She must have known there was no room in your heart . . .'

She left him, and without returning to the house collected her tally-sack from where she had dropped it in the foundry and walked away without a backward glance.

As she marched towards Tur Lacey her disappointment in Nat grew to a fury against the way women and girls were preyed upon and tyrannised by men both inside and outside marriage. She worked herself into such a fever she had to pause and rest to let her mind pursue its own quarrel for she could not deny there were good marriages, good men – her own father, Ben, Sam, John.

'Yes, yes, all right!' she exclaimed aloud. 'But poor, poor, Ginnie! I can't bear it!'

Nat knew beyond any doubt she was blameless – and yet it seemed he would do nothing, or that his love was not after all so great.

She walked on, her thoughts turning ever on the same theme of man's injustice to woman, so she hardly noticed her way. She certainly did not plan any action, but as she reached the main street and saw the lights on in the Stockinger's Arms, she walked straight inside.

As she approached the counter Walter Hobbday raised an arm and pointed imperiously back towards the door. She carried on and David, standing next to his father, recognised the unstoppable when he saw it. 'Not in the bar, Father,' he said, and raised the flap of the counter. 'Come through,' he invited.

Leah strode on with slackening pace. Reaching the room behind the bar, she swung round to expose the truth.

David heard it all on his feet, Walter Hobbday slumped into a chair. When she had finished she looked from one man to the other. 'Nothing to say – and probably nothing you'll do – it seems to be the general reaction from *men*'

She let herself out of the room, through the flap and out past the few gaping customers, taking a deep breath of the fresh air beyond.

She was halfway home when she heard footsteps behind her and her name being called. David came breathlessly up to her and pushed a piece of paper into her hands. 'It's where Ginnie is,' he said.

Chapter Twenty Three

The address had gradually yellowed, tucked into the corner of her dressing-glass. A winter of frustration, thought Leah. She had written, of course, after she and Sam had "debated" the situation shortly before Christmas.

'What do you want me to say?' he had asked. 'Go on, go, be away from your mother and Ben – and everyone else – for Christmas?'

She had not answered, wishing she could tear herself in two, half stay, half go.

'There are times in life when choices also mean sacrifices.' He had looked at her hard and added, 'If there were prizes for glowering, you'd win.'

'If there were prizes for just talk, *you'd* win!' she had retorted – and repented it immediately. 'No, I'm sorry, Sam. I didn't mean that. Not with . . .' Her gesture had been towards the work strewn everywhere, a "trial order" for a dozen pairs of stockings on a sale or return basis from the Prestwich Golf Club. 'You know I don't,' she had added lamely, but knew she had hurt the old man, and must some time make speical reparation.

Choice was ruled out after Christmas. Ben journeyed back to town in the beginnings of a blizzard which in twelve hours cut Tur Lacey off even from its immediate neighbours.

Then came a time of blue skies and brilliant sun. During the day men laboured to dig a way through drifts five, six and more feet deep, eyes screwed tight against the glare from the snow, but come the nights the wind rose and seemed to take a malicious pleasure in blowing it all back again. Then more snow. For many weeks there was no point in writing letters for the mail stayed in the post-box. The village became a closed community, supplies short. The children were excited by the snow and the strangeness, but old folk meeting in the street shook their heads and spoke of "the bad old days", when nobody knew nor cared that folk were half fed and a quarter clothed.'

The mill was cut off and Miriam decided she would winnow and pound the grain they had gleaned in the autumn. Leah punching up at one of the sacks, released the smell of sun-dried straw, and remembered how they had all been together, all sung on the way home, John leading. She saw again the way Ginnie had tipped her head over on to Nat's shoulder.

But Nat had not even come to see his brother at Christmas. Ben had made excuses for him, saying he probably dared not leave the foundry in case Caleb went back. Leah felt he had neither humanity nor imagination enough to reach out to Ginnie. Perhaps, she thought darky, only another woman could understand.

And though they talked of their own wedding, Leah found she could not think of setting a date until she had seen Ginnie. 'We always promised we would have a double wedding, so at the very least I could never be married without her there.' The silence around the dinner table at her announcement had been heavy with doubt, and the matter was left with Leah gaining approval to go to Ginnie as soon as it was possible.

She had not thought she would have to wait until the spring – but now was the time. She plucked the yellowed address from the mirror and put it in her purse. Train to the cathedral city of Litchford, so much she knew, and from there it was a question of enquiry and walking, with the hope of a kindly lift or two.

'Miss Margaret Hobbday, Middle Cottage, Chasewich.' The rotund porter at Litchford station read the address and pursed his lips doubtfully. 'It's a long walk for this time of day. You'll hardly be there before nightfall, and you've some good hills to climb.'

'I'm used to walking,' she reassured him, impatient to be off. 'Please just point me the way I should take out of the town.'

He had beckoned her further out into the station forecourt and pointed above the roofs and church towers to where green hills could be seen in the distance. 'See the great clump of oaks on that hillside? Your road leads up beween them.'

She realised he had not exaggerated either the distance or the hills, for she had walked for a good two hours before she reached the great spreading canopies of the oak copse. The evening sun slanted low, gilding the scalloped curls of new leaves against the gnarled branches. At another time she might have lingered to wonder at ancient things offering up another spring, but halfway up the great hill a signpost indicated Chasewater to her left and Chasewich uphill, 2 miles. The thought that she was so near to Ginnie made her push on faster.

Middle Cottage took no finding at all, though it was no cottage. The row of three large terraced houses were more fitted, in spite of the softening trees and mass of bluebells and primroses, to a town than a hamlet, Leah thought. There were children playing in a stream that ran at the far side of the roadway. She would have liked to have taken a moment or two to collect herself, but as she stood pushing stray ends of hair under her bonnet and shaking the dust from her skirts, the children stopped their play and drew nearer, fingers in mouths, full of curiosity for a stranger.

'Are you the nurse?' a larger girl asked.

Leah shook her head. Her mind full of thoughts of Ginnie, she asked, 'is someone wanting the nurse?'

The child shrugged. 'I don't know,' she answered, then urged her companions back to their dam making. 'Cum on!'

Leah made her way past Trafalgar Cottage and knocked at the middle door of the row. Her heart beat thunderously as she waited, wondering what her reception would be. Arriving this late in the evening threw her very much on the mercy of Walter Hobbday's sister . . . and Ginnie? She drew in her breath in a great gasp of apprehension, then let it out very slowly, listening intently for any sound from within. She had just raised her hand to knock again when there was the sound of something being moved inside the room, then bolts were drawn, and a door which stuck and protested was pulled open.

'Yes?' Miss Margaret Hoddday queried. And as Leah took in the fact that she was as square and aggressive-seeming as her brother, added, 'We don't use the front door.'

'I'm Ginnie's best friend,' she announced.

Miss Hobbday gave a grunt which Leah found impossible to interpret, but the door was dragged wider open.

'Come in then, it's about time!' Leah followed the woman through into a back parlour which she felt had the bareness usually associated with a man living alone, rather than a woman. Margaret was obviously not a woman given to prettying things up – or wasting words in invitation or explanation. She pointed to a chair near the hearth, and swinging the kettle on its trivot tipped the boiling water into a teapot she had ready on the hearth. 'Goes to bed early,' she said. 'I was just making tea for her.'

'Is she . . .'

'You'll see.' Two enormous breakfast cups were well sugared, filled, and put into her hands with the words, 'Back bedroom.'

The staircase ran up from a separate small compartment between the front and back parlour. Leah found she was holding her breath as she hurried up the stairs, both eager and apprehensive about her unannounced visit.

'Ginnie?' Her voice sounded uncertain, echoing in the staircase. 'Ginnie?' she repeated as she reached the half open door of the bedroom.

A figure stood looking out of the window. For a second Leah looked towards the bed, wondering if Ginnie had another visitor, but the bed was empty – and the person at the window did not turn. She put the two cups of tea on the bedside table. 'Ginnie,' she said again quietly, 'it's me, Leah.'

The evening light drained all colour from her hair and clothes as Ginnie slowly turned to face her, and Leah silently acknowledged that she would not have recognised her, so thin, so pale, her hair so lank and unkempt, her figure so grossly swollen. as if reading her thoughts, the girl plucked at the edges of her cotton jacket.

'Ginnie!' Tears started to Leah's eyes and she made as if to rush across the room and take her friend into her arms, but Ginnie shook her head violently and turned away again.

244

'Oh, Ginnie' Leah the comforter sat on the bed, put her head in her hands and cried. She tried to stop herself, to be quiet, while her heart broke for her friend – and the effort of control made it all worse. Then she started as Ginnie touched her shoulder. The next moment she was up on her feet and the two of them were embracing each other and crying together.

'I've come to cheer you up,' she told Ginnie, laughing between sobs.

Ginnie put her head on Leah's shoulder – and neither could speak nor see for a long time.

At length Leah made another effort to stay the flood of tears, wiping her own face and Ginnie's with a sodden handkerchief, then they shared Ginnie's to blow their noses on. Then they just cried again because they were together, touching each other's face and hair and holding hands until Ginnie collapsed awkwardly, half sideways, head down in Leah's lap, and sobbed again. 'I've missed you so much,' she said, 'my heart has ached for you.'

'Why didn't you let me come sooner?'

Ginnie was still and silent, so quiet after the tears that it grew to a bleakness. Leah put her lips down to her friend's cheek. 'Why not much sooner?' she repeated.

Ginnie's sigh came long and ragged. 'It wasn't until David brought your card and note saying Nat and Ben blamed each other that I realised how my keeping silent . . . But I still couldn't bring myself to tell what I'd done.'

'What *you'd* done!' Leah exclaimed.

'I went to their foundry and hid in the spinney. I only suspected until then, but I saw . . . that was just before I waited to talk to Ben in the fields. I thought I could talk to him rather than Nat. I could not bear Nat to know, I loved him so. Then I found I couldn't talk to anyone . . .'

Leah felt at last she shared the utter isolation her friend must have felt: unable to talk to her friends, living in a place where gossip was part of the daily bar parlance, and all the household men.

'Then your letter came, saying you all knew . . .'

She raised herself up. 'I took quinine, you know, tried to get rid of it. Whatever I tried only made me sick. I decided to starve, or if I did eat I made myself vomit, but . . . nothing happened. I just wonder that I have not killed myself. I suppose I'm too much of a coward. Too many lessons about hell fire and damnation from Old Ma Warbo.'

'And Old Pask,' Leah added, stabbing her forefinger at the air. 'He's still poking his messages home.' She watched Ginnie's face carefully but there was no vestige of a smile. Instead her face seemed more darkly shadowed.

'You don't know what it's like to have a child move inside you, a child you hate. A thing that's separated me from all I love.'

How Leah ached to be able to deny this, to say, "No, no, Nat's coming." She wondered if Ginnie had paused in the hope that she brought some message of love or charity from the young man.

'He's not coming is he?' she shook her head. 'No, you would have told me before now. It was a vain hope. No Nat, no life – and he's not able to forgive, is he?'

'Forgive! You've nothing to be forgiven for.'

'Whatever name you give it, the end's the same. He does not want me now. What man would? I've heard the same conversation times enough under the eaves back home. "Better dead", I've heard men say. "Either the child or both", I've heard them say. Go back to Ben, Leah.' She rose very wearily and went to stand at the window again, staring out into the long evening. 'Go back and be happy. Women do die in childbirth. I don't think God would count it as a mortal sin if I just did nothing – just died.'

Leah was appalled and knew nothing would make her leave Ginnie now until after the child was born. 'I'll write home and say I am staying,' she resolved aloud.

'No,' Ginnie shook her head earnestly, 'it's better you go home, Leah.'

'Time will heal, this will all be forgotten.'

'Its not a wound, it's a child,' Ginnie said with a bitter laugh. 'The child of Nat's step-father. I don't want you to see it. I don't want to see it – ever.'

'The child is innocent, too. It will need help in turn,' Leah gently reminded her. 'I'm staying whatever you say, and if your Aunt Margaret won't let me sleep here, I'll ask next door.'

'She will.' Margaret Hobbday stood in the doorway, holding a blanket and a candlestick. 'There's a room for you.'

She lumbered off towards one of the front bedrooms.

'The child . . .' Ginnie began, 'it could live – grow up?' She moved closer to the window, leaned her forehead on the pane.

'Of course,' Leah said very gently. 'We would have to help the child grow in love, in fun, Ginnie! – and – remember Sunday School in all the ways of righteousness.'

Ginnie pressed her face to the glass and would not be drawn to talk further. Eventually Leah went downstairs for supper. Margaret carried Ginnie's basin of warm milk and bread upstairs, commenting, 'She'll not eat it.'

'There's nothing ready,' she stated when she returned.

'For the baby?'

'I've money from my brother, but I never go into town.'

Leah began to see the meaning behind her cryptic greeting "about time". This spinster was out of her depth. 'Would you like me to buy what's needed?'

Margaret rose with lumbering alacrity and reached to the mantelpiece. From under the bobbled plush cover she produced an envelope and gave it to Leah. 'I don't think the baby'll be long.'

'I'll go to Litchford tomorrow,' Leah said. 'is there a good doctor or a nurse?'

'At Litchford.'

'I'll write home tonight and post the letters in town tomorrow.

'I'm glad you've come.' Margaret sat down heavily. 'Glad to have someone here who knows what's to be done.'

Leah pondered whether there could be many girls who knew less! She took a candle, writing paper, pen and ink to her bedroom, and wrote first to Ben and then to her mother. She was just sealing the second letter when there was a sound near her door, a gentle tap. She went to open it, and Ginnie stood there, almost wraithlike, so wan in her voluminous white nightgown.

Leah reached for her and took her over to the double bed and turned back the sheets. 'Which side do you like?' she asked.

247

They fell asleep holding hands.

It was five days later that Leah entering the bedroom, found Ginnie walking around clasping her back.

'Ginnie?'

'Just backache from making the bed.' She straightened, eased her shoulders back. 'I'm all right, it's nothing. It's gone now.'

Later in the morning, she sought Leah out. 'It can't be many days now. I wondered if you would go into Litchford again this afternoon and ask the doctor to come and see me?'

'He would at least know exactly where the house is when we do need him.' Leah tried not to sound too enthusiastic. It had been what she had wanted to do when she had bought the baby's layette, but Ginnie had threatened to leave the house and not come back.

Dr Witts was the name Aunt Margaret had supplied. She had also described where his surgery was in relation to the railway station. Leah anticipated no difficulty finding him, and intended to ask him to call as a matter of some urgency.

She was, she felt, beginning to know the way from Litchford to Chasewich very well indeed, and just as well for it was almost dark again as she turned into the lane where Margaret Hobbday lived. She glanced up to the bedroom she and Ginnie had shared ever since she had arrived, but there was no candlelight. She hurried around to the back door, eager to let Ginnie and her aunt know that she had found the doctor kind, if censorious about there being no contact made before the last days of the pregnancy. She found Aunt Margaret alone.

'Everything's arranged,' she said. 'Dr Witts will come tomorrow morning. Has Ginnie gone to bed?'

'She's hardly been out of her room all day. Said she didn't sleep well last night.'

'Has she eaten?' Leah asked, unease stirring in her.

'She came down midday, took something back upstairs. I thought you would take her something when you got back.'

'I'll run up now. See if there's anything special she'd like.'

248

It was the smell she noticed first, a cross between dough rising and meat beginning to cook. Had it been downstairs she would not have remarked upon it, thinking it might have been something Margaret had cooked. But as she opened the bedroom door there was no doubt the warm smell orginated from here.

'Ginnie?' Though she could see the girl was lying on the bed, there was something tense, and different, and alarming about her stillness. Leah ran to the bedside table, found candle and matches. As she struck the match she glanced at the bed and cried out, for Ginnie lay with staring eyes, only her face and her knuckles visible, gripping the edges of the bedclothes up under her chin. Leah's fingers shook so much she lost the flame of the first match and must strike another. This time she did not look up until the wick of the candle was alight.

'Ginnie?' She put out a tentative hand, touched one of the clenched fists and thanked God as she found it warm. Then, as her hand went to Ginnie's forehead, alarm flared again. Icy sweat wet her fingers, and she realised the other difference: the bulge that had ridden full about Ginnie's middle was surely lower. 'The baby,' she said. 'It's coming isn't it?'

'I'm alright,' Ginnie managed to say, breath held tight. 'Go away!'

'Let me see.' Leah grasped the top of the bedclothes.

Ginnie flared at her: 'Leave me alone. Go away. I don't want you. I don't want anybody. I'm all right!'

Pain took over her body, and Leah saw her fight against the labour her body needed. She ran to the top of the stairs and shouted for Margaret. 'The baby's coming.' She realised now, with the echo of Ginnie's words that morning, "I'm alright", that the baby had started then – and Ginnie had known it – had deliberately schemed to get her out of the house . . .

She took a firmer hold of the bedclothes and pulled them away. The bed was soaked with waters and blood.

Ginnie turned her agonised face first this way then sharply the other, and attempted to cover herself again. 'Leave me alone,' she moaned and as pain came over her again her legs automatically drew up.

'Oh, my God! What can we do?' Margaret sounded near to panic as she arrived in the bedroom.'

'Is there anyone nearby who might help?' Leah asked. 'See if one of the neighbours . . . then light the fire in here – heat water.'

The alarmed woman hurried away. Leah heard her thudding heavily and hastily down the stairs.

She turned back to the bed where Ginnie, like some mortally injured wild creature, seemed determined to cover herself again, to hide and wait for death.

'You've got to help yourself,' Leah told her. 'Stop being so stupid.' She tried to dredge from her memory everything she had ever heard about childbirth. 'Hold on to the bedrails above your head,' she told Ginnie, 'that'll help.' She tried to lift Ginnie's hands and arms, but her friend almost snarled at her as another spasm of pain overtook her.

'Scream if it helps.' Leah had heard that somewhere, but was not prepared for her advice to be taken so quickly, as Ginnie let out a noise that was half a groan, half a screech of utter frustration and anguish – with a dismissal thrown in at the end. 'Go away, Leah. I don't want anyone to see me like this.'

'Ginnie, I'm staying,' she shouted back, then added more quietly, 'I'm staying.'

'Leave me to die in peace. Why did you come back?'

'You'll die in my arms, or not at all,' she said, unsure now whether what they were saying even made sense as again Ginnie struggled to prevent her body arching itself in pain. Leah had the urgent feeling that she was lying all wrong in the bed, and as Margaret came back into the bedroom, she said, 'Come and help me lift her higher on the pillows.'

They stood each side, and putting an arm under each shoulder lifted Ginnie so her body was not so flat. 'No, no, leave me! Leave me! I'm not having it!' Ginnie screamed.

'Is anybody coming?' Leah asked.

'Next door neighbour's gone for his sister. She does . . . these things.'

Leah knelt on the bed to try to prevent Ginnie rolling herself down again. 'How long?' she asked.

'Not too long – if she's at home. I'm praying.'

'Ginnie, help yourself! Push!'

'She bleeding from the mouth,' Margaret said in an awed voice.

'She's bitten through her lip.' Leah heaved Ginnie back into the middle of the pillows as she tried to inch herself into unproductive flatness again. 'Doesn't my love for you count at all, Ginnie Hobbday? Because one man took you, and another won't, you're giving up. I won't let you. Push! Push!

Being shouted at distracted Ginnie and again her knees came up as her body dictated what should be done.

'This baby's going to be born in spite of you!' Leah found the only way Ginnie seemed to react properly was when she was shouted at, making her lose concentration and give her body time to take over.

But as the minutes lengthened to the half hour, and more, and more, Leah was not sure she was really helping. She felt Ginnie was beginning to look as if she had no strength left to obey the urgent call of her body to deliver the child.

'Is that women ever coming?' she asked wearily as Margaret again made up the bedroom fire.

'I'll go again.' Margaret looked as drained as Leah felt. But before she left the room, they heard someone call from below: 'Mrs Wing – you want me?'

'This way, this way!' Margaret went to the head of the stairs with one of the several candles they had lit around the room.

Leah was not reassured as the woman came in for she was small, skinny, looked quite old, but as she came to the bed, slipping off her coat and rolling up her sleeves, it was clear she was no stranger to such a situation.

'When did she start?' she asked, feeling Ginnie's cheeks with the back of her hand.

'I think first thing this morning. She's not trying,' Leah added, 'and I don't think she has the strength now.'

'Didn't want it,' she stated, 'that's nothing new. Help me turn her on her side.'

Leah was relieved to hear the tone of knowledge and authority in Mrs Wing's voice.

'Its well down. Provided she's big enough, we'll soon see. Has the doctor been sent for?

'He's – no – he's coming tomorrow. He doesn't know the baby's started.'

'Huh!' The self-taught midwife dismissed the three of them as little more than useless. 'Go and get water and towels – and are the child's clothes warming? You do that,' she dismissed Margaret. Adding to Leah, 'You stay where you are. I may need you.'

Ginnie seemed suddenly to realise someone else had arrived, and shrank from the woman's touch.

'Come on, my girl.' Mrs Wing raised her voice as if talking to someone a long way off. 'It'll be easier for us all if you *push down*!' Without ceremony, she lifted Ginnie's leg that had fallen clear of the bed and crooked it upwards. Ginnie screamed.

'Next pain, push! We'll help you.' the shouting was lowered to a whispered instruction to Leah. 'Cruel to be kind, my girl. See how I have this leg? I want you to hold it so – all the time – no matter how she shouts. Can you do that?'

Leah hardly had time to nod before Mrs Wing ordered: 'Now!' to both girls. Then, 'Push, you little fool!'

Leah closed her eyes and hung on to the jerking leg. Ginnie screamed as if being torn apart, and as Leah half opened her eyes Mrs Wing, her arm muscles tensed like whip-lashes, seemed to be pushing down on Ginnie's stomach. 'About three more should do it.'

Three more! Leah was horrified. Three more like that? But they were into a repeat before she had time to do more than react as she had been told. But the three came and went, and Leah felt it was the end. Ginnie must die as she wished. Then Mrs Wing exclaimed excitedly above another scream, 'I have the head.'

Leah kept her eyes closed, felt Ginnie give one more convulsion, and suddenly it was as if someone had declared peace after a long conflict.

'It's all over,' Mrs Wing declared. 'You have a little girl.' There was the sound of a slap and the first cry of the newborn mewed in the room.

Ginnie lay back staring fixedly at the ceiling, and Leah stood away as Mrs Wing cut the cord and swaddled the baby tight in a towel before handing it to her. She looked down at the red helpless little creature, and her heart went out to it. 'Poor, poor, little thing,' she whispered.

'Give me a bowl,' Mrs Wing instructed. 'Let's have the afterbirth away and this bed changed. Then this silly young woman can have a rest. I've no doubt it would have been over hours since if you'd had someone who knew what they were doing. And there wouldn't be all this mess to clear up.'

'I think you saved her life – both of their lives,' Leah said, her voice shaky with emotion and exhaustion.

'It was patently clear none of you lot knew what you were doing!' Mrs Wing laughed good-naturedly. 'What about a cup of tea all round, Miss Hobbday? Then the new mum can nurse her baby.'

Chapter Twenty Four

Mrs Wing and Dr Witts were both mistaken in their belief that Ginnie would "take to" her baby. She lay pale and resentful of every effort made to endear the child to her. She ate just enough to stay alive, and little more. Even so, her breasts were hard with milk, but she refused to suckle the baby.

Leah took the child into her own room and painstakingly fed it there with milk fetched warm from a goat. It made the child sick, and feeling quite desperate one weary midnight she marched along the landing to Ginnie. 'You are going to have to see your daughter some time. You can't stay in bed with your arms crossed over your breasts and your eyes closed forever.'

'Why not? It's better than spending the rest of my life looking at Caleb Berridge's child!'

'And yours! It's wicked, Ginnie. Listen to the poor little thing cry. I'm sure she's hungry. She's innocent . . .' Leah's voice rose. She felt she would like to shake Ginnie, shake her until she rattled. Then she realised it was utter weariness that was shouting in that quiet bedroom, with Aunt Margaret next door. She knew if she went on she would regret it. So left the room pointedly repeating, 'And yours!'

By trial and careful observation Leah gradually succeeded in instituting a proper feeding regime, and by the time the child was eighteen days old it was established on a finely measured diet of watered goat's milk. Ginnie showed no improvement. Mrs Wing said she was lucky not to have contracted milk fever, and helped the girl express the surplus milk then bind up her breasts.

What was waste, Leah thought.

The child's greater contentment endeared her to Leah even more, and though Ginnie had several more weeks to lie in, Leah began to carry the baby with her to fetch the milk from the morning and evening milking. Holding her close, she began to feel a keen bond with the child who, as the days passed, had lost her indignant red colour. Satisfied now with her feeding, she became a pleasing, delightful-looking child.

'Poor nameless creature,' Leah whispered as she walked. 'I shall call you Ruth – she did not wish to be sent away.' She cradled the tiny girl tenderly. If only Ginnie knew what she was missing! Leah acknowledged that all this was not what *she* had expected: this yearning for Ben, and a child of her own. She felt she had been prudish in her dealings with him, afraid of pregnancy. The dread would still be there, and she understood now why it was called "labour". But one bad day – and wasn't the end worth the pain?

When she arrived back she took the child again to Ginnie's room and held her up. 'Ginnie, meet Ruth. Ruth, your mother. Aye, well, never mind, little girl. Me and your Great Aunt Margaret love you anyway – and soon you'll have visitors from your home village. Lots of uncles, all full of fun and spirits.'

Leah was only guessing, and if she hoped for any response from Ginnie she was disappointed. She carried the child downstairs to where Margaret wass preparing the feeding bottle. She laid the child in the older woman's arms who with awkward tenderness managed to get the thick teat into its mouth.

'How long can you stay on?' Margaret asked, a touch of anxiety in her voice.

Leah pondered that she had hoped to see Ginnie accept her child, but now doubted that was going to happen at all. 'I thought I'd wait until your brother came – and something's decided about little Ruth.' She reached over and touched the feeding baby's cheek as she spoke. Margaret smiled at the given name, though shook her head over it all. 'What will be the end of it? But I'd not see the child homeless.'

Leah was not sure whether Margaret meant Ginnie, or the baby, or both. She herself began to feel what a strange time this was she had spent in the tiny hamlet, bonding herself to a baby that was not hers. Three women coping alone, yet waiting, she supposed, for the male Hobbdays to condescend to come and give a verdict about what should happen to the child.

The following weekend she was carrying the child and the milk can back to the terrace when she saw a familiar figure coming towards her.

'Ben!' she called, and for once found her burden an encumbrance as she began to run to him.

He clasped her carefully, cradling her burden with one of his arms. Their greetings were punctuated by his glances down at the child. 'Meet Ruth,' she said.

'Motherhood suits you,' he said, taking in her glowing good health.

'I wish she was ours, Ben.'

That same look came over his face that had half-scared, half-delighted her in her bedroom at home – but now her response was all delight. 'I love you. I want to marry you straight away – this minute!'

'What, no "but"?' Desire was in his eyes, and she thrilled to the look. 'And what about waiting for Ginnie?'

'No "buts",' she said very firmly – and went on to tell him all that had happened.

'Then Nat isn't going to get a very good reception . . .'

'Nat?'

He nodded to a figure standing at a distance, on the bank of the small stream. Nat looked up at that moment, waved, and came slowly towards them.

Leah unconsciously lifted her burden a little higher, signalling perhaps both the baby's presence and her own protectiveness towards it. 'He's late coming,' she commented briefly.

'He needed the time. If you'd seen him! He's been like one who died and had to be reborn before he could accept . . .'

'So he has accepted?' Leah's voice was low now, for Nat was almost within hearing distance.

'He thinks he has.'

Leah could see the history of recent trauma on Nat's face. Their eyes met for the first time since she had confronted Caleb in the foundry, but neither of them spoke. Somehow it was too big a moment for an ordinary greeting, and they were too unsure of their old friendship to make any extraordinary show.

Nat's glance fell to the close-wrapped bundle she carried. His hand trembled as, very gingerly, he held back the shawl to see the child. 'Meet Ruth,' she said.

It seemed a very long time that Nat gazed down on the child. 'Ruth,' he repeated, his voice husky, and extended his arms.

'You want to hold her?' Leah questioned, yet handed her over quickly lest he should change his mind.

Nat held her awkwardly, making the shawl bunch up, nearly covering her face. He looked at Leah in alarm, and gently she tucked the shawl down against his jacket on one side and under his forearm the other. The upset made the child pucker her face and struggle to push a fist free, which Nat caught between forefinger and thumb.

'Hello, Ruth,' he said gently. 'you're not going to cry, are you?'

To Leah's surprise, the baby opened its eyes as if to see who spoke. 'She's never done that before,' she said wonderingly.

'I hope to surprise your mother too,' he said.

'You have no worries there. You'll find her very changed – pale and thin. She has neither nursed nor even looked at her baby.'

Nat gave out a low sound of distress, and now Ruth did cry. Leah took her back and led the way to introduce them both to Aunt Margaret.

'The Bellmakers?' she asked 'So you're the young men . . .'

'We've been waiting for,' Leah finished for her, adding, 'I do hope so. Shall I show you up?'

Nat followed her up the stairs. Ginnie's bedroom door was open and seeing Leah coming in empty-handed she roused herself a little. 'Is it Dr Witts downstairs?' she asked, then she saw Nat. Her lips parted and her face coloured with shock.

'Nat! You? I can't believe it.'

'Forgive me, Ginnie. Forgive me for not coming before.' He went quickly to her and gathered her into his arms, holding her gently to him. For long seconds they were both perfectly still, eyes closed, as if afraid to look or move in case they lost the precious moment. It seemed more than their arms that enfolded each ohter, more than their heads that touched; their togetherness held an aura of something larger. 'It's not too late, is it?' he asked.

Leah closed the door after herself, thinking they needed time and privacy, but she had not reached the bottom of the stairs when she heard Nat coming after her. She felt he had hardly given Ginnie time to recover from the shock of seeing him. Now he was rushing away. But this was not quite so, for as she reluctantly preceded him into the back parlour, he announced: 'I want you all to come upstairs.' He stopped to take the baby from Margaret, and repeated, 'All of you.'

Ben caught and squeezed Leah's hand as they followed Margaret in the little procession that returned upstairs.

'Now, Ginnie,' Nat said, sitting on the bed beside her, holding the baby next to her. Leah watched her face as she looked on her daughter for the first time. Her lips opened in wonder and some alarm as Nat gently transferred the baby into her arms. She held it gingerly, as if it might bite. Nat leant down and moved the shawl down from the baby's face as if he had been dealing with infants all his life. 'She's like you, Ginnie,' he murmured.

Ginnie rocked Ruth a little, but it was she who needed the comfort of the movement.

'Are you all right?' Nat asked her. 'Because I want you, all of you, to listen carefully. You are all witnesses.'

'It took a lot of pain and a lot of heartache – a lot of growing-up really – for me to realise how much I love Ginnie. Now I want all of you to know I want to marry her as soon as it can be arranged, and to say that no one will ever know from my lips that Ruth here is not my child. She's Ginnie's so she's mine. And not only that!' he announced, and with a theatrical gesture handed over to Ben.

Ben cleared his throat, and made a bow. Leah wondered at the different atmosphere these two brothers had created in a mere hour or so. Nat seemed almost his old self. It could surely not be so easy, and there could be no better news than that Nat had just given them . . .

'Lionel Champion,' Ben began, 'has agreed to finance us as a partnership in premises we've been to see at the extreme west of our county. We shall take the orders we have outstanding at the Robertsons' foundry and execute them at the new premises, acting as sub-contractors for Mr Champion when he has too much work – and as we get on, we shall pay back his capital for the buildings.'

'But why should he, a stranger . . .?' Leah queried.

'I think he is just a saintly man, who has no family of his own,' Ben answered.

'But not only that,' Nat put in. 'Go on, Ben!'

'Not only that,' Ben repeated obligingly, 'the premises include two vacant cottages . . .'

'One for us,' Nat told Ginnie.

'And one for us,' Ben added.

Leah opened her mouth to form a "but", then stopped. 'When can we go to see them?' she asked.

'As soon as Ginnie's up,' Nat said.

They all looked over to the bed where Ginnie lay cradling her new daughter, half laughing and half crying. 'It will be soon' she told him, then leaning over Ruth rocked and shed tears over her. 'I'm so sorry,' she kept repeating.

They left Nat alone with her then for they sensed their own excitement would prove overwhelming for her.

Margaret dealt with her feelings by energetically slicing bacon from the side hanging in her pantry. Leah volunteered their services in collecting eggs from the coop at the bottom of the garden.

'It was a bit off-putting to find her so like Walter Hobbday,' Ben began. 'So masculine!'

'She's kind enough,' Leah affirmed. 'But what about your step-father?'

'We feel sure he's not going to come back. Nat traced him to Bristol, he sold the horse there, and although he must have changed his name, there was a man of his description travelling aboard an empty timber boat returning to Canada.'

'And your mother?'

'She's . . .' he paused as if trying to find the right words '. . . like a person released from a cage. She's already made and sent clothes for Ginnie's baby, and she's offered Cuddy a home. I'm happy about that. Cuddy's like an animal that's been unjustly treated – he'll never forget that injury, and he'll never let Caleb back into the house again. He's taking to the field and garden work, and my grandfather will have no regrets about being able to give up the foundry work.'

'So the foundry. . .'

'Will just be closed up and left. Nothing will be touched.' His face hardened as he made that judgment. 'No more bells will ever be made there.'

'Yes, that's right. We shall leave all that behind. A new start, as quickly as possible.'

Leah held her grandfather's old tally-book with its neat illustrations and outstanding amounts in one hand, and her own book in the other, bewailing the fact that she had more money outstanding in her book then old Fred had left in his.

'You needn't fret,' Sam told her. 'This mail order is going to take on, I can feel it. And we're organised to deal with it. Look at us.' His gesture encompassed the shop with Clarrie, Nellie and Miriam all hard at work. 'There's many a business has separate office and work address. You can do the writing from t'other side of county and we'll do the work this.'

'Provided there's going to be enough people with time and money enough to play this golf,' Leah said. 'perhaps we should look at other ideas?'

'Well, ideas is your departemnt, Gaffer.'

Leah caught his arm and hung on it. 'It seems it's all going to work out – but I have something to ask you.' Sam looked at her with mock apprehension. 'When I'm married, would you give me away?'

'Aye, I might think about that,' he said after a minute, taking his great red spotted handkerchief out of his pocket and while pretending to wipe his forehead, managing to blot his eyes.

Ginnie and Nat were married quietly at the city register office as soon as Ginnie could travel. David and Leah acted as witnesses, and Walter turned up unexpectedly to be by his daughter's side. He shook hands with his new son-in-law and gave him, 'Five pounds to get you started. And by the way, I'll drop the ban on you at the Stockinger's Arms.' It turned out to be a jolly affair with a high tea arranged at a nearby cafe. As Ginnie confided, 'Not what we planned by a long shot – but in the end, more than I expected.'

'I can't wait until we're all living in the same lane,' Leah said as she hugged her friend hard. 'At last I feel I've really got you back – and I don't want to part with you ever again!'

'It won't be for long!' Nat said, adding to his brother. 'And I shall be hard at work tomorrow, converting those barns for the foundry.' They all smiled but no one doubted that he had found a new commitment – the boy had been forged into a man.

Leah and Ben's own wedding date became difficult to settle, Ben becoming so fraught with work commitments, duties to Lionel Champion, or with traumas such as the collapse of the main barn at Hamelcote. It was Leah who grew steadily more impatient.

She yearned to be at Hamelcote with Ginnie. She managed to journey over there several times, and her stays were delightful times full of preparations in the second cottage, and trips up and down the lane to consult Ginnie, who had assumed the air of knowledgeable matron. She would come running (Ruth under her arm protesting at being scooped up from play) to make decisions about drapes and kitchen utensils.

Ruth was a sturdy thirteen-month-old before the date was finally fixed. Even so, in the final days before the late May wedding, like all brides Leah was convinced she would never be ready.

She knew she had disappointed many people by insisting her wedding be at the church near their new home, but Leah wanted the break with the Lacey villages to be complete. Hamelcote was being kind to Ginnie and Nat – and the new foundry. She could not wait to make a fresh start as Ginnie had done, away from the memory of the gossip and narrow-mindedness they had suffered from people such as the Warburtons; away from all the anguish Edgar Lacey had caused. She did not wish to have the name of Lacey in any form on her marriage certificate.

She longed to be established in her cottage with Ben, thrilled at the thought of being alone with him there. She looked beyond the wedding most of the time, so when the day arrived many things caught her offguard. Sam, resplendent in new suit when he arrived at Ginnie's house to wait with the bride until everyone else was assembled in the church.

'Why, Sam, you look splendid, really . . . Grandfather would have been pleased to have you stand in his place,' she told him, 'No, don't laugh, Sam. I mean it.'

'If I don't laugh, I might cry. I only wish old Fred Dexter might be here to see his favourite wed.'

'Perhaps he is,' Miriam said, coming to take one more look at the bride before going to church.

'No young woman ever looked better,' she said, taking in the plain heavy white satin gown, long sleeves falling to an elongated point over the back of Leah's hands. The slim-cut dress draped gracefully back in a short train, emphasising the bride's tall dark beauty. Her grandmother handed Leah a small white leather bound prayer-book. 'This is for you, my dear. I had it on my wedding day, and you must have something to carry.'

'Oh, Gran, thank you. I shall treasure it all my life. It *is* better with something in my hands.' She had refused to carry flowers. That would have been too reminiscent of the garlands that had led to John White's death.

'Now you mother's here to see you, then we must hurry to take our places.'

'Mum?'

Nellie came hurrying in, looking flushed and not a little flustered. 'Of all things, no one could unlock the organ! Never mind. The key's found now.' She paused. 'Ah, if only your father could see you now.' She stood tip-toe to kiss her daughter's cheek, whispering, 'See you in church then.'

'Mum, I have something for you. Close your eyes and hold out your hands.'

'We really haven't time,' she began, but did as she was told.

'Spread your fingers,' said Leah, then slid her mother's wedding-ring back into place. 'Ben always said he would redeem it before we were married. He got it back yesterday.'

262

'Oh, Leah!' Nellie put the ring to her lips, all her reprimands for the money they had spent, all her joy, flitting across her face with no need to speak them. The ring still next her lips, she said, 'Now I feel your father is here,' then turned and rushed away to take her place in church.

'I hope the rest of the day is going to be easier,' Sam said, giving his nose a hearty blow on his old red and white spotted handkerchief. The sight of the workaday thing made Leah want to laugh aloud. She was glad Clarrie's sharp eye had overlooked it.

'We have a few more minutes,' she said. 'Come and listen to Ben and Nat's first bell.'

The new foundry's first work had been to recast the tenor bell for Hamelcote's church. It rang now, for the first time in concert with its fellows, for her wedding. For Leah it finally laid the curse of the Monk's bell that had so plagued her. She remembered part of the inscription from Soston's bell – "Cursed in bright May by eye of wumman, Evil powers release them that ME again summon".

This bright May morning made a nonsense of the old scratched curse. She drew in a deep breath full of the scent of sweet hawthorn – "May blessing" she thought it ought to be called. She and Sam stood in the open door to listen to the cllamour of the tuneful bells, pealing out across the calm serenity of the green Midlands – ringing out for herself and Ben.

'"Let men and women join together with equal honesty and voice. For Ben and Leah Robertson. May 1880."'

She repeated aloud the inscription Ben had cast into Hamelcote's tenor bell. It had made her proud to read it, proud of its author. 'Partners,' she added, 'that's what it means.'

Sam chuckled, then as the calling bell began to toll he crooked his arm to her. 'Come on, Gaffer.'

Mary Williams

The Bridge Between

From the moment she arrives in the tiny Cornish fishing village of Port Todric in 1904, Julia Kerr loves the place. Through the ups and downs of her own writing career and her marriage to a man who always puts his painting first, she draws strength and encouragement from the unchanging rhythm of village life.

Caroline's daughter Sarah, while very different from her mother, shares the same passionate wilfulness. Will she break Julia's heart by continuing to estrange herself from her family after a quarrel? Or will their shared love for the village bring about a reconciliation?

A warm and realistic love story with a lovingly rendered Cornish background, *The Bridge Between* is a book to touch the heart.

Rose Boucheron

Promise of Summer

It is 1939 and despite the threat of war the future is bright for three South London girls. While Sarah's dreams of fame propel her into a world far removed from her family and friends, her schoolfriend Julie stays closer to home, taking a clerical job in a paper factory. There she soon wins a new admirer Andrew, a RAF pilot officer and the boss's son.

Andrew's sister Olivia is also in love – with a married man – and is forced to conceal her true feelings and agree to her lover's demand for secrecy. But can she really be content to win her own happiness at the expense of another woman's?

A rich and satisfying story woven from the lives of three very different girls, hoping to secure love and futures for themselves despite the heartbreak of war.

Further titles available from Woman's Weekly Fiction

While every effort is made to keep prices low, it is sometimes necessary to increase prices at short notice. Mandarin Paperbacks reserves the right to show new retail prices on covers which may differ from those previously advertised in the text or elsewhere.

The prices shown below were correct at the time of going to press.

☐ 1 86056 000 8	**A Place in the Sun**	Nina Lambert	£1.99
☐ 1 86056 005 9	**The Bellmakers**	Jean Chapman	£1.99
☐ 1 86056 010 5	**The Bridge Between**	Mary Williams	£1.99
☐ 1 86056 015 6	**Promise of Summer**	Rose Boucheron	£1.99
☐ 1 86056 020 2	**Tallie's War**	Jan Webster	£1.99
☐ 1 86056 025 3	**Time Will Tell**	June Barraclough	£1.99
☐ 1 86056 021 0	**Lucky Star**	Betty Paul	£1.99
☐ 1 86056 055 5	**With This Ring**	Jean Saunders	£1.99
☐ 1 86056 065 2	**A Captain's Lady**	Jennifer Wray Bowie	£1.99
☐ 1 86056 060 1	**Lily's Daughter**	Diana Raymond	£1.99

All these books are available at your bookshop or newsagent, or can be ordered direct from the address below. Just tick the titles you want and fill in the form below.

Cash Sales Department, PO Box 5, Rushden, Northants NN10 6YX.
Fax: 0933 414000 : Phone 0933 414047.

Please send cheque, payable to 'Reed Book Services Ltd', or postal order for purchase price quoted and allow the following for postage and packing:

£1.00 for the first book: £1.50 for **two books or more per order.**

NAME (Block letters) ....

ADDRESS ....

.... Postcode ....

☐ I enclose my remittance for £....................

☐ I wish to pay by Access/Visa Card Number

Expiry Date

☐ If you do not wish your name to be used by other carefully selected organisations for promotional purposes please tick this box.

Signature ....
Please quote our reference: 3 503 500 C

Orders are normally dispatched within five working days, but please allow up to twenty days for delivery.

Registered office: Michelin House, 81 Fulham Road, London SW3 6RB

Registered in England. No. 1974080